A Note from the Author

And Thanks

Jara: Quest for the Dagger of Nystia is my first full-length fantasy novel. I began writing this through divine inspiration after my youngest daughter's doctor told my wife and I they would be able to remove a rare tumor she was born with (after previously being told surgery probably wouldn't be a viable option for three and a half years). That same day we returned home and I began writing down ideas that started coming to me about a story with a young lead female which set itself apart from other stories, while remaining original and 'new'. A story about someone who had magic within them, someone that had no choice in the task they were given and did all they could to carry it out nonetheless.

Writing this book provided an amazing escape for me and my wife, bringing us to a magical new world each time I began writing again...it also provided a great supply of bedtime stories (watered-down). I hope it brings each reader the same joy it brought me and my wife as I wrote it. This is the first in a series of books I am writing set in this world, which I cannot wait to share!

I would also like to thank a few people who have helped mold both me and this book... I certainly would have never completed this story had my wife Evie not been at my side, reading over my shoulder and bouncing ideas back and forth with me (not to mention providing the name 'Jara'). My daughters who constantly asked me for new Jara stories each night at bedtime. My parents & in-laws (especially my mother Tracy and my father-in-law Kevin who read through my rough drafts and copy-edited it).

I also want to thank friends and acquaintances who gave me the opportunities and experiences throughout my life which shaped me (even if I didn't quite 'get it' at the time). My grandfather Rosolino for teaching me the importance of fine-detail and honing the edges. Mariela Comitini & Ludovic Littee for introducing me into the world of filmmaking and allowing me to see (and be a part of) how magic is made. Aldo Bruno and the NJ Steel Baron team for introducing me to other knife and sword makers, which in-turn kept my love of steel and times long past alive. All my friends who wrote screenplays and made films by my side, whether they were worthy of acclaim or not.

And of course I need to thank those that let me pile medieval clothes and armor on them for the book cover: Alexis Mourad (Jara), Jason Bischak (Tripp), Marissa DePierro (Runa), Travis Sample (Zuht), and of course Evie Salerno (Toree).

Dedication

This book is dedicated to my Pop, who spent countless hours with me figuring out how to make bows out of PVC pipe and grinding out swords and battle axes with me in his garage.

An Early Morning

Chapter 1

I rolled over with a groan in my bed as heavy knocking began at my door.

"My Lady" a guard's voice said.

I covered my head with my blanket, trying to get back to sleep after the initial knocking woke me from my slumber. As I was about to drift back into my dreams there was another knock.

"My lady, I must speak with you!" the guard said again.

Still groggy from the feast the night before, I stumbled to the quilt hanging over my chair and threw it over my shoulders, making myself somewhat decent.

"Just a moment" I called out, this was not how I envisioned myself waking up this morning.

"There will be no rest this morning it seems" I said out loud to myself, and perhaps just loud enough for the guard to hear.

I took my time, dragging myself to the door. Something inside of me knew whatever the soul on the other side of my door had to say would almost certainly throw off my entire day. I opened the door all at once, startling the guard on the other side.

"What is it that is so important at this time of the morning? The eggs from the coups have not even been harvested yet! Can I have no time to come around from last evenings festivities?" I said.

"My apologies my lady, a messenger from King Ansel arrived at our gates this morning. He requests an urgent audience with you." The guard spoke.

"The king's messenger - here? Does he bring word on the tide of war in Wurth?" I said.

"No my lady, he says he must have an audience with you in private." The guard replied.

"It appears my suspicions were correct" I mused.

"Your 'suspicions' my lady?" replied the guard.

"Yes" I said, "I will indeed not be getting any rest this morning. Tell him we shall break our fast together within the hour."

"Yes m'lady" the guard said, and then walked briskly down the corridor.

The king's messenger here? This is most unusual. King Ansel has been focused on the war in the north with Wurth for nearly eight years. There is hearsay that the garrisons on the border have been dwindling, along with the coffers that fuel them. Perhaps he is requesting that I send men, or maybe even a loan? Either way, I can not imagine a worse way of spending my morning meal, discussing politics after a night of song, dance, food, and drink!

I call in my handmaidens to help me make decent and open the window, the cool early morning air certainly helps my wandering mind to give pause. The maidens' gossip from the feast the night before would usually peak my interest, today however my interest only lays on our new guest and whatever mysterious news he has brought from the king.

As the maidens remove the wash basin from the chambers I walk to my desk and pick up my signet ring and place it carefully on my finger. I watch the worn engraving of the dragon and two battle axes slowly rotate down each knuckle, the light reflecting off each ding and scratch that it has accumulated over the past one hundred and thirty years. I turn my attention to the drawer in my desk. I quite enjoy my morning routine, picking the fine details of my kit become something of a ritual these days. I open my drawer which contains my daggers and various clasps which I have accumulated over time.

I ran my fingertips across the hilts of my daggers, deciding which one I should fashion. A part of me wonders how I fell into this trap; running the castle and village while my brother, Devin, is out protecting the snow-ridden Western Pass from the random bands of marauders and bandits that make their way through from the Grot Mountains to the western-most border towns. The Gods know I can handle a foe as well as him, yet I am still made to stay here. When father returns from his expedition, I expect a full explanation why I am made to stay in the keep and hold court for which farmer's cows got into which farmer's fields while Devin is out living a life of adventure. If mother was still here in mind, I know I would be the one testing my metal while my brother would stay and settle each silly quarrel the villagers had.

Still, today there is mystery! The king's messenger, here! Here in my walls requesting an audience! I know it is likely nothing more than a plea for men-at-arms but until then I will revel in the mystery! I have daydreamed long enough; I mustn't keep my new guest waiting much longer! I grab my oldest dagger, "Alaia", a family heirloom on my mother's side; a beautiful pattern welded blade with a handle of ebony and braided silver strand wrap, a hilt of silver and sapphires, made by Daleon centuries ago. The perfect accessory to impress my guest. I strap my dagger to my belt and splash some flower water over my neck to drown out any remaining scent from the night before.

The Messenger

Chapter 2

The sound of my leather soles are muffled on the rugs that run down the castle corridors. I rushed down in such excitement that had I studded boots on; I would likely sound like a horse at full gallop in tournament. I stop and compose myself, making sure my braids are tied tight before making my way into the gardens.

"What are you doing? Were you not just complaining what a hassle this would be not even an hour ago?" I said to myself aloud.

What seemed like an annoyance this morning has quickly turned into the highlight of my tenure as Lady of the castle. I wonder who has come, I hope that Unul has been sent! Unul was the only of King Ansel's messengers that did not have a pompous bone in his body. My stomach fluttered in excitement!

I walked out the door to the castle gardens and see my hopes are made true! Unul is seated at a stone table surrounded by large hedges. The servants have already brought the fruit, bread, and meat out and placed a beautiful canopy over the table. Unul sees me enter the courtyard and stands from his seat.

He walked over to me, "Lady Jara" he says as he takes my hand with a nod of his head.

"Unul, welcome back to Dragon's Reach! I am glad it is you who has come! Please, come and take a seat, let us eat! Welum, pour us water and mead!" I say.

Welum, the head steward, fills our chalices while Unul and I sit. It has been years since I have seen Unul, he often would come to deliver news to my father before the war began.

"It is good to see a familiar face again" I said to him.

"It is good indeed" Unul said, "The last I walked in these walls you were knee high and sending squires to the infirmary with bloody noses and broken sticks! The war in the north has taken much from this kingdom, time among the losses."

"To broken sticks and bloody noses!" I said as I raised my chalice in toast.

"Aye, to broken sticks and bloody noses" Unul said as he too raised a toast.

We both took a sip and smiled, stuck in memories of a distant past. His smile was the same as I remember, but his face had changed; aged, but more than that... his eyes sank back, the features around them chiseled, dark, wrinkles from endless worry scarring his face in a subtle yet defining way. His smile faded and I could see there was indeed a reason he was here. It was not just an old friend visiting.

"Jara," he said, "I – "

"I know" I said cutting him off, "you are here on the king's request for men to fight in the north. My brother has been burdened with more fighting in the Western Pass than usual. I can not spare any men, but I can offer a loan so the king can secure mercenaries from the Falenik Islands."

Unul did not respond all at once, he took a sip of his drink and a bite into a chop of lamb before responding. He looked amused.

"You have certainly fallen into your parents' footsteps well. You have the gift of your mother's speechcraft and your father's tactical prowess." He said. "if only the reason for my journey here was that simple. I have come to collect you, Jara. King Ansel wishes to speak to you - in person."

"The King wishes to speak with me?" I reply "I'm afraid that's impossible. There will be no one to oversee Dragon's Reach, and with my father still on his expedition I cannot leave."

Unul brought his hand to his chin, rubbing it while staring at the mead in his chalice.

"The king wishes to speak with you about your father." He said

About my father, what could Unul know that I myself do not know already about my father's expedition? It is true that we have not heard from him in over a year, but how could the king know something that we did not?

Unul could see my surprise and concern.

"Do not worry about Dragon's Reach, a legion has been sent to the pass from the south and word sent to your brother to return to the castle. Devin will oversee Dragon's Reach while you are away." He said.

A legion? The king spared a legion to oversee the pass so that I could leave my post and have audience with him?

"Your father saw the war raging on longer than anyone expected and began to look for ways to change the tide. In his research he found a few tales that peaked the king's interest. The expedition your father went on was to seek out the artifacts in one of those tales to shift the war in our favor. The men he took with him were not hired guards, they were the kings own knights. They have been missing for some time now and King Ansel knows that you know the route they were taking. He needs your help to track down and find out what happened to the expedition." Unul said.

I was taken back, how had all of this gone on without my knowledge? My father had always been an open book with me, sharing his plans and ideas.

"Who else knows about this?" I replied.

"You and I, the king – I doubt your father would have made mention of it to anyone else." Said Unul.

There must be more than Unul is letting on, I thought. Even with the war raging king Ansel has many resources, including many skilled trackers.

"What is really at play, Unul? The king does not need me to track an expedition party. There must be something greater at play." I said very matter-of-factly.

"Aye, it is foolish for me to try and play a simple messenger with you. Your gut serves you right, as I hope it does in the coming months ahead. About a month and a half after we had last heard word from the party we began to receive strange reports of creatures from old story tales showing up in the villages just outside of Evanwood Forest." Unul said.

He stared at me for a moment, then down at the king's crest he bore on his ring finger. He was playing with it, twisting from side to side. I remember seeing him do this while he was in deep conversation with my father about matters of great importance, a sort of nervous tick of his.

Unul looked up from the ring and stared me in the eyes, his look was one of both disbelief and despair.

"What sort of creatures?" I replied.

"Wolfmen, Briars, Cythians." He said with complete conviction.

"Surely this must be a case of a tainted well in the village causing hysteria!" I replied. "These beasts are nothing more than tales!"

"They have been gone for hundreds of years, not tales." He said, cutting me off. "Not since your ancestors destroyed them all."

I shook my head in disbelief. I had heard stories from my mother when I was younger, I had always assumed it was just a tale made up to keep my mother's house revered among the villages in the kingdom – nothing more. I found my hand wandering to the hilt of my dagger – surely this must be a joke.

"At first we brushed the reports off as ramblings of hungry and disgruntled villagers. We sent an envoy out to convene with the villages on the border of the forest. Nearly two dozen men were sent, only six returned – all with wounds unlike I have ever seen." Unul continued.

"Why come here and ask for me?" I replied. "Surely the king would be better served by a battalion scouring the wood for the creatures and putting their heads on pikes!"

"Jara," Unul leaned over the table and placed his hand on my wrist. "look back at the training your father and mother put you through. With the war raging and your mother's accident, there was no time to properly induct you into the order. Your mother should be here to do it now, but it seems it is up to me."

The order? Perhaps Unul has had too much to drink on too little sleep! I did have quite an eventful childhood. My father taught me how to use a sword, bow, staff, and knife from the age of six. Unul was not joking when he earlier said that squires would be sent crying from bouts with me. My mother did indeed tell me the stories of the old creatures, adding in 'facts' such as what they were weak to and where they liked to dwell. But some sort of order seems far-fetched.

"What are you on about Unul?" I said. "Creatures, orders, wizards! I think you have had far too much mead this morning and your journey has made you delirious!"

"I wish it were so. Your mother's bloodline is the last of the Order of the Moon. There was a man, Lucian, who was the last known wizard to wreak havoc. The beasts he conjured were a menace like nothing the people of our time have faced. It was thought that he and all of his artifacts were destroyed, and with them any threats. Over the years the deeds and tales were turned into fables, so much so that even I was convinced it was nothing but a story for mothers to tell to keep their children in line.

It was not until I turned the king's library upside down that I found the accounts of what happened. Things that your mother would have already revealed to you. Your mother was the last of the Order of the Moon."

All of this seems like so much, one big joke created at the feast last night… yet a part of me feels it to be true.

"And what does this order do exactly?" I asked.

"The Order of the Moon has always kept an ear to the ground, listening for the return of the supernatural and remnants of Nystia. Long before you or I were born into this world there were two kingdoms. Our own, and Nystia. Nystia was a kingdom of wizards, witches, and magic." Unul explained.

"We were allies until Aludia, the queen of Nystia, was crossed by Lucian. Lucian, her general, assumed the role of Royal Regent and began cutting ties and altering treaties between our kingdoms. Aludia's subjects began to grow weary of Lucian and the problems he was causing. They started to rebel, and as they did, they began to disappear. With each disappearance creatures began to appear as if from a nightmare. Your mother's family was a noble house of Nystia and rebelled against Lucian. They gathered their supporters and created the Order of the Moon to keep watch over Lucian and battle these creatures that appeared. Eventually your ancestors drove a dagger through Lucian's heart.

When Lucian died, something happened. He had casted a spell over the whole of the kingdom, all the subjects and villages disappeared – overcome by the deep darkness of Evanwood Forest all at once. Only your ancestor that defeated Lucian remained. Since then, the story and the task of keeping watch has fallen on your family's order. When you came of age your mother should have inducted you in. Fate had other plans it seems." Unul said.

"Unul, you speak with much confidence, but this sounds like a bard's tale!" I said in disbelief. "You say that my family comes from a magical whimsical kingdom that all-at-once disappeared, yet I have yet to see an ounce of magic fire shoot from my fingertips in all my life. Surely if I am to believe this and venture forth to meet the king you must have some sort of real evidence."

I was skeptical about what Unul had told me, but my soul was lit afire in hope that he did indeed have something more! Could this be what I have been yearning for my whole life? Or some elaborate joke?

"Lady Jara," Unul replied "when you came of age there was to be an induction into the order."

"Why would my father not perform the ceremony?" I quickly chimed, hoping he had a strong answer.

Unul stood from his seat, bringing his right hand to his mouth, his left arm supporting his right elbow. I could tell, he too had struggled with this question on his own. He walked towards the shrubbery and stood there for a moment.

"The truth is I don't know. Perhaps it was because he didn't actually have magic in his blood." He slowly turned and said, his hands still in place. "This is something I have tried to wrap my mind around for weeks. Perhaps he was too distraught with what had happened to your mother, or perhaps he felt it was just wives tales and it was time to put a stop to it…"

Unul began to walk over to me with a look of certainty. He came around to my seat and held his hands out to take hold of mine. I placed my hands in his palms and stood from my seat. He looked me in my eyes, peering into my soul, and spoke –

"What I can tell you is, while I can not initiate you into the order, I have discovered how to connect you to your ancestral powers that lay dormant inside you. What it will bring you I do not know. What I do know is that it is your birth-rite, and it is the proof you seek from my story."

"Last night I was sitting at a feast in the great hall, drinking and eating, perhaps a bit too much. The bards were singing of warriors and wolves, jesters were juggling and stumbling, the guests were speaking of the regions' gossip. This morning I was woken up to a messenger arriving, being summoned by the king, the history of a kingdom only spoken of in tales, and secret orders and magic powers." I said.

"I know all of this comes as a surprise…" Unul interjected.

"A surprise is a cold bath when expecting warm water, or a scantly clad lad waiting with wine in my chambers after a festival. This is a fire bomb from a catapult hurled over the castle walls at dawn." I replied.

"You have always had quite a way with words. Magic kingdoms or not, that has come from your mother." Unul said with a smile.

"I need a moment to think." I said.

I let go of Unul's hands and walked towards the willows next to the pond. It has always been my favorite place for quiet contemplation, or late-night rendezvous that my parents would certainly not approve of. In this instance, I believe I need the energy of both to process my thoughts.

I sat beneath the largest of the willows and stared at my hands. "what power do you behold" I thought to myself, half joking and half seriously. I then pulled out my dagger and laid it in front of me, looking at my reflection on the blade. "…and what secrets do I hold, little friend?" I said out loud to myself. Perhaps what Unul says is true, would it change who I am? Would it change who people think I am?

This could be a waste of my time, or this could change my life forever. I could waste a day performing a ritual that will be boring at worst, or mildly entertaining at best; or everything that I have loathed about everyday castle life could change in an instant…I could have a life of adventure! I only wish this opportunity wasn't tainted by the happenings of late.

"Jara, I know it has only been a short while" Unul said from a short distance behind me. "Neither you, nor I have the luxury of long contemplation. I must know, will you allow me to perform the ceremony?"

I looked down at the dagger in my hands, taking in what he had said. For the first time, it seemed to be calling me, pulling my being to it. It was filling me with a confidence and fire I had never felt holding it before – like a new courtship between two young lovers. I can not live my life not knowing what I am capable of, and I owe it to my father and mother to step up into the position I have been groomed for but never allowed to do – to lead.

"Yes." I said looking up into Unul's eyes. "I will do it."

Unul put his hands together and raised them to his forehead.

"Thank you, Lady Jara," he said. "I will prepare a place to hold the ceremony. We will meet just after dusk. Bring your dagger as it will be bound to you."

"Where shall we meet?" I replied.

Unul looked around the willows, he walked over to a tree and felt it's majestic body.

"This is a place of great importance to you," he said smiling. "We will meet here. Go and rest, gather your supplies for the journey. You will be tired after the ceremony and we leave at first light in the morning."

It was done…I had made my decision. Things were now decided and there was no going back to yesterday. I sheathed Alaia, nodded my head, and began to walk towards the keep. I stopped and turned to Unul.

"Unul," I said, "thank you."

Unul smiled and curtsied, "My Lady." He replied.

"Good evening Unul" I replied "I must say, I expected more than some herbs on the ground and a serving of wine on a table that must have come from the servants quarters!"

Unul looked disapprovingly at me...

"My Lady, I will have you know that this table did not come from the servants' quarters." He said very sternly.

"The miller's home?" I responded joking.

"This fine table was supplied by the finest chef in the castle...along with the herbs." said Unul.

"Well, I am glad that we have got that squared away." I said in a very serious tone.

"I am glad you brought your humor along with you this evening; be sure not to lose it when we leave your lands." Unul said.

Unul then motioned for me to walk up to the chalice on the table.

"Take your dagger and place it on the table." Unul instructed

I pulled the dagger from it's scabbard and lay it on the table. Unul looked at the scroll and then rolled it up and placed it aside. He closed his eyes and held his hands just over the blade.

Unul took three deep breaths and began chanting an incantation, I could not understand what he was saying. It was some strange tongue, beautiful and ancient. As he continued the dagger seemed to start to glow with a blue luminescence. Whatever was in the chalice began to glow the same hue.

The chanting stopped.

With his eyes still closed Unul took the chalice in his hands and held it up, offering it to me.

"Take this and drink it fully." He said while opening his eyes.

He looked right into my eyes, his pupils had the same strange glow. Whatever nonsense I thought he might be up to earlier when he first arrived fled from my thought.

All at once I sobered up to what was taking place around me... my blade was glowing, the wine was glowing, Unul's eyes were glowing. The whole willow grove suddenly felt...different... I felt like I was in a bubble, floating between the clouds and the hills.

I took the cup from Unul's hands and drank all the liquid inside. It tasted...sweet?...tart....fruity....flowery – this was definitely just a wine from the kitchen. It seems this is just a silly jo –

Oh! Oh my! My stomach feels like it is on fire!

"Unul! What have you poisoned me with!" I demanded as I fell to my knees in pain.

"There is no poison, Jara." Unul said reassuringly

"The wine has become the key to open you up to what is locked inside you; your ancestral birthright." He continued

He was right, as quick as the burning began, it dissipated. I could stand up again – but standing felt like flying.

I felt like smoke rising over the fire... Out of my body yet anchored to my hands...

"What is this feeling?" I asked him

"You are connecting." He replied

"Connecting? Connecting to what, to who?" I said in confusion

"To Her." Unul said

I looked around, the entire grove began to glow the same shade as the wine and Unul's eyes earlier. The willows lit up like the full moon after a winter snow storm. The circle with the herbs began to glow. The glow grew brighter and brighter, then all at once there was a flash and a burst of cold wind.

I was blinded by the intensity of the light for a second. When my vision returned even the air around me was glowing softly. There was glowing pollen floating around the air, time seemed to stand still.

I looked to the circle of herbs that was on the ground. In the center was a beautiful glowing woman, she had short hair and was built like a warrior – tall, muscular, in a thin flowing dress. She had on a simple and delicate crown, a wide metal cuff with characters on it I can't decipher, and a belt of golden tiles around her waist. From it hung a slim sword with a simple hilt, as if just for ceremony.

In this moment it was just her and I in the grove. I was face to face with this mysterious glowing woman, surrounded by luminescent nature and pure darkness.

She moved to me in total silence. She looked me in the eyes with a large smile and held her finger up to her mouth as if to shush a crying babe. She reached out with her hand and with two fingers she pushed onto my forehead.

I went blind and I felt a rush of energy enter my body. It felt like an explosion of light from my heart out to my limbs. It radiated out of my body and I felt a heaviness thrown off me. My lungs thrust out all of the old air and I gasped for a fresh breath. My muscles all tensed up and released. My head flung back and I let a new breath enter my body.

I felt as light as a feather, as did my head. I fell to my knees. I was now drunk with the most strange form of substance I had ever encountered. I attempted to get my footing and stand but as I began to stand up my eyes saw white and I fell over in a intoxicated stupor.

The Lake Village

Chapter 4

My eyes were heavy, I felt like I couldn't open them with a pry bar. What had happened last night? Where am I now?

I could hear hooves on dirt, and I felt my body going up and down at a trot. As I slowly began to open my eyes I could see I was tied onto the saddle of my horse, riding just in front was Unul on his. My horse was tethered to his and our sacks were packed behind our saddles.

"Ah! You are awake!" Unul said in a rather cheerful tone, only looking back for a moment.

"There is a pouch of water just to your right." He added.

Still groggy and completely unaware of where it is we were, I looked around to try and get my bearings. Fields of overgrown grass for miles was all I could see on my left, straight ahead we were heading down a small dirt road running parallel with a stream on my right. On the other side of the stream was a colorful small forest that I did not recognize.

I grabbed the water and struggled for a moment to take the cork out, I felt like I had just sparred for a week. The water finally opened with a pop and I took a big swig. The water was warm from the sun beating down on it, but it was refreshing non the less. It seemed to clear the fog from my senses and I could smell the grass and the wet ground from beside the stream. The wind blew from the forest and I could smell the sweetness of the leaves surround me.

We were making our way over a hill, which the stream seemed to cut straight through. At the top I could see a small village in the distance, perched next to a small lake that the stream emptied into. As we drew closer to it I could smell freshly baked bread in the air and the aroma of meat and spices.

As I felt my energy return to me, I could feel my stomach churning so loud it could be mistaken for a wolf stuck in a cage. I had not even thought to look to see where the sun was. I looked up and there it was, just overhead, I had slept until nearly noon!

"Have I been out this whole time?" I asked

"Aye, I could not wake you no matter how I tried!" Unul cracked back at me.

"After the ceremony you collapsed in a slumber. I asked Welum to help me fasten you to the saddle so we could begin our journey." Unul continued.

"Where are we? I do not recall this road nor the town in any previous treks I've made to the capital." I said.

"We are taking a quieter route, since the war began the king's roads have been targets for bands of thieves and small marauding parties from the north. The king's coin has gone to the war effort and little to the safety of the roads. I thought it best to stay off the main paths until you had recovered, so I charted an off the map route." Unul replied.

"Does this route have time for a rest at the local tavern?" I said in a jesting manner, although I was quite serious.

"Yes, as a matter of fact we will be stopping at a lovely tavern called 'The Golden Fish' for a midday meal." Unul answered.

"Mmm, I do like the sound of that!" I said.

"I suggest you get your belly's full; we will be staying in the inn just next door until the morning. From the time we set out tomorrow we will not see a village again until we reach the capital in about a week's time." Said Unul.

These were welcome words; I would certainly eat my weight today. I could not remember the last time I had such hunger! I needed meat, I needed bread, I needed drink! A journey such as this should be started in such a way!

We made our way to a small stable just outside of the village. Unul hopped off his horse and spoke to the stable boy. He handed the boy a couple of coins and came to help me down. I was still fastened in and felt very weak from the night before. I did not have quite the energy back in me yet to even entertain the thought of asking him about it.

I grabbed my bag and sword from my horse and slung them over my shoulder.

"I will go speak with the inn keeper, you go fill your belly with good food and drink. Sit at a table near the corner so that we may talk about last nights' happenings when I join you." Unul told me as I followed him into the center of the village.

"It seems you can read minds now as well!" I said, trotting behind him.

Finally, I could see a painted sign in front of a large tavern that sat just next to the docks at the lake that read 'The Golden Fish.' Unul couldn't even get out a word before I burst through the doors and up to the tavern keeper.

"What can I do you for?" the keeper said

"Two pints of ale, bread, and…"

I looked behind the keeper to see what was over the fire, and then looked through the large window at the dock with the fishing boats tied to it.

"…and whatever came in from that dock today!" I said

"Aye, there was a good haul today. I'll bring it over to you shortly." The keeper said as he filled the tankards.

I grabbed both tankards by their handles with one hand and the fresh bread with the other. I still had my belongings thrown over my shoulder, it was quite the balancing act.

I made my way to the corner where there was a table open and sat on the bench. I put my belongings down, leaned my sword against the wall in the corner, and took what I believe to be the biggest mouthful of bread I have ever had. I followed it up with a large gulp of the ale.

It seemed like everything tasted better on this day! The bread was sweet and the ale refreshing. My hunger and thirst was extreme, I still felt like I had not eaten in a fortnight.

I could see Unul walking through the door, he looked over and saw me, I simply raised my tankard and took a swig. Unul smiled and walked over to me, he took a seat across the table.

"Ah, this ale looks divine!" he said as he reached toward the untouched tankard.

"What are you doing?" I said smacking his hand away. I took a bite of my bread and another large gulp of my ale, finishing it in the process.

"This one is mine! Don't try to steal any of my food as well. You can go get your own!" I stated very blatantly as I grabbed the other tankard and took another sip.

"Hmm, I see the young girl I remember from years ago is still in there..." Unul said looking at me.

The tavern keeper brought over my food. It was redfish! One of my favorites. I remember catching these when fishing with my father and brother on trips to the capital when I was young. We would gut them and throw them right on the fire, eating it with just our hands.

"I would like to trouble you for an ale and a birds breast if you would." Unul said to the keeper.

"No trouble at all" the keeper said, speaking from his belly, and made his way to the back.

"So." I said

"Are you sure you are ready for questions?" Unul said back, motioning his hand towards the dish of fish I was currently devouring.

"I'll have you know I am as curious as I am hungry." I replied.

"What happened last night? I felt like it was some sort of dream. The glowing blades, wine, trees, your eyes…that woman? Who was that woman?" I continued.

"Yes, it was quite real." Unul said, looking up at the keeper who was placing his food and drink on the table.

Unul grabbed his tankard and played with it in his hands for a second.

"You did not imagine anything." He said while taking a swig of his ale.

"It was the first time I have been a part of such a ceremony…if even we should call it that. It is more of a rite of passage for your family. Your family traces back to Nystia, but you are also Nerikian. There are exceptional powers that were locked inside you, powers that you did not know existed. What happened last night unlocked those powers. You may not be aware of what they are right now, but have no doubt they will show themselves to you when appropriate." Unul continued.

"And what of the woman? Was she just a figment of my imagination or was she real?" I said

"I cannot tell you who the woman was. Not because I do not wish to, but because I do not know. She is mentioned in every scripture I found, exactly as she appeared to you and I, but alas, there is no more information than that. It seems that when she touches your head that is the key to unlocking the power inside of you." Unul replied.

"I feel like this is a dream that I have yet to wake from. First a feast, then you turn up at the castle and now a mysterious glowing woman touches my forehead and I wake up a day later in a village I could not even point out on a map!" I said.

"Don't feel so alone in that!" Unul said, "I still feel this way at my age! The days blend together, then all of the sudden you have gone from a snow-covered mountain top to a sandy beach, watching children run in and out of the water's edge. You don't know what happened in between, but you know that somehow, someway, something brought you here."

"So where will we go from here?" I asked.

"We will break our fast in the morning and be off. We will follow the forest where we will intersect with the king's road and take that to the capital. As I said earlier, there have been many issues with the roads of late, but it is the only way to get to Raven's Landing in any decent time." Unul answered.

"Here is a question; if you know all this business about my father and what he was doing – why go to the king at all and not just find him on our own?" I questioned.

"When your father left, he did not leave any trace of his journey in written word or maps. The only person that knows anything of his path is the king. He told King Ansel which paths he would be taking before leaving; and now the king will tell not a soul except for you. Not even I know anything more than I have already told you." Unul replied.

"Well," I said raising my glass, "to the King then!" I said toasting. "We will ride to King Ansel, question him as to my father's whereabouts, and swiftly rescue him from Evanwood Forest!" I stated very matter-of-factly.

"Aye, to King Ansel and your over-simplified rescue plan" Unul replied, raising his glass.

We each took a swig of our drinks. I looked down at my fish and continued to rip into it.

We finished devouring our food and I brought the trays back to the keeper.

"I couldn't help but overhear you and your friend earlier," the keeper said, "if it's Raven's Landing you're heading to, you'd best head to the east side of the lake and follow the stream south through the wood." He continued.

"Through the wood? Would it not be quicker to continue on the path to the King's road?" I replied.

"Well, usually that would be true, 'cept that about a month ago a big storm ripped through there and a river weaseled it's way across the road." He said.

"Has not one made a bridge yet?" I asked

"No, we all figured it would be best to keep it as it is – on account of the bandit attacks on the road." He answered.

"Bandits?" I said.

"Aye, they raid the roads to the south, going in and out of the woods. The river currant will be toe strong and too deep to cross with horse and kit. Follow the stream south through the wood. When you reach the other side you will see Gunter's Tower just off in the distance. It will take you two days' time to venture through the wood, you can rest and restock your water at the tower. There is a barracks there that will allow you rest when you arrive." He continued.

I wondered what Unul would think about this new route.

"Thank you for the information and advice." I said to the keeper. "I believe we will both require another ale now…"

I grabbed both the tankards and head back to the table and handed Unul his tankard.

"So, the road is out and we will need to cut through the wood to Gunter's Tower." I said to Unul.

"Cut through the wood? Who has told you this? The woods and forests in this area are riddled with thieves and bandits." Unul said back.

"The keeper said so, just now." I said.

Unul bit his knuckles for a moment and took a swig of his ale.

"Then it appears we will be going through the wood." He said.

Unul looked a bit annoyed while contemplating this new route.

"Here's to the uncertainty of tomorrow!" He said raising his tankard.

"To the uncertainty of tomorrow!" I mimicked back to him.

We each took a swig. We sat the rest of the time drinking our ales in silence, a sort of meditation. We finished our drinks and left for the inn.

As we walked down the street in this village you would not know there was a war going on, you would not know that anyone was missing from any place, you would not know there was more at all except for the sun rising and setting. Castle life was filled with politics and gossip, pomp and circumstance, excess. Here everyone was just living their life, there was no gossip in the streets, there were no power plays. The people here were talking about what they caught in the lake today, or what they needed to have repaired at the blacksmith. It was refreshing and unfamiliar.

We had spent quite a while in the tavern, the sun was turning orange, signaling to the townsfolk that it was time to return home to their families. We made our way to the inn and into our room. There were two small beds with a fire between them. I threw my rucksack off and leaned my sword against the side of the bed.

I was exhausted. It had not been a tiring day yet I was still tired from the night before. I began opening my rucksack and pulling out a night gown. Unul sat on his bed across from mine, rubbing his eyes and slowly taking his boots off.

"We should get to sleep early and make good time in the morning" I said to him while taking my clothes from the day off and pulling my night gown over my head.

"Aye, you're right. We will leave at first light" he said while kicking his feet on the bed and closing his eyes.

"Unul," I said in a curious tone, "you will continue on this journey with me until we find my father, wont you?" I asked him.

"If it is your wish that I accompany you, I will stay by your side until we return." He said back, still with his eyes closed and not moving a muscle.

"Thank you." I said.

"And so tomorrow begins our journey into the unknown." Unul replied.

I blew out my candle and laid on my back, sheet pulled to my neck. I looked over at Unul, who was still on top of his sheets, clothed, and laying with his legs crossed and his hands folded on his belly. He opened his eyes and turned his head to look at me.

"May good fortune be with us." He said touching his hand to his heart, to his mouth, then to his forehead and up to the air.

He closed his eyes and straightened his head up again. My eyes began to get heavy and I allowed myself to fall into a heavy, restful slumber.

The Path to Gunter's Tower

Chapter 5

I heard the birds chirping outside the window of our room. It was morning. I sat up in my bed and looked out. It was an overcast day. Unul was already sat up in his bed pulling chainmail over his head.

"Put your mail on beneath your clothes." Unul told me.

"It will offer less padding, but keep us less conspicuous on our journey to the tower." He continued.

I took off my gown, pulled up my under garments and threw my mail over my head as well. I adjusted it and tied a loop with a belt around my waist, then threw a slightly oversized shirt over my head and my cloak.

Unul was slipping on his boots, I grabbed my sword belt and fastened it around my hips. I adjusted my clothing to my comfort and moved toward the door.

"Through the woods" I said

"Through the woods." Unul mimicked back.

We fetched our horses from the stable and made our way east toward the bridge the tavern keeper spoke of. I had hoped the clouds would burn off in the morning sun, but it was not the case. It was a dreary day and a wind was blowing. The only part of the trek through the woods I was looking forward to was the wind being tapered back by the trees and growth.

In the distance I could see a small bridge going over a stream which made it's way from the woods. That would be our path. As if on cue, it began to drizzle rain drops down on us. Unul and I pulled our hoods over our heads and kept our trot to the bridge.

"Take a deep breath m'lady." Unul said, "this will be your last view of any open air for the next short while. These woods are thick and old."

"Good, then it will make for a great trial run before we head to Evanwood." I said back.

"Ah! That's the spirit!" Unul cheered.

We moved off the road and onto an overgrown small dirt trail which followed the stream through the woods. We made our way into the woods. Luckily, it seems that because the road is out ahead there has been more travel on this path. For now, it remains mostly clear.

We continued the path for most of the morning. Just before noon the weather began to turn for the worse. Thunder filled the sky and the rain began to fall like buckets from a window. The ground became too muddy to stay on our horses. We dismounted and continued on the trail, that water still fell harder than I had seen in ages. We kept our eyes on the path and the stream, the water level was rising at a fast rate.

"This rain is flooding the stream!" I yelled to Unul.

"You are right!" He said back, "We must move up hill into the forest incase this path is swept away in the current!"

Something mentioned so simply was such a task in practice. The horses were scared from the thunder and the sound of the stream gaining volume and speed. They were bucking and pulling away from us as we tried to lead them up the bank and into the woods a bit more.

As Unul was leading his horse over the ridge of the bank there was a loud CRACK and a tree just on the other side of the stream exploded into smoking pieces of lumber. The ground shook from the sound of the thunder just overhead. His horse reared and pulled away, sprinting towards my steed and I at a full gallop, knocking Unul backwards into the mud.

"Jara! Jump away!" Unul yelled from the mud.

I looked around, there was no where to run to, and if I did not get my horse away with me the two of them would collide and end up in the swollen stream, which now seamed more of a river. Unul's horse was still charging towards me, I could grab the exposed tree roots on the ridge next to the path and pull myself away, but not my horse. There was only one thing I could do.

I pulled my horses reins in the direction we had come from and let out a loud "YAAHH!" and smacked his buttocks as hard as I could. He reared up and ran, Unul's horse just behind him as I threw myself at the exposed roots and held on to not get trampled by the frightened creature.

Unul got up and made his way stumbling back down the hill towards me, I let go of the roots and slid back down to the path, which was now becoming flooded with water.

The horses were gone, and along with them all of the supplies we had fastened to their saddles. We had nothing but a canteen of water, a fire steel, and our blades.

"We must go back and find them!" I said to Unul.

"No, we can not go back! We must continue on by foot until we get to the tower. We can not risk the flood washing away the paths forward more than it already has!" Unul yelled back to me.

I nodded; he was right. The horses would be back in the town by the time we even got to the wood's edge. We needed to press forward. We had enough water to get us to the tower in our canteens, and a day and a half without food would not kill us. Unfortunately, our oil cloths and bed rolls were on our horses. Tonight would not be a very pleasant night's sleep.

We made our way back up the bank to the ridge and into the woods. There was more coverage under the large trees than there was next to the stream. It did a good job keeping us a bit dryer. We made our way through quicker and easier than we would have with the horses in tow.

We walked for hours before stopping again, not saying a word. Just following the winding swollen stream was a task from the woods. The forest was littered with fallen trees and bushes blocking our way. Eventually the weather began clearing and the rain stopped. The sun began poking it's head before setting for the night. That is when we stopped.

"We must find a spot to rest for the night." Unul said to me as he walked towards a large tree that had fallen at an angle, leaving a small triangular shelter between it and a small cliffside on the hill.

"This will do well for tonight." He exclaimed as he felt the large tree to make sure it was sound.

"If you can start a fire with whatever you can find, I will gather some evergreen and moss for bedding." I said to him while handing him my fire steel.

Unul took it and began looking for dry wood around our chosen camp. I began back tracking a bit to wear I saw the materials I needed. I broke off the branches of the evergreens and peeled the moss, carrying it all back to our camp. I laid them down under the tree and created bedding to keep us warm and dry through the night. Unul had managed to get the fire going.

The whole process had become very meditative, there was no space in my mind or time available to think about or do anything else except the tasks at hand. Right now we needed to dry off and get some rest.

I sat by the fire and warmed myself, enjoying a sip of the sweet water from the streams that went through the previous town. After a day like today the water felt like a delicious mead warming my throat and body.

"We must take shifts tonight." He said as he sat next to me, warming his hands over the fire.

"I will take the first shift." He continued.

"If that's the case then I am going to go lay down now." I said, getting up and heading towards the makeshift bedding.

Unul did not say a word. Neither of us needed to, it had been quite a day. I lay on the evergreens and moss and it feels like a warm bed, my eyes are heavy and before I know it I am in a deep slumber.

…

I wake up in my room at Dragon's Reach and sit up, confused.

"What kind of dream was that?" I say aloud to myself.

Magic ceremonies, quaint villages, trekking through the woods in a storm? Perhaps there was something more in that wine last night that no one told me about!

I wrap a quilt around me so I can sneak a piece of bread from the kitchen before anyone else starts eating. As I walk down the halls, I cannot help but notice that the guards and servants are all missing. I suppose I cannot think too much of it, it was quite the feast last night after all, I am sure the whole town needs a slow morning.

I continue making my way to the kitchen, but something catches the corner of my eye and moves around a corner. Most mornings I wouldn't be bothered, but it does seem odd today with how quiet the castle is.

I am going to follow it.

I turn around and move in the same direction the figure moved in. As I turn the corner I see…her? The glowing magical woman from my dream? Except now she just seems to be normal, there's no glow at all.

She stops at the end of the hall and looks at me, smiles, and then turns the corner and keeps walking.

I follow her faster down the halls, as I turn the corner she is stood in front of my mother's room – the door is shut but she just walks through it, as if it's nothing more than an illusion.

I move quickly to the door and feel it – it feels like…a real door?

Impossible.

I open the door and walk in, my mother is sat in her chair staring out the window as always, but the woman is standing next to her.

"Who are you?" I ask

All I get in response is a smile from the woman.

"Can you not speak? Who…what are you? Why have I seen you in my dreams?" I say

She does not answer again, instead she motions for me to come closer to her and my mother. My curiosity gets the better of me and I do her bidding. As I get closer she motions for me to sit on a chair across from my mother. I do as she asks.

"What is this about?" I ask again.

She places her left hand over my mother's heart and her right hand on my mother's shoulder, as if shocked from cold water, my mother takes a quick large inhale and exhale. Her eyes get wide and move around, her pupils move to me!

"H-h-how?" I ask startled, "how are you doing this?"

My mother's lips crack open

"You will know who I am soon, know that I am a friend of your mother's, a friend of your family's, and a friend of yours. I am sorry that I had to bring you here, but it was necessary." She said, using my mother's voice as her own.

"What do you mean 'bring me here'? We are here, right now." I reply

"We don't have much time," she says through my mother's lips again. "Something has been unlocked in you, there is no time for practice now, you must trust your intuition when the time comes. You will feel like you need to do things and you will not know why. Do what you feel and you will discover all of the things you are capable of. They will come to the surface like fish waiting to be fed."

"You sound like Unul in my dream last night." I said to her, seeing what kind of reaction I would get.

"That was no dream…this…this is the dream, Jara. It was the only way to connect to you right now." My mother's lips said.

"Wha-"

"Until next time!" she said through my mother, cutting me off.

…

I am shaken awake by Unul, back in the forest. The fire is out and Unul put's his hand over my mouth and motions for me to be quiet. He looks around, I quietly sit up and hold my breath to listen.

There is a commotion going on not far from us. I can hear the voices of five men that appear to be aggressors, and the voices of an older man and a younger boy. It sounds like they are just over the hill from our camp.

"We must see what is going on." I say to Unul.

"No, we can not interfere with whatever is going on, we have our own obligations first. This will have to play out in whichever way the Gods deem fit" He responded.

I felt my blood boil; I was raised to restore order and help when possible, as were all the children of nobles raised in Dragon's Reach. I would not lay here and sleep while something was going on just over from me. I grabbed my sword from it's scabbard and fastened my dagger to my waist.

"You can sit here and sleep if you would like, I am going to see what is going on!" I replied in an angry whisper.

I made my way up the hill. There were three men with torches and two men tying an older man in a tunic and a younger boy, no more than 14, to two trees facing each other. There was a camp fire going in the middle of the small clearing. It looked like before they got caught, he got his war hammer stuck in one of the group's head. One of the men began talking to the older man.

"It's too bad your coin purse was so light, old man. Maybe if ya had a bit more in it I'd think about letting the two of ya go. But now we's got a bit of coin and one of us's heads smashed in." The man said while the others were jarring him on. "I think it's about time that I return the favor, 'ey?"

The man pulled the war hammer from his fallen comrade and walked over to the old man.

"This will solve nothing, let us go on our way and I won't mention this incident to anyone! You have my word as a knight!" the old man said.

"A knight that can't even protect himself huh? Sounds like you're a bit old to be prancing around in armor now!" the leader of the group said.

"At least let the boy go, he's done nothing to-"

Before the old knight could finish the leader of the group walked over to him and swung the old knight's hammer at his head, again, and again.

"Now that does make me feel a bit better!" The leader said, the others cheering on.

Just then Unul made his way to my position and asked what I had found.

"It seems like the talker is the leader. From what I can gather, they tried to rob these two that are tied up and the old man killed one of theirs before they were caught. The leader just killed him with his own hammer." I whispered

"Do you have a plan yet?" He asked

"If we can take out the leader and the largest of the group that's holding the rope, the other three might scatter and we can get the boy out of there." I said back to him.

"That's a good start. I will use my bow and take out the leader, you get around to the fallen tree next to them. When I let loose my arrow you go after the large one and I will cut the boy loose." Unul added.

I nodded and made my way down to the fallen tree trunk. I could hear the men getting even more rowdy, emboldened by their recent murder. They were sticking the torches in the boy's face, terrorizing him. I signaled to Unul.

The leader of the group walked over to the boy who was shedding tears over the helplessness of the situation and the loss of the old man.

"Don't cry laddy, you be seeing the old man soon enough." The leader said as he held up the hammer, ready to swing it down. Just then the hammer dropped from his grip, the boy looked up to see the tip of an arrow sticking from the man's eye. The man fell to the ground limp.

It took a moment for the rest of the group to realize what was going on. I jumped over the log and drove my sword into the brute's gut. He fell to his knees letting go of the rope. I pulled my sword out and, in a flourish, brought my blade down on his neck, separating his head.

Unul came running down the hill to rescue the boy, but as he got close one of the bandits was able to get to reach him with his make-shift mace and landed a hit right in the gut. Unul dropped to his knees clenching his abdomen and gasping for air.

"This isn't quite how this was supposed to go!" I yelled to Unul, who in turn just let out a whimpering whine and rolled on his side in pain, trying to catch his breath.

It was three against one now, not my best odds. As one of them got close I kicked the coal and ash from their campfire at his face, making him back away. The two others split up, one moved toward me while the other went towards the boy.

The boy was desperately trying to get himself out of the rope now the bandit that had been keeping it taught was dispatched. He managed to free his arms and began kicking his legs out. The bandit made his way towards the boy, but Unul managed to catch his leg and trip him. The boy broke free and grabbed the old man's hammer. The bandit kicked Unul in the face and broke free, as he went to stand, he looked up and the boy was over him. A swift swing of the hammer was the boy's judgement over the bandit. The boy then dropped it to help tend to Unul.

The bandit that was pursuing me pulled out his axe. As he swung his axe I dodged to the right and gave a cut to the back of his leg, bringing him down for a moment. The bandit limped back up and gave another great swing. I caught the beard of his axe with my sword blade and knocked him over the head with the pommel of my sword. He kneed me in the gut and I dropped gasping for air.

I grabbed my sword and stumbled back towards the fire, putting it between us. He limped towards me as his comrade did the same (albeit with only one usable eye and burns from the coals on his face). The boy was still tending to Unul, who was having trouble picking himself up off the ground.

As I propped myself up on my sword I felt a strange sense of calm and warmth in my heart. My dream popped into my head for just a split second. I closed my eyes and followed my intuition. I saw in my mind, in my heart, the campfire grow and heat up like a blacksmith's forge.

I opened my eyes and saw the fire had grown, I made ready my sword and took a deep breath in, as I exhaled the fire bellowed to a shade of white and blew back like a firestorm at the two limping bandits, engulfing them in flames and sending them scattering in the woods.

The skirmish was over, and I had indeed unlocked something that was hiding deep within me.

I made my way to the boy and Unul. The boy and I put him over our shoulders and got him to the camp fire so we could take a look at him. We lay him down and I lifted his shirt, his mail stopped any punctures but the lower portion of his rib cage was bruised. It looked like he had broken a few ribs when he took the hit of the mace.

"Boy, help me take his mail off so he can breathe easier." I said.

We each held him with one arm and took his mail off with the other.

"Thank you" Unul said with a short breath, "Prop me up on this log so I can rest."

I helped him get his back up the log.

"There you go. By the looks of it you must have a couple of broken ribs. Nothing some rest cannot fix! We will continue our journey in the morning. You did surprisingly good for someone your age." I said to him.

"I'm not entirely that old, but I was perhaps a bit more tired than usual. You did well, Jara. You do your father proud." Unul replied in a broken manner, getting the words out between short air gasps.

"We must get him to the tower! We cannot wait with his injuries!" The boy said to me.

"There is no use in making for any refuge now. It is far too dark, and he will not be able to walk with us. His injuries will not kill him. Besides, we still do not know who you are! I was honor bound to save you, but we are not acquaintances." I said to the boy.

"A fair point madam, my name is Tripp. I am…was… Sir Krinn's squire of 8 years. I thank you for my rescue, it is a shame that Sir Krinn had gotten too sickly to put up a good fight, but he died with dignity. I am now duty bound to safely escort you out of these woods and to the barracks at Gunter's Tower. There you will find shelter and –" I had cut the boy off with my own laughter!

I did not try to intentionally laugh, it just erupted from the bottom of my belly and into the air. Unul and I had just saved this boy and he now thinks that he is saving us! This has been quite the day!

"I'm sorry madam, what is so amusing?" the boy said.

"It's Lady, actually. And you are quite amusing! I believe it was I that saved you! We will make our way to the tower together tomorrow at first light." I answered.

"L-l-lady? I am sorry m'lady, I had no idea. What is the plan then? To just sleep? " the boy replied.

"That is exactly what the plan is, Tripp the squire. If we are to reach the tower before nightfall tomorrow, we must be rested and have our wits about us. Help me move these bodies next to the trees there. If you want a proper burial for your Sir Krinn there, I will help you." I said to him.

"Yes, I'd like that. Thank you." He answered.

We dragged the sorry lot of bandits' carcasses over to the trees Tripp and Sir Krinn were tied to before. We carried the Sir Krinn's body to a small clearing close by and we began digging a hole. It was only a shallow grave, but it was with whatever energy we could muster at that point. We lay the old knight's body into the shallow hole and covered him with some of the displaced dirt and some large rocks nearby.

I left the knight-less squire to say his goodbye and made my way back over to the fire were Unul was laying. It seemed he was able to get some rest and it was time for me to as well. Everything that had just transpired seemed only a sidenote; nothing more than a temporary adrenaline rush. My eyes felt heavy, and I allowed them to drift shut.

Out of the Woods

Chapter 6

I felt a warmth on my face and began to open my eyes. I pitched myself up and looked around, the sunrise was making its way through the branches above and glistening all around. Only now could I see the beauty of this area that held such carnage last night. There were downed trees with new seedlings growing in the cracks and crevice's they were littered with. Unul was beginning to stir, Tripp was still fast asleep.

In the chaos and darkness of the night, Tripp looked much younger, perhaps it was his hairless face, or the chivalrous way he spoke. In the morning sun I could see that he was much older, but not quite in his twenties...I did not dwell on it, once we reached the tower we would be rid of him.

I slowly stood up to get a look all around. As I stretched my shoulders, chest, and arms I could see just behind a tree a small hand drawn wagon next to a sack. I moved toward it slowly with my hand on my sword's hilt. I could not be sure there were not more bandits in the distance last night that got away. As I moved closer to it I could see all was safe. I inspected the wagon, checking the wheels and joints; it seemed to be in good order. I opened the sack next to it –

Ah! What good fortune had fallen upon us at last! It seemed that the bandits had a fresh supply of food and drink! Apples, a loaf of bread, cheese, and a bottle of mead. This is what we needed to raise spirits and invigorate our last trek through the woods.

I grabbed the sack and carried it to what was left of the fire. I pulled out the mead and took out the cork, taking a swig for myself.

"A little early to be sipping from the bottle?" I could hear Unul say softly.

"Oh, silly Unul, it's never too early. Would you like an apple or cheese to break your fast?" I replied.

"I think I will stick to the apple, thank you very much." Unul said holding his hands out.

"You are in luck," I said while tossing him an apple, "it seems the bandits had a small wagon that me and the boy can cart you through the rest of the journey in."

"That is auspicious! Who is the boy? Did you find anything out about him and the old man?" Unul asked.

"Yes, the old man was Sir Krinn. The boy said he had been sickly as of late and could not put up a fight. The boy was his squire, Tripp." I answered.

Unul's face changed to one of sadness and contemplation.

"That is a shame…" he said. "Sir Krinn accompanied me on a number of campaigns back in our prime. He was a valiant and honorable man. If this boy was his squire, it would be wise to keep him close for the time being. Krinn was an excellent judge of character, if this boy accompanied him for any length of time he is certainly cut from the same cloth." Unul continued.

I looked at the boy sleeping. He had only a poorly fitted tunic and a bullock dagger on him. Hardly ready for confrontation.

"I have not given him our names." I said to Unul

Unul thought for a moment, "No, it is better that we keep that and our business to ourselves for the time being." He declared.

I took another large bite from my apple and looked around the immediate area. Sir Krinn's sword was in it's sheath and belt leaning against a tree, likely removed by the bandits. The war hammer was next to a puddle of blood and bones from where it was used by Tripp last night.

I collected the weapons and dropped them on the ground next to Tripp. It startled him and he woke up.

"What are you doing with these?" he asked.

"We are not out of the woods yet, Tripp the squire. Sir Krinn will have no use for these anymore and you are under armed. Arm yourself with his sword and hammer for the journey. When we get to the tower you can do what you will with them." I said to him.

"Of course, Lady...lady..." Tripp said, fishing for a name.

"Just Lady, for now." I replied. "Now then, have an apple and help me get this wagon over here." I continued tossing him my half-eaten apple.

He caught the apple and took a bite of it. He stood up and fastened Sir Krinn's sword around his waist.

Tripp followed me to the wagon and we wheeled it to the remnants of last nights fire.

"Gather some of the moss from the ground and spread it around the side of the wagon." I instructed.

As Tripp followed my orders I gathered the food and drink that I found in the sack and placed it in the wagon, along with Sir Krinn's war hammer, and Unul's bow and sword. Tripp returned and began spreading the moss he had collected amongst the base of the wagon.

"There!" I said to Unul, "Now you can enjoy a comfortable journey to the tower!"

"Your generosity knows no bounds, m'lady." Unul replied jokingly. "Now help me up and in so that we may get started." He continued.

Tripp and I helped Unul onto his feet and into the wagon. We each grabbed a handle and began moving at a comfortable pace.

The morning was beautiful, a stark contrast to the prior day. The sunlight glistened red, yellow, and orange through the forest, the pollen in the air shined like fairy dust in the stories. It seemed all of us needed to breathe in this new day's air, it was not until we took a stop break for a midday meal next to the now calm stream that the silence was broken.

"Squire, how was it that you and Sir Krinn found yourself in these woods and into the hands of that scum?" Unul asked Tripp while taking a sip from the bottle of mead.

"Sir Krinn and I have been working to clear the roads of highway men for the better part of a year. Not more than two months ago he became ill and could not recover. We were following the road to the tower so that he could seek care from the healers there. At some point the road had washed out and we needed to turn back and head through these woods. When we entered we had to dismount our horses, as we did there was great thunder and our horses ran off." Tripp paused for a moment as Unul handed him the bottle of mead and took a sip.

"The rains had taken a toll on him, he expended most of his energy just walking in the mud without his horse. I suggested that we stop and rest before moving on, he insisted we continue onward. We kept going until he could not walk anymore.

While we rested the bandits snuck up on us. I had a rope around me before I knew what was happening, Sir Krinn managed to free his hammer and end one of them before being captured himself. The thieves were looking for coin, but all our belongings ran off on our horses. From there it would seem you already know the rest." Tripp continued.

"I am sorry about Sir Krinn, I knew of him well. The kingdom is lesser without him." Unul replied.

"If not for you two I would be rotting at the base of that tree. I thank you both for your actions last night." Tripp said.

I grabbed the mead from Tripp and raised the bottle.

"To Sir Krinn, may he drink with the gods tonight!" I said, taking a sip and passing it to Tripp.

"May he feast with his brother in arms." Tripp declared taking a sip of his own.

"Aye, to Sir Krinn." Unul said solemnly, taking a bite of cheese.

We sat in silence for a short while, eating the apples and cheese, drinking the last of the mead, and staring at the slowly flowing stream. The water was clear and peaceful, you could easily see the fish swimming about. There were deer on the other side drinking from it, one raised it's head and stared into my eyes. It had no fear of us, it was content and unbothered. It broke eye contact with me and they moved on back up the bank and into the woods.

"We are nearly to the tower." Unul declared.

"Then let us get moving again, we can get you some proper care." I replied.

Tripp and I stood up from the rocks we were perched on and took hold of the wagon. As we moved further upstream a trail began to appear again. We continued up the trail for the next three hours, again, in silence.

"There it is!" Tripp said, breaking the silence.

I looked up from the dirt path and could see the peak of the tower and it's flags waving far off in the distance. It would be good to eat some proper food and resupply. This two-day journey felt like a week! I was worried about Unul as well.

A mace to the gut without a gambeson or plate on was certainly a serious injury. Usually, Unul had much more to say, but today he was content being pulled in the wagon. He needed care.

"Great!" I replied, "Let us make haste! My companion must see the healers there."

Tripp and I quickened our pace as best we could without causing Unul more discomfort.

I could see the tree line in the distance and fields before the tower. We were out of the woods at last! We made our way into the fields and towards the gate. The closer we got the more I felt my energy return to me.

At last, I could make out the faces of the two guards. As we grew closer the guards crossed their spears across the gate.

"Identify yourself and state your business here!" The guard shouted as we approached.

Tripp began to speak, "I am Tri – "

"Quiet boy, let me handle this." I said cutting him off with a hand up to his mouth.

"I am Lady Jara of Dragon's Reach," I said pointing to myself.

As I said that Tripp's eyes grew wide and stared me down.

"The boy is Tripp, squire of Sir Krinn, who was slain just last night." I continued. "My companion in the wagon is Sir Unul of Raven's Landing, a member of King Ansel's council."

Tripp's eyes grew even wider as he looked back at Unul.

"Sir Unul was injured when we rescued the boy from bandits and needs to see a healer. The boy needs a wash, fresh clothing, and a bed. I need to speak with the captain of this barracks." I declared.

"Of course, m'lady! Follow me inside!" the guard said.

"You're – " I cut Tripp off before he could continue.

"Not now, I must speak with the captain. I was you're age not that long ago, I know you have questions. This evening in the dining hall you may ask me whatever you wish. I will answer what I can."

The guard ushered Tripp to a washroom while the healers came out and brought Unul into their quarters. Another guard asked me to follow him to the captain's office. He led me up a winding staircase, to the top of the tower. He knocked two times and opened the door.

The captain was sitting at his desk marking up a map that he had spread across it. He looked up at the sudden intrusion into his space.

"Captain Ziis, I introduce Lady Jara of Dragon's Reach. She's only just arrived with Sir Unul of Raven's Landing and a squire." The guard said.

"This was certainly unexpected, please leave us." He said to the guard.

The guard stood up straight and kicked his heels together, then turned face and walked out, closing the door behind him.

"Lady Jara," Captain Ziis said as he walked over, "it is an honor to meet you!" he declared as he took my hand and gave a slight bow.

"You are kind, captain. It was not my intention to intrude. My companions and I are on our way to meet with King Ansel. The road was washed out and we needed to cut through the woods. Along the way we encountered bandits. Sir Unul was injured and we saved the squire of Sir Krinn. I ask that you give us shelter and supplies so that we can continue to the capitol." I said.

The captain looked unphased.

"Yes, I've heard about these bandits. It seems the road washed out not long ago. We've had many a traveler pass through here as of late. Most of them have complained about being prayed on in the woods. I have not been able to spare any of my troops to take care of it." He said.

"Well, then you will be pleased to know that Sir Unul and I took care of it for you!" I said.

The captain's expression changed and a large smile grew over his face.

"That is welcome news!" he said.

He walked to a table beneath a window and poured two glasses of wine. He handed me one of them.

"Welcome to Gunter's Tower, Lady Jara!" he said joyfully, toasting my glass.

"When you walked in, I was mapping out my troops journey back to Raven's Landing. A new batch of men are arriving in a few days' time and these men will be returning to the capitol. We have the extra beds and supplies; you are welcome to stay here and make the final leg of your journey with my men." The captain offered.

This was better news than I could have hoped for. Without horses it would take us a week to get back to Raven's Landing. With a garrison we would have protection in numbers and make better time. Unul would also be able to ride in a proper wagon.

"Thank you, Captain, I gladly accept your hospitality! I must go check on Sir Unul. If ever you find yourself traveling near Dragon's Reach, know that our gates are always open to you!" I replied.

I swallowed my glass of wine and placed it on the table and left the captain to his work. I walked back down the winding staircase and into the healers' chambers. As I walked though the door I could see Unul propped up in his bed, he looked much better than the last I saw him.

"Ah you've found me!" Unul said

"Yes, it appears I have. I just spoke with the captain, he has offered to let us stay until his garrison changes in a few days' time. I suspect you will even have your own proper carriage for the trip!" I replied.

"You must talk with the boy, the healer tells me that he has not moved from his bed since we arrived here." Unul added.

"And what will I say to him? I am sorry your mentor had his head smashed in? I have nothing to offer, Unul. I can answer all he asks except for the whole reason we're on this journey." I said.

"No, I think you do have something to offer him. I knew Sir Krinn in his prime. The boy must have skill and a fire inside. This quest will be long…and it will be hard…and I will not be with you to help." Unul added.

"What do you mean you will not be with me?" I asked.

"The healers say it will be months before I am back to my best. Months that you can not wait. I have already sent a messenger bird to the king so that he may pull a couple of skilled warriors and adventurers from the kingdom to aid you on your journey. I think the boy will be an asset." Unul answered.

"An asset? When we found him he was tied to a tree crying!" I responded in protest.

"He had spent four years of his young life in the service of a mentor that he learned from every day. Someone that shaped who he is, someone that, if not ill, could have certainly bested those barbarians in the woods. And this I add, yes you saved him, but he also saved me. If not for Tripp I would be spread around the clearing in those woods. Take him with you, let him learn from you and if he has proven himself when you return I will knight him myself as a knight of Dragon's Reach to help guard the pass." Unul answered calmly.

"You have become more a member of the court than a warrior it seems." I said. "If you can not make the journey, then you are right. I will need a group of companions to venture forth with me, and we can use another knight at Dragon's Reach – should he prove himself."

I went to walk away but paused for a moment.

"Damn your logic." I said to Unul.

I walked out of the room to find Tripp. I made my way down the corridor and to the guard barracks. I looked inside but there was no one there. I continued to look around the tower until I found someone passing by.

"Excuse me," I said grabbing the shoulder of a man walking down the hall with a crate in his hand. "Do you know where the boy I came in with is?"

"O'course m'lady," he responded, "the barracks was filled up so we's set ye up in the store room on account of it being empty. The lad's been there the whole time he has."

"Thank you." I said and let him continue is tasks.

I walked to the store room, as I walked in I saw two makeshift cots, two chests to store whatever items we had, and a lantern on a table with one leg cut far too short. There was Tripp, sat on his cot closest to the door. As I walked in he looked up at me.

"We have some things to discuss." I said to him before he could open his mouth.

"Yes, but I need some real food in my belly first." He replied.

Just then there was a knock on the door frame, one of the stewards had brought us fresh clothes and a wash basin with two sponges.

"The captain thought you both might appreciate a wash and some clean clothes." The steward said.

"There will be food in the hall shortly, when you're done." He added, shutting the door behind him.

"Ah, great! I need to get the weight of this mail off my shoulders." I said.

I pulled off my mud-covered cloak and shirt, undid my belt and pulled my mail off me for the first time in two days. It was a literal weight off my shoulders and I could breath easy again. I grabbed a sponge and began cleaning the dirty and blood off my skin. As I did I noticed Tripp had turned to face the wall and held his hand over his eyes.

"What are you doing?" I asked sarcastically.

"My lady, you are not decent! I must advert my eyes!" he answered.

"Tripp, you are a fool. We are warriors, we have seen and will see again men and women split in two, guts spilled over an old man's belt, a body with a missing head. Least you be worried about a pair of breasts! Clean yourself and put on these new clothes. We will talk over our meal." I said.

This was not my first time on campaign, and I knew well that there was no room for pleasantries and high court manners when things needed to be done. The quicker Tripp was to learn it the better.

"Yes, my lady, as you say." Tripp responded.

He began getting himself cleaned up and in new clothes, the whole time still doing his best to avert his eyes and keep his back toward me. I giggled at his prudeness masquerading as honor.

It felt good to be clean again and in fresh clothes. It was revitalizing. Tripp and I made our way to the hall where there was meat, bread, and vegetables waiting for us. We sat at the end of a rather empty table and filled our plates.

For food that looks quite good, it was perhaps the most bland I have had in my life. The vegetables were over-cooked, the meat had no flavor, and even the bread was tasteless. The cheese and apples from the bandits' sack had more character than this.

I reached over and grabbed the pitcher of ale and filled my cup and Tripp's cup. I could tell he had just as hard of a time with his food as I and could use something to wash it down with. We both took a big swig and got our dry meat into our bellies.

As we took that swig both our eyes widened – the ale was delicious. I suppose it makes sense, if the food is bad the drink must be good or the captain would have a mutiny on his hands. With each bite we took, another sip was taken. We took our time eating and drinking as to not end up on the floor. Eventually it was just a couple of guards telling stories off in the corner, Tripp, and I left in the hall. I could tell from Tripp's energy he was itching to ask me a slew of questions.

"Go on," I said, "ask away."

"You are Lady Jara! You." He said to me.

"Well, when you say it like that I feel as if I should be questioning it!" I replied.

"I'm sorry m'lady, it's just I've heard so much about you at the tournaments. They say that you are one of the best skilled women in the kingdom with a dagger or sword! And that you and a small scouting party held off nearly three dozen marauders at the pass!" Tripp said in excitement.

"It was more like two dozen, but yes. That is I." I said.

"And Sir Unul! Sir Krinn would speak of him often and fondly. He told me stories about their time fighting together. He would tell me about Sir Unul's skill as a tactician and with a bow, he would say that Sir Unul could read a book one time and remember everything in it!" Tripp continued.

"I would say most of that is true." I chirped.

"I must ask, how is it that I am rescued in the woods by the two of you, seemingly in the middle of nowhere?" He asked.

"That was divine coincidence. We were heading to this tower the same as you after learning the bridge was out. We stopped at a town by the lake where they gave us that information ahead of time. We were resting when Unul heard the commotion and woke me up. The rest you know." I answered.

"Yes, but why?" Tripp asked again.

I pulled out my dagger and put it on the table between Tripp and myself.

"This dagger is Alaia, it is an ancient relic passed through the generations of my family. Many lords, ladies, knights, even kings have made oaths upon it. Before we continue this conversation, you must swear before it that you will tell no one of what we speak of." I said very sternly.

Tripp did not even wait a second after I said that before his hands were on the dagger.

"I swear upon this blade, and my life that I will not reveal anything you tell me to another soul." Tripp said, staring directly into my eyes.

"I was summed by King Ansel to go to the capital and see him. Sir Unul was sent by him to see to it that I got to Raven's

Landing safely. My father left for an expedition under King Ansel's orders and never returned. We are to find him and see what happened to him and his men. He was also meant to bring an artifact back that could aid with the war in the north." I told him.

"Outstanding!" Tripp replied.

"You are not surprised by this at all?" I asked, surprised by his reaction myself.

"When I learned both of your names at the gate earlier, I knew there must be an important reason why the two of you were together here." Tripp responded.

"Unul and I have spoken, we have a proposition for you. You are a squire without a knight now that Sir Krinn is gone, and Unul is a knight with no squire. Unul's injuries will prevent him from going further than Raven's Landing on this quest. When we get to the capital there will be a group of warriors selected by the king himself to accompany me on the journey. Come with us – I cannot guarantee your safety, but if and when you return, Unul has given his word that he will make you a knight of Dragon's Reach. What say you?" I said to Tripp.

Tripp did not even hesitate before saying "I accept!"

"I accept, absolutely. I am ready to prove myself, Sir Krinn's sword and hammer will once again draw blood for a noble cause. I will join you." Tripp continued.

"There is more, but the rest must wait until we speak with the king." I added cautiously.

"Understood, my lady." Tripp answered.

"One more thing, while on the journey we will not use titles or places we are from. After we leave the capital and in private you will refer to us only by our names. We must try to keep our task secret." I added.

"Of course, my lady." Tripp said.

I gave him a look over his use of my title and stood up from the table.

"Tomorrow morning we will meet in the armory. I must know what you are capable of, we will spar in the courtyard. Now, I must get some rest. Good night, Tripp." I said.

"Good night, Jara." Tripp said, he had obviously gotten the point.

I smiled at him and made my way back to our room. I pulled the ill-fitting nightgown that the captain gave me to replace my lost clothes from when our horses ran off. As large as it was, it was far better than wet clothes and chainmail. I lay on the cot and let my eyes drift shut.

The Proving Grounds

Chapter 7

I woke to the sound of the door closing. I looked over and Tripp's cot was tidy and he was gone, likely to fill his belly. I sat up and grabbed my clothing, quickly getting changed and tying my hair into a braid to keep it from my face.

I stood up and made my way to the armory. The tower was especially well stocked; there were walls of swords, spears, bows, arrows, bearded axes, hammers, maces, and shields. I could spend my whole day here, but there were things to be done.

I grabbed two spears, two shields, two training swords, and a bow and a quiver of arrows. I slung most of it over my shoulders and had the rest under my arms. I must have looked like a mad woman armed to the teeth leaving the armory. I made my way to the training grounds in the courtyard just outside.

I leaned the spears and swords against the weapons rack and strung the bow. I looked around, no sign of Tripp yet. I decided to shoot some arrows until he arrived. I stuck the arrows into the ground beside me and notched my first arrow. I took a slow methodical stretch back, pulling the bowstring, when my hand got to position, I let a slow breath out and let loose the arrow.

A hit, center mass.

I continued to fire arrows as a sort of meditation until I heard Tripp's voice behind me.

"If that target had a heart, it would have more holes than a sponge." Tripp said.

"Let's see your skill with a bow." I said to him.

"As you wish." Tripp replied, taking the bow from my hands.

He pulled an arrow from the ground and notched it rather unsteadily. As he drew back his form was amateur at best. He let loose his arrow too soon with his shoulders raised far too much. The arrow shot a yard over the target.

"If that target had a heart," I said mimicking Tripp's previous comment, "it would be beating as calmly as a monk in the garden."

Tripp gave me an embarrassed look.

"Sir Krinn never focused much on ranged weapons. He said that battles are won with steel and wits, not with arrows." Tripp explained.

I shook my head.

"That's an ancient approach at best." I said, "Battles are won by any means necessary, and not all battles are on the battlefield, some are in the woods, alone, tied to a tree. After all, it was Unul's arrow that saved your life."

Tripp looked slightly surprised. He took a moment in reflection about what I had said. I was pleasantly surprised myself. I have met many squires that balk when questioned about things they are told. He seemed to take a comment like this as a learning experience.

"I never thought about it like that. I will practice my archery." Tripp answered.

"I don't think there is much point in continuing with the bow today. How is your skill with a spear?" I asked.

Tripp smiled, "Now that is something I can do."

We each grabbed a spear and moved into a sparring pen. I circled around, lightly tapping his spear. He was quick to repel the taps. He was defending, he might have thought I was playing with him before going in for a strike. While yes, true to an extent, I wanted to see his stance and footwork. He held the spear well, and his footwork was impeccable. I felt it was time to go in for it.

I circled my spear, knocking his aside and went for a jab at the chest. He quickly used the shaft of his weapon to repel my thrust and followed up with a strike to my side, which I avoided by extending my arm and jumping backward. We each got back into stance and began circling again.

I charged at him using the shaft of my spear to butt him in the head. He blocked my blow, as he tried to catch his balance behind him, I turned and hooked my leg behind his. He fell backward onto the dirt. As he landed, he flourished his spear to keep me at a distance. I moved out of the way but was able to get my foot on his spear as he was pushing himself off the ground. He was standing but had no weapon, moving around in a defensive position still looking to continue the fight.

At this point a crowd of the soldiers had gathered to watch. The soldiers primarily ran formation drills and practiced unit warfare, so when officers or knights sparred it was quite the spectacle for them. This spar was one such special event. They grabbed the shield and training sword from the rack and tossed it into the ring. Tripp dashed towards them.

As he tried to pick up the sword and shield I struck down at the area he was reaching toward, keeping him at bay. When he realized I was not giving him a chance to arm himself again he quickly changed tactics. I went in for a thrust and he caught my spear with his hands, pulling back and swinging me off balance.

He had bought himself enough time to pick up the sword. I came down with a strike from above and he parried with the sword. I continued with a barrage of strikes and stabs, which he fended off extremely competently with the sword.

He was able to keep my spear at bay long enough to grab the shield. Now fully armed he decided to go on the attack. He quickly moved toward me, deflecting my blows with the spear. He was able to get close enough to hook my spear with the cross guard of his sword and pull it from my hands. As he did, I kicked into his shield, knocking him back enough for me to move away.

It appeared the soldiers were rooting for the underdog this day; they threw in a sword with no shield. I quickly ran and slid to grab it and was back on my feet. I flourished my blade and adjusted my stance to a half sword technique. As Tripp moved in, he slashed from above. I parried and managed to get to his side without a bind, using my pommel I knocked him in the back of his shoulder and sent him stumbling slightly.

He swung his shield around, as his arm exposed itself, I used my guard to pull his arm down and in a swift motion caught his leg. He flipped onto the ground and the wind knocked out of him. I lightly pressed the tip of the blunt sword into his back.

The crowd was cheering and laughing. Tripp rolled over and I helped him up.

"You are much better with hand weapons." I said to him in approval. "Sir Krinn taught you well."

"I don't think he ever went quite as hard as this." Tripp replied. "After one round of this, I can see why you have the reputation you do."

"I think you will do well with us. Let us take a break and then we will get back to your abysmal archery." I said.

The crowd was still gathered around the ring laughing and clapping. Tripp was obviously over it and yelled out to the crowd, "I am glad that you all enjoyed that, but the show is over now. You can go back to whatever it is you do!"

The crowd scattered Tripp went off to sit under a tree. I decided to use this time and escape out to the fields outside the tower. It was a perfect sunny day and there were questions I needed to ask myself about the night of the skirmish in the woods.

The fields were filled with tall grass and flowers, just down a small hill was the stream again where it gathered into a small pool before heading into the forest, a beautiful hidden gem.

I sat on a rock beside the pool and closed my eyes. I could feel the sunlight beams through the trees in patches of scattered warmth, the sound of the water created a soothing ambience. I let the water clear my mind with my muscles now relaxed after the intense sparring session.

I let my attention drift to thoughts of what happened in the woods. I recalled everything I could about the dream of the glowing woman and the fire in the clearing. I played back the moment the flames roared and bustled into a fireball. What had I felt? Where did my intention lay?

Just before the flames burst up I remember feeling angry, and a need to protect Unul, Tripp, and myself. I could feel the fire, the flames. I connected to it. I felt my voice become one with the fire, the flames grew and burst out with my breath.

What if I could do that with water…or with the earth beneath me…or create it from thin air?

I was both filled with excitement and skepticism. I needed to try and hone this new part of me the same way I needed to help Tripp hone his abilities with a bow. I suppose we were both starting from the ground up with our training, but mine was to be in secret. No one could know until I had control over this gift.

"Let's give it a try…" I said aloud.

I looked at the water and a large stone that sat a short distance away from the water's edge. I took a deep breath and brought my mind and heart into harmony with the water. I closed my eyes and could feel the current in my chest, the ripples in my hands, I could feel the coolness of it from the mountains it ran down from.

I visualized it breaking through the pool's edge and around the stone. As I let my breath out, I felt the water push through the dirt and creating a channel around the stone. I opened my eyes and continued to hold my focus as if I was leading an animal on a hunt.

The water was cutting around the stone and rejoining the pool. I brought my focus from my heart to my eyes and looked angrily at the center of the pool. The water that had broken away to go around the stone flew from the ground all at once. It wrapped itself as if a sling around the stone and sent it hurtling to the center of the pond where I had directed my aggressive gaze.

"It worked!" I gasped.

It. Worked.

I could control fire and water for a period of time, and in doing so other objects around it. I wondered, could I do this with objects like stones?

I needed to try.

I took a small stone for the pool's edge and placed it in front of me. I brought my attention to the stone but could not feel it. I tried to connect to it but there was nothing. I visualized it flying through the air and against a tree.

I opened my eyes and saw the rock at my feet, much to my dismay. It appeared I could not control just any objects, just elements.

I decided to try the water once more. I cut out the initial step and tried just remembering the feeling of the water from the first try. I let the feeling move from my memory to my hand. I raised my hand up and focused, a small stream of water shot up from the pool like the fountains back at the castle!

Progress!

It would take time for sure, but I had figured out the basics I needed to practice. For now, it was time to get back and go over proper stance and technique with Tripp.

I started walking back up to the tower. As I walked, I remembered a time that my mother took it upon herself to help the villages next to the rivers during the rainy season. I wondered if she had this same ability and used it to help.

I made my way to the target area where Tripp was waiting. We spent the next few days shooting arrows, grappling, eating poorly prepared dinners, and drinking great ale. Unul rested and seemed to get better food than us, which was prepared by the healers especially for him. I asked the armorer to measure Tripp and I for new armor, since everything we had was lost. I had the sizes sent to the capital via messenger bird so the blacksmiths there could begin working on them before we arrived.

I did not have much free time as the captain asked to go over different strategy tactics with him. He had been posted to the tower for quite some time and it appeared he did not have much interaction with other leaders during his tenure there.

With more raids down from Wurth he wanted to be sure he had battle plans ready at moment's notice. When possible, I had Tripp join in the meetings. Physical training was only a part of a knight's repertoire, he would need to learn strategy as well. It also helped to build the trust between us.

I escaped to the pool by the river every opportunity I had. I would bring a lantern down and practice manipulating the fire and the water. Soon the connection became instinctual, I could bend them both to my will quickly, but only in short bursts.

After five days' time word arrived that the new troops were to arrive the next day, and that everyone that had served their time at the tower was to return to the capital. We all slept well our last night there, thinking about what the next leg of our journey would bring (mostly we thought it would be better food and our own quarters).

The King's Road

Chapter 8

The tower was roaring the next morning. Most of the men had been stationed there for four months, and all were excited to be getting back to Raven's Landing. The men were grabbing and stashing fruits from the dining hall in their tunics and bed rolls for the journey.

Tripp and I got ourselves decent, grabbed our belongings, and head out the door to the road. Unul was walking slowly, his hand on a walking stick, and slightly hunched over.

"I hear you two will be joining me in the carriage." Unul said.

"You heard correct! Your healers requested that your feet are rubbed, and your neck kneaded every two hours!" I replied.

"They are very skilled at their profession; it would be best to do as they request." Unul said sarcastically.

"Well, it is a good thing we have Tripp with us now, he can perform his squirely duties by rubbing our feet and kneading our shoulders!" I boasted.

Tripp looked confused.

"Is that really what they said?" Tripp asked.

Unul and I looked at each other and then stared him down with a very serious look, making him think that we were disappointed in him for taking the comments as a joke.

"You would question the healers of Gunter's Tower?" Unul said to Tripp.

"I would never – I – I just didn't…" Tripp stuttered.

The laughter that bellowed from Unul and I cut Tripp off.

"Ah yes, I vaguely recall Sir Krinn being very literal and direct when he spoke." Unul said to Tripp. "You will find no such luxuries with us!" Unul continued as he laughed.

"Noted." Tripp said while rolling his eyes and loading our belongings onto the carriage.

"Do you think you can manage a three days' ride to the capital?" I asked Unul. "That is a long time to be sat in a wagon with a bandage around your chest."

"Usually yes, luckily I arranged for some entertainment along the way." Unul replied.

"Entertainment?" I asked.

"Boy!" Unul said shouting to Tripp, who was still loading their belongings. "Pull that blanket back!"

Tripp pulled the blanket on the side of the carriage back as Unul requested. Underneath it was a small barrel of the ale!

"How on earth?" I asked Unul.

"The healers were very nice… I also saved one of them from a band of raiders as a young boy. That usually helps." He said with a big smile.

I helped Unul into the carriage and took a seat up front next to Tripp, who was steering the horses. A horn sounded and we began our trek down the King's Road.

We had been travelling for a few hours. There was a calming cadence to the sounds of the marching feet and the horses' hooves on the cobble stone. I sat and looked to the distance while biting into an apple that, I myself, smuggled out of the tower.

"Did you take that from the tower?" Tripp asked, stunned that I would be up to the same antics as the soldiers that were stationed there.

"Mhm." I mumbled with my mouth full of the apple.

I pulled another apple from the folds of my shirt and presented it to him.

"I brought one for you too!" I said with my mouth still full of my oversized bite.

Tripped looked over at me in slight disbelief.

"Isn't it a bit...pardon my wording, but...common of you?" Tripp said.

It was a bit comical; Tripp was the prim and proper squire of the fairytales.

"Oh, you poor boy!" I said, "Sir Krinn must have never let you have any fun!"

"Oh no, we had fun. We would help the townspeople we came across with their tasks and carry out trials in villages and there was one time that we needed to help move a cow that had gotten into the blacksmith's forge..."

Tripp rambled.

"Yes, that definitely sounds like fun. It sounds like you were nearly one step away from being tarred and feathered for all of your antics..." I said sarcastically.

Tripp looked confused.

"You mean to tell me you've never gotten wild or caused some small mischief?" I asked.

"Like stealing two apples from a place that gave me shelter for a week? No, I don't believe so." Tripp said with his own sarcastic tone.

"Come on, surely you must have had a short romance with a fair maiden at a tournament and snuck to the stables for a bit of fun! Nothing too extreme like stealing a piece of fruit..." I said edging him on.

"What! I would never do such a thing!" Tripp exclaimed.

"Oh? Not a maiden then, perhaps another squire? Sneaking away to play with your swords?" I laughed.

"Excuse me! I am an honorable squire! Not some common farmer's son! And you, you are a lady!" Tripp said, clearly flustered.

"That's right! I am a lady, a lady that has lived life and continues to enjoy every aspect of it!" I said back sternly.

"Titles are just titles, Tripp. We are warriors not bloody sages! Each day people like you and I spend outside the walls of a castle is a day that could be our last. Sir Krinn did not wake up that morning knowing that he would not see the next sunrise. People like you and I must live our lives to the fullest. If no one is hurt in what we do, and we are happier for it, then there is no wrongdoing." I said to him earnestly. "Live your life and love, tomorrow is not guaranteed."

Tripp brought his eyes to the horses. He stared in quiet contemplation for a short while. I felt sorry for him, never having stepped outside the lines. Or maybe he had and was put back in place so never questioned it again... no he is here, nearly two decades old and has just been told to live his life.

Tripp looked up from the horses and the road ahead.

"I'll take that apple now." he said, extending his hand out.

I smiled and placed it in his hand.

"That's a good boy!" I said rubbing his head.

He let out a small laugh.

The day had passed, and we had stopped and made camp next to the road. The soldiers pitched their tents, Tripp and I pitched ours. There were cured meats and vegetables sent with the troops for the journey to the castle. One of the men came over and handed us our rations.

I grabbed our cups and walked to the barrel of ale Unul had secured us, filling them to the top. I handed Unul and Tripp their drinks and we all took a slow long sip, savoring the flavor after a long boring day on the road.

We all ate at our own pace with little talk. As I bit into the cured meats I was pleasantly surprised. They had been holding out the good food at the tower! This was perfectly seasoned and expertly smoked and cured. I could live off this food. I looked around, and judging by the quickness Unul and Tripp were eating, they agreed.

After our meal Tripp excused himself and left us. It seemed he had an inner dialogue playing in his head after our talk earlier. Unul used this opportunity to bring up what happened with the fire the night we found Tripp.

"In the woods, that small fire became a rather large fire very quickly. I assume that had something to do with you?" Unul asked me.

"Very perceptive!" I replied.

"What else have you found since that night? I'm sure you have been quite busy giving yourself tests when no one is looking." said Unul.

Unul knew me well. Apart from doing nothing the day after a feast, I needed to keep my time filled with things to do. The whole week had been filled with exploring my new abilities and training with Tripp (it had been very productive on both accounts).

"So far I've found that I can manipulate fire and water. I've tried to conjure a flame from the air but was not able to. I have been practicing every chance I've had." I said.

"Amazing..." Unul replied with a smile. "Don't stop honing your abilities, these are more valuable than any sword or bow."

"I'm having quite a lot of fun actually." I said as I tip-toed to the opening of the tent, making sure no one was coming our way.

"Would you like to see some of it?" I asked him.

"Oh I'd very much like that!" Unul answered.

The excitement! I had been practicing all week with tiny flames and water. I had just the show to put on! I grabbed a candle off the barrel we were using as a table and placed it on the floor in front of me.

I looked at the flame and raised my hand slowly, the flame moved from the candle into the air. I twisted my hand and spread my fingers and the flame turned into a small ball of fire, like a tiny sun floating in our tent.

I began to close my fist and the tiny sun started to shrink until it was nearly out. All at once I opened my hand again and pulled it back; the small ball of fire grew to the size of a shield and filled the tent with warmth and light. The ball of fire spun around slowly, creating mesmerizing colors and shadows on the walls of the tent.

Unul was looking on in wonder. I myself was impressed with the control I was able to garner over this element in the short time I had to practice.

I brought the tips of my fingers together and pulled my hand down. The ball of fire shrunk and changed shape – back to a flame fitting of a candle. I lowered the flame onto the candle's wick and broke my connection with it.

"…Magnificent…" Unul stuttered.

I smiled; happy my work had paid off.

"Unul, did my mother have this ability?" I asked.

Unul stared off to the corner of our tent.

"I am not sure… she was always very secretive. I do know that when there were floods or wildfires, she was the first one off to help. Coincidence? Only she knows the answer." Unul responded.

"My hope is, one day, she will be able to tell us herself." I replied.

"I will drink to that!" Unul said, raising his cup in the air.

"Aye…" I said raising my cup up to meet his.

We both took a sip as Tripp walked back into the tent.

"What are we toasting to, then?" Tripp asked, pouring himself a fresh cup of ale.

"To a full night's sleep!" Unul quickly responded.

"Now that," Tripp said while bringing his cup to his mouth, "…that is something I will drink to!"

We all finished our ales and made our way to our cots. It seemed that just as quick as I had shut my eyes, the bell was ringing, and we were pulling ourselves out of our blankets. Tripp and I broke down our tent and loaded it into the wagon before helping Unul into it. The weather was not as kind today as it had been. The skies were dark and grey, the rain began falling almost immediately.

Today we were warned to keep our eyes out. The road would take us around a mountain and through a section that raiders from Wurth had been frequently terrorizing. We trotted on for most of the day without incident. Most of the conversation was Tripp asking Unul about he and Sir Krinn's exploits. As Unul was in the middle of the first story I actually found interesting, we noticed smoke rising ahead. We could not see what it was from, it was beyond a hill some distance away. The soldiers saw it too. We all picked up our pace and the soldiers made ready their weapons.

As we got closer the rain began to get heavier. It felt like we were in a monsoon during the rainy season. The sky grew darker and there was thunder from the mountains. The company of soldiers we were with separated, a small group stayed behind with the wagons and supplies while the larger group began marching in battle formation towards the smoke.

Tripp and I left Unul with his sword and mounted the two horses that were pulling our wagon.

"You stay with the men here incase this is an ambush. We can not allow these supplies to be taken!" I yelled to Tripp, trying to raise my voice over the pounding rain and thunder.

"And what will you do, my lady?" Tripp yelled back.

"I will scout ahead and see what is going on before the troops are too far from the wagons. I want to make sure it is not a trap!" I yelled back.

Tripp nodded and rode off to circle the wagons. I galloped ahead to the top of the hill. There in the distance I could see five wagons, all alight. It looked like there was a battle. As I rode closer, I could see butchered bodies laying around the wagons, some half hanging off. They were not soldiers that were cut to pieces, they were regular women and men, elderly, and children. Even the kingdom's thieves did not commit atrocities of this nature.

In the distance I saw a broad man in torn clothing swinging a spear around. The spear was moving so quickly it looked like lighting across the air as it reflected the flames surrounding them. He looked older and had on similar clothes as the unfortunate travelers that lay lifeless amongst the mud.

There were easily nine or ten soldiers, all wearing the colors of Wurth. They were closing in on the man in the center, his spear was keeping them at bay. One of the soldiers got too close and the man drove the tip of the spear through his eye socket. I rode as quick as my horse would go. As I drew near the horses' legs got caught in the mud and he had trouble moving forward. I jumped off and slowly made my way through the mud.

The men from Wurth inched their way closer in a formation to repeal the man's spear flourishes. The man started backing up but slipped and fell on his rear. I was too far to help – I closed my eyes and focused on the rain. With my hand extended I caught the droplets of rain and massed them into a wall of water. I propelled the wall against the soldiers with all the force I could, knocking them all back against one of the wagons that was in flames. As they hit the wagon, I brought my attention to the fire. I raised my hand and slammed it downwards.

The fire bellowed and roared, coming down against the offending soldiers. There were screams as the flames unrelentingly engulfed them where they stood. Those who wore only leather and linen were charred quickly. Those that wore armor were quite unlucky, the metal heated to a color of white, cooking the men inside as they fell shrieking.

Eventually the screams and cries stopped. The bodies lay there in the mud, smoking. Some were black and white ash, some were bone, some were charcoal shapes inside armor that had cooled to a deep blue and purple color. I stood there…in the mud…looking at the damage I had done.

I was both in awe and disgust. I had let my rage and eagerness to conclude the massacre I had rode up to, only to create a massacre of my own. My anger came down like a hand from one of the Gods against my foe, and they felt my judgement. I had seen many horrific events in my life, but this was different. It was raw, it was brutal, it was unrelenting, and it was my doing.

As I stood there, in the mud, looking on at what my powers had done, the man had stood up from the mud, running over to one of the wagons. He was ripping it apart, picking up a slain woman and pulling her to his chest. He let out a roar and shriek from his belly, reminiscent of the men I had just burned alive. What happened to his foe on this impromptu battlefield did not matter, all that mattered to him in this moment was the loss of someone, who by the looks of it, he loved very much.

It was then that the detachment of soldiers had made it over the hill.

"Check the wagons for survivors!" I yelled.

They did as I commanded. I made my way to the slaughtered caravan as well. I looked at the carnage the raiding soldiers had caused, their total disregard for life. I walked over to their remains, upon looking down at them all the disgust I felt vanished. I was justified, these men were feral animals and needed to be put down.

One of the soldiers ran up to me, "My lady, we have checked all the wagons, there are no survivors. What would you have us do?"

"These were innocent people, likely fleeing to the capital. They were undeserving of this fate, let us at least give them a deserving burial. Send word to Tripp to lead the rest here. We will need everyone's help."

"Yes, my Lady." The solider said, running off.

I walked to the man I had saved. He was obviously still in shock from what had happened. He said in the mud, leaning against one of the wheels of a wagon. He stared at the raindrops bouncing off the surface of the mud, splashing and puddling.

I bent down in front of him, bringing myself to his eyelevel. I studied him for a moment before speaking. He was broad and muscular, he was not particularly old, yet he was not particularly young either. He had a great grey, black, and white beard (which was now covered in blood). His head was clean shaven and shone a tattoo that ran from his left temple, around his head and down his neck to his shoulders and back. He was a disciple of the God of Fire and Light. All these people must have been disciples, pushed from their homes in the north in Wurth's genocidal crusade to spread their new religion. They all bore similar tattoos, jewelry, and the same style clothing.

They wore tunics and dresses of grey with red and yellow trim. Their jewelry adorned with citrine and ruby stones. They were fleeing the north for a haven. If only they had left one day sooner, they would have missed this group of raiders and made it to the castle, or at the very least a well-guarded village along the way.

"I know this must be hard for you, but I need to know what happened here." I said to him softly.

He looked up at me, his eyes blank.

"I am Lady Jara of Dragon's Reach. We are on our way to the capital. We can take you with us, but you must tell me what happened before we arrived..." I said again.

The man's gaze went back to the same spot on the ground he was previously looking at, again in total silence. I called to one of the passing men.

"Take this man to Sir Unul, then continue collecting the bodies to be buried."

This made the man lift his head all at once and his mouth opened.

"No...no. They must be burned on a pyre. It is our way..." he said broken and slowly.

I looked at him, let out a small smile, and nodded.

"You heard him," I said to the man I had hailed, "let everyone know. Break down the damaged wagons and build a pyre for the bodies."

"...th..thank you..." the man stuttered.

Two of the soldiers helped him up and brought him to Unul. If anyone could help him it would be Unul.

I spent the rest of the day overseeing the preparations of the funeral pyre. I had the men bury whatever was left of the raiders from Wurth in a ditch together. Their helmets were blackened, and the steel made soft by the flames I sent down on them. I impaled one of the helmets on a spear and drove it into the ground above where they lay, it would be the only headstone they would receive, and serve as a warning to other would-be raiders of what would happen if caught.

By the evening we were ready to light the pyre. I made my way to Unul to let him know and see how the man was faring. The camp had been set on the hill, about two hundred yards from the massacre. The sun was beginning to set, and the rain had stopped a short while before. I walked up the road in the warm red light, the site of tents, fires, and lanterns in the distance.

I made my way to the tent. When I arrived Unul pulled himself up from a stool and wobbled over to me. He was obviously feeling well enough to move on his own, albeit slowly. He took my arm and walked me out of the tent.

"I heard about what you did out there." Unul said to me.

"He knew it was me?" I replied, stunned.

"No, he believes the hand of the God of fire and light himself judged the men." Unul assured me.

"I don't blame him; it did look like that." I said.

"Yes, it seems your feelings definitely influence the strength of your abilities. This can be very useful, or very dangerous. You should take note and work to master your abilities, less it lead to an action you might regret." He lectured.

He wasn't wrong. It was something I was thinking about the whole day. I had directed all my anger and aggression towards the raiders, but what if I had a quarrel with my own men? Would I be capable of the same carnage then? It seemed to me I needed to master my mind more than my powers. This was hard to do not knowing what we were being sent to look for, aside from my father.

"I think knowing what this object we're looking for is would help keep my mind more clear." I said.

"The king will – "

"Unul, do not play with me anymore. You may not have the authority by royal decree to send me on this quest, or to tell me what it is we are doing in detail, but I know that you are holding back information. You are one of the king's most trusted knights, and you would not have agreed to come fetch me had you not known more." I said, cutting Unul off.

Unul looked over his shoulder and then down to his hands. He raised his head back up and took a deep breath.

"This is why King Ansel picked you for this job." He said. "You are right. I cannot and will not go into more detail about the journey, as I will not be a part of it after we get to the castle. I will tell you that the object we are looking for is the dagger of Nystia. The legends written on the scrolls and books at the castle speak of a dagger that was used just before Lucian's death to cast the spell that made the entire kingdom disappear and become Evanwood forest."

It all made sense now, this was why my father's mission was so important. With that the king could send a spy north into Wurth and simply make the entire kingdom vanish. It would end the war instantly.

"I can see why he would want to do that, finding and using such a relic would end the war...but at what cost? If the goal is accomplished, everyone and everything in the kingdom would disappear – the innocents included." I said.

"I don't disagree with what you've said, however with each day Wurth becomes more bold. This is not the first raiding party they have sent down in the name of their new gods! The entire north of the kingdom is littered with scenes like this. We believe that most of the men and women that wanted to escape have already fled south. If it can end the war and bring peace to the land then it is something we must try." Unul said.

He was never one to make uncalculated decisions. This one would have taken him quite a while to settle on.

"I will search for and find my father and this relic, but I can not promise what I will do when it is found." I said.

"I respect that." Unul replied, slapping my shoulder.

I walked into the tent. The man was there, sat on the floor in front of a small fire eating a rabbit that was likely caught while stuck in the mud earlier.

"I want to come with you." The man said.

"I don't even know who you are!" I replied.

"I am Zuht, son of Rojon, priest of Tristi, God of Fire and Light." The man said, very matter of fact.

"Well, Zuht, son of Rojon. I am glad you are doing better than last I laid eyes upon you. However, you do not know of what you ask." I said to him.

"I heard what you said to Sir Unul. I want to join you and make the Wurth kingdom pay." He said with calm resolve.

"You heard what I told Unul?" I questioned. "How much did you hear…."

"Just that you are on a mission to find some sort of object that can wipe the entirety of Wurth off the map forever." He said.

"So, this is just about revenge?" I questioned.

"Those people your men collected from the wagons and mud; those people are…. were…my people. They were my neighbors, my friends, my wife. We left the north to find peace in the south of the kingdom. We had no desires to be involved in any conflicts. Now they are all gone. What was, is no longer, and who I was, I am no longer. I have no purpose, no mission…the only thing I want…need… is to exact my revenge on Wurth." He answered.

I would like to say he was the first person I met in this situation, but the fact was that he wasn't. Actually, this was becoming quite common in the north of the kingdom. I thought about what the man, Zuht, had asked. A fire priest could be very useful on the journey as we pass through different villages.

"On Tristi, God of Fire and Light, I swear that I will join your side until your quest is carried out or I die defending you." He said, obviously seeing I was thinking about his request longer than he had anticipated.

"This is to ensure I remember this oath." Zuht said as he picked up a red and white ember, bringing it to the back of his left hand and squeezing it on his skin.

"Stop stop stop! That's enough." I said.

The truth was I had smelt enough burning flesh for the day and could do without anymore. Besides, there was still a funeral pyre to be lit. I would accept his request, since Unul had said he would be staying back at the capital to heal, my thoughts had been on building up numbers. Unul had the value of two or three men easily in a battle. Without him I would need help.

"I accept, you may join us. You may call me Jara, just Jara." I said to Zuht.

Zuht smiled and dropped the ember back into the fire. He nodded to me with gratitude.

"You may call me Zuht." He said blatantly.

"The pyre is ready. Do you want to light it or should I?" I asked him, changing the subject.

"No, I will light it. They were my people; I will send them off myself. It is my duty." Zuht said.

I nodded and walked him out of the tent. We made our way to the edge of the camp. The darkness of night had set in, the only thing breaking the blackness were three torches burning in the distance. Zuht stopped me about twenty yards from the camp.

"Why are you following me?" he asked.

"I'm accompanying you on your task, the same as you are on mine. I will not get in the way, but I will be there." I said.

Zuht looked at me, made a small smile, and walked on. I stood far enough away for Zuht to have his privacy. He took one of the torches and walked towards the pyre. He stopped and said a prayer over the pyre and tossed his torch in it.

The flames started spreading slowly at first, then started spreading faster. Eventually the entire pyre was up in a roar of flames. As far back as I stood, I could still feel the heat of the flames against my skin. Zuht stood directly in front, no more than a stone's throw away. How he withstood the heat without burns of his own I do not know.

We stood there for two hours watching the fire roar and jump into the black sky, down to a small pile of smoking red, white, and orange embers. Zuht turned and walked away, back toward the camp.

"It is done." He said solemnly, never breaking his stride towards the camp.

I nodded and followed him back. He was given a spare bedroll, which he laid out under the now clear night sky. I could see why, there was something very peaceful and serene about the sky while on the road.

The two moons glowed brightly, one blue and one white, and the clusters of stars shimmered like the sun reflecting off gems set in silver and gold. I always looked at it as a reminder that even after the hardest days and the bloodiest battles, there is always peace beyond the clouds and fog. The stars are there, always present, always looking down from above.

I made my way back to my own tent after a short while, Tripp and Unul were already asleep. I threw all my extra clothing off except for my under garments and got under the blanket. That night I had a much more difficult time falling asleep, and while I did my mind went back to the color of the soldiers' helms changing in the heat of the flames, smoke slowly rising from the eyelets. The images in my head did not make me feel any particular emotions, it was more of a replay and in-depth study of the scene in my mind; until, eventually, I fell asleep.

I woke up the next morning uncertain how long I had lay awake the night before. It certainly felt like I had been up for quite a while as I felt absolutely exhausted. I sat up and looked around, the tent was empty, and I could hear Tripp going on about something just outside. I got up and wrapped my blanket around me, leaving the tent.

As I walked out the warmth of the sun felt refreshing and healing. Tripp, Unul, and Zuht were sat on stools around a small fire. There were some rabbits skewered on sticks perched just over the flame. Tripp was singing praise over some story Unul had just been telling him, while Zuht sat brewing a concoction over the fire that had an interesting aroma.

"Jara!" Tripp said excitedly when he saw that I had come to the fire. "Can you believe that Unul was at the battle of Mad Pauper? He was the one that dealt the final blows that sent the slime back to where they came!"

"Yes, I know." I replied, yawning.

"You…did you say you know?" Tripp said in both excitement and confusion.

"Yes. I know, I was there." I added.

"But…how? I heard it was a bloodbath! And you would have only been…" Tripp said perplexed.

"She was there." Unul stated.

"She was there!?" Tripp said confused and pointing to me.

"She was but a lass, her father asked me to bring her and her brother to study tactics and experience battle firsthand." Unul added.

"How did you think I earned my reputation? By sparring with squires in the courtyard?" I said sarcastically.

"I…I had no idea…" Tripp said in awe.

"Life is about learning new things every day, Tripp. Today you learned that, and I want to learn what this is that Zuht is brewing…" I said.

"It is 'jin-jap-tu', a morning brew to awaken your senses. A delicacy where I am from." Zuht answered.

Zuht poured some of his concoction into my mug.

"Drink it slowly, it is hot." Zuht warned.

I held it to my nose, taking a whiff. It smelled different; like burnt leaves, mud, and crushed flowers mixed together. I took a sip...

"Wow..." I said, taken back by the bitterness of the drink. It turns out, it did taste like all of those scents put together.

"Ah, good. You enjoy it. I will make it for you every morning to help you harness your energy!" Zuht said without waiting for any more response from me.

I was taken back by Zuht's energy. He lost everything but his life yesterday, this day he was uplifted and energized.

"You are very cheerful this morning, considering what happened yesterday..." I said cautiously, not wanting to upset him.

His smile turned into a serious face as he stared directly into my eyes.

"I am a priest of Tristi, and Tristi does not do things for no reason." Zuht stopped for a moment and looked at the ground before continuing. "Yesterday, yesterday was a day of death and endings. Last evening was an evening of mourning and laying to rest, cleansing. When the men that attacked were burning and I rose from the mud, I saw you standing there. Behind my grief and hurt, I knew you were somehow part of a new beginning to this end. Tristi does not play games with those who he follows. Yesterday I lost my entire life, but today... Today Jara, today is my new birth. Tristi has given me direction, I am to accompany you and your companions on your journey.

Yesterday I only wanted revenge, today I know it is more. If Tristi sees fit to grant me revenge, I will have it along side you and your companions. If he does not, I will still go forth with you until your task is completed. So today, today we will drink jin-jap-tu together and I will start my new life."

I was taken back, he looked much older yesterday than he did today; perhaps it was the stress of the fight and the trauma he endured. Now I could see, he must be younger than Unul, yet how he spoke and what he said was filled with much more wisdom than I had heard Unul or my own father utter in the past. I had never seen someone overcome devastation like that in one evening, but I had heard rumors that priests and priestesses of the Gods had such devotion they questioned nothing.

"Thank you, Zuht. You are most welcome as a companion." I said, taking a gulp of the rest of the drink.

Zuht smiled and went back to his brew, eager to share it with whomever he could convince. I grabbed one of the skewered rabbits and began walking around the camp while I chewed. The men were all in better spirits, it seemed a few of them got together and went on an early morning hunt, there was a rabbit, squirrel, or bird for each soul in our party.

The men joked and told stories, making ready for the rest of the trip. I looked forward to getting to Raven's Landing now. Zuht's strange enthusiasm for his God's will seemed to rub off on me. I made my way back to the tent to prepare for the rest of our trip.

Raven's Landing

Chapter 9

The rest of the journey to the capital was unremarkable. The skies were blue and there was a refreshing breeze. It kept the men in good spirits and our pace quick, we were able to cut nearly an entire day off our journey. I spent much of my time in a silent meditation or honing my powers in private when camped, preparing myself for whatever was to come.

The same could not be said for Tripp, Unul, and Zuht. Tripp spent most of the time he wasn't focused steering our wagon in conversation with Unul and Zuht. It seemed they were a trio that could never run out of things to say. A very large part of me was sad that Unul could not continue with us after we depart the capital… an even larger part of me was relieved that there would be one less voice in constant conversation. I swear, the three of them were worse than a group of handmaidens at a joust.

Eventually we made it to the stables outside of Raven's Landing. The capital was made up of two islands sat within a lake, with a series of bridges connecting them. The main port city was on the shore of the lake, most of the inhabitants simply called this section 'The Lower City'. In reality, this area was named 'Raven's Port'. It was the main trading route from the north of the kingdom down to the isles just off the coast in the south.

As we made our way into the city most of the guard detail from the tower said farewell and reported to their barracks before having some time with their families. We however, continued in our wagon. This was Tripp's first time in Raven's

Landing and he was having a hard time focusing on the road. Unul eventually took over the reins so he could look around.

The lower city was filled with beggars, artists, cooks selling their goods, traders getting food, and sailors getting drunk. The smell was a mix of fish, urine, delicious food, old beer, and body odor. The buildings were old or in disrepair, and the streets were dirty. Despite all of this, the crime in the lower city was no higher than any other small town or village.

As we made our way through the square a small child ran beside our wagon peddling meat pies. The sweet rich aroma of the pies stood out from the stink of fish at the wet market we had just made our way through a minute prior. The tiny vendor seemed to garner Tripp's attention.

"You there, child. I'll take four of the warmest pies you have!" Tripp yelled out, throwing a few coins to the child.

"Aye sir, four of me mum's finest pies for ye!" the child replied, counting the coins and stuffing them in his coin purse.

The boy ran beside the wagon handing up the pies to Tripp, who began distributing them to Unul, Zuht, and I. I had not realized how hungry I was for market food until I had that warm pie in my hand, smelling the freshly baked crust and the scent of herbs wafting up from it. I took a large bite into it and my entire body warmed up with comfort, it was as if I was back in Dragon's Reach market. The pies here had a fattier meat than the lean, gamey meat I was accustomed to, but it warmed my belly and heart all the same. I looked around and could see my companions all felt the same.

"I have not tasted such flavors in all my life!" Zuht exclaimed.

"Well then, you best prepare your stomach priest! We are in Raven's Landing now, there will be plenty more to come!" Unul said to Zuht.

We continued down the main avenue that ran through Raven's Port, over a bridge and to the first of the islands. This area was very creatively named 'The Upper City' by the common folk. Its actual name was Raven's Grand.

This section of the capital was a city of it's own. The upper city was where the wealthy traders, nobles, and artists with rich patrons lived and worked. The streets were clean, the buildings were built well and with beautiful architecture, there were small plantings of flowers everywhere to fill the roads and alleys with a lovely aroma.

There were jewelry shops or fine clothing shops everywhere, and some traders who were selling some of the finest swords and armor in the kingdom had storefronts on the main avenue. There was the occasional bard singing and playing songs or reciting poems at the intersections or gardens. The people going about their life here were clean and well dressed.

"Look at that!" Tripp said, pointing to a suit of armor on display.

The armor was indeed beautiful, it was intricately decorated and had gilded details. A suit of armor like this could easily cost the yearly wage of a knight.

"Don't look too hard," Unul said to Tripp, "that's for the nobles and knights that spend all their time balancing the kings books instead of on the battlefield."

"You are right," Tripp replied, "still, could you imagine…"

We made our way through the upper city and to the gate of the final bridge to Raven's Crown, the capitals castle. The commoners simply referred to this area as 'the castle'.

There was a gatehouse with guards blocking our path down the final bridge.

"Oy! You lot - state y'er bus'ness!" The guard shouted.

At this point, everyone we had left with from the tower had slowly funneled out to their posts or homes. It was just our wagon with Unul, Tripp, Zuht, and myself.

"It is I, Sir Unul. I am back with my companions to see King Ansel immediately. Open this gate at once!" Unul shouted from the reins.

The guard looked horrified and lowered his head and shoulders while moving out of the way.

"I am sorry Sir Unul, I did not recognize you! Please take my apologies… I'll open the gate right away Sir." The guard responded.

The guard opened the gate, and we made our way over the bridge, through the second gatehouse, and into the courtyard of Raven's Landing.

We were there.

Tripp and Zuht's eyes moved skyward as they looked at the inner castle. The walls and towers stood tall and glowed white and orange as the early autumn sun reflected off of their limestone walls, casting shadows on the intricate carvings which adorned them. The peaks were a deep and rich blue, mimicking the raven's feathers the city was named after. Flags stood on each gate and tower. Every other flag was the king's coat of arms, between them the coat of arms of each great house within the kingdom.

I felt a great sense of pride as I looked up myself and saw my family's arms flying in the wind. After a moment that pride turned into a great weight, as I remember the reason I was here now. A moment later, the weight became resilience, as I knew that I could handle whatever was thrown at me – easy or difficult as it may be.

We approached a large staircase with two sculptures of hero's from times past on either end and a large gilded door in the center. There were guards on either side of the staircase and the doors. As our wagon drew to a stop and we began to dismount it, a figure opened the doors with a small entourage of servants and they began making their way down the stairs.

"My lords, my lady," the figure called out as I made my way around the wagon.

I recognized the voice and made my way around the wagon.

"Josan!" I exclaimed.

"Lady Jara, it has been quite some time, and by the looks of it you have grown quite a bit as well!" Josan said with a large smile on his face.

Josan was the king's head house steward. He was tasked with running every aspect of the castle and making sure he knew everything about everyone that stepped inside of it. I had last seen him nearly ten years prior at a tournament here in the Raven's Landing.

"What sort of tonics are you taking to keep your features so untouched by the years?" I asked coyly. "Or have you perhaps found some sort of ancient magic to keep you forever youthful?" I added, the irony of the joke only known by Unul and myself.

"My lady, you are far too much! …but if you must know, I believe it's an herbal tea concocted by Yusel the alchemist, after all, first impressions are everything!" Josan replied blushing.

One lesson I learned early on was to develop a good report with the head stewards when visiting. Too many courtiers focused on only the nobles and knights, but if you needed the most recent gossip or a favor in the castle the servants were your eyes and ears. Simple flatteries and polite conversations would get you further in one hour with a steward than a week with a noble in court.

"You will have to procure me some before I leave." I replied in jest.

"Sir Unul, I have received word about your injuries, you will find the castle physician waiting in your chambers." Josan said with a warmth in his voice.

"Young Tripp," Josan said turning to Tripp while fixing his posture, "I am sorry to hear about Sir Krinn. I had the good fortune of being in his company many-a-time. He was a good and honest man, truly the pinnacle of chivalry. He will be sorely missed. I am glad that you survived, Sir Unul wrote highly of you in his messages and I believe you will fit right into Sir Krinn's footsteps! We all look forward to seeing how you grow into a knight of the realm!" Josan said earnestly to Tripp.

"Thank you for your kind words. They warm my heart and strengthen my resolve. I am glad to be welcomed into Raven's Landing." Tripp replied.

"Master Zuht, I am without words for what you have experienced." Josan said, approaching Zuht. "If only our men were closer and stopped those events from ever happening." Josan said solemnly.

"Do not be full of sorrow, mister Josan... Tristi sees to it that all moves on to tomorrow. Had nothing happened, I would not be here making your acquaintance! My life yesterday was my life yesterday, my life today is my life today. Today, I am most pleased to meet you!" Zuht said with the energy only a true devotee could possibly muster.

Josan smiled and nodded.

"Please, now that we are all well met let us go in. I will have you all shown to your quarters for your duration here and send chamber aids to come and provide you with fresh clothing after your long journey. Warm baths will be poured for you all and meals brought into your rooms so you may fill your bellies in peace." Josan said to the four of us. He motioned with his arms for us to head up the stairs and into the castle.

"Lady Jara…" Josan said after we entered the main hall of the keep. "I will send a maid to come gather you in the morning, King Ansel has requested to meet with you after breakfast."

"Thank you, Josan." I replied, winking. I continued making my way to my chambers.

I was led through the hall and down a long corridor. On either side of the corridor hung the portraits of kings of old, knights and nobles of notoriety, and some of the weapons they wielded in their time. The corridor floors were lined with fabric, which helped to keep the footsteps in a busy castle muffled. At the end of the corridor was an alcove with a sculpture of a dragon perched on a tower, a visual representation of my home, now a comforting reminder in this temporary residence.

To the right of the sculpture was a winding staircase to a tower which was reserved for visiting nobles and high-profile guests. The chambers in the tower were well furnished and offered views of the lake and the city. I remembered visiting with my father when I was a child, climbing up onto the windowsill and staring out to the city with a spyglass, watching the people go about their lives.

I was led up the staircase to my chambers, as the maid opened the door, I felt the weight of the trip here fall off my shoulders and my chest open. There was a large bed with furs covering it, a fireplace alight with a warm fire, two chairs on either side of the fire with tables beside each of them, a large circular table near a window on which to eat, and a desk with paper and quill. In front of the fire, a copper tub was placed and filled with steaming water.

I could hardly wait, I took my sword belt off and placed it against the chair at the desk, then disrobed as quickly as I could. I tossed my dirty clothing to the maid and jumped into the tub before she had even left the room. The warm water felt like a light from the Gods warming me up from the inside out. I spread out my toes and stretched my legs, then submerged my head.

The silence under the water was peaceful and meditative. It had been weeks since I had left Dragon's Reach, and the whole time in the company of one person or another...or a dozen... It was nice to have time for myself. I knew it was temporary, so I soaked it all in the best I could.

I raised my head from the water feeling anew, and off to the side of the tub was a small table with some fruit and a bottle of wine. I picked up my glass and sipped the wine, and like a child throwing saw dust in the fire, began using my abilities to stoke and calm the fire. I had found that more than fun or useful in vital situations, these powers offered me an outlet for my ever-wandering mind. It was peaceful and entrancing, bringing me both clarity and amusement.

I sat in the tub until the tips of my fingers looked like prunes. There was a knock at the door.

"Excuse me, my lady." The voice was that of the maid that had led me here. "I have supper, where would you like me to leave it for you?" the maid continued.

It was perfect timing, the fullness of the meat pie from earlier had passed and I was ready for a properly cooked meal again. Especially now that I felt clean for the first time in weeks.

"On the table beside the fireplace will do." I answered to her.

The maid placed a platter of roast pheasant, baked vegetables, and a loaf of bread on the table.

"You get yourself comfortable my lady, I will be back in a short while." the maid said before leaving the room.

I got out of the tub and dried myself, then pulled out fresh clothing from the wardrobe. I quickly got myself dressed, it felt good to wear clean clothes again. I sat down in the fur covered chair beside the fireplace and began eating my meal.

A short while later the maid returned.

"Is there anything else I can fetch for you, my lady?" the maid asked.

"Yes, I'd like to know your name." I answered.

"Oh, of course my lady, my name is Grace. Josan has instructed me to assist you with anything you need." Grace, the maid, responded.

"Well, Grace, you may call me Lady Jara. While on our travels, Sir Unul mentioned that the king had gathered a few others to come meet with us. I pray you can tell me who else has arrived." I said to her.

"Of course, Lady Jara." Grace said before rattling off the roster in her head. "Sir Alor of Stag's Leap arrived earlier in the week, Lady Toree from the College of Vir last week, and Lady Runa of Glushal just two days ago."

...Runa...

The name lit a fire in my heart that had previously been but a simmer.

"Thank you, Grace, that is all. Please wake me in the morning." I said to her.

"Of course, my lady." She said as she turned and left the room.

It was quite a roster the king had put together. Sir Alor was a giant of a man, middle aged, bald with a great beard, and as muscular as a barbarian. He was known around the kingdom for his skill in hand-to-hand combat and his skillful use of the great sword. He would certainly be a force to be reckoned with on our journey.

Lady Toree was tall and fit, in her prime, and was a scholar and explorer. While not an official at the College of Vir, she was as well respected there as any other dean or headmaster. She would be exceptionally helpful while in Evanwood.

Then there was Lady Runa...

Lady Runa was the youngest of her siblings of the great house of Glushal, she was a knight of the kingdom. She was elegant in her movements and speech, known for her beauty. She was of similar stature to me, but with long braided red hair, icy blue eyes, and warm fascial features. She was an expert with a longsword and spear. She was my rival at every tournament, bound to make it to the final round against me.

She was my equal in every way and it made every tournament a challenge. I had not seen her in nearly three years. Runa was dispatched to the boarder to stop raids coming down on the coast, while I was sent back to Dragon's Reach to defend the pass. With the war continuing on, tournaments were put on hold.

Despite the games coming to a halt, what we lacked in public rivalry we made up for with battle's we were caught up in. For each skirmish she took part in I made sure I was in one just as grand. For every notch in her spear, I made sure I had two. As deep as our rivalry was, our respect and admiration for each other was equal. We had known each other since young teens, competing in tournaments against each other or being brought to battlefields with our fathers, debating which one of our strategies was best.

I sat there, staring at the fire, sipping my wine and fondling the handle of my dagger. By this point the sun had set and the bed looked enticing. I stripped down and got into the bed.

No sooner had I felt the linens and furs on the bed against my skin, then I found myself awaken with the sunrise. I felt refreshed and ready for adventure again. I lay there but could not stay still. It would be some time before Grace would come to wake me, but here I was, awake already.

I decided to go for a walk through the gardens. I got up and dressed myself, pouring a glass of water and eating some of the left-over fruit from the day before. As I sat and ate, I found myself craving the jin-jap-tu that Zuht brewed every morning. As off-putting as it smelled, and sometimes tasted, I now found it hard to get my day started without it.

With some food in my belly, I decided to make my way outside. The castle was nearly silent this morning, with only some muffled footsteps on the corridor runners. I made my way outside; the sky was a beautiful pink and orange and the air brisk. The gardens on the main island were large and filled with sculptures and often had seasonal flower arrangements. Back when the kingdom was not at war, people from the upper city would often come and walk through the gardens, now it was a sight for only invited guests. The war had changed much, but the beauty of the gardens remained intact, however sheltered they may be now.

I began walking into the hedges, following a trail of purple and blue flowers along the wall. This mornings walk helped to clear my head before my meeting with the king, until I heard a voice call to me.

"Lady Jara!" the familiar voice called.

The hair on my neck stood up at the sound of the voice and I slowed my pace.

"Jara, do not pretend you didn't hear me call you! You're not envious I arrived at the castle before you, are you?" the voice called out.

I stopped walking entirely and stood there. I could hear the footsteps make their way to me, but I did not turn around.

"Lady Runa." I said very matter-of-factly.

Runa walked around to my front, and looked me up and down.

"Jara, don't you look ravishing as ever." Runa said to me sarcastically.

"Lady Runa," I said, "...your braids are so...nice..." I continued sarcastically myself.

"You certainly have not lost your way with words. I can't say I've missed that." Runa replied.

"Ah! So you have missed me!" I said to her giggling.

Runa let out a chuckle.

"Come, walk with me a bit." I said to her while beginning to walk through the gardens.

"How has the fight against Wurth been up in the north?" I asked.

Runa took a deep breath, "It has been weathering on me. The warriors we have fought fear no death, their only focus is on either forcing their adversaries into their ranks and religion or slaughter. They do not behave like warriors, more like bees protecting their queen with no regard for their lives." She said.

"I saw little of that until we came across a caravan of slaughtered followers of Tristi. The only survivor is now traveling with us. They were ruthless, unarmed devotees cut down like rabid hounds." I said.

Runa stopped walking and stared at one of the sculptures in the garden, although I could tell her gaze was nothing more than a direction; her mind was on other thoughts.

"Speak your mind then..." I prompted.

"I will be blunt with you," she started, still gazing at the sculpture, "we have seen much in our short time in this world, you and I. This war is the first time I have felt like I am chained to an anchor and cast into the sea. Each skirmish, battle, and raid, another wave keeping me from a full breath. Their ranks are never ending and I worry that despite our resolve, at some point we will be overrun by zealots with no mind of their own."

"It may not be my place to say this, but your thoughts are in good company. I have word that the king seems to feel this as well." I replied, sympathetically.

"I don't know if that brings comfort or distress...who's loose lips did you pry that from?" Runa asked.

"Oh, you know me, I have my sources." I said slyly.

"Well," she said, "It sounds to me as if you have spent a good deal of time with Sir Unul."

"Sir Unul! Please! Why on the moons would you think... Am I really that easy to read?" I responded.

"To others, no. I, however, read you like a book." Runa said while looking at me and gently moving my hair from over my eye and letting the side of her hand slightly brush my cheek. I can't help but feel a rush of energy force me to miss a breath.

"And how is it that you are capable of what others are not?" I asked, genuinely curious.

"Because you and I are the same, Jara. We two are warriors, Ladies of our houses, leaders, strategists! And because Unul is always full of the latest gossip, for a knight of the king he is worse than a hand maiden!" Runa answered, laughing and slowly walking away.

"And where are you going, Lady warrior of your house?" I said in jest.

"To find some good meat to eat and wine to drink before our meeting with the king!" She yelled while walking down the path alone.

Before she was completely out of reach I thought I would use my abilities for a bit of fun. As she walked next to a fountain I manipulated the water to splash up onto her shirt.

"What on the moons!" Runa shouted.

"Lady Runa, you must be cautious near the fountains! Shame on you getting so close on a windy day like this!" I yelled out.

Runa looked visably confused as there was no wind on this morning. She looked around for signs of a breeze, upon seeing and feeling nothing she shook her head and walked around a corner.

With her out of sight a feeling of calm washed over me. Not because I was on edge while she was within eyesight, but because I was truly happy she was asked to join us. Yes, we were often at odds, but I would rather have her beside me in battle than be facing her.

I noticed the sun was beginning to rise higher in the sky and made my way back to my room to change into finer clothes before meeting with the king. I was eager to hear more about my father and how we could end this war.

The King's Request

Chapter 10

The corridors leading to the great hall were barren, the only things which lined the oversized castle pathways were portraits, tapestries, statues, and guards. The castle had always been bustling with courtiers, nobles, and wealthy merchants. It was not until that moment, walking through in mostly silence, that I saw the effect the war had. If not essential, the castle was barred from visitors after two consecutive assassination attempts.

When I arrived at the doors to the great hall I was greeted by a captain of the guard and Lady Toree.

"Lady Jara, I have heard much about you! I am glad we can finally meet!" Toree said to me with a curtsy.

"Lady Toree, my father had told me all about you - I am honored to be here with you!" I replied.

"Lady Jara, Lady Toree, his majesty has asked me to guide you to his private meeting room. Please follow me." the captain said.

I nodded and followed in step with the captain and Toree. He guided us through the great hall and to a corner in the room, he pushed a piece of a carving on the wall and a hidden door popped open.

"Oh my! Has this been here all this time?" Toree exclaimed. "I can't believe I never caught sight of this pathway before! The work is absolutely exquisite, there is not one sign this entrance exists..." Toree continued with no sign of stopping.

"Er Hmm..." the captain sounded, clearing his throat in an obvious attempt to get Toree's attention. "Just follow the spiral up and you will find his majesty with all of your companions." the captain said as I walked through.

"Oh, of course, sorry..." Toree said, aware of where she was placing her attention.

The door had led to a spiral staircase, which I began to make my way up. As I started up the door closed behind me. The spiral seemed to go on forever before I eventually made my way to a gilded door, which I opened slowly, Toree in tow.

On the other side of the door was a room beautifully decorated and warm. There were two fireplaces, bookcases all around, large stained glass windows, a large table, and a carved desk. At the table sat King Ansel, Unul, Tripp, Zuht, Sir Alor, and Runa.

"Your majesty" we said in tandem with a curtsy.

"Ah! Lady Jara, Lady Toree! Welcome, please come take a seat! We have much to discuss." King Ansel said to us, motioning his arm towards two empty chairs at the table.

We made our way to the empty chairs and sat. As I looked around the table nods were given by each of the souls there, as not to interrupt anything King Ansel would say.

"Now that all are in attendance, let us discuss the reason I have called you all here." The king said, addressing all of us. "Some time ago, a rumor of an enchanted dagger from Nystia made it's way to the castle."

"Nystia? Nystia is but a myth told to children at night!" Sir Alor exclaimed.

It was not unusual for Sir Alor to speak out to the King. Sir Alor had fought side by side with King Ansel in many battles and was named a High Protector of the kingdom.

"No Alor, it is more! I too thought that, until I heard a story about a dagger that made the entire kingdom disappear in a moment. I asked Lady Toree and Lord Mistaan to search the ancient archives here in Raven's Landing. What they found was a treasure trove of documents and treaties made with a kingdom that had somehow disappeared." The king replied.

"Is this true, Lady Toree?" Sir Alor asked.

"It is, and from my research, it appears the legends are true; it was a kingdom of supernatural powers and enchantment that some how vanished without a trace." Lady Toree responded.

"But why seal away all records of it ever existing?" Runa asked.

"Because," Unul said in a commanding voice, "The reason the kingdom disappeared in the first place was because of an enchanted dagger that was created to save the kingdom was used in haste and made it vanish!"

"Sir Unul is correct. The dagger of Nystia was created to save the kingdom from Lucian, the Queen's head general. From what I gathered from various notes made by diplomats we had there at that time, Lucian had a romance with one of the Queen's commanders, the Queen soon after disappeared and Lucian began acting as regent. He was breaking the treaties with neighboring kingdoms and becoming more powerful and barbaric each day.

A secret order was created and had a dagger forged which could stop Lucian and bring the kingdom peace again. Something happened when it was used and the entire kingdom of Nystia disappeared in an instant." Lady Toree explained.

"Exactly." The king pronounced. "An enchanted object that had the power to make an entire kingdom just cease to exist! You can imagine why my forefathers felt it necessary to make it seem like a children's story! If someone were to try and find this dagger and use it on us it would spell disaster!" King Ansel continued.

"Yet here we are, talking about a magical dagger that is capable of making a whole kingdom disappear, are we not?" Zuht chimed in.

Unul stood up from his seat at the table and walked towards a wall where a map of the known continent was hanging and looked at it. His motions and direct trajectory made everyone at the table go silent and watch him. Unul was wise beyond his years, in truth he had the best traits of each person at the table. He knew that he would get everyone's attention in an effort to quell the questioning and move forward onto the task at hand.

"Yes, here we are. Except we are not just talking about a magical dagger, we are going to find the dagger. Some time ago, Lady Jara's father, Lord Mistaan, was tasked with taking a number of men into Evanwood Forest. Their task was simple in theory, journey to the forest, which according to our research is where Nystia lay, find the keep where Lucian was defeated, take the dagger, and finally use it to make Wurth disappear." Unul said very matter-of-fact.

Everyone remained silent, waiting to see where he would move from there. Unul turned around and faced us all.

"The fact of the matter is, as I am sure you are all keenly aware, Wurth has been relentless in this crusade they have launched on the world. We have depleted most of our treasury and made little progress. A special secret council consisting of His Majesty, myself, Lord Mistaan, Lady Runa's mother - Lady Liika, and Lady Toree, deemed it necessary to take the risk and try to end this war before it destroys the world.

Lord Mistaan was tasked with tracking and finding the dagger because his wife, Lady Elia is a Nystian descendant and might have heard stories through her family. It has been quite some time since he made his way into the forest and we have not had any reports since. What we have had is a slew of reports from villages bordering the forest speaking of fairy tail creatures attacking villages and wrecking havoc. Reports that are consistent with logs we have dating back to Lucian's short reign before Nystia vanished.

Our fear is that something has happened to Lord Mistaan, we do not know whether it was Wurth spies, these creatures, or some other unknown circumstance. What we do know is the dagger must be found. Much like Lucian's reign, Wurth has brought much destruction and malice to our world, and we need to stop them, using any means possible." Unul said in a very straight forward manner.

"Are you saying that this magic is real? Surely you can not be serious!" Runa questioned.

Unul planted his hands on the table and stared Runa in the eyes.

"I have seen much that you have not, Lady Runa. I have seen battles and atrocities you could not imagine, I have committed atrocities you can not imagine, I have read the ancient scrolls about a magical kingdom, and I have since seen such magic first hand!" Unul spurred back.

"First hand? When?" Tripp asked, opening his mouth for the first time since I entered the room.

"Such things are not for me to reveal." He said, avoiding any gaze in my direction. "I give you my word as a knight of Raven's Landing that I have seen such magic with my own eyes. When the time is right all shall be revealed." Unul stated.

"Of course," Tripp said with a face red of embarrassment, "how foolish of me to question you my lord."

King Ansel cleared his throat.

"Everyone at this table is either one of my most competent and trusted warriors, leaders, or have found themselves stumbling into something by divine intervention. I am not one to question the Gods, so if you sit here with me, the Gods and I task you with this quest.

I ask that you all venture forth to Evanwood Forest, track down the lost keep of Nystia with Lady Toree's help, and find this dagger so we can learn how to use it to put an end to this senseless war!" King Ansel said with inspiring charisma.

Everyone looked resolute, despite how outlandish anyone else thought this task was, Unul and King Ansel seemed to dispel any skepticism.

"I have no interest in forcing anyone into this quest. I will ask you each only once and will accept only one yay or nay response; so choose your answer wisely." King Ansel said, addressing all of us.

"Lady Jara," King Ansel said, addressing me first, "do you accept this quest on behalf of your father and myself?"

"I am your Lady, your Majesty." I said bringing my hand to my chest and bowing my head. "I will find my father and help you stop this war by any means necessary!" I added.

"Lady Toree," the king said, "you have aided me in this endeavor since the beginning, your comfort is in libraries and archives, but now I ask you to risk your life in the field while aiding others. Will you guide the others on their journey as if they were your students?"

"I will, your majesty. I fear if I do not, there will be no libraries to return to." Lady Toree answered, bowing her head.

"Lady Runa, you and your family have fought valiantly in this war, will you fight for me now when the time is most dire?" King Ansel asked Runa.

"Your Majesty, I have always strived to do the best I can for Nerick and Glushal, if this is what you believe the right path is I will walk it. Besides, if this does work, I can not let Lady Jara take all the credit. I accept." Runa said bowing with her fist to her heart.

"Your long rivalry with Lady Jara is both endearing and entertaining. My heart his full of hope that you both we will succeed!" King Ansel said.

"Your Majesty, you need not waste words on me. I am your man." Sir Alor stated bowing his head and tapping his chest.

The king nodded in approval.

"Zuht, Master Tripp, you stepped foot into this journey unknowingly, yet the Gods have deemed it so. This is why you are here, in my private room, amongst the most noble of my kingdom. I will not press you, if you do not wish to go you may stay here in Raven's Landing." King Ansel said.

"My King," Zuht said, "Tristi deemed it that I accompany Lady Jara, I will follow his will." he continued, raising his hand to his forehead and bowing.

Tripp looked at Zuht and at me, then at the king.

"Your Majesty, Lady Jara and Sir Unul saved my life and took me in after my liege was murdered. No matter the danger, I will follow them." Tripp said with a quick fist to his chest and firm bow.

"Your Majesty..." Unul began.

"Sir Unul, my most trusted confidant. As you yourself know, your injuries require too much time to heal. You will stay with me here and oversee battle plans should this quest turn up empty handed."

"Your Majesty." Unul said bowing his head slightly.

"It has been decided then, you all shall journey together. You will leave in two days time. I entrust both Sir Alor and Lady Toree to lead this quest jointly. I will be honest with you all, we have little left to give. What we have in skill and heart, Wurth has beaten us with sheer numbers of bodies. I would not look to such efforts if there were other options. The kingdom's fate is tied with yours. If you should fail, Sir Unul and I will put up such a final fight that it will be spoken of through the ages!

Go, prepare, and know that you all have my trust, my hopes, and my gratitude. I thank you all. Should you be successful, you will be hero's of the kingdom and never want for more." King Ansel said to us all earnestly.

"Your Majesty." We all said with a bow.

"Lady Jara, Sir Unul, Lady Toree, stay here so we may speak. The rest of you will find food and drink waiting for you in the hall outside the stairwell." The king said.

As the room emptied I wondered, aside from Unul, who else here knew the extent of my involvement. I was not even sure the king himself knew. I felt a comfort in Unul staying along with me. Everyone had made their way out and the king took a seat at the table.

"I wanted the others to leave because I fear if they know the whole story they might look at this as nothing more than an ill-timed joke. The war in the north is a very real problem, however the disturbances in the east, towards Evanwood have been even more worrisome." King Ansel said to us.

"So the rumors are true then?" Toree asked.

"Yes, there are unnatural creatures coming from the forest and causing carnage in the surrounding towns and villages. I have sent men to quell the problems but it has done little to curb the violence." The king continued.

"If there are indeed wolfmen, briars, and cythians destroying villages, how is it we have not heard more rumor from the soldiers or townspeople on our journey here?" I asked, confused as to how something like this could stay so quiet.

"I could not let this information get out into the populous, it would break the morale of the whole kingdom and Wurth would march right over us. I sent men, hand picked and sworn to secrecy, to blockade the path to the eastern villages. They stop anyone trying to travel to the east and stop anyone trying to leave the villages that have been shut in. The secret must stay a secret." The king answered.

"You shut them in?" I said surprised and disgusted. "They are fighting creatures from children's tales and you are keeping them locked in?"

"Lady Jara, it was not a decision I made lightly, but it was one I had to make. The soldiers standing guard have provisions to provide the villages and townsfolk to make their lives as easy as possible during this time." The king replied.

"Jara," Unul said, "if Wurth knew what was going on there, they would launch an immediate assault, both physical and mentally on the kingdom. They would use this knowledge to break the people's minds and then come in and take them as slaughter or to indoctrinate."

"I understand leadership and decisions made for the greater good. What I don't understand is why no other soldiers have been sent to help the townspeople and villagers fend off these beasts." I replied.

"We have," Toree said, joining into the conversation. "We have sent one hundred and fifty men. None have returned. The only people left are those that sought it wise to hide and move sparingly."

"The last report I was given stated they were torn apart. Armor made little difference to the beasts. What makes this so troublesome is that these attacks only began after your father disappeared into the forest." The king said.

"We believe he stumbled upon something in the forest that unlocked some sort of portal or gateway, allowing the beasts into the world. From the texts I have read, this has happened before, when Lucian came to power." Toree added.

"This is why your family's order was created. The texts we've recovered mention Lucian using some form of magic to turn his opponents into these beasts and letting them loose, all traces of who they were before, gone. The Order of the Moon was created to destroy the beasts and stop Lucian." Unul said.

"You are the last remaining member of the order, and as such it is your sacred duty to follow this quest through." Lady Toree said to me.

"I am a member of an order without anyone to teach me it's knowledge. The order was dead before Unul performed the ritual." I said back.

"Yes, but you didn't have me before! I will help guide you where others can not, using the path your ancestors took and noted." Lady Toree said from her heart.

"Thank you, Lady Toree. In truth this has been much to take in, I will gladly accept your assistance." I replied back.

"There is one more thing, Lady Jara." The king said, obviously angling for some information. "The ritual, the texts we've read say something about it unlocking a gift for those born of Nystian blood. What have you found has been your gift? I would not ask if I did not think it important on this quest."

I hesitated, my hair stood on end, and I looked at Unul. Unul looked back at me and gave me an expression of reassurance. A part of me felt naked in front of the world, another part felt like an anvil was lifted off my shoulders.

"Yes, of course Your Majesty. I have found that I can manipulate the elements. If there is a candle flame, I can make it a roaring fire. If there is water, I can have it split through a stone. I am still practicing, still learning. That is how Zuht was saved. It was not Tristi that brought fire and flames down on the enemy, it was me. I used the flames already alight on the wagons to cook the men alive in their armor and stop the fight immediately." I said.

"Truly incredible!" the king said in amazement.

"I will not ask you to reveal these gifts to anyone else until you are ready to do so, but when you choose to, you will find these powers you have extremely useful on our journey." Lady Toree said.

"Lady Toree, what we have discussed here today must stay a secret. Do not tell anyone what you are headed into until you are on your journey and have gained their trust. They must know that you are serious. I will give Sir Alor some notice to ease him into the situation, but the others must stay unaware until Alor is made aware." The king said.

"Of course, Your Majesty." Toree replied.

"Thank you for your time, now please leave me to my studies and join the others in the hall." King Ansel said, dismissing us all from the room.

"Your Majesty." I said with a curtsy, and made my way to out.

Ghosts of the Past

Chapter 11

It was dusk and I could see Runa in the distance. She was beating a pole with her wooden sword, practicing her form. Next to her, her mother Liika was speaking with my father and Sir Unul. There was a rumor going around that Wurth wanted to attack us. Our parents were probably talking about that because no one yelled at us when we were practicing throwing stones to catch birds and accidentally broke one of the bottles of wine.

A hand touched my shoulder...

"C'mon! Let's get Runa and play monster hunter in the forest!" my brother Devin exclaimed, running to the wood's edge.

I nodded and ran toward Runa.

"Runa! Runa!" I yelled out in what I imagined was a very secretive tone.

"Hold on! I need to get this cut right so I can get beat you and your brother at the next tournament!" Runa said.

"Oh please, a donkey with a stick could beat my little brother. But you could not beat me with even the finest sword in the world!" I boasted.

"Really?" Runa said sarcastically. "I bet you three meat pies that I can best you before the bell of the first round!"

"I accept your bet!" I replied. "But first - Devin has run to the wood to play monster hunter! He and you are the monsters! Go hide, the winner gets an extra sugar loaf I snatched from the kitchen earlier!"

"That sugar pie is mine!" Runa exclaimed, tossing her wooden sword to the ground and running into the forest.

I don't know why we were betting, they wouldn't let us compete until we were at least thirteen, which worked perfectly; it would give me three more years to come up with my plan to beat Runa in every category!

I counted to one hundred before I chased after. As I ran into the woods I was pulled into another direction. What it was that made me go out of the clear path Devin and Runa took I do not know. I went into a bushier section of the woods, careful to not tear my clothing on any thorns.

It was getting darker and I knew I needed to turn back and find Runa and my brother before it was too late. As I was about to turn around a blue-green glow was illuminating from a small clearing with some stones littering the area. I could hear two women speaking in a language I couldn't decipher.

I decided to take a closer peak and snuck down the hill a bit. I could make out two young looking women. One of them had her back turned in my direction, the other was facing me but it was too dark to make out a face. They were speaking something in unison, some sort of incantation. As they continued the glow grew brighter and brighter, the second woman's face lit up....it was my mothers!

What in the world was she doing? Before I could say anything or move from my spot everything around me stopped. The chanting ceased, the air stood still, not a bird moved. The world around me grew silent. I cautiously stepped forward, and with each step my feet did not make a single sound on the ground.

It was silent...

The glow continued to grow, and as I got closer to it I could clearly see my mother's face, as it was when I was but ten. The glow erupted into a heatless flame and I covered my eyes with my arm. When I moved my arm the flame was gone and I was transformed to my current age. I was so confused I almost didn't notice the glowing woman was there again, smiling.

"You again?" I said, "You are not a part of this memory..."

The glowing woman walked to my frozen mother and put her hand on her shoulder.

"I am, but it is not a part of your memory." The words rang out from my mother's lips, but I knew it was the woman speaking through her.

"I am proud of you, Jara." The woman said through my mother. "You have done well to trust your instincts, and your control over your abilities has grown."

"Why can you only speak through my mother?" I asked. "Have you no voice of your own?"

The glowing woman could see a resentment in my eyes, and her face showed me empathy.

"I have no voice, not anymore. Elia allows me to use her as a vessel to speak with you."

"How could my mother allow you to use her as your mouth? She has not spoken in four years!" I announced.

"No, she has not spoken to anyone in your realm. Elia and I are quite close. I know you do not understand now, but all will be revealed." the woman said.

"Revealed? You sound like nothing more than a conjurer of tricks!" I proclaimed.

"It is not my place to share it with you. When the time is right you will know. I am here to help you before you leave on your quest."

"I can not say I enjoy your stoicism. How can you aid me if you can not even speak to me yourself?" I replied.

"The creatures that have been spoken of. They are the children of Lucian. The men sent to kill them did not have the means to destroy them. They can only be killed by fire or a blade forged with magic."

"A blade forged with magic? There would not have been any weapons forged with magic for at least two hundred years!"

"No, they still exist. Your dagger is one such weapon. Alaia was forged by Aldonis, who was much more than the smith you know him to be. Being half Nystian and half Nericki, Aldonis infused everything he made with an essence of magic, giving it life through the ages and the ability to cut down any beast created with dark ambition." She said.

"So you are saying, Alaia is the only tool that can be used to destroy these beasts?" I asked.

"It is the only tool you have now; there are others. Aldonis had a vision of beasts returning to the world, so he made a small number of weapons that could defeat them and hid them away, entrusting them to only his apprentice, Daal. When Aldonis died, Daal took the weapons he made and brought them to the Order of the Moon to hide away until they were needed again. With the help of the Baron of Petre, the blades eventually made their way here to the castle."

"The castle is a city unto itself, how will I find them?" I asked.

"I do not know where they were placed. The only information I can give you is a riddle that was passed down through the order."

"Tell me the riddle, and I will do my best to uncover the blades." I said.

"Where the path ends and the dragon sits,

There is but one moon the dagger slits,

When the dragon moves in rage,

You have reached the final stage,

Hold your hands up towards the sky,

Do not let the dragon fly,

Then down in darkness lays the flame,

Aldonis lit to find hope again."

"Do you have any other clues you can give me?" I asked, trying to make sense of the riddle.

"Yes, your friends. The order was at it's most powerful in small numbers of trusted friends. Ask and they will help. Now, it is time for you to go." The woman said.

"Will we speak again?" I asked.

"Yes." she said.

The woman let go of my mother and walked toward me with a smile. She held her hand up and pushed me on the head. I felt like I was flying backwards and as I was about to hit the ground...

I jumped up out of my bed. I would not make the same mistake thinking this had been just a dream again. I needed to speak with Unul right away. I got myself dressed and strapped my dagger to my waist. I had no intention of ever letting it leave my side again. Once dressed I headed straight to Unul's room.

It was still early and none of my other companions had woken up yet. I opened Unul's door and slammed it shut behind me, startling him in his bed.

"Jara? What in the Gods are you doing in here at this hour?" he questioned while rubbing his face.

"Where the path ends and the dragon sits,

There is but one moon the dagger slits,

When the dragon moves in rage,

You have reached the final stage,

Hold your hands up towards the sky,

Do not let the dragon fly,

Then down in darkness lays the flame,

Aldonis lit to find hope again." I recited to him.

"...where did you hear this?" he asked me.

"The glowing woman came to me last night. She said this was a riddle passed down in my order through the ages. Solving this riddle is the only way we survive the beasts of the forest." I said very matter-of-factly.

"We don't even know what the riddle refers to, the meaning behind it was forgotten decades ago..." Unul said confused.

"No, I know what it's about. Aldonis forged blades imbued with magic before he died. He had a vision and knew that the beasts Lucian created would return so he forged them in secret and had them hidden after his death. They are here in the castle, solving that riddle is how we find the blades. Without them we can not kill the creatures tormenting the villages or anything else in that forest." I said.

"Well then, it sounds like we have some work to do." Unul said.

"Do you have any thoughts on where to start?" I asked him.

"Yes," Unul said, pausing for a moment, "but I doubt you will like it."

"Try me." I replied.

"We need to get Runa. There are three people that can put this together, and we are two of them." He said.

"Runa?" I asked, "She will never let me live it down if she solves it first!"

"Jara, sometimes I think you let your old rivalries take control over what you need to do to get things done. If you continue to let the past dictate your future you will never accomplish what you are capable of. You and Runa are kindred spirits, you have the same heart, the same drive, and the same goals." Unul said to me.

"But were you not the one that said competition is good amongst peers?" I replied.

"Yes, when you were sixteen and still learning how to kick a soldiers teeth in! You are both ladies now, you can achieve far more joining in harmony than at odds with each other. Just look at Alor and King Ansel, they grew up together here at the castle, sparring and fighting against each other every day. It made them both strong and respectful of each others abilities despite titles, but when they put the rivalry aside and joined in friendship they created a more powerful force, one which could be seen at battles fought side by side." Unul exclaimed.

I was quiet for a minute, I knew Unul was right. The truth was, I had known for a long time that we had outgrown our childhood rivalry. But something about a close friendship with Runa made me uneasy. I couldn't put my finger on what it was, but it made me keep my guard up. Unul suggesting Runa also made me aware of my dream; it was surely no coincidence that I was brought to a memory with Runa in it. There must have been some significance in it.

"Very well, we will get Runa." I conceded

"Go, tell Runa about a riddle to find some ancient swords and nothing more. I will meet you at her chamber once I am decent." He said to me, sending me off out the door.

I made my way down the corridors to Runa's chambers. I could see the door already ajar as I grew closer, the light of the sunrise shining like a painting through into the hall. I heard the sound of a whetstone being dragged across a blade's edge. She was restless. Since we were children this had been a habit of hers on mornings of tournaments, in the yurts on battlefields, and important ceremonies. She had always remarked how calm the slow honing of an edge made her feel.

A part of me wanted to make a joke of it, some sort of witty comment. On any normal day I would have, but the words of the glowing woman and Unul sat heavily on me.

"Did you not sleep well?" I asked poking my head through the door.

Runa was sat on a chair honing her dagger, just as I had suspected. She was already dressed for the day.

"By the looks of it, you didn't sleep well either." Runa said, looking over to me, pointing out that I too was awake and dressed.

"May I come in?" I asked her.

Runa nodded with a smile and motioned to the empty chair across from hers.

I walked in and took a seat. I made notes of my feelings as I sat down; her energy was different this morning. I couldn't help but think that it was perhaps my own habit of needing to one-up everyone all the time that spurred the competitive side in her.

"What woke you so early?" I asked her.

"To be honest, I don't know. Something felt different last night. I was restless and could feel the change in the air. The last time I felt like this was before my father died, before that when your mother went into her state. My mind spent the entire night racing around, trying to decipher what was about to happen." Runa said to me in a troubling tone.

"Why is it you are awake at this hour and in my chambers?" She asked me.

I quickly decided it would be best to not mention the glowing woman, and instead bring up the riddle.

"I heard a riddle just recently," I began, "and it has been playing over in my head. I brought it up with Unul and he said we should investigate it today. It has been the only thing in my mind. It's connected to this castle and hides a treasure of steel. Unul believes that the three of us can solve it together."

"You mean to say, you don't want to solve it first? Take all the glory?" Runa asked sarcastically.

"Yesterday, perhaps." I said. "But what you said about a change in the air, I felt it too. Many things have changed since we saw each other last and we will be campaigning together in a small group. I would much rather be on the road with a friend and companion instead of a rival." I continued earnestly.

"I would like that very much... Since I have been campaigning in the north, I have not had much in the way of friends. The servants just do as I say, and those under my command are afraid to speak truth to me. The truth is, I have always appreciated how open you are with your thoughts when we talk or spar." Runa admitted.

"Then lets do this together, and start a new chapter today." I said nodding with a smile.

It felt good to finally let my guard down with someone. I did not realize the burden I had been carrying until this moment. I couldn't admit it fully aloud, but the truth was I also was lonely. Childhood friends in Dragon's Reach became subordinates or went out on campaign and did not return. In truth, Runa was the only person with whom I had a connection with and was my equal.

"Now, what's this riddle?" She asked me.

"Where the path ends and the dragon sits,

There is but one moon the dagger slits,

When the dragon moves in rage,

You have reached the final stage,

Hold your hands up towards the sky,

Do not let the dragon fly,

Then down in darkness lays the flame,

Aldonis lit to find hope again." Unul said as he walked through the door.

"Aldonis?" Runa repeated.

"I thought that would peak your interest!" I exclaimed.

Runa placed her whetstone on the table and sheathed her dagger. She stood up and began pacing around.

"Why not ask Lady Toree? Surely she would have this figured out right away." Runa said.

"No, Lady Toree is making preparations for your departure." Unul responded.

"Well then, let's start with the beginning. Where the path ends and the dragon sits.... Unul, where are all the dragon statues in the castle?" I asked.

Unul paced around thinking for a moment.

"There is one dragon down at the base of the stairwell here, there is one that sits behind the kings throne, there are two in the courtyard - but those are not in a dead end....." Unul muttered aloud.

"But add in the second line, that's what will narrow the search down! There is but one moon the dagger slits. Unul, what sculptures have a sky motif behind?" Runa asked.

Unul stood and thought for a moment, rubbing his eyes with his hand. His face lit up and he walked toward us.

"There is only one dragon statue in this castle with a sky behind. In the library study! Come, both of you follow me!" Unul proclaimed.

We got up and followed Unul down the corridor and to the entrance of the library's second floor. He took us down a winding path of book cases and to a small stairwell that went to the main floor of the library. Once on the main floor he lead us straight to a small door in the corner. We went down yet another stairwell, this one lit only by a candle he took from a table next to the door.

We had entered the lower library, a section reserved for only scholars and nobles. It was surrounded with elaborately carved stone bookcases set against the walls and equally beautiful carved stone tables. Unul lit four torches around the room, as the light became stronger we saw a circular alcove with a large iron dragon sculpture in it. The statue was a dragon sat on a rock, the mouth open, his wings spread. The walls around were a depiction of the night sky in all mosaic tile. There were two moons amongst the stars. One moon was full, the other crescent.

"This is it!" Runa exclaimed. "The path ends and the dragon sits, and the sky mosaic behind!"

"Yes, but the moons are made of stone, what is meant by 'a dagger slits'?" Unul questioned looking at the mosaic.

"There must be some sort of clue here..." Runa said, looking around the rest of the room to see if she could decipher the next line somehow.

I grabbed a lantern and held it up to the wall to study the motif. It was all solid stone tiles, the artist had done an exquisite job. Each tile was completely flat and smoothed off. I felt my hand glide across the smooth surface. The moons were so well polished it looked like a mirror made of stone.

I ran my hand along the full moon and felt something give way under my finger. I held my lantern up to it, in the center of the moon was a small crack I had made with the pressure of my finger.

"Come here!" I called.

Runa and Unul gathered round, I ran my finger up and down with more pressure and more stone began to fall away as dust.

"Jara, use your dagger!" Runa said.

I looked at her and pulled out Alaia, slowly inserting it's blade into the emerging slit in the moon. The entire dagger blade fit in as well as it does in it's own sheath.

"How did you know?" I asked Runa.

"Your dagger is Alaia, one of Aldonis's works. It would make sense that one of his pieces would be the key." Runa answered.

"Yes but, nothing's happened..." I said.

"No! Runa is right, it's a key!" Unul said excitedly.

Unul touched the dagger's handle and began to turn it slowly. The whole moon spun clockwise and a loud roar sounded from beneath the dragon. The entire sculpture spun around clockwise in unison with the moon. The wings on the dragon creaked as they extended upwards as if it was about to take flight.

"When the dragon moves in rage,

You have reached the final stage,

Hold your hands up towards the sky,

Do not let the dragon fly..." Runa said aloud.

"The wings!" I said, "Do not let the dragon fly, grab his wings and pull them down!"

Runa took hold of the dragon's wings and pulled them downwards with all of her strength. They screeched as they were closed. We heard a loud click and a stone grinding. I pulled my dagger from the wall and we moved into the main study. One of the large stone bookcases had moved over from it's location revealing a staircase heading downwards.

"Then down in darkness lays the flame,

Aldonis lit to find hope again." Unul recited.

We each grabbed a lantern and made our way down the stairs. When we reached the bottom there was a small room with glowing stones set into the ceiling, replicating the night sky. Against the wall was a weapon rack adorned with carvings, it's contents covered by a silk cloth.

"Can this be?" Asked Runa aloud.

"There is only one way to find out..." Unul answered while pulling the cloth off the rack, exposing the last makings of a master smith.

There stood exquisite swords and matching dagger sets sat in beautiful scabbards. They were different lengths and styles, about a dozen in all. Each of them radiated an energy, almost as if they were alive. They yearned for attention and love, offering protection in return.

Each of us stood there staring at the blades, unable to make a move in front of this ancient treasure gifted to us. Unul looked over to me.

"Go ahead Jara, pick your sword." he said to me.

I walked toward the rack and stopped for a moment, feeling my hand on the handle of my dagger.

"No," I said looking at Unul, and then to Runa, "I already have a dagger made by Aldonis. It would be selfish of me to choose first. Runa, you choose what calls out to you first."

Runa looked at me with a smile and a star in her eye. It's a look I had not seen since we were teens, sneaking bottles of mead and wine from the great halls and getting into trouble after tournaments. She was right earlier, something had shifted in the air.

Runa walked to the rack with intention, waiting for a something to speak to her. She closed her eyes and held out her hand, letting herself be guided. She picked up a longsword and dagger, the hilt and scabbard a deep red that matched her hair with gold fittings. She pulled out the sword from the scabbard and its glow in the low light illuminated the room.

"Kalya, this swords name is Kalya. The dagger is Nuii. Thank you, Jara." Runa said

"We found this together." I replied.

I could see a faint smile on Unul's face for a moment but pretended I had not. I walked up to the rack and let my hand float over all the hilts, allowing it to be pulled like a magnet. I was guided to a longsword with dark black wood, white inlays, and silver fittings. There was no dagger along with it, it was alone, calling to me. I could feel it speak to me, quietly in my mind.

"I am Laku," the blade called out, "I was made for the one who wields Alaia."

All was silent yet I could hear the sword speak clear as day.

"This is Laku, made to be Alaia's companion." I said.

Unul walked up to the rack and immediately picked up a short sword and oversized dagger, the hilts white with gold wire inlay.

"Jotir and Rotir," Unul said, "I can not say I have had a blade that can speak its name to the wielder before. Now come, we must bring the rest of these with us to the king and call your companions. You all will need them on your journey!" Unul continued while gathering a few of the weapons.

Runa and I each grabbed the remaining sets and brought them to the king and the rest of our group.

The Companions

Chapter 12

King Ansel was grateful for the weapons we found. I explained their usefulness on our quest in private, understanding the importance, he agreed to give each member of our quest a set.

"Now that your bellies are full for your journey tomorrow, I have gifts for you all. Sir Unul, Lady Jara, and Lady Runa have precured a number of blades that were previously lost to time. I would like you all to take a set for your journey. I am sure you will find them useful on your journey! Come, each of you come up and pick!" The king boasted.

"Thank you, but I already have a blade at my side." Alor said to the king

"Yes, you are right, but these are blades made by Aldonis himself! Left here, hidden for centuries." The king replied.

"Aldonis? You must be joking..." Alor said as he walked to a sword and pulled it from the sheath.

Alor froze in awe, he held the blade out into the air and stared at it, studying every part of it.

"This...this is the work of Aldonis!" Alor said while giving the sword a flourish before putting it back in it's sheath. "Thank you your majesty!" He added.

The rest of the group was astonished, except for Zuht, who was visibly confused.

"Aldonis? What is an Aldonis?" Zuht asked.

"Aldonis was a master smith ages ago, his blades have been said to cut through ghosts and flesh alike. So skilled with a hammer his blades felt like extensions of your own body." Tripp answered.

"They say he was so skilled and connected to his steel that each blade he made inherited a soul, and they greet the one who inherits them." added Toree.

"By Tristi, let this be so!" Zuht said as he walked up and picked his blade.

He stood holding it for a minute before exclaiming with a large smile: "It is true! They speak, how wonderful!"

Toree and Tripp each went up and took their own blades and thanked the king. After some night time pleasantries we all dispersed to our own chambers for the night. Tomorrow at sunrise we would leave for the villages on the outskirts of Evanwood. Properly prepared, it would only take us two days' ride.

I was unable to sleep after the excitement of the day, and knowing tomorrow meant being on the road again. I walked around my room, swinging Laku around, it really did feel like an extension of my own arm. It was nimble, quick, and felt lighter than any sword of the size I had held before. I was sheathing it when I heard a knock at my door.

"Come in." I called out.

The door opened and Runa stepped in.

"Runa, we started the day in your chambers, I suppose it's fitting that we end it in mine! Shall I turn down my bedding?" I said in jest to her.

"Hmm, tempting, yet I think not." Runa said sarcastically.

"Go ahead, speak your mind. I can see there's something on it." I said.

"I wanted to come and thank you for today." Runa said.

"There's no need for thanks." I replied.

"No, no there is. I have not had a day like this since we were children running about. Thank you for being a bigger woman than I; we need not more rivals than we already have." She said to me.

"Runa," I began walking towards her and took her hands in mine, "I am glad you are on this quest with me." I said with a smile.

Runa smiled back.

"But I must confess, I don't know if I can remove all the competition from our friendship... I am sure there will be tallies we are counting." I continued.

"Of course," she said back, "we must still have some fun!"

"Good." I replied

"I am off to bed, good night Jara." Runa said with a earnest smile.

"Good night, Runa." I said back and closed the door as she exited my room.

After closing the door I felt warm and happy. It had been so long since I had a friend of equal status to speak and spend time with. Runa's feelings echoed mine, it had been years since I had a day such as this.

The hour was late and I needed to get my rest. I tossed in my bed a bit, as much as the peril of battling unknown beasts weighed on my mind, the group I was a part of gave my mind ease. Eventually I slept and the next morning came, I found myself in the courtyard of the castle.

The rest of my companions were saying goodbyes to anyone they needed to. I finished packing my horse and double checked all the strappings.

"Good luck on your quest Lady Jara!" Unul called while walking closer.

"Don't cause too much trouble while you are stuck here at the castle." I said back as he got near.

"I will do my best to behave!" He said joking. "You take care of yourself, and when you find your father give him a piece of my mind for me!"

"Thank you Unul, for everything. Without you none of us would be here, and I would be waking up, hung over again, switching spots with my brother at the Western Pass. It is good to be a part of something much larger now." I said honestly to him.

"You are special Jara, and you now hold a great deal of responsibility. In truth, I believe you are the one who should be leading this. The fate of this kingdom falls in your hands. I will see you on the other end. May the Gods be with you on your journey, my friend." Unul said to me.

I smiled at Unul and embraced him in a hug. I wrapped my arms tight around him, probably a bit too tight. As I held him I could hear a muted whimper and felt him shift his wounds away from where my body was.

"I will see you again." I said with a smile and pulling away.

Unul nodded in response and I mounted my horse. I steered my horse to the rest of the group, we all sat mounted as the king addressed us.

"Go now, my companions. Go and know that you have my hopes and blessings with you. Seek what must be found, open your minds from all beliefs you have known to be truths, and above all trust in each other and your cause. Our fates are tied with yours. I pray to see you all when the sun rises on Nerick once again!" The king said to us.

Each of us nodded our heads and we turned, heading out the castle gates, through each level of the city and into the countryside. We road well into the afternoon, stopping only to let the horses drink or to relieve ourselves. We aimed to make it to the Hyrik River before nightfall so that we could cross in the morning.

The area we rode was not too remarkable. Mainly filled with hills of grass, some trees and small patches of woodland, the occasional creek or pond. There were no breakthrough attacks by Wurth in this area of the kingdom. I did rather enjoy the silence of the journey as well. I think everyone was in silent meditation on our trek, simply listening to each one of the horses hoofs clamper on the road.

Eventually we did reach the river and Tripp found a clearing for us to make camp on the banks. Tripp and I pitched the tents, Zuht and Toree made a fire, and Alor and Runa took their bows into the woodland to find dinner for the night. The king had provided us with food rations, but it would be better to save that for the forest. The woodlands in the area we made camp were known for being overrun with all sorts of animals.

"What do you make of this quest, m'lady?" Tripp asked me as we were finishing the second tent.

"I think tomorrow is the last day we will be able to not look over our shoulders." I said honestly to him.

"What do you mean by that?" Tripp asked.

"Tomorrow afternoon we make it to the outskirts of the forest. From there much will change. Make no mistake, you will be earning your knighthood. King Ansel asked that I do not share this information, but I think it is important that you know - the tales of creatures and monsters coming from Evanwood forest are true." I said quietly to him. Zuht and Toree were making too much noise getting the fire started to overhear.

"What do you mean the stories are true?" Tripp asked.

"Whatever was done by the previous group, which included my father, somehow brought these creatures from story to reality." I explained.

"How do you know this?" Tripp asked me, stopping what he was doing.

"First, get back to work." I said pointing to the next and last tent that had to be pitched.

"Right, I'm on it." Tripp said.

"When the king dismissed you all except for Unul, Toree, and myself, he kept us to fill us all in. The towns we are heading to on the border of the forest might not have anyone left in them. Creatures have been killing in the night, and the guard was wiped out by them. Before we get to the town we will come upon a barricade. The way has been sealed off so the kingdom does not panic in fear." I said very honestly to him.

"Is this some sort of joke that you and Unul devised?" Tripp asked with a frown.

I put my hand on his shoulder and looked him in the eyes. "You have my word." I said to him.

"S...so why not tell us all when we were at the castle?" Tripp asked.

"I asked the same question, the King and Toree said it was not to make everyone question the entire quest. They were afraid everyone would think it was a joke and a waste of time. He had already asked us to find a magic dagger, do you think if he brought up monsters that would have bode well?" I replied.

"No, I suppose you are right. How do we defeat these creatures if they destroyed a whole guard?" Tripp responded.

"With these!" I said, gripping the hilt of my sword. "Aldonis was a child of Nystia, he made his blades with a hint of magic in them, it gave them the power to slay beasts made by magic." I continued.

"So that is why the king gave them all to us!" Tripp said.

"Exactly. This must remain a secret, Tripp." I replied. "The others can not know about this yet. They will find out tomorrow when we arrive at the blockade."

"Of course m'lady." Tripp said nodding.

I paused for a moment, staring at Tripp.

"You seem very calm for someone that just learned about monsters being real..." I said inquisitively.

"Well, I can see why you'd think that. While you've been busy with your own tasks, I've spent a lot of time these past weeks speaking with Sir Unul and Zuht. Sir Unul believes when you are faced with a situation of dire circumstance do what you can do for the greatest good, no matter your own outcome.

Zuht believes that there are no coincidences, just mysteries. Zuht says that when you end up in a situation you could not imagine, it is the Gods' doing, and that we must do all we can to earn our place in their plans, even if we can not make sense of it. I suppose I've resonated with both... don't get me wrong, the thought of fighting monsters from fairytales makes me feel like I am going to soil myself, but I am adopting a different outlook." Tripp explained.

"I am impressed, I think I am beginning to understand what Unul saw in you!" I said, crossing my arms and standing tall.

"Thank you?" Tripp said, unsure if it was a compliment or an insult.

"Now!" I exclaimed, "let's finish pegging this tent up!" I remarked.

Tripp and I finished pitching the tents and laid out the bedrolls. I was impressed with how far he has come in such a short amount of time. Sir Krinn was a great knight, but too rigid in his beliefs and chivalry over anything else. Tripp had great training under Krinn, but not theory. It was good to see him evolve into a more well-rounded, not so stuck-up warrior.

By the time we finished the fire was roaring. Runa and Alor were returning from the wood with two rabbits and a pheasant. Tripp helped Alor dress the animals and we roasted them over the fire, picking food off as it cooked, sharing stories from our pasts, and laughing through the evening.

"So there we were, King Ansel and I, walking through the woods with our bows looking for the stag...not more than ten years of age..." Alor began, "We were so loud talking amongst ourselves that we did not even hear what was behind us... and before we knew it - POW! A small hog had knocked his tusk right up Ansel's arse!" He exclaimed laughing.

"He was so surprised he didn't even stop to see what it was that hit him! He grabbed his ass and ran back to the manor screaming like a wee babe!" Alor continued.

We had all consumed quite a bit of mead this night and could not control our laughter. Each one of us took our turn telling an embarrassing or fun story. Some were better than others, Toree spoke about a dispute at one of the colleges that she found amusing, it was a bit above the rest of our heads. Tripp told the story about the cows again, Zuht had us all laughing about a story about a follower being too drunk at the fire temple and his belches lit aflame when he was too close to the candles at the alter.

I told a story about me helping my brother woe the scullery maid at Dragon's Reach before setting up a meeting between my father and Unul at the same rendezvous point so he would be caught. Alor and Runa found that one particularly comical.

Runa had us all laughing about how she swindled a gang of thieves in their own dice game before sending guards in and having them arrested. It was a night of bonding through the stories of our past. For a moment we all seemed to forget the task at hand, all felt well. Eventually each of us retired to our bedrolls in our tent. Runa had already fallen asleep in hers, as I approached the tent I was sharing with her, I could hear her snoring. Luckily, I was happy enough from the drinks that I could sleep through a bear attack.

"Time to rise!" I heard over me with a hand pinching my cheek. I was still inebriated because I did not know where I was, who I was with, or even what year it was.

"Lina? Is that you?" I asked, thinking I was still at a tournament three years prior...

"Lina? Who is that? I'm heartbroken, you must have had more to drink than I thought!" the voice said.

"Where am I?" I asked trying to sit up.

"Oh you definitely did drink more than I thought! Your name is Jara, you are on a secret quest to find a magic knife in a big forest." I could see and comprehend that it was Runa waking me up.

"Yeah, I guess I did... get me some of that smelly stuff Zuht brews every morning please..." I said.

"Oh, of course my lady..." Runa said sarcastically before walking to get a cup.

I had noticed while on the road with Zuht, his concoction could cut through a hangover in about five minutes. Whatever was in that had more than one medicinal value.

"Here you go." said Runa, handing me the brew.

"Thank you" I said, taking it from her and battling the heat of the drink to get it in my belly and attack the headache I had as quickly as possible.

"Really though, Lina? Who is Lina?" Runa asked me.

I let out a small chuckle before I realized how much that hurt my head.

"Just some fun from the Kurpiz tournament a few years back." I answered quietly, my hand on my head.

"If you thought she was waking you up outside on the ground she must have been some fun." Runa said giggling.

"Come, finish that up, we're packing now to get back on the move." Runa added.

I nodded and drank up.

Eventually the pain in my head subsided and I pulled myself together, rolling up my bed mat, strapping my sword belt on, and taking down the tent. I joined the others by the horses as Toree was sticking out her chest, an obvious motion to show that she wanted to make herself heard before we leave the camp.

"I hope all of you had a good night's sleep. I am afraid it might be the last for a while. Today we ride towards the town of Enex. We will come across an outpost before we reach the town limits, the king has instructed me to have you all listen to what the captain has to say with open ears when we arrive...however...I think it is a mistake so I am telling you all this now. Since Jara's father entered the forest creatures from fairytales have been appearing, tormenting the town and surrounding area. A large group of soldiers were sent in to kill the beasts but none returned. The king has had the path to Enex blockaded to all save us. Our swords and fire are the only things that can kill the beasts." Toree said.

"Strange that the king would not fill me in on this rather elaborate joke." Alor stated.

"I am sorry Alor, but is not a joke. King Ansel has become somewhat paranoid at this point in the war and his decisions, while having the best intentions, would be likely to cause damage. When we reach the outpost at the blockade you will see what I speak of." Toree elaborated.

"I should have you know, I'm not one for ill-timed jokes." Alor said in a passive-aggressive manner.

"I can assure you, neither am I. That is why I call on Lady Jara as my witness, she was there when the King spoke of it." Toree responded.

Tripp looked over at me, keenly aware of what Toree was referring to. In truth I told Tripp both so he could prepare himself, and because he would be the first one to question something abnormal. It had worked because Tripp did not rally behind Alor's arguments. It seemed Zuht and Runa took Tripp's calmness and my word without question, since they did not speak up about it.

"Lady Toree speaks the truth. The king and sir Unul both spoke of it. That is what led me to seek these blades out with Unul and Runa, that they might be our light in the dark of battle." I said.

"Bullocks, absolute bullocks..." Alor muttered.

Throughout the war and assassination attempts it had made the king slightly paranoid. As a result he trusts some far too much, and others far too little. I did not realize this until I spoke with Unul at supper the last night in the castle. We had recapped our recent time together from the gardens in my home to our drinks in Ansel's court. When I asked him why it was necessary for us to stay hidden on the road to the castle from Dragon's Reach he said that the king was afraid that an enemy agent targeted my father. Since my father was missing he thought they might come for me next while traveling to Raven's Landing.

While someone targeting my father could be plausible, targeting me for anything other than weakening the command of an army was unlikely. However, Unul had pointed out that if not for our roundabout path Tripp would be dead, and by association Zuht would be too. It did make me question fate and how all small decisions, no matter how far away are made, are somehow connected to much bigger events.

Eventually some of the distrust between Alor and Toree was swept away. It did not seem to plant any seeds with other members of the group, but the attitude between Alor and Toree had shifted. In my opinion, it was a terrible idea for the king to only tell me and Toree about this and leaving Alor out. If that was the plan Toree should be leading us without a partner. This war had indeed worn down the king, five years ago such a poor leadership decision would have never been made.

We began our ride towards Enex. Runa rode beside Zuht, who was talking her ear off. Alor rode beside Tripp, who was trying to calm Alor's mistrust over Toree's short speech. I was trailing the group but rode up to Toree, who was leading.

"I am glad you told them the truth." I said, steering my horse towards her.

"I could not blindly follow the king's orders." Toree said.

"I know, but even now with the truth out his orders are proving to sow division between you and Alor. He has spent too much time devising theories in a tower surrounded by stone walls." I replied back.

"Lady Jara, this is not your quest to lead, yet I can't help but feel you are capable of doing so." Toree said very matter-of-factly to me.

I pulled my reigns away and stood apart, allowing my position in the line to fall behind before getting back in next to Zuht, who was still talking Runa's ear off. Toree had obviously spent too much time indoors, away from danger, only studying tactics. Now on the road, it seemed to me that her time in the colleges also gave her a chip on her shoulder, not willing to take opinion aside from her own. I could let it all be known at that moment, but the reality was all would be revealed before nightfall anyway.

We rode on, Toree kept to herself in the front, while Alor and Tripp continued to speak. Runa and I kept Zuht busy with stories of tournaments and battles past that we were in together. Prior to the battle on the road, Zuht had never conversed with any warriors before, let alone travel as one.

The sky began to turn red and in the distance we could see the outpost. It was strategically positioned between two densely wooded areas overgrown with vine and thorn. A cart sat across the thin road running through the dense woods, the smoke from a fire nearly out was rising from within the make-shift camp. As we drew closer we could see that the road was unguarded. Our attention immediately heightened, as this was a blockade put in place by the king.

"Why have you all turned so tense?" Zuht asked.

"Lady Toree said there would be an outpost here, and she was right, but there is no one guarding the road." Runa said.

Alor had rode up to Toree and I rode up to meet them. Tripp and Runa stayed behind with Zuht to watch our back.

"You said this was one of the king's outposts?" Alor asked Toree.

"Yes, guarding the road to Enex..." She said wearily.

"Yet the blockade is empty of guards, and the night sets upon us with no roaring fire... something is wrong. Stay back with the others while I check ahead!" Alor said to Toree and then rode towards the outpost.

"Alor does not believe what we are up against!" I said to Toree in frustration.

"I know, the stubborn fool! He will need my help..." Toree said and rode towards the outpost behind Alor.

"You are bloody daft Toree!" I yelled out.

I turned and rode to the others, as I made my way I noticed tracks leading around a fork in the road. I made an on-the-spot assumption that whatever survivors there were made the tracks and could offer reinforcements.

"I fear something amiss far worse than Wurth here! There are tracks around the bend - follow them and have them with torches ready!" I said to Tripp, turning and riding to the outpost.

There was no sight of anyone at the blockade or in the tents as we rode in. We all sat on our horses at a slow trot, we did not unsheathe our swords incase the king's men were there. We did not want to be deemed a threat and be thrust into an altercation with our own brethren, especially as the sky was becoming darker. It seemed an unnecessary precaution however, as the fires around the camps were smoldering and had clearly been left for some hours now. Rainclouds moved overhead and would soon put out any remains of the fires.

"I will search toward the head tent, you continue searching here for anyone you can find." Alor said to me.

"Wait!" I called, "You must believe what it is we face!" I said to him.

Just at that moment we heard a loud screeching sound that seemed to come from all around us. We all stopped and stood still, trying to keep our horses calm. We drew our swords and looked around to find the source. The rain started to come down and the sky grew black.

It was dead silent except for the tip tap of a drizzle starting.

Alor drew his horse closer to mine.

"What is it?" Alor asked me.

"Cythians, briars, even reports of wolf-men." I said blatantly.

"You can't be serious..." Alor said to me while looking around, sword in hand, keeping his horse in check with his other hand.

"It's true." Toree chimed in.

"How?" Alor asked.

"It started when the first expedition went missing, that's why they blockaded the town, we went over this earlier..." I said.

"Our blades and fire are the only things that can destroy them." Toree said to us.

Alor trotted towards Toree.

"If this is true, you must get out onto the road now. Jara and I will check this post ourselves. Leave." Alor demanded to Toree.

Toree stared at Alor defiantly.

"Now!" Alor ordered again.

"I will not! We must stay tog-" before Toree could finish there was another loud shriek and screech.

Our horses reared as something bustled through the trees and came at a charge, tearing down the tent next to us. In an instant the horse Toree was on had no head, and she was thrown under the body of her steed. She yelled in shock and surprise, her sword was thrown from her hand and she tried to get herself out from under her horse.

"Be ready!" Alor yelled to me.

I circled my horse around looking for where the creature came from. The shrieking began again and I looked around frantically.

"Your left!" Yelled Alor charging towards me.

Before I could look over my shoulder I felt a strong impact and I was spun around. It took me a moment to get my bearing, I realized my horse was on the ground neighing. I tapped her shoulder.

"Up!" I said to my horse, "Get up now!" I said pulling the reins.

The horse struggled getting it's front legs up, as it tried to lift it's back legs it fell down again, trapping my leg under it. I looked to where I felt the impact before, the horse had a gash stretching from her belly to her buttock, all of her tendons were sliced through. I could hear the shrieking again and quickly dislodged my leg from under the horse, sword still in hand I ran towards Toree who's lower half was completely stuck under the motionless carcass.

"Pull your legs out while I lift!" I said to Toree, beginning to lift the body of the horse off her.

The shrieking got closer and I heard a thump. I looked back and saw Alor thrown to the ground and in a daze, the horse he was on split nearly in half. The rain got heavier and the ground began to get muddy.

"On your feet Alor!" I yelled to him, weary of where the next attack would come from.

Alor managed to get up and stumbled through the tents to where the last creature had come from.

I could hear calling for us by the others, who had now made their way into the outpost.

"Cythians!" I called out to them, "Cythians!" I repeated again.

The shrieking began again and I could hear one charging me. I dropped the horse, unaware of Toree managed to get free or not, and picked up my sword. I turned around and saw the figure speeding toward me. I could see what I could only describe as a human-dragon hybrid, covered in scales with arms that had protruding bones, this must have been what they were attacking the horses with. As it charged it knocked a lantern that was hanging on a tent pole and set the tent next to us aflame.

I quickly raised my guard as it approached me. I blocked a slash from it's arm and rode the bone to it's neck, cleaving the head off. Up close these creatures were smaller in stature than their blows made it seem. They stood only three quarters the size of the average human but were fast and savage. The body fell to the ground and I heard another shout, this time sounding like an injured bear.

I looked to my side and saw a massive briar, a creature that could only be described as a giant half human half stag. I turned to face it, sword ready. It marched up with large steps and swung it's clenched fist at me. I attempted to knock his arm down and get in for a thrust but the mass of his arm knocked my sword from my hands and threw my balance off.

"Jara look out!" I heard Toree yell.

As I regained my balance I brought my vision back to the briar. His other arm was raised back he began to swing it towards me. Confronted with a beast from nightmares, I had forgotten all the gifts that were bestowed upon me, I could have used the burning tent beside me to sling a whirlwind of fire at the briar, instead I held my bracers up to take the blow.

I felt my arms jolt to the size and an impact across my torso. I heard a 'thud.' My body went numb, my hearing muted, and my legs gave out from under me. My vision began to blur as I saw the briar walk closer. Everything turned red, my body grew warm, I could vaguely feel the tapping of the rain on my face, then suddenly all was black.

Secrets Learned

Chapter 13

I heard a woman's voice singing quietly over me while a cold cloth ran gently across my face, down my neck, and on my shoulders. I could feel some soreness on my side, but any pain I felt subsided with the warm sunlight on my body and the gentle singing. I tried to open my eyes and move my head, but I was only able to let out a moan.

"Shh, rest now..." I heard the voice say.

I felt a caressing of my hair and face while I fell back into a slumber.

I woke up in a field outside of Dragon's Reach, feeling no pain I got up from the grass I had been laying in. I made my way to the courtyard where I met Unul at the beginning of my journey. My mother was sat there, I sat across from her and leaned back in my chair.

"Am I dead?" I asked, for the first time aware that I was not where I perceived myself to be.

The glowing woman appeared within a blink of my eye and put her hand on my mother's shoulder again.

"No, you are alive, but injured." She said through my mother.

"Did everyone survive?" I asked,

"Yes, your companions are alive. You did well, but you did not use your gifts."

"I was preoccupied with a monster from the tales my mother told me as a child standing in front of me..." I said in defense.

"You must see your abilities as much a part of you as your nose. It is out of sight but doing it's work when you need it to."

"It certainly would have made things easier if that were the case." I replied.

"Your trust and commitment to your companions saved you. Since we last spoke you have done well, do not let a small punch on the side make you waiver."

"The blades we found," I began, changing the subject, "they were able to slay the beasts, but the beasts were so fast!"

"The blades know what to do. You must put trust in them, don't think when battling the beasts, just feel, you will know when to strike. Now, you must go back Jara. I will see you again..."

My vision went black again.

My eyes opened slowly, the soft gentle singing seemed to pull me back into reality. I saw a shadow walk toward me while my vision was still blurred, the singing stopped and I felt my head lifted onto someone's lap. The cold cloth wiped the staleness from my eyes and I was able to open them.

"Was that you singing?" I asked

"Yes." Runa said with a smile, brushing a hair from my face. "It's a song my mother sang me when I was young."

"Beautiful..." I replied looking at her smile while I drifted back into a slumber.

I had more dreams of home, playing games with my brother, studying with my father, and walking through the forest with my mother. In each place I visited, I could hear Runa's song echoing in the air, it was calling me back.

I opened my eyes and saw Tripp sat next to the cot I was on.

"Lady Jara, don't move!" Tripp said to me, leaving his seat and walking out the door.

"Not a problem..." I moaned out as I tried to prop myself up, feeling the soreness of laying down for what must have been a day.

Tripp came back with Toree and Runa.

"Thank the Gods you are awake!" Tripp said.

"Me too..." I replied.

"You have healed, what you feel are just the aches from being in bed for five days." Runa said to me.

"Five days?" I asked surprised.

"You got hit pretty hard, Lady Toree and Zuht put together a concoction to speed up the healing process." Tripp said.

"Thank you." I said to Toree. "What happened after I went down?" I asked.

"The briar you fought burst into flames, it must have knocked over a barrel of oil before it could finish it's attack. There were two more cythians running around, Sir Alor ran one through but lost two fingers in the process, the other Runa cut down." Tripp answered.

The realization had only then occurred to me, I was on a cot in a tent.

"Where are we?" I asked.

"You both can go, I'll help her from here." Runa said to Tripp and Toree.

They both nodded and left the tent, Runa sat at the foot of the cot and smiled at me, taking my hand in hers.

"I was worried about you. Truth be told, it's the first time I was genuinely worried about someone else. Your wounds had healed quick, but a fever took you until today." she said.

"I jumped through time and memories, the only thing that kept pulling me back here was your song echoing in the air everywhere I was..." I said truthfully.

We both smiled for a moment.

"But really, where are we?" I asked changing the subject.

"We're at the outpost. After you rode off we found a scout from the outpost. They said when they spotted the briar slowly heading toward their camp they retreated back.

They were returning to see if the camp was clear when they bumped into us. We could see a tent aflame in the distance and the guards showed us another way to get in, behind anything you were facing. I was able to surprise and cut the cythian down. We created enough of a diversion that Alor was able to find an opening and slay the last of the creatures.

We searched to make sure the outpost was clear, that's when we found you and Toree. She was knelt over you, repeating some sort of prayer. One of the guards showed me where the healers quarters were and I carried you here." Runa explained.

"And how are the others?" I asked.

"Alor's hand has healed very quickly with Zuht and Toree's help. Other than that we are all in good condition. How do you feel now?" Runa questioned.

"I feel tired, but otherwise well. I think I'd like to get up and see everyone outside." I said.

Runa nodded and helped me up. My body did not hurt from any wounds but the fever had made me weak. I walked out the tent leaning on her and felt the sun hit my face, the warmth brought some energy back to me.

"Ah, Lady Jara!" Alor said as he walked towards me. "It is good to see you on your feet! You must feel good about having a new feather in your hat!"

"Just the feathers in my pillow." I joked.

"Lady Jara, you are the first to kill a cythian and survive a briar!" Tripp boasted from a barrel he was perched on.

"Three cythians were slain, and not all by me. As far as surviving the briar, it's not an experience I would recommend." I said with some humility.

Zuht walked over to me and took hold of my arm, placing it under his.

"Come with me my lady, let me walk you around in the light. I would very much like to hear what it was like taking the head off of a demon and facing a giant!" Zuht said to me, ushering me away from the others.

I began to recant the story for Zuht, but as soon as we got out of earshot he cut me off.

"There is more to Lady Toree than she has told us." Zuht said.

"What makes you say that?" I asked inquisitively, not letting on I had the same feeling after my vision of the glowing woman.

"Lady Jara, Tristi brought you to me, and I respect you. Tristi gave me the gift of keen sight, I am not so easily fooled as young Tripp and the others. Tristi has given you gifts too." Zuht began.

"Zuht you -"

"No no Lady Jara, you must let me speak." Zuht said, cutting me off.

"I know, that day we met, that it was not Tristi himself sending the fire down from the sky. I know it was you!" He continued.

"Zuht, listen-" I was cut off again by Zuht.

"Ah, yes listen! Tristi gave you that gift, and you hide it. I understand why, and I have not said, even to you, a word about it. I know the things you can do, this is part of the reason I follow you. When I entered this place with the others I saw a fire roar and take down the beast. I thought at that moment it was you!" Zuht said.

"But I fought with only my sword..." I said.

"Yes, I know. When I arrived where you were on the ground unconscious, I know you have a great gift but I think not one you can use it when asleep... it is not just this, I saw you there on the ground before the others found you. Your shoulder and side were smashed in and your face was turning white." Zuht explained.

I was taken back, that was not the account Runa gave me, some bruising and soreness but nothing more. I certainly didn't feel like I had half my side beating in...

"You were dying Jara, I watched Lady Toree kneel over your body, muttering a prayer, and breath into your mouth. She had a hand on your head and chest and then began saying the prayer, over and over again. It was in a tongue I have not heard. Before my eyes your body fixed itself and your color returned. That is when Lady Runa arrived and carried you away."

"What you're saying is that I was dying?" I asked confused.

"Dying or dead. What I am saying is, whatever gift Tristi bestowed on you he also gave to Lady Toree. You could not have sent the flame down on the beast, and if I had not watched your body transform with my own eyes I would call myself crazy!" He said very definitively.

I tried to replay the encounter back in my mind... I knew that I did not use anything other than my sword that night, and the last thing I remembered was seeing red. It would make sense that it was fire but how did Toree have that ability, and why not tell me? More confusing was what Zuht was saying about my body being smashed in. He has been honest with me since we met, he certainly wouldn't lie to me now. As far as I knew, healing using magic was not possible.

"I'm sorry I'm so quiet, this just doesn't make sense to me." I said to Zuht.

"Do not be sorry, and do not try to make sense of it. Look at it as it is and do what you must to uncover the truth." Zuht replied.

I nodded my head in agreement and we turned a corner back to where our companions were sitting. They were all there talking, laughing amongst themselves.

"That woman right there, That is a true friend." Zuht said, nodding his head in Runa's direction. "I know you must keep secrets for a time, but to those closest, you must reveal your truth."

"Why do you say that?" I asked curiously.

"When she found you she pushed Lady Toree off and carried you herself to the healer's quarters. Young Tripp and I offered to help, she refused. She nursed you from your fever. If any of us came in to check on you Lady Runa was there too." Zuht informed me.

"Is that so?" I said, intrigued.

"I had a friend like this, she was killed some time ago. It still weighs heavy on me. A friendship such as that needs truth instead of water, and trust instead of sun." He counseled.

"Thank you." I said to Zuht as he escorted me back to the group.

As we walked back I was unsure of how to process the information I was just given. I knew that before anything, I needed food and drink. It seemed as though my companions felt the same. Over the fire was meat roasting, and a broth collecting the juice below.

"My lady, you must be hungry! Sit! Have some food!" Alor said, handing me a spoon and bowl filled with meat and broth.

I sat and ate the fastest I had ever eaten.

"How is your hand?" I asked Alor with a mouth full of meat.

"Thanks to the healer, Zuht, and Toree it is feeling good. I might be a few fingers short, but it seems I don't need them with my sword!" he replied.

"Oh? What do you mean?" I asked, confused as it was his pinky an ring finger on his sword hand that were lost. One missing finger on a sword hand could be troublesome, let alone two!

"This sword..." he began, pulling his from it's scabbard. "It's a strange thing, it feels as comfortable and nimble in my hand now as it did when I first drew it..."

He did a quick flourish and looked at it in his three fingered hand before sheathing it.

"Truly a magnificent work of art." he said.

"What is the plan, Alor?" Toree asked.

"Now that Jara is up, we will rest tomorrow. After that we move onto Enex. We will do what we can for any survivors still in the town before moving into the woods." Alor announced.

"That is a good idea, we can use the day to gather any supplies we may need once in the forest. I will gather some healing herbs and candles." Toree added.

"I will join you." added Zuht.

"That would be most appreciated!" Toree said to Zuht.

Now that I was awake and in better condition, the healer of the outpost took his quarters back. Runa offered her tent to me. I went to the tent and walked up to a tall mirror standing to the side of the cot.

I looked at myself in the mirror, remembering the condition Zuht said he saw me in. I stripped off my top and studied my body's reflection. I could not see one sign of injury.

I can remember vividly bracing myself and the beasts heavy arm coming down on me with such force...I should have been broken like an egg over a skillet...yet here I was, not a trace of anything.

I put my top back on and began to button it up.

"Do you need help with anything?" I heard Runa ask as she made her way into the tent.

"No, thank you." I said, "I just need to speak to Toree about something before retiring for the night."

I smiled and left Runa with some privacy.

I walked to the tent Toree was using and went inside. She was sat in a chair next to a wooden table reading.

"Lady Jara, how can I help you?" she asked me.

"I had some questions that I thought you might answer for me..." I said.

"Of course, what kind of questions?" She asked, putting down her book.

I had not thought this far ahead in truth. I was running on impulse since Zuht spoke to me, but I thought following the glowing woman's advice and trusting my instincts and trusting my friends would bode me well.

"Why did you not tell me?" I asked her while staring in her eyes.

"Tell you what?" she asked innocently.

I looked her in the eyes and made the flame of the candle grow into a ball of fire before sending it hurling at her. She caught it in her hand and shrunk it down to a candle flame again, placing the flame back on the candlewick like she was lighting it with a stick.

"That." I said.

"How did you know?" She asked me.

"My friends tell me things that might be important to know." I said, an obvious jab at her previous decisions.

"I am so sorry..." she said to me earnestly.

"The fire that took down the briar, that wasn't an accident, that was you." I stated.

"Yes..." she replied.

"And the reason I am not dead right now is because of you." I stated again.

"...yes..." she replied again.

"...thank you..." I said, breaking down into tears.

I walked up to her and put my arms around her, embracing the only other person in the world that knew what I felt hiding my abilities. I could not control my emotions, having this power and not knowing anyone else that knew what it was like to wield it was silently tearing me apart without me even realizing.

"I know what it is you feel, Jara. I have been there for longer than you can imagine." she said, kindly.

"But how did you heal me?" I asked her.

"There are a great many things you do not yet know." she said.

"How did you learn, how did you keep it a secret?" I asked.

"Now is not the time. Tomorrow, in the woods, come with me to pick the herbs, leave Zuht to help Alor. It is a story too long to share with words, I will show you." Toree said to me.

"Tomorrow." I said, releasing her and walking towards the tent's entrance.

"Tomorrow." She repeated after me.

I began to walk out and Toree called out: "Jara, you are not alone."

I smiled and continued back to Runa's tent.

I heard the cock crow the next morning and rubbed my face awake. I rolled over and faced Runa on the cot we shared. She was already awake, laying and staring at the top of our tent.

"Do you ever wonder what would be, had this war never started?" Runa asked me.

"I feel it has been so long, I can not remember much of what it was like before." I said.

Runa took a deep breath and turned over, facing me.

"Yes, but what do you think life would be like if the north had just stayed in the north?" she asked again.

"I don't know, I'd like to think it would be a lot like when we were children, running about in the woods and stealing wine from the cellar. Except it would be boring political games and wild boar hunts." I suggested.

"I lay awake some nights imagining it. I imagine my family intact, I imagine walking in armlock with a lover through the gardens of Glushal, sharing a kiss next to the waterfalls at river's edge." she lamented.

"When was the last time you were romanced?" I asked, intrigued by her day dreams.

"Too long." She sighed. "It is my own doing. Some have tried, but I have pushed them all away. Without bringing the war to an end I fear there would be no peace for me with someone else."

"You should just give in to your feelings and enjoy life while you live it." I said back.

"How do you do it? You seem to go about each day like there is nothing larger looming over you." She asked me.

"Honestly, we are stuck in roles in our lives we did not choose to take on. It was all thrown at us out of the womb. I like to feel that freedom over who to love or who to lay with is something that I get to choose, not decided for me." I confessed to her.

"I never looked at it like that before... does the constant fighting never get to you?" she inquired.

"In truth, it doesn't. The other nobles are always fighting over something. If there was not a war with Wurth there would be a feud with someone else. Yes there would be a peace for a time, but to me knowing at some point trouble would break out again and not knowing when is a far worse burden than constantly being at war." I admitted.

"It seems our circumstances have made us both too hard. It would do us both well to let the flowing water break down our walls a bit." Runa said, then she sat up and kicked herself out of the bed.

"I'm off for food!" she sang in a tune before throwing a cloak on and rushing out the tent.

I laid there unsure of what had just transpired. I did feel that the water was in fact wearing down my wall. I pulled myself out of the bed and got myself together to meet Toree.

At the wood's edge Toree stood with a basket to collect the herbs in.

"Come," she said, "let us head toward the stream."

We made our way into the woods, I could hear the stream flowing nearby. Toree gave me a list of the herbs to look for and pick that would be near the water's edge.

"So how did you come into these powers? And how did you learn to use them so effectively?" I asked her while picking the herbs she listed.

"Like you, I was born into it." she said to me openly.

Her secretive demeaner had fallen by the wayside and she was relatively open with me.

"But how did you make them so strong? The healing, I have heard nothing of it before!" I said again.

"I've been practicing for a long time, and had many great teachers." She said back to me.

"What do you mean a long time? You can't be more than thirty five!" I said.

Toree chuckled to herself.

"Thirty seven?" I asked

She shook her head from side to side, never stopping from her herb collecting.

"Surely you can't be forty?" I asked again.

"No, no, I am not forty." she answered.

"I thought not, thirty eight then?" adding one more guess.

Toree put her basket down and walked up to me, placed one hand on my shoulder, and stared me in the eyes.

"I am three hundred and sixty eight." she said completely serious.

My look of confusion had obviously spoke for me.

"Well, give or take a few years. I lost track at some point." she added.

"...bu...wha...how? Surely you are joking!" I stuttered.

"No, I am one of the few pieces of Nystia left in this world. How my life has been lengthened like this I do not know. I am the head of your order, and I am the one who initiated your mother. That is how your father knew me. I was the one that gave Unul his instructions for your initiation ritual, it was under the guise of being found in an old scroll, but me none the less." she informed me.

"But why keep it a secret?" I asked.

"People turn on what they can't understand. I was hunted for generations after Nystia disappeared for what I could do. Eventually I began to hide it, only revealing who I was and what I could do to those in the order. With our situation, I was weary to reveal myself to you or anyone else. I am happy with who I am in this 'life' and did not want to have to run away again and start over next generation." she explained.

"But why get involved with this quest then?" I asked. "Surely this has given you the greatest risk of exposing yourself."

She looked at me calmly with a certainty in her eyes.

"I am putting an end to a story that I should have wrapped up over three hundred years ago." she said.

"You said your story was too long to explain, so you would show me. What did you mean by that?" I asked, with a million other questions bouncing around my head.

"Yes, you should know what happened all those years ago, and what role you and I play now. If you are ready I will show you, if not we will continue picking our herbs and join the others at camp."

"Show me." I said.

Toree walked up to me, held my head in her hands and touched her forehead on mine. I felt a rush of energy to my head and felt faint. The wind was knocked out of me through some internal force and when I inhaled I was somewhere all together different.

What Was

Chapter 14

I stood in a room with two others, one I recognized as Toree, the other a man I did not recognize. The architecture was unlike anything I have seen in Nerick.

"Toree, where are we? And who is this?" I asked.

There was no response. I walked to Toree and went to put my hand on her shoulder but it just fell through her like she was made of smoke.

"Show you" I thought to myself, Toree must have somehow connected me to her memories.

Toree was in a gorgeous blue dress that draped her body like a silk cloth, around her neck was a necklace with a pendant that glowed bright with polished silver, her hand held a chalice. She drank all its contents at once, then turned around.

"But what do you expect to gain that you do not have now? You have the queen in your pocket, you have control over the armies, why make a play for the throne?" Toree said to the man.

The man walked toward her, he was tall, slim and fit, he wore robes of deep purple and had a chain of silver stars around his shoulders.

"My love," he said, "the other kingdoms use our powers, our inventions, our skills, and they offer nothing in return. We could have such a kingdom that it would extend across the continent!"

Toree was visibly troubled.

"And what of everyone in those kingdoms?" she asked him.

"My subjects, my happy subjects. They would be a part of the greatest kingdom the world has seen!" he said enthusiastically.

"And what of me?" Toree asked him.

"And you..." he said, caressing her hair and giving her a sensual kiss on the neck.

"You will be my queen, my confidant..." he said between kisses down her neck to her shoulder.

He gently slipped the dress off of her shoulders and it slid down her naked body, the dress pooled at her feet on the floor. His hands caressing her sweetly as her eyes closed and she began to embrace the moment. As the man went to kiss her, her eyes shot open and she backed away, crossing her legs and half covering her breasts with her arms.

"I have seen kings go through women like arrows through a bow. Would I be your only woman?" Toree asked him.

The man smiled and gently pulled her closer, whispering in her ear "The only one, the bearer of my heirs..."

Their lips locked and they embraced in passion. As Toree began to slip the man's robes off I was suddenly in a dark and cold chamber. It seemed like I was in a cellar underground. I heard footsteps and saw the glowing woman walk up - except she was not glowing, and she was in a light blue flowing gown. On her head sat a nimble crown of white and gold. Over my shoulder was Toree in the same dress I saw her in previously.

"Toree," the woman said, "what have you found?"

"My Queen." Toree said, bowing her head.

The glowing woman I had been seeing was the queen of Nystia! The questions in my head were too many to count, but I knew whatever was being shown was for a reason.

"Your instincts serve you well, your grace. Lucian plans to take the throne and expand the kingdom. I don't know how yet, but I will find out before he can make his move." Toree said to her.

"How did you get this information? Can you be certain?" The queen asked her.

"I spent the night in his chambers, he admitted his ambitions to me before he took me to his bed..." Toree admitted.

I was in disbelief for a moment, the man Toree went to bed with was the Lucian everyone had been speaking of, the reason behind Nystia's problems...

"Toree," the queen said empathetically, "what you have done already for me and Nystia I can never repay, but we must know what his next move is. He holds too much power over the armies for me to just remove him, there would be revolt without proof of his actions."

"I understand my queen." Toree said bowing her head.

"You have a big heart, be careful as to not lose sight when in the darkness." the queen said, then turned around and made her way down a dark hall.

"Your grace." Toree replied with a bow.

The dark cellar became clear skies over a grotto in the woods. Toree was standing there with two others, a woman and man. They were in everyday attire with daggers at their hips. The woman looked familiar for some reason, though I could not place her.

"Have you found where these creatures are coming from?" The woman asked the man. "A whole town was reduced to rubble in a day!"

"No." he said, shaking his head from side to side. "One single creature killed three of my men, we could only best it using fire. Toree, have you learned anything about these?"

"He hasn't told me, but I am sure this is Lucian's doing. He has spent all his time the last few weeks in his laboratory or riding out into Nerick. I will ride out to his camp tonight and learn what I can." Toree said to them both.

"You should know, Queen Aludia has Aldonis working on a secret weapon if all else fails." the other woman said.

"What kind of weapon?" the man asked.

"A dagger, plunge it into him and recite an incantation. Channel fire, water, and wind around you to create a portal to the spirit realm. When the incantation is finished pull the dagger and Lucian, along with all those corrupted by him will be sent to the other realm, locked inside with no trace left here." the woman explained.

"We must wait, Lucian can still be dealt with in other ways!" Toree remarked.

"Why wait? This may solve all our problems quicker than playing these games with him!" the man argued.

"No, Toree is right. I have spoken with Aldonis. There is too much that can go wrong, if the vortex creating the portal is not maintained, if the incantation is broken apart too slowly, if you miss your target. All of these things could wreak havoc." the woman warned...

I looked around again, it was evening and Toree was hooded, walking towards a noble's tent in an encampment. The guards bowed their heads as Toree walked passed them into the tent.

Suddenly I was inside the tent, she was removing her hood as she strode up to Lucian.

"My love, these creatures are destroying our towns. The queen is growing anxious and wants you to quell the attacks." Toree said to Lucian, laying a hand on his shoulder as he sat over a scroll at his desk.

"It is beautiful isn't it..." Lucian said to her.

"....beautiful?" Toree said, stepping back repulsed and confused.

"Yes, honestly the pieces could not fall into place better. It wasn't even my intention! By some miraculous twist of fates I laid a seed and a forest grew!" Lucian remarked proudly.

"I'm confused, what seed did you plant exactly?" Toree asked visibly concerned.

"Sit, my love, and I will tell you." he said to her, guiding her to his bedside.

"Lucian, what have you done?" she asked calmly.

This time there was a different kind of emotion behind her concern. It wasn't concern for herself or her kingdom, it was a concern for Lucian. Toree stared at Lucian with open eyes, calm lips, and dropped shoulders. I realized there was more here, Toree was genuinely in love with him.

"I have been trying to find a way to avoid the surrounding kingdoms from uniting and beating back our armies through sheer numbers. Their love of their royal titles would deter them from ever joining us peacefully. That's when the idea occurred to me, curse what they all desire most! I found a way to put a spell on simple gold coins. The happiness in finding them is all the energy that's needed to begin the transformation." Lucian explained.

I watched tears of sadness roll down Toree's cheeks as she sat there in silence.

"The spell was simple! I thought they would turn into beasts of nature, deer, rabbits, birds. Our opposition would just disappear into nature! I took some to the bordering villages of Nerick to try. The townspeople behaved as I thought they would, but I did not count on their greed. It was not joy that activated the spell on the gold, it was greed. Instead of transforming into the animals around us, they transformed into the beasts they most feared. Their greed fuels them, and instead of lust for gold they lust for blood. Now only fire and magic steel can tame them." he continued.

"Lucian..." Toree said standing and holding his face with two hands. "These monsters you created are destroying our lands, our homes..."

"They created themselves!" Lucian barked out at Toree, knocking her hands away with his arm. "They did it with their greed, their fears, their lust for our powers! How long would it be before the other kingdoms turned on us? Five years? Twenty years? A hundred? At some point they would turn us into their slaves out of the fear we would do the same! Setting them into the woods seemed the most humane option, but it was they who spoiled the spell!"

"You don't know that!" Toree barked back.

"Don't be so short-sighted! This is a blessing Toree! A blessing! There is enough tainted gold to spread across all of the continent if need be!" Lucian said enthusiastically.

"What you have done is set off a beacon of war with Nerick! How is that a blessing?!" Toree argued.

There was a rustle at the door and one of the guards stepped through inquisitively.

"Is everything alright, my lord?" the guard asked.

"GET OUT!" Toree ordered, conjuring a powerful gust of wind from her hand that practically threw the guard off his feet and out the doorway.

Lucian began pacing back and forth...

"You simple-minded little girl! Can you not see how this works in our favor? These beasts now attack our towns, fear and distrust in the queen's ability to keep her subjects protected is spreading around the kingdom like wildfire... They are looking for their saviors! You are the most skilled in the magics of all Nystia, and I have control of the armies. Together you and I are those saviors, Toree!" Lucian boasted.

"You underestimate the Aludia, she would have us run through and encased in ice beside her throne!" Toree shouted.

"Ah, that's the best part, as we speak two of my spies are trapping her in the spirit realm!" Lucian said, delighted.

All the color withdrew from Toree's face.

"Yes, I know about her little spell, I've had spies in her court for months, even her last lover was one of my eyes and ears in the keep. Oh, you should hear the things your queen does behind her bedroom door, even you would blush! I've known her every move, this whole secret order nonsense..." he rambled on...

"Lucian, please you -" Toree was cut off by Lucian.

"Shh, I know you tried to handle her own your own, but it's okay - I did it for you." Lucian said caressing her face.

Toree was white, the blood had withdrawn from her face and she was as still as a statue.

"...what did you do..." she muttered under her breath.

Her legs began to fall out from under her, so she sat on the bed. It looked like Toree had just been sentenced to death.

"My love," Lucian said, sitting next to Toree on the bed and turning her head to face his, "Nystia is ours..."

Toree stared blankly at Lucian as he eyed her body up and down. He kissed her lips as she sat idly.

"Nystia, and soon the whole continent... all ours..." continued as he undid Toree's blouse.

I watched Lucian push Toree backward onto the bed and pull her blouse down...

"Let us celebrate by creating an heir on this night..." Lucian suggested to a still expressionless Toree.

Lucian kissed her from cheek to neck, and as he began to caress her exposed breast Toree's face filled with a fire... the tent ballooned outward and the lanterns flared brightly... her hand grabbed his and glowed a bright yellow, creating smoke that rose up.

Lucian screamed in pain and grabbed his hand as Toree kicked him off of her, pulling up her blouse and throwing a ball of fire at the scrolls on his desk.

"You have lost your mind, Lucian!" She yelled in rage. "You have done nothing but condemn Nystia to death!"

"No! I did this for us!" Lucian decried, standing on his feet cradling his burnt hand.

"You did it for greed!" she said, using the fire to melt the gold on his desk...

"You did it for lust!" she continued, engulfing the bed in flames...

"You did it for your own power!" she shouted, conjuring a wind that brought Lucian to his knees.

At that moment I watched another guard walk through the door, his sword drawn.

"My liege!" the guard yelled, but he could hardly take two steps before Toree used the wind to send Lucian's sword hurling through the air, lobbing the guards head off. The blade of the sword stuck into the wooden post bracing the sides of the tent.

"Think about this Toree!" Lucian cried out.

"I have! It was not the peoples greed that turned them into nightmares, it was your greed! You put your own fear and greed, your lust for power into your spell! That is what created these monsters! They are just reflections of who you have become!" Toree yelled.

"It's too late, Toree... it is done, together we can create a prosperous kingdom!" Lucian called to her, grasping to the air.

"Of that you are right, it is too late, Lucian, my love. It is done...." Toree said sternly, setting the room alight.

She grabbed her cloak and walked out the tent. Suddenly I was in a forge, in front of me was Aldonis himself speaking to Toree and the woman from the earlier memory. Aldonis was a large man with a balding head covered by a cap, and a great big mustache. In his teeth he clenched a pipe.

"It is not ready yet, the energy inside has not been balanced. If you two use this there is no telling what it might do!" Aldonis said.

"I understand, but if we do nothing Lucian's beasts will consume this world. There are unknown risks, yes, however what we know to be a threat is the bigger risk now." the woman said.

"Ren is right, we have been left with no other choice. We must use any means necessary to stop him." Toree said, revealing the other woman's name to me.

Aldonis took a deep breath, sat on his anvil, and puffed his pipe for a moment, lost in thought. His eyes got wide as an idea came to him. He stood up and walked to his work bench, grabbing three pieces of steel and tying a cord to them. He put one of them on his own neck and handed the other two to Toree and Ren.

"If this is what must be done, take these and wear them. Do not take them off until the deed is done. They are left over steel from this blade and hold the same powers. If something should go wrong these pendants will protect you from any ill-effects." Aldonis said.

"Thank you, my friend." Toree said, putting on her pendant and taking the dagger.

"How did it get to this?" Aldonis questioned.

"Truth be told, I loved a demon that could not find his salvation. Now I must set it right." Toree said, defeated in her words.

"There is always hope for salvation, we just don't know what kind until it is upon us." Aldonis said to Toree, patting his hand on her shoulder.

Toree let out a faint smile and I was suddenly in the midst of a battle. I was outside a keep unknown to me. Toree and

Ren were in battle armor with an army of their own. The small army seemed to be lead by the man from the forest memory.

It was dusk and the sun was setting over a pink and purple sky, I could smell the fires and blood in the air. It was a battle not just of steel, but magic too. There was fire and ice thrown about like spears and arrows. A soldier would attack with a blade and defend with an element from their off-hand.

The gates were blown open and Toree's army was funneling into the keep's courtyard, fighting Lucian's army as they progressed. Behind them Lucian's reserve forces made their way to block them in the castle walls. The man from the memory ran up to Toree and Ren.

"I will do my best to hold them off, you must get into the throne room and stop Lucian! Do not look back!" he yelled to them before turning and leading a charge into Lucian's men.

"Gruun is right, it does not matter what happens here, if we do not stop him the fight is lost!" Ren said to Toree.

"With me then!" Toree shouted.

Toree turned and sent a wall of flame at the reinforcements Gruun and his men were fighting, then ran into the keep.

I found myself now in the keep with them. Lucian's men ran towards them swords drawn, sending the blades down onto Toree and Ren. The two didn't flinch, they stood tall and continued walking towards the throne room, turning the swords into molten steel before it could reach them, heating their armor, burning them alive.

I had flashbacks to when I used the same method saving Zuht. It gave me shivers as I watched Toree and Ren burn two dozen men this way, all the while showing no emotion. It was carnage.

They made their way to the entrance of the throne room. Three of Lucian's men ran to attack them but Ren used a gust of wind and threw them from the window. She looked below into the courtyard, closing her eyes for a moment before turning back towards Toree.

"They've been overrun." Ren said to Toree.

"All of them?" Toree asked.

"...all of them." Ren confirmed.

"This is it then..." Toree said to her.

"This is it... I will hold the door for as long as I can." Ren said.

Toree nodded, "You have been a good friend, thank you..."

"Toree!" Ren shouted before heading back towards to keep's entrance.

Toree turned around and looked at Ren.

"If you survive tonight...my daughter is hidden at Dragon's Reach in Nerick. Teach her our ways." Ren requested.

Toree nodded and Ren ran off.

Now it made sense! I recognized her because she was my ancestor, the one Unul spoke of. I now also knew intimately how my family had these powers. Toree must have come and gone through the years, teaching each generation how to harness our power.

I followed Toree as she blew the doors of the throne room wide open. Inside sat Lucian on the throne, a crown on his head.

"Stop playing pretend, Lucian! You have no right to wear that crown!" Toree shouted.

"Have you come here to sit next to me as queen, or for retribution?" Lucian questioned aloud.

"You destroyed Nystia! You destroyed this world! You destroyed our world! You were so consumed with what you wanted you could not see what you had!" Toree yelled as she walked closer.

"I did what needed to be done! For Nystia, for you and I, for the world I wanted our children to grow up in! The queen was weak and a fool! She let the other kingdoms walk all over us! I was the one that made Nystia strong, I was the one that made Nystia great!" Lucian said, standing from the throne and banging on his chest.

"No! You were the one that proved me the fool! I thought I could steer you away from this path of destruction, I thought I could give you redemption! I was a...how did you put it?

Yes...yes that's right, a simple-minded little girl..." Toree replied.

"Toree, my love! Join me as my queen and I will forgive all you have done... Together with my wits and your power we can control from ocean to ocean! We will rule this world, as will our children!" Lucian pleaded.

"You forgive me? Everyone I have loved is dead, all because I believed in someone you used to be! The other kingdoms are ready to go to war with us because you turned their subjects into beasts! You would rule dirt and nightmares!" Toree said as she began a vortex of fire around the two of them.

"Toree, think about your actions..." Lucian warned.

"I am." Toree replied as she grabbed Lucian and kissed him passionately.

Lucian froze, as did I as the scene unfolded. When he let his guard down Toree pulled the dagger from her belt and drove it into his abdomen.

"Toree, what have you done?" Lucian moaned while trying to pull the dagger from his body.

"What needed to be done..." Toree said with tears in her eyes, using her strength to keep the dagger in him.

Toree began to chant the incantation and a portal to another dimension opened up above them.

"If you are to decide my fate, I will decide yours!" a rageful Lucian declared.

Lucian grabbed Toree's lower abdomen and lit it aflame. Toree screamed in pain as she forced herself to continue the incantation.

"I curse you to walk the world alone, loveless, ageless, and childless! Your lovers will grow old and die, you will never mother a child, and you will be hunted through the ages simply because you are different!" Lucian said as he burned her womb from the inside out.

Toree fell to her knees, screaming and crying while maintaining the incantation, her hand still on the dagger. Lucian fell to his knees in front of her as well and drew his face to hers.

"You did this Toree, you." Lucian said in her ear.

There was a big flash and everything went white. When it cleared Toree was knelt in a forest, her medallion from Aldonis glowing, and the dagger clean and in her hand. She rolled to the ground screaming in agony. It was the same scream Zuht let out when he saw there were no survivors.

She lay there alone.

There was another jump and I was following her, she had found Ren's body and was carrying it through the woods.

Another jump, this time we were at Dragon's Reach in it's early days. Toree was dirty, beaten, her clothes were torn, and she still carried Ren's body. As she got to the gate she collapsed.

Suddenly I was in the study at Dragon's Reach. Toree was clean, fed, and in fresh clothes. She handed a man who must have been my ancestor the dagger...

"Take this, when Ren's daughter is of age give this to her. This is the dagger Alaia, forged by Aldonis, it is her birthright. I will return when she is old enough to learn the ways and teach her." Toree said.

"Of course my lady. Worry not for the child, I will raise her as my own. You are always welcome here." the man said.

I turned my head and found myself back in Aldonis's forge.

"Where is the blade?" Aldonis asked Toree, smoke from his ever-lit pipe circling his face.

"It is safe, hidden with Ren's family." Toree informed him.

"Was Lucian wearing the crown when you sent him through the portal?" Aldonis asked with heavy pipe smoke leaking through his lips, a curious look was on his face.

"Yes, why?" Toree asked.

"After the rest of the Kingdom vanished I tried to work out what had gone wrong. I looked through my drawings and calculations, nothing made sense...until I worked in the possibility of him crowning himself king. The dagger should have broken his physical body and his curses - taking them all with him, and the incantation should have sealed him in the spirit realm. By him crowning himself, he extended his curse and energy to all of Nystia. All are gone, save us." Aldonis explained.

"Is there no way to set the rest free?" Toree asked in desperation.

"No, I'm afraid not. Anything living cursed by Lucian would have been destroyed the moment the dagger pierced him." Aldonis said with sorrow.

"But I am still here...he cursed me right before everything disappeared..." Toree said confused.

"He cursed you?" Aldonis said surprised. "...the shard of steel must have kept you safe from destruction as well... what did he curse you with?"

Toree's face sank as she looked into the forge fire.

"...I will walk this world until the end of days...ageless and childless..." Toree said woefully.

"My dear..." Aldonis said with empathy, placing his pipe on his anvil and holding Toree by the shoulders, "I am sorry..."

Aldonis embraced Toree in an affectionate hug.

"Where will you go now?" Aldonis asked her.

"I will go to the kings and inform them of what has happened, from there I know not. Perhaps I will walk the lands, help where I can." Toree said to Aldonis.

She reached into a pouch on her belt and pulled out the two shards of steel Aldonis had given her and Ren before their assault on the keep.

"Thank you for your help, these are the two shards, it is better if you keep them." she said, handing the two shards to Aldonis. "If you ever need me, I have made a vow to return to Dragon's Reach to train Ren's child. Leave word for me there." she added.

Time shifted again and I found myself back at Dragon's Reach. I could see Toree walking into the castle, which had changed some since the last vision. I followed her inside where she was greeted by an older version of the man she spoke to in the last memory of this place.

"My Lord." Toree greeted.

"Lady Toree...it seems you have not aged a moment since I saw you last..." the man said.

"I am here to fulfil my word and train the child, Yewn." Toree stated.

"Yes, yes so you have...though I would hardly call her a child anymore. She's become quite the woman, and quite the handful!" the man said robustly.

"Her mother's blood must run strong in her then..." Toree replied, cracking a small smile.

"Before you greet her, this parcel arrived for you two years ago. I have made sure the wax seal has stayed in place." the man said, motioning his servant to hand her a bound leather package, there was a cord ceiling it with Aldonis's mark.

I was thrust to yet another scene, we were now in Toree's chambers in Dragon's Reach. The decor was rather different than it is now. She sat at the desk in the room and cut the cord, carefully unwrapping it. She opened the leather flap and reached in, there was a small pouch and a letter inside.

She read it in silence so I walked around her and read the letter myself...

My dear Toree,

I write this letter to you now, during my last days in this world. I know not when you will get it, so I have entrusted the Lord of Dragon's Reach with this to hold in confidence. The events nearly two decades ago have weighed heavy on my mind... I have not stopped working out the possibilities since we last parted.

I did not give you all the information back then, not for a lack of thought, because I hadn't quite figured it out yet. I have discovered there are two yet alive... Lucian and Aludia... Lucian was only locked away, Aludia was sealed away before she could be corrupted by Lucian's curses. They are in the spirit realm, locked away in their own cells. In this parcel there is a pouch that holds our three shards of Alaia's steel, I have crafted them into proper pendants.

When worn, you can take your consciousness into their realm and communicate with them. Do not remove them while in the spirit realm or your consciousness will be trapped there. I have also created a ritual, when completed you or anyone with Nystian blood will be able to communicate with Aludia in dreams, though she can only communicate through a proxy, a thought of a person close to you to serve as her voice. I have included the ritual instructions below...

I read through Aldonis's instructions, it was as Unul had prepared for me. Suddenly more missing pieces appeared to me. I continued on...

I must warn you, I have had a vision... the dagger and spell were never meant to lock away so much as an entire kingdom. Physical objects from Nystia will appear again someday, including some of Lucian's cursed objects. I do not know how it will come to be, but I fear that because he still lives in another realm and you in this one, his curses will become realized once more.

I have made new blades that can destroy Lucian's creatures, blades that can be wielded by anyone. I have sent my apprentice to Raven's Landing to hide them. When the time is right and they are needed they will be found. I have used the pendant to speak with Aludia and have given her a riddle to their location. She will know when it is right.

When the time comes, Lucian must be destroyed once and for all to end the curses. There is one more thing you should know... Lucian's life is what binds you to your curse, and this world. When he is gone your curse will be gone, and the world will correct what he has altered...

I hope you find some happiness in the world, and that this information I've given provides new meaning for you.

Salvation appears in many ways.

-Aldonis, the last Master Smith of Nystia & Nerick

I watched Toree open the pouch and pull out three pendants... I recognized them immediately, one of them my mother wore up until she became locked away in her mind. I remember playing with her pendant as a child, she would tell me when it is time I would have my own, that they were passed down in the family...

Toree held them tightly in her hand, a tear streaming down her face.

Suddenly I was on the edge of a clearing the woods, looking from a hill down at Toree and a teenage girl. The woods around me felt familiar, as did the hill I was on, though not the foliage. The teenage girl must have been Yewn, the girl mentioned previously. She had the features of Ren but appeared not quite as adept in her abilities.

They had a rickety wooden table set up in the center which had an assortment of herbs and items on it, I watched them as Toree appeared to train her in the different magics. I could only watch at afar, each time I attempted to walk down the hill to the clearing I would suddenly find myself back at the top of the hill.

Within blinks of the eye I watched time move forward. Yewn grew older, the trees around grew larger, and what was grass in the clearing was down trampled soil. In what only felt like a few moments to me, a decade seemed to pass. Yewn was now a woman, perhaps my age. She was just as resourceful with her magic as Ren was. The rickety wooden table was now a substantial wooden table and the trampled soil was now covered with tiny broken stones. It was dusk, and there were candles and torches around.

Toree had the table and surrounding set up for what appeared to be the same ceremony Aldonis wrote about, which I had gone through with Unul. She performed the ritual and Alaia was there on the table, used as Yewn's blade for the ritual. I watched the same thing unfold for Yewn as it had for me; except after she collapsed at it's completion, Toree put one hand to the ground and one hand on her, there was a slight golden glow pulsing from her hand to the ground to her hand on Yewn.

In not more than a minute Yewn was awake. Toree helped her up and they spoke. I was too far away to hear what was said, but after they finished speaking Yewn lowered her head and Toree placed one of the amulets on her. When they finished conversing they embraced in an emotional hug, Toree grabbed a bag from behind the wooden table and left.

I was thrown to time again but remained on the hill in the clearing. The crushed stone on the ground was now cobblestone, the wooden table was an elaborately chiseled stone alter, and the overgrowth around the trees (which were now substantially larger in all directions) was kept trim and neat. There was an older woman at the alter with a lot of grey in her hair, when she turned her head towards my direction I could see it was a much older Yewn. With her were two other teenage girls.

I could not hear what they were saying, but I saw Toree, just as young as she was before, walk onto the cobblestone. I watched as time appeared to fly forward again. The two teen girls became young women and both underwent the ritual. After the ritual both Toree and Yewn placed a hand on the ground and a hand on the girls, reviving them. They did not receive the the pendants though, Toree wore one and Yewn the other, the third was not given out.

This same scene played out over and over again with every breath, each time the people, number of people, the woods, and the clearing changing, aging...all except Toree who's only change was her clothing. Sometimes it was all women, sometimes it was all men, sometimes it was a mix. Eventually time slowed again and I could see two figures I recognized. An older man who I recognized as my grandfather by the portraits that hung in Dragon's Reach, and a teenage girl who had all my features.

It was my mother.

The stone alter was now worn and weathered, the intricate detail long gone; the cobblestones rubble and dirt, the trees old and dying or fallen, new growth was poking through and wild vines and bushes had taken over. I tried walking down again, this time I made it to the clearing. Toree walked in, her appearance the same as the generations prior, all except her expressions. She was worn down and tired, despite her everlasting youth. She didn't seem to have the same vigor she had previously when training the next generation.

None the less, she trained my mother. I watched her transform from a novice teen to a force to be reckoned with. Time went by and she became a young woman. Eventually her ceremony came, afterwards Toree presented her with one of the pendants.

Suddenly I was back to the dream I had at the castle, the clearing was severely over-grown and my mother was chanting with someone else in a language I couldn't decipher. I walked around and saw the other figure was Toree. Their pendants glowed blue and green as they spoke with the glowing queen, who seemingly stood at the broken and weathered alter with them.

I was again thrown through time. I was now in a small cottage in the woods. Sat at a desk was Toree, she was writing in a journal as rain trickled down outside. I looked over to see the significance of this moment and read her thoughts as she put them to the paper.

Elia and I have spoken with Aludia. It continues, her son Devin shows no aptitude for her bloodline's magic. It is too soon to tell yet whether her daughter Jara holds the power in her or not. Ren's descendants have been strong but over the last century or so, all but a few of the children hold any power.

I have read all I could find in the libraries around the kingdom but have not found anything about this. Perhaps it is because their Nystian blood has been diluted over the centuries, or perhaps the longer Nystia is gone the power it held dwindles. My own abilities seem to show no issues, but I can not be certain that's not another part of my curse.

In my searches of the old texts hidden away I garnered king Ansel's attention. He insisted on accompanying me and read about the disappearance of Nystia...at least the version given to his ancestors. He has become enamored with the dagger and wants to use it to end his war. He has become desperate in his effort. The last time there was a conflict like this I was one of the few at the helm, the result was a loss of my kingdom.

Elia's husband Mistaan has become very interested in this as well. He has asked to head an expedition into Evanwood. The things Aldonis spoke of all those years ago have begun to pass. I have heard word from the towns boarding the forest that small structures, objects, statues have begun to appear - scattered through the woods. I have been unable to bring myself to go back there for over three centuries.

I have given Mistaan and Ansel just enough information to keep them busy without causing trouble. Hopefully this will give me more time to find out what is happening to Ren's bloodline.

As I read her journal the pages seemed to turn and fill with scribbles on their own, the days and weeks and years carried on before it stopped at a new page...

Much has happened since I was last at the capital. King Ansel appointed Mistaan to carry out his expedition of Nystia's ruins. It seems over the last ten years Elia's body sits dormant of all consciousness. I fear Mistaan unknowingly removed her pendant to take it with him while she was with Aludia and accidentally locked her away in the other realm.

Mistaan disappeared after entering the forest and Lucian's creatures have begun to appear again. I fear his cursed gold reappeared and transformed them all. For Mistaan I hope for the best, but expect the worst. The only way to know for certain is to get the last two pendants from their hiding spot in the woods near Enex.

It seems it is time for me to get involved again. I have met with Unul, whom I believe is one of the few pure-of-heart knights in this lifetime. I asked him to go to Dragon's Reach under the king's orders to perform the ritual with Elia's daughter Jara. She knows not any of her family's past. She has had no training, I do not know if she will even survive the ritual without healing afterwards or a connection with her powers. Truth be told I do not even know if she has Ren's legacy in her blood.

This is not a situation I ever wanted to be in, yet my only other option is to sit on the sideline for eternity, living in solitude until the world falls apart. I am tired of creating myself anew with each generation. I must go into the fray again.

Transported through time again, I found myself standing in the rain. I looked down and saw myself in the mud...just as Zuht said, I was dying. My entire side was smashed, my color white and my eyes rolling. Toree was still under her horse but used a massive gust of wind to toss the carcass off of her. She got to her feet and created a huge twister of fire to engulf the briar, then fell to the ground and placed one hand on me, one hand in the mud. Her hands glowed and she muttered something in the language from earlier. I watched as my body transformed back to it's normal state, and the color almost finished returning to my face. I could see Toree stop the healing when Runa ran over.

To Enex

Chapter 15

In an instant I was back where we started, next to a creek in the woods outside Enex. Toree was standing in front of me and I reached out to touch her. As I did my hand stopped when it hit her clothing.

"No more memories, you are back." Toree said with a chuckle.

"...all of that...this...everything..." I stuttered, trying to take everything in.

"Yes...that is the real story of the past. Pieces of it anyway." Toree confirmed

"But what did you do in between for all of those years?" I asked

"I traveled, healed people, stopped some small disasters, strived to bring some good into the world. Other times I ran away - hunted by townsfolk and knights alike for my abilities. A handful of times I tried to leave the past behind and start anew, always reinventing myself and looking for love again." Toree answered

"Did you find it? Love again?" I asked her

"Yes." She said bluntly.

"...and..." I prompted

"And I realized I was a fool again. Made up childhoods, keeping my abilities a secret, saying my womb was barren each time someone looked for an heir...all things I could manage. The only thing I could not control was time. Each instance was the same, I would create a new life with someone and the years would pass. They would begin to grow grey yet I would stay the same. Some I would tell of my curse, and they would curse me themselves, some I watched wither and die, with others I simply went for a walk in the forest and 'disappeared'. A victim of bandits or an angry bear.

I sought connection without worrying about outliving a partner, so I eventually began to court older nobles. I quickly realized they had no interest in emotions, they were just after a young fuck to boast about or chance of dying with a set of tits in their face...but it did allow me to gain access to the colleges and archives. I threw my life into books and gaining knowledge, always reinventing myself as a scholar so that my solitude would not be questioned." Toree lamented

"I am sorry, Toree, for all that you have been made to go through..." I said with my hand on her shoulder, then embraced her in a hug.

"Thank you, but there is no time for past now. Did you understand all you saw?" Toree asked me

"Yes, but how was it that these elements could be conjured up with no source?" I asked her

"You are the source. Life itself is the source of all magic. I am proud that you have learned to manipulate the elements on your own, however now it's time to step into your family's legacy. I can not offer you the years of training I have to generations past, but you have a fire in your heart, a fire I have not seen since Ren herself. Years of training can not compare to entering a hot crucible. You will learn much of yourself and your powers on this journey. I will show you who you are, it is up to you whether or not to share who you are with the others." Toree answered

She stepped back and held a hand out to her side with an open palm. In it she manifested a twisting ball of flame.

"You can not only create the elements, but you can manipulate what you have created. A ball of flame, it is not fires natural state, yet here it is. Shape it like a piece of clay, direct it like an arrow, then let it loose." She said, hurling the ball of fire into the stream.

I nodded and held my hand out, putting intense focus into it...nothing was happening...

"Stop, stop." Toree directed, "Do not focus on it, feel it. You have spoken with Aludia in dreams have you not? What was it she told you when you first discovered your powers?"

"She told me to follow my instincts and intuition." I replied

"Yes, and what do your instincts tell you to do right now?" She asked me

"To let loose..." I said shaking the tension from my muscles.

I closed my eyes and held out my hand, I felt a fire from my chest project over my palm. I opened my eyes and there was a flame spinning like a globe over my hand... I had done it... I had created an element on my own!

"Good!" She exclaimed creating her own ball of fire, "Now do two!"

Toree held out her other hand and created a ball of water.

"Two elements at once? Should I not practice with one at a time?" I asked

"There is no time for practice, the inner fire you posses will fuel you. You saw the power your ancestors held, that same power is in you, in your blood, in your breath!" Toree declared encouragingly.

I felt the fire inside me again and created a second ball over my other hand...except I had created two balls of fire...

"Is there a secret to this or something?" I asked her

"There might be, but there is only one way to find out..." she said muttering to herself

Toree flicked her hand and sent a wave of water at me, completely soaking me and extinguishing the flames I held.

"Was that absolutely necessary?" I said with an attitude

"Yes! Together Ren and I pushed back armies all while never lifting a sword! Together you and I can light every candle in the kingdom without a matchstick!" Toree mocked.

I was so angry, my whole body felt aflame and a rage came over me. The visions of watching my family's order being built up only to dwindle down to just myself played in my mind, I replayed my fierceness in battle where I have proven my worth, and reminded myself that I was called on this quest by others, not by myself.

I was so overcome by my emotions of what I had just watched in Toree's memories and the anger of her insult, I did not even realize that I had created a whirlwind of fire and water around me, spinning in the air. I took a breath and let it fade.

"There's your secret!" Toree said to me.

"What do you mean?" I asked confused, and still slightly annoyed.

"You have gained strength through your accomplishments and failures, from your family's past and your present. When I downplayed what you are capable of, you pulled on your past and that of your family. That is your secret to your power, pull on the strength you know you have, and the line you know you come from. See yourself on the wall in Dragon's Reach just next to the other greats in your family. That is your source of power." Toree explained.

"What else can I do with these powers?" I asked her

"Come with me to the water's edge, I will show you." She said.

We spent the rest of the day practicing, breaking to collect herbs, then practicing some more. Eventually we began to make our way out of the woods and back to the outpost. I used this opportunity before we reached our destination to ask about my mother and what I read in Toree's diary.

"Toree, when I was in your memories, I saw you write about my mother being locked away with Aludia..." I began

"Yes, your father learned of the pendants and thought it would be wise to find one and take it with him. He realized that your mother's necklace was one of the pendants in question. He could not use it in any way other than a protective charm since he has no magic in his blood. I believe she may have been in the middle of a shift to the spirit realm to speak with Aludia when he took it, believing she was actually asleep. That is why one day her body woke up but her consciousness did not." Toree said, keenly aware of what I was about to ask.

"How do you know for sure?" I asked her

"I don't, we will have to find out tonight." She said to me

"Tonight, how? Aludia only ever comes to me in dreams and my mother is never there, although the last time she did elude that she is in close contact with her..." I said

"You will need this..." she said as she pulled a pendant out of her waistband and handed it to me.

"Where did this come from?" I asked

"A long time ago I came to these woods. I was intent on leaving my past behind and starting anew, these pendants were a piece of my past I no longer wanted to remember. I hid them away safely next to the creak, the third has always remained with your family's matriarch or patriarch. While you were picking your herbs I retrieved them...put this on and never take it off. It is yours now." she said while placing the second around her own neck.

"They are just like my mother's..." I said

"Yes, your mother wore Ren's pendant, you now wear the pendant of Aldonis. It is fitting on you. I will teach you how to use it to shift your consciousness to the spirit realm and speak with Aludia. We will find out what has happened tonight. After you have eaten come to my quarters." Toree instructed.

I nodded and we made our way back to the outpost. As we got closer dusk began to set in and the sky turned colors of pink and orange. The soldiers were going about their tasks before rolling out the barrels of ale and wine for the evening's dinner. We made our way to where our tents were located and found Runa and Alor had already taken the liberty of helping themselves to some of the wine.

"There you two are! Come, you must be thirsty after harvesting weeds all day!" Alor greeted, obviously merry from a few helpings of wine already.

"I am sorry ladies, the captain of the guard challenged Alor to a drinking game..." Zuht began, seemingly the only sober member of our party, apart from Toree and I.

"Aye! And Sir Alor never backs down when challenged!" Alor proclaimed.

"So why does everyone else seem just as intoxicated?" Toree asked.

"Well...you see..." said Tripp, obviously inebriated, "the captain challenged our good leader to a game of drink...and when he saw Sir Alor outlast him he challenged the rest of us against his officers..."

"...and where are they, exactly?" I asked Tripp

"They couldn't hold their drink more than a babe at the tit! They fell one by one and went off to their cots!" Runa chimed in raising a glass. This motion made the rest of the group cheer and drink again.

"Well, this day has been full of bonding experiences..." I said sarcastically.

"Do not get drunk tonight, you will need to be sober to use the amulet..." Toree whispered in my ear.

"Will you not join us then?" Asked Alor.

"Thank you, but these herbs will not process themselves. I will go to my tent to begin my work with them for tomorrow's trek. Zuht, you are the only one with a steady hand here, would you mind bringing me a plate of food and some of that wonderful brew you are so good at making?" Toree replied

"It would be my pleasure my lady." Zuht replied.

"Aye, if you change your mind I'll have a cup set aside for you!" Alor said to Toree.

"And what about you?" Runa said, passing me a cup of wine and pushing my shoulder.

"Oh, I suppose I can have one or two glasses. But then I did promise Toree I would help her..." I replied to Runa, taking the glass of wine and sipping it slowly.

Toree made her way back to her tent while me and the others ate around the fire. They indulged in their drink while I sipped mine steadily. As much as I wanted to partake in full, I did not want to ruin any opportunity Toree had to give. There was much laughter through the evening, everyone stripped their cares away for the joy of the night.

Tripp seemed to be listening to every word that came out of Alor's mouth as if it was a gospel, Zuht had gone off to pray for the evening, and Runa sat beside me as merry as I had ever seen her. It was good to see everyone laugh on this night, and it was good to be here to laugh with them...even though I was sober... It was good to be a part of this group of companions. As we laughed at jokes and situations told, Runa would look at me with a smile...it made me wish there was no actual danger in our quest and that we could live this each and every evening together.

Eventually the hour grew late and we started retiring for the evening...

"Shall we....go back to our tent?" Runa asked me, pulling my hand and stumbling backwards.

I'm sure there was some sort of gossip she wanted to discuss, and as much as I liked drunken gossip, what I needed to do with Toree was more important.

"I'm sorry, but I've promised Toree that I would help her with the herbs..." I said to her, not letting onto what I actually needed to see her for.

"Oh...that's too bad... well, I will try to wait up! Don't be long!" Runa said disappointed.

"Don't worry, I will see you shortly!" I said waving to her as I made my way to Toree's tent.

I entered the tent and Toree was sat at the foot of her bed.

"I was wondering when you would make your way here, I almost thought you weren't coming!" Toree said

"A year ago I would have been stumbling back to my bed, now there are reasons for me to stay sober more." I said to her.

"Come, lay on my bed." Toree said, motioning to her cot.

"...did I misinterpret something earlier?" I asked sarcastically.

"Come silly girl, laying is the easiest way to do this for someone new." she replied to me.

I walked to the bed and lay on top of the sheet.

"So how do I do this?" I asked her

"Close your eyes and place your hands over the pendant, then take three deep breaths..." she said

I followed her instructions and felt my body begin to relax. She continued to guide me into a deep relaxation before directing me to tap into the amulet.

"...now, bring all of your focus from your body and mind and move it into your heart... when you feel it all there move it into your amulet..." she directed

I did as she instructed and focused all of my consciousness into the amulet. It felt like all of my energy was draining from my body and my breathing slowed. The amulet became increasingly warmer and bright lights shone through my closed eyes. Suddenly the amulet went ice cold and all of the light disappeared, leaving only blackness.

"Open your eyes..." I heard Toree's voice call.

I opened my eyes slowly and found myself in a familiar looking corridor. Toree was standing just in front of me.

"Just like your memories?" I asked as I tried to swat my hand through Toree's shoulder as had been the case earlier.

"...no... and that was quite unnecessary..." Toree said amused as my hand actually made contact with her body.

"...oh...sorry..." I said to her, embarrassed by my action.

"Worry yourself not, you did well. It is easier than it seems isn't it?" Toree asked

"So that's it? That's all I need to do to come here?" I asked, confused as to how easy it was.

"With that pendant, yes. Aldonis was a master, just as his swords made the wielder adept in their use, these pendants hold the same qualities true. If you have the power you can easily move between the veil of the worlds. For those without magic in their blood it is just a protective charm. With practice on your focus you will be able to journey in a moment sat at the table." Toree explained

"...this is magnificent..." I exclaimed

"Yes, but beware, only your consciousness has traveled here. Your physical body remains laying on the bed. Only travel here when you know you are in certain safety." She warned me

"I understand, but why does this place look so familiar?" I asked

"We are in the halls of Nystia. When Lucian was trapped, the kingdom that he crowned himself ruler of disappeared with him. While Lucian is locked within his own prison here created by the dagger, the rest of the kingdom moved from our waking world to this realm. Follow me." She said guiding me down the corridor.

We walked through a silent and lifeless castle, to a stairwell that led to a doorway outside. Toree led me through the doorway and into a courtyard. As we walked out I looked up and saw a purple, pink, and blue sky covered in stars. There were no moons or suns, but some stars shone like a torch in a black cave. The courtyard around was illuminated as if it was the middle of a summer day.

As we made our way deeper into a seemingly endless garden I noticed that I could hear the sounds of birds in the air and crickets in the bushes, yet I saw not one living thing around. We made our way through some shrubbery and I could see two figures sat at what appeared to be a chess table.

"Is that..." I began

"Go." Toree said

I ran to the table as fast as my legs could take me. Sitting there was Aludia, the glowing woman who I now knew to be the queen of Nystia, and my mother.

"Mother!" I cried running up to her.

"Jara!" my mother said standing up from her seat and moving towards me.

We ran and embraced, she pulled me into her like a bear protecting it's cub from a lion on the mountain. I could not hold back the tears that poured down my face as I felt her in my arms. Eventually we were able to pull away long enough to get a look at each other.

"My sweet Jara, you've grown so much...how long has it been?" she asked me with tears still coming from her eyes.

"It's been years...I've missed you so much..." I sobbed

"Aludia said you've come into your own...look at you, a grown woman, a warrior, and a sorceress! Have you found love yet?" she asked me

"Not yet, things haven't been easy since you disappeared..." I said, admitting it for the first time aloud to someone else and myself.

"Don't worry, have fun when you can. When love comes it is like a hammer on an anvil!" she said wiping the tears on my cheeks.

"What happened to you? I know that you are here, but how did you get stuck here? We thought you became sick or had been poisoned..." I asked her

"My dear, I wish I could give you an answer but I can not. I journeyed and could not return. When I reached for my pendant to call myself back it was gone, taken from my body in the waking world." she replied

"Surely there must be a way to bring you back! If I find your pendant and return it to your body? Would that work?" I asked

"Yes, it would. But I am sorry that I must tell you it is unlikely." Aludia said, walking closer to us.

"You! This is what you meant earlier when you came to me in my fevers!" I exclaimed, fitting all the puzzle pieces together.

"Yes, and while I have enjoyed your mother's company, I would very much like to see you all reunited in the waking world. But I fear you do not know the full extent to which we are all tied together..." Aludia said to me

"Something has happened and the veil between the waking world and the spirit world is thinning. Parts of Nystia are returning to what you know as the Evanwood forest. The magical lock that keeps Lucian sealed is beginning to fail as well. He needs to be destroyed, and with him his curses.

This journey will end with either his death or ours, and we will not be able to return home until one of them has come. When his curses are broken, everything and everyone in this realm will move fully into the spirit world..." Toree explained

"Wait, I'm confused...are we not in the spirit realm now?" I asked

"This is a prison within the spirit realm, a moment and place transported beyond time through Lucian's curse. We are indeed here, but not integrated into this world." Aludia said

"When the curse is broken, this place will melt into the rest of the spirit realm, along with Aludia and your mother..." Toree said woefully

"There must be some way to stop that from happening!" I pleaded

"Jara...I wish it were so... but Toree is right, your quest is greater than me. Lucian would destroy the world if he is allowed to return. When that time comes, I will be with our ancestors and my body in Dragon's Reach can finally rest..." my mother said to me

"But we don't even know how you were trapped here!" I lamented

"How I came to be here matters not, I am here now. I can not help you run a keep, I can not help you lead an army, I can not help you braid your hair before a betrothal, but I can give you whatever powers I still possess in this realm so you may use them in your fight!" my mother exclaimed

"What do you mean?" I asked her

"Come, place your hand on my heart as I place mine on yours and feel my power fill you..." she said to me, grabbing my hand and placing it on her chest for me

My mother began to mutter an incantation I could not understand. As she did so, I felt warm light moving into my chest and through my body, her hand and mine began to glow gold and I felt as if I had just quenched my thirst after a week in the desert. I looked up to see my mother smiling and her eyes glowing.

"It is done." she said with a smile and a tear.

"What did you do?" I asked her.

"I gave you whatever power I had. It is up to you, Toree, and your friends to put an end to this curse. Then rebuild the order. There are others, descendents of Nystia that have not been found, people who's ancestors left the kingdom before the curse. Rebuild the order and use it to create good in the world..." she answered back

"Thank you, mother. I will miss you..." I said solemnly

"I am glad to have lived a life worth missing, but I would much rather know that you are celebrating." she said with eyes full of water

"We should go, Jara..." Toree urged.

I embraced my mother again, holding her tight, knowing this might be my last opportunity to do so. As we embraced I saw Toree and Aludia whisper to each other and touch their foreheads against the opposite. Toree then walked over to me.

"It was a privilege to know you, Elia. Your daughter is special..." Toree said to my mother

"When you are ready, grab your amulet and bring your focus back into it, you will wake up back on the bed." Toree said to me.

Toree smiled, nodded her head to us and vanished. I looked over at them with tears still coming from my eyes, I could not remember a time so much water shed from them. I grabbed my amulet and smiled.

"Jara, I love you." my mother said to me before I returned.

I smiled and said "We'll see each other again, someday..." focusing on my amulet and returned to Toree's bed.

I rose up from the bed and looked around, I felt just awake as I had before we journeyed to the spirit realm. Toree sat where she was with her eyes closed. I was unsure if she was still in the spirit realm until I noticed her hands were clenched tightly in a fist. She was back here, but her thoughts must have been on the past. I placed my hand on her shoulder and a tear ran down her cheek, her only acknowledgement was a light forced smile and her eyes opening, red with emotion. I sat beside her and embraced her in a long and tight hug, I could feel her forcing her breathing to be shallow, unwilling to let herself break down in front of me. What she wanted now was some solitude with her feelings, but could not bring herself to ask.

"Good night, Toree." I said, then left her.

The hour was late and the camp had gone quiet. Just the night sentries remained vigil around the post as I returned to the tent Runa and I shared. When I walked in there were still two candles lit, they were almost completely melted away. I looked down at the bed Runa and I shared; she was spread across the fur blanket, snoring, and half naked. She had not quite managed to get her clothing from the day off and a night dress on before the effects of her drinking consumed her.

Her tankard was spilled over on a small wooden stool next to the bed, her hair covered her face and blew up and down with each exhale, one boot was still on her leg which hung off the bed, and her top was halfway pulled off.

"Runa?" I said poking her.

My calling and prodding only elicited a groan and a snore. I pulled her boot off along with her trousers, which were covered in drink. I walked around and finished pulling her top off (which also had drink spilled all over it) and brushed the hair from the front of her face. Once I had her down to her bottoms and clean from her spills I managed to pull the blanket from underneath and get her into the bedding.

"So this must be what it is like to be responsible, so boring..." I chuckled to myself, wondering how many times the tables had been reversed and I was the one being put into a bed.

It had grown later yet and I could not be bothered to find a nightgown in my pack, so I stripped down to my own bottoms and lay into the other side of the bed. I blew the last candle out and lay my head down. As I did, Runa let out a large snore and mumbled something incoherent from her drunken dream before rolling over, grabbing one of my breasts, and pulling my back to her chest. I let out a giggle, wondering what she was dreaming of before trying to pull her hand away. When I grabbed her hand to move it she mumbled something else and pulled me to her tighter yet.

It seemed Runa resolved to cuddle someone or something in her drunken slumber and nothing would change that. I chose to embrace the moment and enjoy the warmth and connection of someone else's body and touch. I could feel the warmth of her chest against my back, her forehead buried in the back of my hair, and her arm which kept me pulled into her embrace, her heart beating behind me. Drunken dreams or not, I felt warm and safe like a babe in it's mother's arms for the first time in years. Within minutes I had fallen soundly asleep until morning.

The tent had lit up with the sun's glow as the guards sounded the morning drum. I opened my eyes slowly and let my body wake up with me. The drum had not woken Runa, who was still against my back, her hand still firmly grasped on my chest. I placed my hand over hand on my breast and squeezed it. A groan came from Runa and she removed her hand and rolled onto her back, rubbing her face awake.

"Is it morning already? I have not let loose like that in ages..." Runa said in a raspy morning voice.

"Oh, I could tell..." I said sarcastically.

Runa stretched and looked down, realizing that her and I were just in bottoms. She quickly grabbed the blanket and pulled it up covering her chest.

"Jara...." she said concerned.

"Yes..." I said back.

"...did we...did we do anything last night?" she asked me.

"Hmm... well... when I returned to the tent you were half clothed, and whatever clothing you still had on contained the contents of your tankard. So if by 'do anything' you mean strip you out of your dirty clothing and put you to bed, yes. If you mean exploring each others bodies and bringing ourselves to ecstasy in a drunken state then no. Although I am fairly certain if tits could be suffocated; my left tit would have been! You didn't let me go all night!" I replied giggling.

With the truth revealed to her, Runa let the blanket drop and put her hands on her face shaking her head.

"I'm sorry!" she said, embarrassed.

"Don't be, truth be told, I found it comforting. That is the best I have slept in a long while. You can hold me in your big strong arms any night!" I said with a smile, patting her thigh over the blanket.

"Don't tempt me! I could use a teddy bear these days!" she said, obviously finding relief and comfort in my response.

"Maybe just give my tits a bit of air next time though?" I said jokingly.

"I cannot make any promises." she said in a sarcastically serious tone.

"Come! We must make ready and be on our way." I said to her as I hopped out of the bed and splashed some water on my face from the wash basin.

Today we would be making our way to Enex, and with our arrival would come the danger of a greater number of the cursed beasts. We put on the light armor we brought with us and strapped on our blades. Zuht had brought us left over meat on a piece of bread from the night before, which we ate as if there would be no food in sight for the next week. Runa braided her hair so it would not impede her, and I tied my own back.

"It is strange, isn't it? Suiting up for battle against a foe not natural to this world..." Runa said to me as she finished her last braid.

"It is, and hopefully this time I'm not hammered down by a giant beast!" I said trying to lighten where I thought the conversation was going.

"Yes, let's not do that again!" she said to me, delivering a soft punch to my shoulder.

We grabbed our belongings and put them in our rucksacks. We only packed the essentials, as we would be making the rest of our journey on foot. We threw the sacks on our backs and made our way to the others.

Everyone stood around a small fire where Zuht made his usual morning drink.

"Oh thank the Gods! This is just what I need this morning!" Runa said to Zuht.

"I thought this might benefit everyone!" Zuht exclaimed

"It pains me to say this, but in the short time we have been together I have grown to enjoy this quite a lot!" Alor said to Zuht.

"It honors me that you say this, but I am sorry to say this will be the last time I can make this until we return." Zuht said to the group, being met with a genuine sorrow from the companions.

"What! But why?!" Tripp exclaimed.

"The ingredients; I did not bring enough. I did not expect to stay in one place for so long, or maybe I did not bring enough for Master Tripp to drink three times a day!" Zuht said with a belly laugh.

It was true, somehow in the short time I had known Zuht I had come to not just respect his opinion and insight, but also his morning drinks. I found it hard to fathom going back to a morning herbal tea or water. I truthfully did not know how I would survive without his brews.

"Well Zuht, it is with great sorrow that I must depart our group of fine companions and head back to Raven's Landing where I can precure the ingredients to make more of your heavenly mixture!" I said in jest.

"Lady Jara, your jokes warm my heart. Tristi truly did deliver me to you!" Zuht said humbly.

"Come, the lot of you. Finish your drinks and let us be off! If we depart within the hour we shall be at the gates of Enex by the noon sun." Toree declared.

"Aye, Lady Toree is right. Let us toast and be on our way, we have lingered here too long already!" Alor said, raising his drink.

"To Nerick!" Runa exclaimed.

"To Nerick!" the rest of us mimicked in a toast.

We all gulped down our drinks and made our way out of the camp. As we reached the blockade at the path the captain met Alor and spoke with him. They were too far to overhear their conversation but a bird was given to Alor before he rejoined us.

"What did he say?" asked Toree.

"The captain asked us to send word back with this bird about the state of Enex. I told him once we had cleared the town we would send word so he and his men could help anyone that was left...or clear all trace of the town..." Alor said.

"Clear all trace of the town? How could you possibly do that?" Tripp asked

"Well, I suppose the same way an entire magical kingdom was turned into a fairytale!" Alor stated.

I looked at Toree, who had remained completely stone faced. Now knowing the truth, I knew how much every step forward from this point would hurt her. Although I had only known her personally since Raven's Landing, I felt like I have known her intimately my whole life after seeing her memories. My heart ached for her on this journey as it did knowing my mother was truly lost.

"Let us continue." Runa simply stated.

"Aye, we'll make our way to Enex. Use your blades or fire against any creature we find there. If there are still townsfolk we will do our best to help them." Alor said.

With that we began our way through the narrow woods path. Truth be told it was not a dangerous path, it seemed like the only creatures that ventured forward from the town were the ones we already faced. We made our way through, in mostly silence. We all were completely aware of the dangers we faced from here and welcomed the element of surprise on our side. The wood path was filled with birds chirping, deer roaming, and nothing out of the ordinary.

"Do you think we've killed all the creatures there were?" Runa whispered to me.

"I doubt it, I think there will be at least two or three dozen yet ahead." I said to Runa, pulling from my memory how many soldiers ventured forth with my father that might have been cursed.

"If we are surrounded, go back to back with me. We will not be overtaken as easily as we were before." Runa said very seriously to me.

I nodded to her and kept walking. I played situations in my head that could come to be, wondering if I would only use my sword or call on my powers to help us. A part of me wanted to feel powerful and use them in a grand display of destruction and awe, another part was afraid that I would be branded a beast like the ones we were on our way to dispatch and the group would turn...

Toree had hidden her powers for decades, if not hundreds of years. Would those that were once my friends turn on me? I know Zuht would not, as well as Toree. But I had formed an even deeper friendship with Runa and budded a friendship with Tripp, would they brand me a monster and take my head as well? I suddenly realized why Toree had removed herself from all others for so long, diving instead into books. I decided that what would happen would happen; if I needed to use my powers to save myself or my companions I would, and I would take whatever hand was dealt after the fact.

Each of us walked slowly and quietly, our hands ready to pull our swords from their scabbards at a moments notice. The sun was rising as we grew closer,, and with each foot the sun rose in the sky the woods grew increasingly quiet. At some point Alor drew his sword and kept moving forward with it in-hand, ready to go at a moment's notice.

Eventually we reached the area between the woods and the gates. It was a clearing created so that the town could see any would-be attackers before they reached the gates and could storm the town. The gates were wide open with no guard in place, the air was audible, no other sounds could be heard. The wildlife had steered clear of this place. Not even a bird circled overhead, the only living animal in the area was the bird that had moved from Alor's hand to Toree's shoulder to be sent back to the captain.

We slowed our pace and all drew our weapons, our senses were heightened as we got closer to the open gate. We walked through two at a time, ready to fight. The town was in disarray... the blacksmith's anvil was in the town square, which sat just through the front gate, a bucket knocked against the side of the well - echoing through the square... shutters were torn off the windows and doors were broken, hanging on their hinges...

The town belltower was battered, the beam that held the bell was broken in two and the bell sat smashed into the wooden floorboards beneath it. Food from the vendors stands were covered in mold, bottles of wine on the ground some smashed. The textile merchant's stall still had it's wares, but they were black with old blood.

"This town is large, let us split in two." Alor whispered to us while giving the messenger bird a lift to the sky.

"I will take Jara and Zuht, we will make our way around the town walls and come from the other end. You go with Runa and Tripp and check the rest of the market." Toree added.

Alor nodded and we split up. They crept off and began checking the store fronts off the market and we made our way to the homes against the town walls. We were all silent as we opened the first door to a house and headed inside.

It took a moment for our eyes to adjust to the dim interior of the home after the bright noon sun outside. We moved silently through the small home, which only consisted of two rooms. It was empty and there was no sign of anyone being there in weeks. We left through the door and made our way to the next home in silence, again it was empty.

As we moved on, we came across the town brothel. As we walked through the door we all noticed the strong odor of wet dogs. The air in the brothel had a strange feel to it and I felt as if we were being watched by someone. The sitting area through the door was quiet and the chairs were strewn about. We went through the parlor and up the stairs to the rooms.

The hall was narrow and there were about seven rooms in all. Toree motioned to me and Zuht to each take our own room. It was too narrow for all of us to try and swing a sword around together. We each entered the bedrooms, the one I took had ripped sheets, paintings knocked off the wall, and the window outside was broken. None of us found anything.

We did the same in the next group of rooms, but there was a growl and a snarl from the room Zuht took. I rushed out to see what was happening, meeting Toree in the hallway doing the same. I ran into the next room over as there was a loud bang and a louder snarl. Zuht was thrown against the wall, across from him there was a wolfman, large and with the muscles of a barbarian, the jaws and teeth of the biggest wolf I had ever seen.

On the floor was the wolfman's arm, Zuht had taken it before he was thrown and the wolf was lashing out with his other claw. I came down with my sword on his other arm, cutting it clean off. At that moment we heard another door smash open and a loud growl make its way to the room we were in.

I heard a belly growl and the floor boards bending, then felt a wind fill the room. The wolf in front came at me with his teeth, now armless. I pounded it's scull with my swords pommel, then swept up, cutting it's protruding jaw off of it's face, then cut down in a swift motion, cutting it's head and shoulder off the rest of it's body.

I turned around and Zuht was standing up again with his sword in his hand, Toree had created a whirlwind around the other beast which kept it slightly lifted off the floor and contained. Zuht walked up to it and drove his blade through the creatures heart, gave it a twist, and pulled it out. Toree let the whirlwind cease and the beast fell to the ground lifeless.

"Ah I knew it! How splendid! I fight with two beautiful sorceresses at my side!" Zuht exclaimed.

"How did you know?" Toree asked him.

"It is a secret, but I suppose since I know yours I can share mine... It is very simple, I just keep my eyes open!" he said with a chuckle while wiping the blood off his blade on the torn sheets in the room.

"What a rarity, someone that walks around with eyes actually open!" Toree responded.

I wiped my own sword off and began to walk out of the room when we heard something fall from the lower floor. We made our way back downstairs cautiously, looking around and seeing nothing. We all stopped and stood still, careful to make no sound. We then heard another sound from behind a wall in the parlor...

We walked to the bar in the parlor and noticed a large tapestry hanging on one wall. I cut it down with a swoosh of my sword and it fell, revealing what appeared to be a false wall. I conjured the wind as Toree did earlier and forced it against the wall. A secret door was flung open and a set of steps ran down to a cellar behind. It was dark, save for the light peaking through the floorboards above.

Toree conjured up a flame and held it over her hand as we walked down the stairs and around the corner. There were ale barrels lining the walls along with some food storage. We walked together slowly, looking between each barrel. I saw toward the back a pale foot from under a barrel.

"There!" I whispered to Toree.

Toree sent the flame through the air and kept it floating above where the feet were. We heard a whimper and the feet bunched up and curled in. I had a feeling that it was not actually one of the beasts, but instead a survivor. I sheathed my sword and walked to the corner behind the barrels.

There was a pale young woman curled up in a ball on top of a blanket which lay on the floor. She was filthy and completely naked, her hair knotted and her belly slim and malnourished. She covered her face with one arm and her throat and chest with the other. She was shaking, probably both out of fear and from the chill of the cellar.

"Shh, it's okay, we're hear to help..." I said in a comforting tone to her.

"...no...you can't help...just leave me alone...they already tried..." the young woman stuttered, still not looking at me.

"Who tried to help? What do you mean?" I asked.

"The soldiers...they came... they drove the monsters off, then they came back with more and killed them... you should have left me alone! Now they know where I am!" the young woman said.

"Zuht, get a blanket from upstairs and bring it down here for this girl." Toree ordered.

"Who came back, dear? The monsters returned and killed everyone?" Toree then asked the young woman.

"It doesn't matter, we will all be slaughtered like animals before the night falls!" the young woman said to her.

"The soldiers may have come, but they could not do this..." Toree said while creating three small flames in her hand, dancing around each other in circles.

The young woman looked up in amazement. As she watched the flames dance around Toree's palm, Zuht returned with a blanket and draped it over the young woman's naked shoulders.

"Now tell me, what happened here." Toree said to her.

"A long while back a lord and a bunch of soldiers passed through here and into the forest. Not long after there was talk from the farmers outside the walls about seeing monsters.

Everyone thought they had been drinking too much... but then people outside the walls started to disappear, everyone had to stay within the town walls.

We sent a messenger to the king for help. When his soldiers came they drove off whatever beasts there were and we all celebrated. Just before sunset the gates were knocked open and the town was overrun by beasts, some lizard like, some like dogs, and some giants like I have never seen! They killed almost everyone." the young woman explained.

"How did you survive, and where are your clothes?" Toree asked.

"I... I work here... I was in bed with one of the soldiers when the door was knocked open. One of the lizard people came in and cut his head nearly off and his body fell on me. I was too scared to scream. Before the same happened to me the madame came in and stabbed the creature in the back - but it didn't do anything! It just turned around and cut her in two from her groin to her neck...

Then it left after one of the other girls working here who tried to escape down the hall. I pushed myself from under the soldiers body and hid beneath the bed. The screams stopped, the lizard creatures returned and carried the bodies away with them. I don't know where they went with them.

When I didn't hear anything else I grabbed a blanket to wrap myself in and snuck into the hidden cellar. I thought the king would send more men, but none ever came. I stayed hidden, drinking the ale and eating the cheese and raw potatoes stored here in the cellar. I lost track of how long it has been..." the young woman explained.

"Come, I am Toree, this is Jara and Zuht, what is your name?" Toree asked her.

"I am Kirr..." the young woman said.

"Well, Kirr, Zuht will take you upstairs to clean yourself and put on clothes, eat some of our fresh food." Toree said to her.

"Zuht, you keep an eye on the girl, Jara, you and I shall continue to check on the town." Toree said to us.

"As you wish." Zuht said, helping the girl up and taking her upstairs.

I nodded and Toree and I made our way out of the brothel. Once outside we stood outside of the cleared houses so we could speak.

"Why would the Cythians come and carry the bodies out?" I asked Toree.

"I've seen this before, they are making a nest." Toree said to me.

"A nest? What do you mean?" I asked her

"They kill, then they carry the bodies of their prey to their lair. They keep the bodies there to feed on without having to leave, when they've eaten all their victims they go out and kill again. That might be why we haven't seen any here, perhaps they are almost through with their victims from this village and sent two to find another food source..." Toree explained.

"...that does not sound good... where would their lair be?" I asked her.

"Just that fight with those two wolfmen would have been enough to set them out on us if it was in the town... no... no I think it must be outside these walls. It has been at least a hundred years since I have been here, but I recall a crypt the entire town uses not far beyond the town walls. It is cool and dark, it would keep the bodies from decomposing too quickly. If they are near, it must be there." Toree concluded.

"We must check there!" I said.

"Yes, but first this town must be cleared. There are no signs of briars, so it seems we are only dealing with wolfmen here. As you saw, they are the easiest of the beasts to dispatch, but they are smart. They will be hiding as the two in the brother were." Toree said to me.

"Then let us continue on." I said to her.

We set off to check the remaining houses, which were all empty. We came upon one of the inns and stopped at the door, there were multiple snarls coming from inside, it seemed that unlike the other two, these were not worried about the element of surprise.

Before we walked in, swords drawn, Toree created a ball of fire in her hand as I did mine. We both burst through the open door and saw a den of the creatures. There were a dozen of varying size and color, all with sharp white and yellow teeth, drool falling from their open mouths as they hunched over and closed in on us.

One ran out towards Toree with an open mouth, ready to bite. She raised her hand and shoved the ball of fire that was levitating over her palm into the beasts mouth - it struggled to breath and could only groan as it cooked from the inside out. The beast fell to the floor smoking from the inside out and Toree conjured a new flame in her hand.

It was an exceptional display of power, one which I thought would put the other beasts off of their attack... but it seemed to not have that effect. The beasts instead snarled and growled louder. Two lunged out, one I cut down with my sword, the other Toree sent hurling through the air with a gust of wind, smashing its head apart on the stone hearth over the fireplace.

They kept coming, two and three at a time, Toree used her flame to blind a few before dispatching them with her sword. In an effort to throw the beasts off, I used my own fire to engulf a couple of the wolves that had not yet engaged. It worked to distract them and allowed me to carve my way through the others in the room.

There were two left, one which I then cut in two at the waist, the other Toree caught in another whirlwind. While the beast was spinning in circles she took her sword and placed the edge against the creatures neck, slowly cutting into it like a butcher carving meat over a spit. She calmly worked the blade through until the beasts head fell to the floor and the inn became silent.

"...I think this place is empty now..." I said to her.

"I do believe you are correct." she responded in her most proper voice.

We left the inn, with an entire den there we knew there would be no survivors inside. We went building to building looking for more creatures or survivors, in each we found none. We eventually cleared out every space we intended to and made our way back to the brothel. Zuht was sat with the girl while she rested.

"Come, let us join the others at the square again." Toree said to us.

"Yes, I hope there are more survivors." Zuht agreed.

Zuht and I put the girl over our shoulders and helped her to the square. Once there we saw Alor, Tripp, and Runa. With them were four other survivors, one child and three adults of varying ages. They were huddled together next to the wine merchants stand. Zuht and I brought the girl to them and left her with them so we could rejoin our companions.

"Is this all there was?" Alor asked us, nodding his head toward the survivors.

"Yes, the rest were carried away." I answered.

"Carried away, carried away where?" Alor asked.

"A cythian nest. They take the bodies of those they kill and bring them to their lair to feed on. There is a town crypt not far from the gates, I believe they are there. If I'm correct you did not see any in the town?" Toree responded.

"Aye, just wolfmen, six of them." Alor said.

"Only six?" I questioned.

"Yes...how many did you come by?" Runa asked.

"...about twenty..." I answered.

"What?! Twenty?" Tripp exclaimed.

"I don't know, maybe a couple more, maybe a couple less. I lost count after a dozen." I boasted in a friendly manner.

"We came across a den of them at the inn. Jara and I dispatched them all while Zuht stayed with the girl from the brothel." Toree said.

"Wow, and I thought I should be proud slaying two..." Tripp said woefully.

"Tripp, you are a brilliant warrior, and I am very proud of you." I said very plain-faced with my hand on his shoulder.

Tripp turned red and Runa and Alor let out a chuckle.

"We should take the survivors back." Runa said.

"The king was worried about them spreading the news of the attacks. The guards may not let them pass." Toree said.

"There was no telling how many were left. Now knowing there were only five survivors, anything they could say about this would be taken as crazy talk." I said.

"True, but the captain would not let them pass on their own. They will need an escort and an explanation to plead their case without a note from the king." Toree said.

"There is nothing left in this town to save, let us raze it to the ground once they leave for the outpost. Send two of us to go with the survivors and speak with the captain. This evening the rest of us will go to the crypt and destroy the cythian nest. In the morning we will burn the town to ash." I suggested.

"You have quite a head on your shoulders young lady! I think that is a good plan." Alor said.

"I will go with Zuht to the captain." Tripp said.

"No, he would not take a priest and a squire seriously... Runa, you go with Tripp to the outpost. I would not risk you both being made prey in the night walking back, spend the night at the camp and return as soon as the sky lights with the suns morning rise. The rest of us will go to the nest." Toree said.

"We will see it done." Runa said to her.

Runa motioned for Tripp to go to the survivors and get them up, then walked towards me and put her forehead against mine.

"Be careful, I expect to see you here in one piece tomorrow!" Runa said quietly to me.

I gave her a friendly tap on her shoulder with my fist and smiled. They made their way out of the town and down the road to the outpost. I walked back towards the others, who were now deep in conversation.

"What did I miss?" I asked them.

"Toree here knows how to make a mixture that can create an explosion like lightning hitting a warehouse filled with barrels of oil!" Alor exclaimed.

"Wow, that's great...but for what?" I asked.

"The cythians stay in their nest to eat and sleep until they run out of food; that's when they start looking for new prey." Toree said.

"Yes, and that is probably the reason we were not overrun when attacked at the outpost." Zuht added.

"Exactly, they haven't finished feasting on the townspeople yet, but if they sent some hunters out to look for a new food source it won't be long before they do all emerge. The outpost will not stop them at that point." Toree continued.

"So where does the explosive mix come into play?" I questioned again.

"We could not face any great amount of cythians head to head and survive...the crypts here are old, some of the oldest in the kingdom. If we are careful and quiet we can sneak in to the two main caverns and destroy the stone pillars holding them up..." Alor explained.

"...and the caverns would collapse, crushing all the creatures inside!" I exclaimed.

"Precisely." Toree said.

"But how do we get through into the main caverns without them detecting us?" I asked.

"Cythians have poor eyesight and smell, but exceptional hearing. If we are very very quiet we can get through undisturbed. Leave anything unnecessary here and we will move forward after I've collected the ingredients for the explosive mix. Jara, I'd like you to come with me." Toree said.

"I'd love to, let's get moving!" I replied, always eager to learn something new.

Toree explained what it was we needed to put together this mix, an iron dust powder here, a lyme oxide there, pieces of flint, some saw dust and dry manure from the stables, a couple of other little odds and ends. We walked through the remnants of the town scavenging the ingredients we required.

Once we had gathered everything we went to the alchemist's shop and used the equipment there to breakdown and blend the ingredients. Toree showed me very carefully how to make the mixture. We took our time and created four sacks of the explosive mix. What must have been a few hours later our task was complete, and the sun began to set.

"Here, each of us must take one, we can't fail our task at hand. If they get out they will overrun the countryside. When you see the pillars swing and throw these sacks. The flint rocks inside will trigger the compound and will set off the explosion. Make sure you are nowhere near it when they go off, it will destroy everything in a 30 step radius." Toree explained, handing each of us our sacks.

"This would have made many a battle much shorter, Toree!" said Alor, enamored by the perceived effectiveness of these devices.

"Yes, but there is much that could go wrong; put one drunk guard in front of a wagon carrying these and he could decimate a whole battalion." Toree warned.

"Are they really that powerful?" Zuht asked.

"I would imagine there is a reason these have been lost to time..." I chimed in.

"Jara is right, these were put aside and forgotten because of the unintended casualties. In small specialized groups like ours they can change the tides for the better. Give them to a thrown together mob of men-at-arms and farmers, you will likely be rebuilding half the city you are trying to protect." Toree said.

"Aye, that makes sense. Best to leave this secret as our own. I know the king, and if Ansel finds out about these he would see them mass produced and sent to every garrison. I can only imagine what damage a few drunken lads could cause." Alor relented.

"We must not be detected by the creatures until the explosives have been set off. Remove anything that is likely to make unnecessary noise. Any armor should be left here, strap your sword to your back so the scabbard does not knock to your side, and tie your dagger to your chest. We must move quickly and lightly." Toree directed.

"Toree, how will we see once in the crypts? Poor sight and scent make things easier, but with better hearing the creatures would surely hear a torch burning." I asked.

"You are quite right, Jara. Some of the herbs you helped me pick in the woods near the outpost were for just this reason. We can mix three of the herbs we picked with a wine bottle filled with a white wine. The reaction will make it glow for at least five hours. We will use these in place of torches on this mission." Toree explained.

"How in the world did you learn about this mix?" Alor asked.

"It was a trick the bar keeps would use at the taverns where I was raised. Came in quite handy a few times." Toree said with a chuckle.

"And here people say nothing good can come from a night at the tavern!" I exclaimed.

"I've never seen this before...I have been meaning to ask, where was it that you were raised? There's so many different stories about Lady Toree of Vir, I've never known which was the true story..." Alor asked Toree.

"My dear Sir Alor, while I would truly love to reminisce about my past, we have far more pressing matters at hand. I suppose you should take a bit of the best parts from each story and put them together! I'm sure it would be spectacular - you must write it all down for me when your done!" Toree said sarcastically.

"Sorry, you are right. Another story for another day, lady. Let us get started with the preparations!" Alor stated.

I headed to the wine merchant's stand in the market and sifted through the bottles, searching for bottles that only contained white wine as Toree had instructed. Toree was busy grounding down the herbs we picked the day prior to mix in while Zuht and Alor began to remove any equipment not essential to the objective at hand. I searched the stand entirely and only found two bottles suited for the mixture.

"These were the only two I could find with white wine." I said to Toree, bringing her the bottles.

"I was hoping at least one for each of us. We will have to move in twos." Toree declared.

"Aye, that works for us." Alor said walking towards Toree and I with Zuht in tow.

"Very well. I will take Zuht with me, Alor, you take Jara. We will need to split up once inside so we can take down both main caverns at the same time. Here, take this..." Toree said, handing Alor a small piece of rope.

"What am I to do with this?" Alor asked her.

This will burn at a slow pace. If we light them together before we enter the crypts, they will burn for about fifteen minutes. That will give us enough time to get to the two columns supporting the whole crypt. They make no sound so they will not garner the attention of the creatures within, but will allow us to stay on track with each other. Once we split up this will be the only way to know when to use the satchels." Toree explained.

"Lady Toree, my hat is off to you! You have the wisdom of a scholar and the tactics of a general! You have missed your calling, you belong on the battle field not sitting in a library!" Alor complimented, impressed by Toree's plan.

"That is kind of you to say. Perhaps in a past life I was a general..." Toree said sarcastically to Alor, aware that only her and I knew the truth.

"Come! We must make our way to the crypts!" Toree exclaimed.

"Aye, we will follow you." Alor said to Toree.

The Crypts of Enex

Chapter 16

Toree now led the group through the town and out the gate towards the forest. Before we got too near the forest we went south. The town fell out of sight and the sun began to set on us. As we walked the terrain became more rocky, we passed small stones with different inscriptions and prayers written on them and torches that had long since burnt out, no one left alive to refuel them.

As the sun was about to set we arrived at a large open door to the crypts. We could tell that Toree was correct and this was in fact the cythians lair by the smell coming through the dark doorway. It made me step back and recount my own buried memories.

Only once in my life had I smelled a stench so foul in air and in spirit, that was at the battle of Skitzbak. It was a fierce battle in the midsummer sun. Both my father's force and the forces of Wurth were decimated, either succumbing to the sword or the heat. The whole fight lasted no longer than two hours, yet it took three days to work up the energy and stomach to clean the dead from the battle field.

The battle had taken place in the Skitzbak valley, there were no trees, there was no breeze, and there were no clouds. It was the hottest day I could remember throughout my life. Our men fought valiantly, and Wurth fought without restraint. The only reason my men and I survived was because we only wore chainmail and linen.

Had we donned our padding or gambesons we surely would have fell pray to the sun's heat. The men of Wurth cooked in their armor, all those that did not die by our blades fell prey to their own armor. By the end of the battle the guard of the Wurth standard fell, not by our hands, but by the will of the Gods and the sun's light. For two days the heat trapped the bodies of the fallen, allowing only the smell of their corpses into our camp.

Toree seemed to notice that the smell from the crypts had sent me into a memory I could not pull myself out of. She walked over and put her forearm on my shoulder, grabbing the back of my head with her hand pulling my head close.

"You can do this, Jara." she said to me.

I snapped out of it and nodded. Toree pulled a small pouch from her belt and opened it, holding it out to me.

"Dip you fingers in and rub this mix under your nostrils. Inside these crypts are the decomposing corpses of the whole of Enex. This herb blend will keep the air through your noses fresh." Toree directed.

I dipped my finger in and rubbed it beneath my nose. Immediately my nostrils filled with the smell of lavender, thyme, and two other herbs I could not place. Alor, Zuht, and Toree herself followed suit. The stench of decomposing bodies disappeared and my mind moved back to the task at hand.

"Lady Toree, you are full of surprises!" Zuht exclaimed, impressed by the herbal concoction that could eliminate the stench of the dead.

"Now that we are all cleansed of distractions, let us light the cords and destroy this nest!" Toree exclaimed.

"Aye, here you go. When this reaches it's end so will these beasts!" Alor exclaimed.

"I will light the cords, Jara, take the two bottles and shake them vigorously. It will make the concoction glow." Toree directed.

I did as she asked. As I did so the bottles began to glow a bright blue and shone as bright as two torches. A tavern trick indeed! I would need to remember this one. Toree lit the cords and Alor took his while I gave Zuht the second bottle of illuminated wine. We walked quietly and cautiously through the door and into the crypts...

We walked down a long wide stairway carved into the natural cave system. As we descended we could all see rivers of bright blue glowing. At the bottom of the stairs was the main crypt foyer where there stood a sculpture of the ancient god of death. In one hand he held a sword, in the other an hourglass. On either side of his stretched arms were two paths leading to the crypts.

"Ah, Lord Harpo, the god of Death. The path on the left beside his sword will lead to the crypts of the warriors that fell before us, the path on the right beside his hour glass will lead to those that walked this world and died naturally. Which would you choose, Lady Toree?" Zuht asked her in a whisper.

"Let Alor and Jara take the path of the warriors; it is fitting that two of the kingdom's finest would be the ones to close the crypt and let them slumber forever. You and I will take the path of time...I find it more fitting." Toree whispered back.

"Aye, we will collapse the tunnels and make our way back above ground. May the Gods go with you, my friends!" Alor whispered.

"Use these rivers of blue to navigate the catacombs quicker." Toree added.

"What is it? I've never seen anything like it before..." I asked.

"The light shows the dried blood from the bodies that were dragged through. Follow the trail and you will find the creatures location." Toree answered.

We nodded and split up. Toree and Zuht disappeared through the passage to the right - the blue glow fading down the hall as they crept through. Alor and I made our way slowly down the warriors path. It was long and twisted through the natural cave system. Every so often there was a sarcophagus or an exposed skeleton of a warrior still in full armor propped up, as if a guardian of the dead.

We came to a section of the passage which had been littered with pieces of broken tombs and the skeletons of those laid to rest previously. We cautiously stepped between the bones and rock, careful to not accidentally make any racket that could echo through the tunnels. The trek was taking longer than expected, we looked at the cordage which had burned over the halfway mark.

We reached a fork, it was a natural clearing in the rock. This area must have been used for ceremonies, there was an alter, two torch baskets, and two gilded skeletons in armor on display. We approached slowly before quickly stopping short.

Ahead of us was a cythian emerging from the tunnel which the blue trail led down.

Alor and I looked at the creature and then at each other. We each gave a nod in silent agreement we would have to dispatch the beast before we could move forward. How to do this in silence would be something else all together. If the beast could manage to let out one of their shrieks we would be overrun before we made it to the entrance.

I looked around, the path we were in was too small to use our swords, and my magic would not kill the beast quick enough that it couldn't call out. Our only option was to somehow kill it using only our daggers. I looked at the small space by the alter, there was an old offering of bread on it. It would likely be as hard as a rock. I nodded toward it and Alor gave me an approving nod of his own.

I felt the ground for a soft section of dirt or sand, when I found it I placed the illuminated bottle on it so that there would be even light for us both. I controlled my breathing and very slowly made my way to the alter. The creature that had emerged was standing sentry over the passage we needed to go down, unmoving. My eyes constantly moved between my own footing, careful to not give myself away, and the beast - making sure it had not moved.

I reached the alter and carefully picked up the bread, it was indeed hard as a stone. I moved back towards Alor carefully, as I did he slowly withdrew his dagger and made it ready. We stared at each other and then down at the lit cord; it was nearly out. We both nodded and I carefully rolled the piece of bread just beside Alor.

The creature immediately raised it's head and let out a quiet hiss as it made it's way slowly toward where the bread had stopped. Time moved slowly and my heart beat so hard I feared the creature would turn and head toward me. Sweat beaded from my brow, hitting my hand as it fell. Alor made ready, the creature was only a few steps away before stopping and standing as still as the dead inhabiting the crypt.

We looked at each other with wide eyes, the cord was getting short and the beast was ever so slightly out of reach for a clean kill. Alor looked at me and then down to the ground, then nodded toward my hands. Considering we had to do all of this in silence, I thought I had a good idea of what his plan was.

Alor stepped his foot off to the side and rubbed the ball of his foot on the stone. The beast immediately turned it's head towards the direction and took two more steps, still not enough to cleanly kill it. Alor nodded to me and I thrust forward, shoving the creature towards Alor. Alor gave it an uppercut with his palm to reveal the beast's neck and immediately sliced it to the bone with his dagger.

The beast stumbled backward and I rushed to catch it before it fell, quietly placing it on the ground. Alor quickly knelt over it and drove his dagger through the creatures heart and gave it a twist. In a moment it stopped writhing and was completely still. We both nodded to each other and I grabbed the lit bottle to continue forward.

We followed the blue trail through the fork in the road and found ourselves descending down yet another steep staircase. This one looked different than the one before. It was more natural, the steps were roughly carved into the stone and the attention to detail was not the same. We were entering the lowest and oldest part of the crypt.

There were tombs carved into the side of the path we walked down, stone basins covered with wood half disintegrated or thin broken stone sheets. We were getting closer, the smell of the villager corpses was beginning to make its way past the herbal barrier Toree had given us. I now smelled a mix of herbs, rotting flesh, and feces.

The path became wider and the walls were carved through. As we circled down we could see the large main cavern in the crypt. The glow faintly illuminated a pile of half eaten, half decomposed bodies. It was made up of men, women and the livestock. Crawling over them was a mass of cythians, picking at the bodies like a lord picking apart a pheasant at a feast.

Just past the pile was the column which supported the whole lower level. Alor and I looked at each other with a smile, ready to move within throwing range of our explosives. As we took our first step into the cavern the ground began to shake and dust fell from the walls...a roar filled the halls a moment after...

I looked at Alor, who's eyes had gone wide. We looked down at the cord, it hat burned down completely...we were late! Toree and Zuht had set off their explosive! The cythians that were content feeding on their victims stood up on high alert, they began to screech and flail their bodies around. It was as if a drunkard had kicked over a hornets nest in the midst of summer. The creatures swarmed together and began to move toward our position near the cavern entrance, ready to investigate what they had just felt and heard.

Alor pulled me against him and spoke in a whisper straight to my face.

"Take these and make sure my family gets them..." he said, pulling off his signet ring and dagger, shoving them into my arms.

"Don't, we can throw them from here!" I urged, knowing full well what he was about to do.

"You and I both know we can't." he said, placing a hand on my shoulder. "You must succeed, may the Gods look fondly on you, Jara..." he continued, grabbing my explosive satchel and pushing me towards the path we had just come down.

I began frantically trying to devise a last minute plan, but Alor was right, we could not reach the column from here. We needed to be closer. The creatures were moving toward our position and I stood frozen for a moment. Alor looked back at me, he put both the explosive satchels in one hand and pulled his sword, he gave me a wink and shouted...

"RUN!" he yelled to me, then began dragging his sword on the ground to get the creatures attention as he made his way closer to the column.

"Come here ya whore's sons! Ye never feasted on meat as good as mine!" he shouted, slicing the arm off a cythian that had gotten closer to him.

The beasts approached him cautiously, unaware of how he was able to get to this point undetected. He continued to shout slurs at them as they slowly encircled him near the pillar. He looked over and saw me still standing there.

"Run, Jara! Ya daft girl!" he yelled as he wound up the two satchels in his hand.

I turned and ran as fast as I could the way we came. I heard him yell something inaudible and then heard what I could only describe as lighting in a canyon. The entire crypt shook, knocking me on the ground. I dropped the glowing bottle, which broke and spread across the stone floor.

I tried to quickly regain my balance and stand back up, dust had filled the path and stones were falling from above. I conjured a flame to guide me back, it seemed the main cavern behind me had collapsed immediately. I could hear no screeches or shrieks. Whatever beasts there were had been buried under the dirt and rock.

I tried to make my way upward, but even with the flame I could not see past the dust. I created a flow of wind to clear a small space around me, enough to see where I was going. I was knocked to the ground and to the walls repeatedly as the crypt collapsed around me. I created more wind around me to form a sort of bubble, protecting me from some of the smaller stones and dust as I raced out as quick as I could.

I had made my way past the cythian Alor killed at the fork and began up the final path. I was nearly at the end when the cave collapsed in front of me. I looked around but there was no other way out. I began to claw at the collapsed rock and dirt in front. I could see the path still stood beyond this collapse. I focused all the energy I could to create a massive gust of wind, like a hurricane at the summer's end. I focused it on the weak point in the cave-in and made a hole big enough to fit my body through. I squeezed through the opening and crawled down the other end.

I made my way through and past the statues sword. The entire crypt was shaking and falling, the statue of Harpo fell behind me as I raced up the stairs, tripping up a couple of times. I could see the entrance and ran through it, collapsing onto the dirt as I exited. Toree and Zuht stood waiting, swords drawn.

"Where is Alor?" Toree asked.

I shook my head from side to side and tossed his dagger on the ground, still coughing out dust and dirt. Toree looked slightly broken for a moment before shaking her own head. She walked to the entrance and took their last explosive satchel, swung it around, and tossed it at the stairwell ceiling. The explosion shook the ground beneath us and the entire entrance collapsed, dust and dirt flew from the doorway I had just ran through. It was done, the cythian nest was destroyed in the quiet of night. It was a task necessary for the good of Nerick's people, yet completely unknown to them...and at the cost of our companion.

Zuht and Toree helped me up and sat me on a boulder.

"Drink." Toree said to me.

"Drink what?" I asked, confused. We had brought nothing with us that wasn't vital for our mission, water or wine being such an item.

"Water..." Toree responded.

"We didn't bring any..." I replied.

"We don't need to bring it, you can make it. Here, drink..." she said again, this time creating a small orb of water over her hand and holding it out.

I took control over the small ball of water and drank it like water from the falls of a river over a cliffside. It was comforting to clear out the left over dust from my throat. I had thought of many ways I could be killed in battle, none of which involved being buried underground.

"Are you okay?" Toree asked.

"Yes, escaping the tunnels proved quite a task." I answered, ignoring undertones referring to Alor's sacrifice.

"You know what I mean. What happened?" Toree asked again.

"Our path was littered with bones of the dead, we needed to move slowly to not alert the beasts. We came to a fork near an alter before reaching the nest. Before we could follow the blood trail one of the creatures appeared from the passage. We needed to kill it in complete silence. By the time we made it to the main cavern at the end the cord had burned out.

Before we could make it to the pillar the ground shook from the shock of your explosives. The beasts were alerted and began to move towards the path out. Alor handed me his ring and dagger, then took my satchel and drew his sword. He lured them to him as he walked towards the pillar. He told me to run, then destroyed the cavern and everything in it. I barely made it out, if not for my powers I would be resting for eternity there myself. Alor sacrificed his life to save ours." I said.

"Jara, there was nothing that could have been done differently..." Toree said, putting her hand on my shoulder.

"No, I could have used my powers to do something different. I let my adrenaline take me over, it clouded my mind and all I could think about was that damn pillar and the beasts not escaping. I can do better, I need to make my powers as a third arm, natural and swift." I said, lamenting on my shortcomings with my gift.

"You are learning, I was raised with this, honing it over too many lifetimes to count. A dozen wolfmen do not compare to a nest of cythians..." Toree said, trying to comfort me.

"I appreciate your thought, but the truth is I need to learn from this. Both to help more in the future and so that Alor's death was not in vain...I need to clear my head. If you need me, I will be at the pond in the woods just outside Enex. I will meet you back in the town shortly after sunrise to help burn it down. Please take this ring and dagger back with you." I said, handing the ring to Toree, who already had picked up Alor's dagger.

Toree nodded in an understanding manner toward me. I stood up and began to make my way down the moonlit path when Zuht called out...

"Lady Jara!" he shouted.

I stopped but did not look back.

"Remember, there are no accidents. All is by divine decree. All things play out as they should." he said, referring to his past conversations with me.

I did not acknowledge with any physical or verbal ques, I just stood there for a minute, remembering how it was that Zuht himself came to be a member of our party. Then I conjured a flame to light my way and continued on.

I often would leave battlefields on my own, seeking some peace in solitude to process the beginning and the outcome, playing through the ways I could improve myself. It was not often that a knight in such high esteem would be lost. In small intimate fights there was no room for error. Sometimes I felt the Gods really did aspire to push one outcome over another for whatever game they had chosen to play.

I wondered what game they were playing tonight. I was by no means close with Alor, but he was my partner in the crypts. It does not matter how intimately or not you know someone, when you fight side by side you are bound to them. The truth was that while I could have used my powers in the nest, that pillar needed to come down. The only way was with the explosives. Sure, I could have used my powers to help Alor to the pillar, but the outcome would have been the same. There were too many and I was too inexperienced with my own abilities for a group that large. One of us would have needed to make that sacrifice, and I knew that I was needed yet to help put an end to Lucian's curse, and by proxy end the war with Wurth.

I flung flames into the air around me as I walked, hurling them in gusts of wind to see just how high I could get them before they burned out. I was going to work on mastering these skills, as Toree had done many ages ago. I tossed boulders aside with the wind, burned through leaves as I entered the forest - then extinguishing them with a wall of water.

I approached the pond in the woods and began to send flames dancing across the water's surface, then dousing them with a ball of water, practicing my aim. I felt as if every single loss I had ever suffered was scratching me from the inside out as I filled with rage and exhaustion. I screamed out my anguish as tears fell down my cheeks. Everything I had held down was released at that moment and I wanted the world to know. I released a wave of fire and aimed it at the pond, I wanted it to boil as my rage and emotions boiled within myself...

I could feel the coolness from the tears on my skin, and then feel them steam off as the heat from the flames intensified. The pond began to steam and bubble as my emotions took me over. I created a whirlwind with the flames and drove it down into the very center of the pond, as if it was a fountain of fire in some exquisite garden. I let out another scream from the bottom of my stomach and fell to the ground, the flame and wind dissipating with my collapse.

As quickly as the pond had steamed up and bubbled in the heat and wind, it cooled and calmed. I chuckled as my emotions seemed to calm as quickly as the pond had. The night had exhausted me and exposed my shortcomings. Exhausted, I lay beside the water's edge and closed my eyes, allowing myself to drift to sleep as I felt the cool breeze flow over me.

In what seemed like only a moment, I felt the warmth of the sun on me as it glistened through the spotty tree canopy above. The sounds of birds chirping was a welcome invitation to this new day. I sat up and drank some of the pond's water from where the stream entered.

I felt different on this morning, I felt like a weight had been lifted off of me. Letting out my anger and emotions the night before removed chains that I had let bind me for far too long. I stripped my clothes off and stepped into the pond. The water was brisk and brought life back into my muscles and face. I submerged myself, scrubbing the dirt and dust from the crypts off my skin and hair, then let myself float around.

As I floated I watched the beams of sun around me stretch from the canopy to the ground. Some of the smaller animals came to drink the water before rushing back to their burrows or nests. I felt alive again, and it felt good. I stepped out and beat my clothing to knock off any dust on them that I could, then dressed again.

I sat for awhile, breathing the fresh air and enjoying the silence. I decided that I did need to practice large scale magic should we encounter more foes in great numbers again. I waded into the pond to my thighs and created a wall of water around me that stretched as high as the tallest trees...I let it shift from side to side, completely blocking out all beyond.

While keeping the wall of water up I had the wind push the water from my feet and around me, exposing the pond bed. I then had it follow me as I walked deeper into the pond. I switched from a wall of water around to a shallow wall of fire around. I manipulated the fire so that it pulsed around me with my heartbeat, flaring out each beat. With each flare I felt more intimately connected to my abilities. They were as connected to me as I was to them.

I switched back to a wall of water, having it splash up with each heartbeat. The wind blew back and forth with each breath I took. I was lost in the splendor of the elements and my ability to connect with them instead of simply controlling them. It was a new level of understanding between my conscious mind and the world around me.

I kept the pulsating wall of water around me as I walked up from the pond and back onto the banks. That's when I heard a loud war cry from just beside me. As I turned my head to look, I saw the tip of a sword pierce through wall of water. I quickly used a the wind to send the sword hurling into a nearby tree and allowed the wall to fly out in all directions, creating a heavy spray of water to disorient whoever had tried to attack.

As the mist of water fell I was knocked off my feet and onto the ground, my attacker on me. My eyes went black for a moment as my head hit the mud, but even still I created a ball of fire in my hand, ready to lay it on my attacker...but then the attack stopped...

"Jara!" I heard a voice say.

My vision quickly returned and I looked up to see Runa sitting on top of me. I quickly let the flame extinguish and propped myself up on my elbows.

"Runa? What are you doing here?" I asked, surprised and caught off-guard.

"When Tripp and I returned we found Toree and Zuht at the market square...they told us what had happened. Toree told me where to find you, I came as fast as I could to...check on you..." Runa said.

"I don't need to be checked on..." I replied to her.

"Well, not exactly to check on...I wanted to be here for you...if you needed me to be..." she elaborated while standing up.

"Thank you, Runa." I replied with a smile as Runa helped me up.

"What was that around you? The water...the flames...my sword literally flew out my hands and into that tree..." Runa questioned.

"That was me..." I answered honestly, unsure of how she would react.

"...That was you? Wha- how?" she asked confused.

"The reason I know that the dagger is real, and the legends are real, is because I am connected to it all. My family are descendants from Nystia, Toree is from Nystia, and we all have this magic in us. We can conjure and control the elements..." I said, nervously awaiting her reply.

"...You mean that you were the one creating the fire, the wind, and the water? Not some beast?" Runa asked.

"Yes." I said honestly, conjuring up a ball of water of my hand.

Runa took a step back as the water levitated above my palm, spinning like the moons in orbit. She stayed silent, and her silence made me uneasy. I could see now why Toree had gone so long without mentioning anything about her powers.

"This is how Toree and I were able to defeat so many wolfmen in the town. We used our steel and our powers..." I added, desperate to break the silence.

"Who else knows about this?" She asked me.

"Zuht, King Ansel, Unul, Toree, myself, and now you...do you think me a beast like those we've been sent to destroy?" I responded to her.

"What I think is that just a few months ago, these creatures were nothing but bedtime stories. I think that this task we've all been sent on was worth Alor sacrificing his life for. I think that I have rethought everything I have ever known...I thought that I was about to loose you to one of those creatures just now..." Runa said, walking up to me and cupping her hand gently on the side of my face.

"But...what I know...what I know is that over this time together I have realized that I care very, very deeply about you...and just because you can boast about having magic powers does not change that..." Runa said in a soft and truthful tone.

She pulled me against her and pressed her lips against mine... in a moment all of our past rivalries from our youth disappeared. I felt warm and safe as I did when she held me and cared for me at the outpost. Her lips were warm, and her hands on my head and body radiated acceptance for who I was.

I embraced her, rubbing my hands along her back and neck, running one hand through her hair. We kissed passionately and I felt truly connected to both myself and someone else for the first time in my life. I don't know how long we stood there, but at the time I felt I could stand there forever.

She ran both hands along my face and gently pulled back.

"I care about you too, Runa...very, very deeply..." I said to her, giving her small passionate kisses between my words.

She smiled at me, rubbing my cheek with her thumb.

"We need to get back to the others...perhaps you can show me more of these powers when we raze the town?" she said to me.

"I would very much like that..." I said back, placing my hand over hers on my face and giving her hand a kiss.

We let each other go. Runa pulled her sword from the tree it was lodged in, and I threw my sword over my shoulder. Each step I took beside Runa felt lighter than any step I had taken before. We walked in silence back, our smiles saying everything we could not vocalize.

However, while my body and heart felt lighter, the closer we came to the town gates the more my mind weighed on the rest of our quest. We were one sword less, and the weight Alor carried on this journey would be split between the remaining five of us. What we would be greeted with once in Evanwood, none of us knew.

We reached the town gates and walked through. Toree, Zuht, and Tripp were talking as we entered the market square.

"Well, you two look content. What were you both up to?" Toree asked, referring to the smiles that Runa and I were unable to wipe from our faces.

"Oh, just trading some stories...you know, from one lady to another..." I said, knowing that Toree would see through anything I said regardless.

"Yes, Jara had some really great ones..." Runa said, glancing over at me, her pale cheeks turning a slight red.

"Hmm...yes...I'm sure..." Toree said in a sarcastic tone.

Zuht smiled, as aware as Toree was. It did seem the two knew of our connection while it was yet a mystery to Runa and myself. I was indeed glad fate transpired that they travelled with us. Their presence was comforting and their input most welcome.

"So what stories were you two sharing? Anything good? Unul had so many amazing tales...I would love to hear more!" Tripp said, completely oblivious.

"By the Gods, Tripp. You are hopeless..." I muttered shaking my head.

Runa let out a giggle and patted Tripp's head as she walked towards Toree.

"What did I say? Was it some sort of secret story you have to be knighted to be privy to?" Tripp continued.

"Young master Tripp, perhaps you and I may have a conversation sometime...you know...in private. I think there are maybe a few things that your last teacher did not get to teach you..." Zuht said to Tripp, putting one hand around his shoulder and patting his chest with his other hand.

"Am I missing something? Have you all gone mad? ...no...no you are all in on some sort of joke!" Tripp continued.

"I think Zuht is right, here is a quick lesson: sometimes it's better to stop talking and just observe..." Toree said before walking off with Runa and I.

We walked to a table and chairs that were knocked over in the square. We picked up the chairs and sat to discuss our plans.

"Jara, are you feeling better?" Toree asked me earnestly.

"Yes, I just needed some time to connect with myself again." I responded.

"And have you?" Toree asked.

"Yes...and then some. This is me, and I will not hide who I am from anyone." I said very matter-of-factly.

Toree smiled at me.

"Then you are braver than I have been in a very long time." she said.

"Toree, Jara told me that you have the same gifts she has, and that you are actually from Nystia?" Runa said inquisitively.

"Yes, all true, but stories for another time. Surely not exciting as the stories you both were telling in the woods earlier..." Toree said with a grin.

"Yes, but as you've said, perhaps those are stories for another time..." Runa said to Toree.

"I quite like games, but what are we going to do with this village?" I asked.

"We checked all the structures for hideaways again, and we called out while walking the town to give warning. We found no one else, it is empty. In the town hall there is oil storage. We can roll a few barrels out and break them open in the dense areas. Jara, you and I will start the fires while everyone else waits outside the gates.

Once the fires are going we will stay until the town has burnt to ash. We can not risk anyone finding a standing building here. Enex will be rebuilt, someday, but today we must cleanse the canvas for the next artist." Toree laid out to us.

"Brilliant, I have but one request." Runa chimed in.

"Speak freely, Runa." Toree responded.

"I would like to see your abilities in action as you set the town alight..." Runa requested.

"Well, I was planning on just using a flint and striker on the oil, but I suppose we could do that for you." Toree said with a smile.

Runa smiled and jumped up.

"You two! Help me to the town hall, we need to get their oil supply out and amongst the town!" Runa yelled to Tripp and Zuht.

"At your request." Zuht said with a hand to his shoulder.

Runa led Tripp and Zuht to the building to retrieve the oil. Toree and I stayed sitting at the table in the square.

"So you told her everything?" Toree asked me.

"No, not everything. But she found me using my powers, I do not want to hide who I am. Are you angry with me?" I responded.

"No, I am proud of you. You do have more courage than I have had in a long time." Toree said.

"Yes, but you have been through such hills and valleys when you have told others about your magic, I understand why you would keep it a secret for so long." I said to her.

"No, I'm not talking about that. Our companions would all know of our powers sooner or later. I am talking about Runa. Anyone in the world aside from Tripp could see how you two feel about each other. I am glad you are acknowledging your feelings with her, and to her. It is something I have not been able to do in a very long time. Let it be a source of your strength!" Toree said with a hand on my shoulder.

"Thank you, Toree." I said with a smile.

The truth was Toree's opinion had become important to me. In the short time that I had known her she had filled a void that had been in me since my mother was locked away in the spirit realm. Perhaps my level of respect and connection had grown faster than normal because I spent so much time in her memories, and saw how she was in one way or another connected to my own. In the end it did not matter, I knew what I felt was my truth, and I was okay with that.

"Now, there is one thing..." Toree said to me.

"What is that?" I asked.

"It seems the only member of our group that does not know about our powers is Tripp. Would you like to have a bit of fun when they bring the barrels out?" she asked me.

"It's almost as if you are still somehow connected to my mind..." I said with a mischievous grin.

Toree stood up and began walking to the town hall where the others were bringing the barrels up from. Tripp and Zuht emerged pushing one large barrel together. Runa walked behind them, directing the barrel's placement.

"I can take over if you'd like, you two can start on the next one." Toree said walking up to them.

"Thank you my lady, but I don't think you will be able to manage this on your own." Tripp said.

"Oh, I think the lady can manage just fine." Zuht said with a smile.

"I feel like I am living in an alternate world right now, one where you can just burn down an entire town, monsters are real, and physics don't apply. You have all gone mad!" Tripp getting flustered.

"Please, I insist, Jara can help me." Toree said to Tripp, then looked over at me.

"Jara! Would you mind helping me place this barrel beside the tavern over there?" Toree called out.

"Of course! I'll wait here for you!" I shouted back.

"I was right, you are all mad! The lot of you!" Tripp said with his hand on his head.

"It'll just take a second, don't worry." Toree said with a pat on Tripp's shoulder.

Toree conjured up the wind and lifted the barrel with it. Tripp's eyes opened wide as he watched the barrel float into the air. Toree flicked her wrist and the barrel was flung through the air toward me. I took control of the wind as it came near and gently guided it to the ground beside the tavern. With that Tripp's jaw dropped and he stood as still as a statue. His grip on his own chin began to make his face red and white.

"I was wrong, I was completely wrong! You haven't gone mad, I have! This is an alternate reality and no rules apply." Tripp said, as if his world was turned upside down.

Tripp walked over to Zuht and poked his cheek with his finger. Zuht let out a laugh and smacked his hand away.

"Some rules still apply, let's not try poking any of us with a sword, yes?" Zuht said laughing.

"How did you do that?" Tripp demanded as he walked around looking for some sort of system in place that could play such a trick.

"It's magic, and you are the last one to know, so we thought we would have a bit of fun." I said to Tripp as I walked over.

"You call that fun? You can't be serious. Magic? They can't be serious!" Tripp said, turning to Zuht and Runa.

"Young master, it is real. We are lucky to travel with two sorceresses! You should see how amazing it is in combat!" Zuht said to Tripp.

"It's true, I only just found out this morning, but it is real." Runa said.

"We are on a secret quest for a magical dagger, in a kingdom that disappeared centuries ago, and have fought monsters. Is it so far fetched to think it real?" Toree said to Tripp.

"You could have just told me, perhaps say: 'Oh by the way, we can use magic powers and make monsters explode from the inside out.' instead." Tripp said.

"Oh Tripp..." I said walking to him and holding his arms with both hands.

"That's not quite how it works, and beside, where would be the fun in that?" I said to him.

"Oh yes, we must not all forget to have fun right?" Tripp said sarcastically and annoyed.

"Exactly! Now come, we can't play around all day. You can ask Toree any questions you have while the town is burning, now we must continue putting the oil barrels in place." I said.

"Why did I agree to come along with you all..." Tripp said, shaking his head and turning to go grab more barrels with Zuht.

We all helped move the oil into positions around the town. Once in place we all feathered out across the town calling for any last survivors. After we had no reply for a few minutes Zuht took a small hatchet that he carried on the small of his back and began to break the lids of the barrels. As the oil flowed we took small buckets we found around the town and filled them. We doused the floor and furniture in the bell tower with it, as well as other stone structures that were either too far removed from the other structures or that would not burn down with the rest of the wooden village.

We were sure to include the carts in the market, there could be no structure that could show what had happened here left standing. After a short while we had finished spreading the oil, and the ground beside the most dense areas was soaked. Toree gave the order for Tripp and Zuht to head out the gates and set up camp for the remainder of the day and and night up-wind. We would stay to make sure the entire town had turned to ash before moving on.

Runa grabbed a torch from one of the cauldrons by the gate and tipped it on the oil-soaked ground, then walked over.

"I'm sure you can both handle this, but I'd like to help out myself. I'll light the bell tower and the town hall since they stand away from the rest, you both can concentrate on the main town area." Runa said to us.

"I think that is a good plan." Toree said.

I created a flame in my hand and held it out to Runa, who held her torch out to be lit with a smile in awe of the magic. Her torch lit and I threw the flame I used into one of the alleys we had emptied a barrel in. The alley erupted in a flame like a blacksmith bellowing his forge.

Toree and I spit between the two sides of the town, setting alight both the oil below and some particularly dry areas above. Runa lit the oil that covered the bell tower and the town hall, then made her way to the square to light the merchants stands that stood there. The flames began to take over the town and the three of us retreated out the gates and to the area Tripp and Zuht chose to set up camp.

The flames were so intense we could feel it's heat even two hundred paces away from the gates. It was a roaring pit of fire that rose high into the sky, the flames only contained by the ancient stone walls that encircled Enex. We stopped to look at the fire before we reached Tripp and Zuht.

"What do you think will happen when people try to come back to the town?" Runa asked.

"Enex was the main trading post between Nystia and Nerick. It stood here centuries before I was born; and since I first walked through it, nearly four hundred years ago, it has changed many times. Only the walls that surround it have remained constant.

People will return out of curiosity, and when they do they will see the walls still standing and clear out the debris. Enex will be rebuilt as something more than it was previously and the cycle will begin again." Toree said in a melancholy tone.

Toree didn't say it, but I could tell that having to burn a town she had known since she was young had an effect on her she didn't think it would. Seeing the flames triggered the unknown feeling in her, Runa's question just helped to pull that out.

"Toree, would you mind telling me more of your past?" Runa asked hesitantly.

"We can not move forward until we can be sure Enex is all ash. I can think of no better time than now." Toree said with a smile breaking through her blank stare.

Runa smiled and nodded in appreciation, then began walking to the others. When we reached them they had a small fire going with some meat cooking over it. I smelled the meat and realized I had not eaten anything since the day prior.

"What is this?" I asked.

"The captain gave us a cut of lamb to bring back before we go into the forest. I didn't want it to spoil so I thought now would be the best time." Tripp explained.

"Mmm, how long until it is cooked?" Runa said, licking her lips.

"Just a few minutes." Tripp answered.

"Great, in the meantime help me set up these tents." I said to him.

"You mean you don't have some magical power that can set it up for you?" Tripp said sarcastically to me.

"It's funny that you should ask, I do! It's a very simple spell, I just say the words 'Tripp, help me set up the tents' and then magically you have to walk over and help me set up the tents." I said with enthusiastic sarcasm.

"Now that is a magical ability we all share!" Toree exclaimed walking over, using the exchange to help her raise her own spirits.

"I'm sorry, I did not realize I was on a quest with four jesters! Who would be at the other side of your jokes had I not come along?" Tripp shot out.

"We would probably all be very serious the entire time. It's a good thing that you did come along, it would have been terribly boring otherwise!" I rebutted.

"Yes, I'm sure it would have been..." Tripp responded.

"Now come, I do need help with these tents. I will let you ask me anything you'd like while we erect them." I said in earnest.

Tripp helped me unfold and lay out the tarps and posts.

"So, why did you not tell me about these powers earlier? Why wait until now?" Tripp asked me as he knocked one post into the ground with a small rock.

"In truth I had only just learned of my powers a week prior to us meeting in the woods. The first time I used them was fighting the bandits to save you. Unul and I thought it was best kept secret until I learned what I was actually capable of." I answered honestly.

"How did you get so powerful then? I have been near you almost constantly since that night." Tripp questioned.

"Each night when I was alone, each morning when I woke, every walk in the woods or the fields. When I met Toree she taught me how to grow my powers even more. That is how Toree and I managed to slay all those wolfmen in the town on our own." I explained.

"Well, honestly, I am glad. I thought we would need a miracle on this quest and it seems you and Lady Toree are that miracle." Tripp said with a smile.

I smiled back as we continued to pitch our tents. We continued to work in silence together, by the time we completed our task Zuht was cutting pieces of meat for each one of us.

"Come, eat! Let us fill our bellies today so that we may not go hungry tomorrow!" Zuht said to us.

We all sat and enjoyed our meal in peace, feeling the waning sun shine against our backs. The sky was now a golden hue and the shadows began to grow long. In the distance the town still burned, what were multi-story buildings now had fallen like logs. It was as if there was a bonfire slowly burning itself down to the dirt.

We had finished our meals and Toree used the opportunity to fill Tripp, Runa, and Zuht in on her past (albeit, the abridged version). I sat there for a long while, hearing her voice but not making out the words. My mind was lost on the landscape; to one side a burning town, a stream and pond in the woods on another, a large ravine which led to the crypts we recently destroyed on the third, and to our backs lay the Evanwood Forest.

It seemed as we sat with Toree recounting her ages old tale, that we were in a new world. It was a world void of fanatical kingdoms and rivalries. Instead we were as children listening to their mother's bedtime story of magic and wonder, living alone in the wilds. I sat there and took it all in with each breath, ensuring that should I survive what was to come I would remember this moment in time for the rest of my life.

Eventually the sky turned red, then purple, then only the blue glow of the stars, our campfire, and the embers of the town remained. The past days had been long and I needed to rest, so I said goodnight and excused myself to my tent.

I took off my sword belt and placed it next to the cot, then managed to pull off my boots and tossed them to the side. As I was about to undress Runa walked into the tent, her sword belt was already in her hand and she tossed it beside the cot as well. She kicked her boots off and looked at me.

"About this morning..." she said to me.

My heart began to sink as I wondered where this would lead.

"...Did you regret it?" I asked.

"No. I just regret that it has taken me so long to realize what I want has been right in front of me the whole time." she answered.

"My new abilities don't scare you off?" I asked, anxious that I sounded arrogant.

"Lady Jara of Dragon's Reach, the only power you can use on me is blowing me away in bed," she said to me, gently pulling my body to hers.

She placed one hand on the back of my head and the other on my hip, then connected her lips to mine as she closed her eyes. Her hands held me softly and I let my guard fall. I placed my hands on her body and let my lips merge completely with hers. I could feel my heart beating nearly out of my body and my chest felt as if it was filled with glowing fireflies. I gently pulled my head away for a moment.

"Seriously, is there anything about my powers you want to talk about?" I asked, subconsciously trying to divert. I had realized how my feelings have avalanched so quickly for Runa.

"Shh..." she replied quietly and sweetly.

Runa pulled me back in and our lips locked. I could feel my breathing getting heavier. She pulled back and looked at me. I gave her a nod and let myself be vulnerable for the first time in my life, letting her take control. She untied my top gently and pulled it over my head. She pulled her own off and slid her leggings down. I ran my hands down my side and let my own bottoms fall to the ground.

We stood there for a moment, fighting a feeling of two magnets pulling to become one again. It was a strange feeling, I had laid with others in the past, but being with Runa now made me feel as if I had allowed every inch of my being to be exposed to her. There was nothing to hide, I felt as if she now could see all of me, inside and out.

In my life I could not remember someone as beautiful as she was this night. We embraced each other and fell onto our bedding. We kissed, caressed, and explored each others bodies with wonder and awe. Our arms and legs intertwined, our bodies pressed tight, our breathing more intense and in harmony. I felt like I was a puzzle piece that was set correctly for the first time in my life.

Eventually the late hour took over and we fell asleep embracing each other.

Evanwood

Chapter 17

Birds chirped outside as I lay with my eyes closed, I took a deep breath with my arms still wrapped around Runa. As I inhaled my nose was filled with the scent of the lavender oil Runa used in her hair and stale smoke. I could hear the others assembling their kit outside the tent, we would be moving shortly.

I nestled my face against the back of Runa's neck and cheek, running my hand from her thigh, up her abdomen, over her breasts, and placed it on her heart. She let out a soft sigh as she rolled over toward me.

"Is it morning already?" She asked, still half asleep.

"Mmm, I'm afraid so." I answered as I traced my fingers over her body.

"No! I'd much rather spend the day here, in this tent with you." Runa protested like a teen procrastinating her studies.

"You and I both. Can you imagine how little we would have gotten done had we connected like this when we were younger? We would have accomplished nothing." I hypothesized.

"I'm too busy imagining how little we will get done after we have completed this quest..." Runa said with a grin, pulling me against her.

Our lips locked for the second morning in a row, and our bodies warmed each other. This was the first time the passion of a first kiss continued to the second day. I allowed myself to begin melting into the moment as our passion became more intense. Just then we heard a call from outside the tent.

"My Ladies, Lady Toree would like to begin the rest of our journey shortly." Tripp called.

We were too enthralled with each other's body's to pay the call any attention. Runa ran her hand through my hair as she pushed my lips deeper against hers... We were so lost in the moment we did not hear our tent's entrance be pushed open...

"Lady Runa, Lady Jara..." Tripp said, poking his head through into the tent.

We pulled our lips apart and sighed. Runa made a grumpy face, I tried to do the same but there was another smile on my face that would not be wiped off.

"Oh dear, were you both cold last night?" Tripp asked rhetorically after seeing us embraced beneath the blanket.

"I slept quite comfortably, perhaps I could switch tents with you so that you stay warmer! Anyway, Lady Toree would like to depart soon!" Tripp said before pulling his head out from the tent, blissfully oblivious to what we were up to.

"We will have to finish this later..." Runa said to me.

"You can count on that!" I said through my smile.

We tossed the blanket to the side and sat up. The air was cool in the tent and we hustled to get dressed. Once in our gear we went outside to begin breaking down the tent. Tripp walked over to us.

"I hope you both got some sleep in that dreadfully cold tent! We'll have quite the journey after this morning!" Tripp said to us, still unaware.

"You! You owe me!" Runa said sternly to Tripp as she pressed her finger into his chest.

"Owe you? For what?" Tripp asked.

I began to chuckle and shook my head. I was not the only one, Zuht overheard and began to laugh himself.

"Master Tripp, perhaps you and I should have a talk about that which you can not perceive..." Zuht said as gently guided Tripp away.

"Has he always had his head buried in a haystack?" Runa asked me.

"Since I have known him." I responded.

We continued to pack our belongings. In the distance Toree was walking up from the town. It seemed like the town burning and heading into the forest woke something hidden inside Toree. Her stride and expression was the same that I saw when I was in her memories, back during the fall of Nystia.

"They what!?" We heard Tripp exclaim.

"I see Tripp is now fully up to speed..." Toree said sarcastically.

"That boy could not find a rock in a quarry..." Runa joked.

"Oh, don't make fun of him! He's like my little puppy!" I said in defense.

It was good to start the day with jokes and laughter. The mornings often set the mood for the day, and my view of the day was optimistic. We would move into the forest. What made the forest dangerous was not usually the beasts in it, but the sheer size. It was after all once the entire kingdom of Nystia. Hunters and woodsmen that ventured too far in would get lost and often not return. Our blessing was Toree, with her intimate knowledge of the forest and the kingdom it took over we could remain on track.

We were fully packed and in any kit we brought with us. I positioned my sword so that I would be comfortable in the trek through the forest. To travel light and largely unnoticed, we only carried the armor elements we deemed to be most necessary. My companions gathered, ready to begin.

"Zuht and I have already surveyed the town, all traces of what happened are gone. I think it best to not delay our journey onward any longer." Toree said to us all.

"Toree, can you tell us what we may expect in the forest?" I asked.

"I can not say for certain, but I have heard that some structures from Nystia have returned from the spirit realm as the prison begins to weaken. This will be helpful, but also dangerous. If there are briars or other creatures scouring the forest they might be using these as their dens.

We will use the path near the town's mill, from there we will go north until sunset. Your father's expedition would have followed this same route. With any luck we can pick up signs of their party and track them." Toree explained.

We all nodded to show that we understood and picked up what we needed. We began walking towards the mill, now on a slightly overgrown dirt path. The forest seemed like an immense cliffside just to our left, the stone walls of Enex on our right paled in comparison. The wind blew from the forest, with it a spiral of red and orange leaves flew through the air. It was not until this moment that I realized how much time had actually passed on this journey.

When Unul arrived in Dragon's Reach the summer had only just begun. Now as the colors of the trees grew warmer and the air colder I felt like I jumped in time, much like my time in Toree's memories. Each day the trees were becoming more bare, and soon snow would flurry down.

While winter would certainly make our journey less enjoyable, it would benefit the kingdom. The snow would bring a reprieve from the fighting with Wurth. The mountains the approaching armies would have to wind through would be impassable until the spring thaw. Nerick would be safe for the time being.

We passed the mill, which lay barren and in disrepair. Just on the other side was an entrance into the forest that the woodsmen would use. We got to the forest's edge when Toree stopped for a moment. She adjusted her collar and walked through into the forest. We all fell in line behind and stepped into the forest one by one.

The light in the forest was dimmer, the thick tree canopy blocking much of the sun's light. The air felt thicker as well. We followed a barely visible dirt path through the thick bush that sat on the outskirts of the forest. We travelled at a reasonable pace in relative peace and quiet for a few hours. As the glow of the sun shone through the canopy overhead, Runa, Tripp, and Zuht began to show signs of confusion.

"It feels different in here..." Runa said holding her hand on the side of her head.

"Yes, I feel it too. It's like a band wrapped too tightly around my head..." Tripp added.

"It's the magic. With the spells that were put in place weakening, you are feeling the weight of the spirit realm amongst the trees. The veil between our world and spirit world is the thinnest I can ever recall. Things might not be as you see them. You may hear or see people that are not really here." Toree said to them.

"Ah, that would explain the wagon wheels and distant conversations I am hearing..." Zuht said.

"You're hearing the sounds of moments long passed. It's a moment in time that plays on a loop, never ending and never beginning. This has always gone on in this forest, that is why it has a reputation for being haunted. This is the strongest it's ever been." Toree explained.

"I feel the heaviness of the air, but can not hear or see anything abnormal..." I interjected.

"That is because you and I are immune from the phantom loops. Tripp, Runa, Zuht, stay close to either Jara or myself." Toree added.

I certainly found this interesting. Now was not the time, but I would need to find out more about this from Toree later. Toree led the group on, I stayed at the rear to ensure no one fell prey to the disorientation they were feeling. Each of them were looking around, sometimes jolting to attention. They're faces changing from area to area, sometimes on high alert, sometimes calm. None of us spoke unless we needed to.

After what had only felt like a few hours more the sun was beginning to set. It surely could not be evening yet, even with the sun setting earlier this just seemed far too early. We all seemed to notice it, yet Toree continued on. The light filling the sky was now orange and it seemed we were out of the thickest part of the forest. The trees began to space further apart and the air was not as heavy. I noticed the others had stopped reacting to the phantom sounds as we entered this new area.

In the distance I could hear a river flowing, and from what I could tell we were walking parallel to it. There were no signs of life in the dense area of the forest that we had just left. Here there were deer, rabbits, and birds completely unphased by our presence. Ahead was a clearing beside a pond, which was fed by a stream from the nearby river.

The sun had gone down and the last of it's glow was fading quickly.

"Jara, your fire, use it to help light the way." Toree directed, creating a flame herself.

I conjured a ball of fire and held it above my palm as we continued, the red glow from our fires illuminating the area around us. We soon reached the clearing and Toree stopped. She looked around the area, sending her ball of fire around in a circle to light her way. Around us were the foundations of buildings. Toree was muttering to herself too far away for me to overhear.

"Have these always been here?" I called out to her.

"Not in a very long time..." She said studying the stone formations around us.

"You mean...these are from Nystia?" Tripp asked.

"Yes, this was a trading town, similar to Enex but within Nystia's boarders. It seems that this area has begun to return." Toree explained.

"How do these return here? Does it just appear?" Tripp added.

"No, there is usually a break in the veil. The whole area will light up like a thunderstorm, there will be sounds that sound like thunder and your stomach will feel like you were just thrown off a cliff. Within the flashes of light the remnants of the past will reappear. Sometimes it's all at once, other times it's pieces - that's what we have here." Toree said with more detail.

"Is it safe to stop here?" Runa asked.

"Yes, we can rest here for the night." Toree responded.

"Lady Toree, perhaps my perception is not what it used to be, but how did it get so late so quickly?" Zuht asked.

"You would not be wrong! The outskirts of the forest skew the perception of time. What feels like a short while to us has actually been the better part of a day. That is why we did not stop there. Had we made camp there, one night to us would have actually been three days. Now that we have passed we can rest." Toree said to Zuht.

"How wonderous this forest is..." Zuht said in awe.

We set our gear down within one of the foundations and Tripp walked around nearby collecting fallen branches and sticks to start a fire with. The presence of animals around us meant there would be no beasts nearby so there was no need to hide a fire. After some short deliberation we decided not to set up any tents, instead we would lay out our bedrolls and sleep beside the fire. This would help us move faster in the morning.

Toree wanted to reach a mountainous area in two days time, but to do so we would have to traverse the river that ran nearby the first day, and the second we would have to make our way through marshland and to the foot of the mountain. To cross the river we would have to move much further north; Toree said without a boat or raft to ford the river with we would have to cross a days march further near an ancient quarry that was used for much of Nystia's stone structures. We would cross before dusk and make camp once on the other side.

"What was it that you saw or heard earlier, in the denser part of the forest?" I asked Runa and Zuht.

"It was a spectrum, I could hear children laughing and playing, adults bartering, tall tales being told, but then also screams, war shouts, crying and grief." Runa answered.

"Yes, I had the same, but the trees and bushes would rustle with life, figures of people not there in the corner of my eyes. To be honest if I was not looking at Toree and yourself I would have pulled my sword at some of it!" Zuht elaborated.

"Did you really not hear or see anything?" Runa asked me.

"No, I could feel a difference in the air around us, time moved the same for me as it did for you, but I did not see or hear anything." I told them.

"Hmm, how strange...I wonder why this is..." Zuht responded.

"It doesn't matter now that we are past it, let's prepare our camp for the night." Runa said.

Zuht nodded and they began to pull out and lay their bedrolls, pulling out some of the cured meat we had taken with us for when they were done. I decided that it would be a good opportunity to speak with Toree in relative privacy again. Toree had taken a seat on a fallen tree trunk that lay beside the pond.

"Toree, why was it that the others were influenced by the forest earlier but we were not?" I asked her rather directly.

"I had a feeling I would be asked this. Had your mother and I trained you like it had been in the past you would have learned early on; our powers come from the spirit realm. We are linked to it from birth, that is why I locked Lucian in it, that's why the kingdom disappeared into it, and that's why Aludia and your mother are trapped there now." Toree explained.

"Yes, but that did not really answer my question, what does our connection to the spirit realm have to do with not being influenced by the forest?" I reiterated.

"We already walk with one foot in each world. We channel that power in our fire, our wind, our water. Because of this we walk in harmony between the two worlds. What the others experienced was a rift in the veil between the worlds; they are without Nystian blood, and because of that their presence amplified the rift. The spirit realm let out ancient memories to create a balance, their senses interpreted it as shadows and sounds.

When we walk through we create our own balance, that is why there is no phantom reaction from the forest. It is not a phenomenon exclusive to this forest, even in Nystia there were sections where the veil was thin or ruptured. Those from other kingdoms could not endure them for any length of time without being driven mad." Toree explained in more detail.

"I see, are we likely to traverse any more of these rifts?" I asked her.

"No, not until we reach the keep. There was much torment and destruction there at the end...I myself do not know what we will encounter when we arrive." Toree said.

"Well, whatever we encounter, we will do so together." I said with a smile, putting my hand on her shoulder.

"Jara, you truly are a living gift that fate has given me." Toree said with a smile back.

"Runa and Zuht have pulled out some of the rations if you want to fill your belly before bed." I said, looking over seeing that the two had already begun to dig into the meats.

"Go, I will be there shortly." Toree said.

I nodded and walked towards the campsite. In truth I did not want to leave Toree alone for too long. This was her first time within the forest for many lifetimes; I felt that she should be with friends... and at this point in our journey I felt like we were a small family.

Tripp was now trying to spark the tinder to get the fire going. Runa and Zuht were sat on their bedding tearing away at their ration for the day. One exceedingly nice bonus to carrying out royal expeditions were the rations. Cured meat, salted fish, and spice if we hunt our own game. Normally we would be left with hardtack and compressed berry cakes. Good food certainly kept the moral up at the end of each day.

"Would you like some help with that?" I asked Tripp.

"Yes that would be great!" Tripp said.

I knelt beside the small pit Tripp had dug and extended my hand towards the kindling. I let a flame form within the ball of dried grass and twigs and then gave some wind to it. Within a minute the fire had formed and could survive on it's own.

"How is it you create these elements?" Tripp asked me.

"I don't really know how to describe it...it's a feeling in me. I feel the element I want inside and give it a destination, then it just sort of appears..." I explained.

"That is fascinating..." Tripp mumbled, looking at the fire.

"Come here! Have some food!" Runa said in a jovial tone.

"You don't have to tell me twice!" I said, sitting on the bedding beside her.

She handed me my ration and I bit into it like a wolf into a sheep.

"You know what this is missing?" I said to Runa.

"A side of greens?" Runa joked.

"No, although some greens would elevate it." I said, rubbing my chin as if in deep thought.

"Well, what then?" Runa asked.

"A good ale! A good ale and a loaf of fresh bread, right from the bakers oven...slather some lowland butter on it, from the cows that graze beside the sea..." I said, using my hands to mime the scenario.

"Mmm...no, now you need to stop! You will drive us all mad with your stories of bread and ale!" Runa said, shoving me playfully.

"I'm sorry, I can not help myself!" I said chuckling.

Toree joined us and the five of us joked about for a while. We all felt the time suddenly catch up to us and decided it was time to sleep. Toree assured us there were no beasts in the area, so we could all rest without having to take turns on watch.

I pulled my bedding right beside Runa so we could share our blanket. We both lay facing each other, holding our hands together. Runa had a grin on her face, a grin that I had seen before, usually when there was gossip she wanted to get out.

"Go on then, what is it?" I whispered to her.

"I think Tripp fancies Toree..." she whispered, holding back a giggle.

"What? Why do you think that?" I asked her.

"You both have been so focused on the quest that you haven't paid attention to Tripp's body language. He is always looking at her, when she walks over to him he corrects his posture, and when she looks towards him he diverts his eyes to another direction." Runa explained.

"No...really?" I said in somewhat disbelief.

"Mhm, really." Runa said with certainty.

"Well this will make for an interesting journey..." I mused.

Eventually we all drifted to sleep until the morning light illuminated the forest. The sky was grey, only a rough outline of the sun could be seen and it was much crisper this morning than it had been previously. We rolled up the bedding and prepared to move on.

As we funneled out of our campsite and followed Toree a hawk flew from the canopy above and landed on the trail in front of us. The bird stared at us for a moment before flying away again.

"It is an omen..." Zuht said.

"An omen of what?" Tripp asked him.

"We must keep our eyes open, like the hawk. If we do not, we will be the prey this day." Zuht explained.

"Could it not be a coincidence?" Runa asked Zuht.

"No, this was no coincidence. I can feel it, we must be on guard today." Zuht said, confirming his stance.

"Very well, let us all be on alert today. We must get to the quarry before sundown." Toree directed.

We began moving forward. As we trotted along I looked for signs of my father's expedition on our path. Despite being over a day into the forest I could not find any clues yet. We made our way up and down hills, over fallen trees, and crossing small streams. It was just after midday when Tripp called out.

"I've found a buckle!" He called, digging a small object from the dirt.

Toree and I walked up to him to have a look.

"This is from armor, we are on your father's trail!" Toree said to me.

"Good job Tripp!" I said giving him a knock on his shoulder.

"Come, we must not stop until we have crossed the river." Toree said, bringing us back on task.

We moved on, Runa squeezed my shoulder in encouragement. A fire in me was lit again! Finally a clue to show we were on the right track! I wanted to yell as loud as I could, but that would certainly put me at odds with Toree. Instead I walked with a skip in my step and a smile on my face.

We all looked about for more signs of my father's expedition as we made our way up a path that only Toree seemed to know. To my dismay, we had not encountered any more clues in the following hours. The reality was we would likely find few more, if any. The expedition would have travelled through this area nearly a year prior to us, and most traces would have been claimed by the forest.

The terrain began to change as the day went on. What was a light airy wood in the morning had now transformed into a rocky uphill trek with scattered trees. We took care with our footing and made our way over the hill.

"Toree, you may want to see this!" Runa said, the first to make it to the top of the hill.

We all scurried to meet her at the top. Once beside her we looked out over a valley. On one side of the valley was a waterfall which created rapids in the river, on the other side was a nearly vertical stone mountain. Neither of those concerned Runa, what stood out to her were the faint lines of a town covered in a purple, blue, and green mist. The town sat in the center of the valley, but the mist filled the valley almost entirely. Sounds of laughter and music rolled through the valley and up the hill to our ears.

"What is that?" I asked Toree.

Toree looked perplexed and stood silent for a minute.

"This town was home to the laborers from the quarry on the other side of the river. Even before Nystia fell it was destroyed. Lucian tried to enslave the people here to work night and day for him, they rose against his troops and were slaughtered, the village razed to the ground..." Toree said in confusion.

"Can you be certain you are thinking of the right town?" Tripp asked her.

"Yes, because I was there as a leader of the Queen's resistance. Lucian's men were greater in numbers and arms, but their hearts held less resolve than those fighting for their freedom and home. We held them off until Lucian's curse soldiers, wolfmen, ran into the town and surrounding valley. They rampaged, tearing the villages inhabitants apart limb from limb.

The beasts were ruthless, even some of Lucian's forces averted their eyes, other's put their fingers in their ears to not hear the screams of women and men being torn in two. We could not fight them back, anyone that could I led in a retreat to the quarry. We destroyed the bridge that led over the river after crossing to slow down Lucian's army." Toree lamented.

"I thought all Nystian's were capable of magic, why did the town not use their magic on the beasts?" Runa asked.

"We are...were. The amount of magic that runs through each of us is different depending on the family you are born into. My family and Jara's family were some of the most powerful. Others could only bring water to a boil, some were more art-inclined, and then there were those like Lucian and Aldonis; who had a moderate amount of power but were exceptionally skilled in spells and incantations.

Those from houses with more powerful magic became nobles and leaders, those without the same level of magic carried out the everyday tasks. It was not unlike Nerick's hierarchy is now. That day only I and two others had any form of significant power, and battle was still new to us.

Magic or not; war is war, there will be life and death, victory and loss." Toree explained to us.

"If the village was destroyed and the people gone, why does this appear full of life and laughter?" Tripp asked.

"I'd like to add to that question as well, I thought you and I could not be affected by a thin veil, but we both see and hear this?" I chimed in.

"Yes, you're both right. There is only one thing I can think of, and I have never witnessed it myself... when I was young one of my mentors told me a story about Nystia before it formed under one banner. These lands were once three kingdoms, all frequently at war with each other.

Eventually the three armies met in the middle of the winter, at the foot of the mountain range we are heading to. They sought to conquer each other for power over all the lands. When the battle began the leader of one of the armies created a spell which melted the winter snows on the mountain. His men thawed the ground with flames and used their powers to guide the water toward the other armies.

The waters tore up the earth and carved a path for the river waters to flow into. The opposing armies were soaked in the waters, then became stuck in the thick, deep mud that followed. They were unable to escape an onslaught of arrow fire. Anyone that did not survive the volleys of arrows froze to death before the sun went down. With water now trickling in from the river, the bodies could not be recovered and were left.

Eventually that battle led to the creation of Nystia, and the Winter Marsh. The water continued to flow in slowly, turning the battlefield into a marshland. The extreme nature of the battle had put so much woe and anger into the lands that it created an actual break into the spirit world.

For decades a mist like this covered the Winter Marsh, any who travelled through found themselves in the midst of the battle that had been years prior. More than that, they would not emerge for days or weeks after, but when questioned they said they were only on the battlefield for as long as it took to evade the fighting and reach a safe area.

My mentor said the mist broke through time itself, you were not in a memory, you were temporarily walking through a completely different age. Sometimes these mists are of terrible events like that battle, and sometimes the mist will take you to the jolliest of times. The common factor was always unexpected traumatic events." Toree informed us like the scholar she had made herself in Vir.

"I have to assume the Winter Marsh you speak of is the marsh you are having us make our way through... does this mist still have hold over it?" Zuht asked.

"No, not long after Nystia came to be an order of monks formed to heal breaks in the veil between worlds. It took nearly a century, but eventually seven monks were able to repair the veil. However, even after the mist was lifted the ghosts of those perished remained. They are tied to the marsh itself and cannot escape it. They can not do anything to us, and do not even know that we are there." Toree said to Zuht.

"Well, the sounds I hear don't sound like the battle you described at all..." Tripp noted.

"Trust me, they are not. This break must be connected to an equinox festival. The people that lived here were a happy jovial bunch; it would make sense that if there was a break from the trauma it would connect to a joyous occasion." Toree affirmed.

"But you said that those who walked through the marsh would be gone for days or weeks, is that likely to happen here?" Runa asked.

"I don't know for certain, but I have to assume it will be the case..." Toree said, troubled.

"Is there no other way around it then?" Tripp asked.

"It does not look like it. There is no way we can traverse that steep of a mountain to the right, and the river is too wide and too wild to try to cross, we would be sucked down the rapids." I said, having already eyed up any visable options.

"Jara is correct, there is no safe way to pass without going through this break." Toree said in agreement.

"Then we must take our chances!" Tripp chimed in.

"I agree, what waits for us when we are on the other side is for Tristi to decide." Zuht proclaimed.

All of us nodded in agreement and began to walk into the valley. As we descended the rocky hill we could hear the music getting louder and the scent of meat on a fire in the air. We had begun to enter the mists.

"Before we go further, you must all remember- we are walking into a time long passed. Everything around us will be real. Do not speak of our quest or our time. The quicker we can exit the town the better." Toree warned us all.

She turned and continued to lead us into the town. The mist grew thicker and thicker, until suddenly it was gone. It was dusk, there were open skies and fields around the town.

The forest was gone. Hanging from the town gates and posts were lanterns and ribbons in celebration.

We walked through the gate and into the town. It was unlike any town I had seen before. Many of the same architecture styles I saw in Toree's memories were present here. There were bards playing beside a beautiful fountain, vendors handing out mead and meat skewers, children ran around the town playing games. I felt as if I was a child again in Dragon's Reach during the fair season.

As we walked through we had many confused stares, our 'modern' fashion and dirty clothing ensured that we stood out from the others. Despite standing out for the wrong reasons, it was apparent that Toree was indeed known here. As we walked most people bowed their heads to her or acknowledge her with an off-the-hip circular motion.

"Why are they doing that?" I whispered to Toree as I walked up beside her.

"We are in Nystia, and in Nystia I am one of the queen's royal advisors. The wave from their hips and the head bows are a symbol of respect here." Toree informed me.

We continued to walk with Toree, smiling at the townspeople as they glanced at us walking through their celebration. As we were on the stone path through the town we were suddenly stopped as a theater troupe jumped in front of us. They all did a big bow in front of Toree and then proceeded to do an acrobatic act for us, right then and their, unprompted. I looked over and saw Toree's eye trickling tears.

"Are you okay?" I asked her quietly while the others laughed and clapped for the performers.

"There is no word I can use to describe simultaneous joy and immense pain I feel at this moment." Toree said as she watched the performers toss each other into the air.

I looked at Toree and then at the festival unfolding around us. I tried to put myself in her shoes, loosing everything, walking the world alone, then being forced to walk through the joys of her youth again. Would it be easier if it was a break to a battle instead of a celebration? Or is being able to live this moment from three and a half centuries ago a gift? There was no real way to put myself in her shoes, she was the only woman in the world that would ever be forced to live through anything like this.

"I can tell, you want a more clear answer." Toree said in my ear. I must have let my inner thoughts show.

"How would you know that?" I asked.

"Because you are the same as your ancestors, and curiosity was a defining trait of you all. What I want to do is give you everything I have on me and send you to complete the quest so that I can relive this night never ending. What I need to do is finish the last mission queen Aludia tasked me with. Make of that what you will." She said in honesty.

The troupe moved on and we continued forward through the town. We were stopped by a vendor handing us all small birds roasted on sticks.

"Lady Toree, please take these for you and your companions! Come, don't be in a rush, enjoy the celebration!" The vendor said.

"Thank you!" She said to him, accepting the food.

"Well, go ahead then. We must act like we belong here." Toree said to us all as she took a bite from her food.

We all stopped and sat on a raised flowerbed as we ate the food the vendor handed us. It was unlike any roast birds I had ever tasted. The seasoning was sensational and full of flavor, and the bird was as juicy as it could be. For a moment I forgot we were in a break and not back in Nerick.

As we sat eating a familiar looking figure jogged forward to us. As the figure got closer I could see who from Toree's memories it was.

"Toree! Toree!"

"Ren?" Toree questioned.

"What on the white mountains are you doing here? I thought you were at court with Aludia this equinox! I have not seen you in months!" Ren said to Toree.

"It feels more like centuries to me!" Toree said, trying but not able to hold back tears of joy.

Toree stood up and gave Ren an embrace that could not be penetrated.

"Okay, I get it, you missed me too. Who are your friends?" Ren asked.

"Oh, these are...delegates...from Nerick... Aludia asked me to collect them from Enex...I thought it would be nice to bring them through this way for the festival!" Toree said, quickly improvising a back story.

"Why are you all so dirty? And are you wearing a sword?" Ren asked Toree.

"Robbed! We were robbed by bandits before we got to Enex, kicked us in the dirt and everything..." Tripp blurted out.

"Oh my, well you should stop into the shops tomorrow and get fresh clothing! I will speak with the shop keepers, you won't need to worry about anything!" Ren said.

"Thank you, we'll be sure to do that." Toree said, now trying to get back on task.

"Wait, what poor manners Toree, you haven't even introduced us properly. I am Lady Ren." She said to us all.

"I am Lady Runa, a commander for the king in the northern regions." Runa said.

"I am Tripp, a squire from Raven's Landing." Tripp added.

"I am Zuht, priest of Tristi. It is a pleasure to meet you Lady Ren." Zuht said charmingly.

"Oh I am so happy to have met you, Zuht! I have heard about this new religion in the north but have not met anyone familiar with it. I would love to speak with you about it tomorrow at the midday feast!" Ren said to Zuht.

"It would be my pleasure, my lady." Zuht responded, fully aware tomorrow would never arrive.

"And I am Lady Jara." I added.

"Lady Jara..." Ren said, walking right up to me and studying my face.

"I'm sorry, you just look so familiar...but I can't seem to place your face..." Ren said as she searched her mind for an instance that didn't exist.

"You know what, you look familiar too! Are you in Dragon's Reach often?" I asked her, fully aware she was.

"Ah! Yes, I work with the Lord of Dragon's Reach quite a bit! Is that where you are from?" Ren asked.

"Yes, that must be it! I am from that area and find myself at the castle frequently. I must have seen you there at some point!" I said.

"That's it, I knew it! Toree, you have quite the group of delegates here tonight. Go and enjoy the festival! There is much dancing and drinking to be enjoyed, but fear not- we will catch up in the morning! It was a pleasure meeting you all, I hope your luck turns around after tonight, be sure to replace those battered clothes!" Ren said.

With that Ren performed a lively curtsy and skipped off to the sound of the music. Toree reached out and grabbed my hand, giving it a light squeeze.

"We need to leave..." Toree said in my ear.

"Can we stay for just a bit longer? Imagine the things I could learn from Ren in just a short conversation with her!" I rebutted.

Toree let go of my hand and put her hands on my shoulders, looking at me face to face.

"Jara...I know this place is tempting, but this is not a place we belong." Toree said to me empathetically.

"But you are from this place and time, surely that gives us a reason to stay a while longer..." I said, desperate to speak with my ancestor and live a night in her lifetime.

"No, we are only meant to live each moment once; we must savor the pleasure it brings us. If we do not, the regret we live with after will teach us how to. This was my place and time, long long ago. Now my place and time are with you and the others, making our way to Aludia's keep. We must leave, we have already lingered here far too long." Toree said.

I knew she was right, and I knew her speech was for herself as much as it was for me.

"You are right...we should move." I agreed.

Toree nodded with a smile and corralled the others. We began to walk towards the open gate. I took one last look back at the beauty of the town, the people within it's walls, and Ren; who was now dancing in the square with a group of others.

Looking back at this all made me feel the real weight of our quest. The war with Wurth took much of the joy out of the kingdom. In my childhood there would be festivals such as this all the time, but it has been many years since such events took place. Ending the war meant we could rebuild our communities and bring laughter back.

I followed my companions out the gate, beside the stables, and across the open fields. The mist began to set in as we continued on, becoming denser with each step. I could no longer see my feet and the temperature went from a warm summer evening to a cold winter day. My steps led me from cushy summer grass to a crunchy snow. The fog began to dissipate and the clouded sun was overhead.

I could see the others in front of me already, they were looking around, finding their bearings. Now out of the fog I could see we had indeed lost time in the break. The trees were bare, a shallow snow covered the ground and flurries fell from the sky.

"Toree, how long were we in the break for?" I asked.

"By the weather and where the sun is sat, I am guessing it has been a month and a half, maybe two..." Toree said shaking her head.

"That would put us halfway through the winter snows..." Runa said.

"Yes, and our timetable now running much shorter than anticipated." Toree confirmed.

"Ladies, please do not despair! Tristi only gives obstacles that are necessary for our growth. There is divine reason for this." Zuht preached.

"Unfortunately he doesn't give us furs to warm us, my tits are freezing off my chest!" Runa exclaimed.

"The best thing we can do right now is to double time it to the quarry and set up camp. If we keep moving we will stay warm." I said.

"Jara is right, we must keep moving. Once we cross the river we will warm by a fire and figure out a way to stay warm while we travel." Toree agreed.

"Which way then?" Tripp asked.

"We must get over the hill and out of the valley. The river bends around the hills here and becomes thinner, we can cross there." Toree informed us.

The snow crunched as we hiked out of the valley. We were moving at a much faster pace now to stay warm. Toree suggested at this pace we would make it to the river's edge within the hour.

"Toree, do you think my father's party passed through that break as well?" I asked.

"There's no way to be certain, but this break was not there the last time I was here. I believe most of this did not start until the expedition reached the keep." Toree replied.

"Why is that?" I prodded.

"I'm not entirely sure... I have theories, but none to share yet. What I will say is the closer we get to the keep, I believe we will find more structures and activity." Toree shared.

"One more thing..." I added.

"Does asking questions in the snow help keep you warm? Because you must be sweating." Toree said sarcastically.

"Why the quarry? What significance, aside from being the location for much of the kingdom's stone supply, does it hold that we must make camp there for the night?" I asked, ignoring the sarcasm.

"It was a royal quarry; as such there was a guard post there to keep it safe. If these structures and breaks are appearing back in this world there is a chance that the structure is there and we can rest and regroup in safety. If it is not, the quarry is littered with caves, we could set up in one of them. We will need to dry in cover, especially now that we have walked into the winter. The only way to cross the river is to wade through the shallow area at the bend." Toree explained.

"How 1 -" I was cut off by Tripp

"Everyone stop..." Tripp whispered, his head swiveling around the forest, sword drawn.

We each drew our swords and looked around. We were now halfway down the hill on the other side of the valley. The river's thin shallow point was in view through the bare trees, only a short hike away.

"What did you see?" Runa quietly asked Tripp.

"Nothing, that's the problem..." Tripp replied.

"Why is that a problem?" Runa followed up.

"Back at our last campsite, Toree told us we would be safe because there were animals all around us. I didn't notice right away because of the time jump, but since we exited the break there have been no animals in sight, not even a bird..." Tripp explained.

"Well done Tripp." I said, giving him a congratulatory knock with my elbow.

"When we went into the break this place was covered with deer and rabbits, could it not just be the snow has forced them out?" Runa questioned.

"It's unlikely that's the case, we must have been in the break longer than I thought. While we were there something must have moved into the area, we are not alone here... We must get across the river, once on the other side Jara and I can torch anything that comes upon the water's edge. Straight to the river on my count...

3...   2...   1...MOVE!" Toree
ordered.

We all shot down the hill as fast as our legs could take us. It was only now that I could sense we were being watched. As we ran the footsteps seemed to multiply. I looked over my shoulder, to our rear was a small pack of wolfmen, chasing us on all fours. For every one step we took the pack ran three.

We were nearly down the hill and to the flats before the river when the beasts made there way beside us. To my right was one of the beasts, as it drew closer I created a flame in it's face which singed some of its hair and eyes, drawing it off for a moment. Toree used the wind to help steer the beasts away from her side; it all proved to be to no avail.

Two of the creatures cut us off by leaping overhead. As they landed in front of our path Toree turned around and lit a wall of fire behind us so we could not be overwhelmed. One of the beasts in front tried to bite at Runa's neck, she quickly used the cross guard of her sword to break the creatures snout, then in one fluid motion brought the blade down - cleaving the creatures head clean off.

The other wolfman then lashed out at Tripp. Tripp attempted to side-step and block with his blade, but slipped on a patch of ice that was hidden beneath the snow and fell on his back. Zuht tried to step in front but was knocked aside by the wolfman's backhand, and before any of us could come to his aid the beast followed up with another slash of it's claws. The beast sliced Tripp from his neck to the bottom of his rib cage. Tripp let out a shriek and grabbed his throat, the snow below him turning red and black as his blood rushed out.

I conjured a wind so strong it held the beast horizontally in the air above us. Runa then plunged her sword into the wolfman's belly, then dragged it forward to it's heart and pulled the blade out. The beast's bowels fell from it as it was helplessly suspended in the air. I then sent a flame through the open cavity in it's belly and burned him from the inside out; his skin smoked and his fur singed as I sent the flames barreling through his chest cavity, blowing flames through his eyes, nose, and mouth before allowing it to drop, charred and smoking to the ground.

After seeing the display I made of the beast, the others from the pack retreated back up the hill, howling at us the whole time. Zuht crawled over to Tripp and looked at the damage that was done to him. Tripp was beginning to go pale as the blood continued to trickle through his fingers that covered the wound.

"It is bad, I do not think he will survive this..." Zuht said to us with a serious look in his eyes.

"Get him across the river, they will regroup and be back soon." Toree said to us.

I cut a piece of my shirt off with my sword and handed it to Runa. She stuffed it into his wound and helped Zuht pick him up. I grabbed Tripp's sword from the snow and we all made our way to the river's edge as fast as we could manage. Behind us we could hear the pack of wolfman beginning to make their way down the hill again.

"The waters run fast, but it is shallow enough to walk through. We must all lock together as we cross." Toree said

With the beasts nearly at the bottom of the hill we locked arms and wadded across the river. The water was so cold it felt like I myself was stabbed. It took the breath from all of us as we tried to control our breathing and make it to the other side.

Runa and Zuht struggled to keep hold of Tripp, who was now unconscious and could not hold himself up any longer.

"Keep moving!" Toree yelled.

We were all now in the center of the river and the wolfmen had arrived at the water's edge. We ignored the beasts, who for the time-being were put off by the freezing waters. It was a struggle to stay in the path across while fighting the strong current, but Zuht was the first of us to touch the bank on the other side, followed by Runa and Tripp, then myself and Toree.

Runa and Zuht laid Tripp down and cut his shirt off. Toree looked back over the river and saw the beasts were beginning to step into the water.

"What should we do now?" I asked Toree.

"Does he still live?" Toree yelled to Runa and Zuht.

Runa put her head to Tripp's chest and listened for a heartbeat.

"Yes, but just barely!" Runa yelled over.

"Jara, go heal Tripp, I will hold the beasts off." Toree ordered.

"You haven't taught me how! Let me hold them off!" I protested.

"You can't channel your powers as much as I can, you will not be able to hold off the whole pack. Beside, you do know how to heal him. Your mother imparted all her knowledge to you in the spirit realm. Follow your intuition and Tripp will survive!" She said, shoving me off in Tripp's direction while she turned to face the beasts.

Toree put her hand to the ground and seemingly pulled a golden light from it, then using the light created a wall of fire that was reminiscent of a castle's wall. She then sent it barreling over the river. The beasts tried to turn and run in a wild frenzy but could not outrun the flames. The wall of fire engulfed not just the pack of wolfmen, but the entire side of the hill. All the snow melted in an instant and the trees were set alight. There was nothing left of the beasts except charred carcasses.

I ran to Tripp and dropped on the ground beside him.

"Do you know what you're doing?" Runa asked me.

"No, but if I don't try he will die." I answered honestly.

"Have faith, Lady Jara." Zuht said softly with his hand on my shoulder.

I nodded in appreciation and closed my eyes. Placing one hand on the ground and one hand on his chest, with each breath in I visualized myself pulling that same golden light from the ground, and with each exhale I put it into Tripp's body. I don't know how long I did this for, but no one said a word and I did not stop until I could see his whole body filled with the golden light like a pitcher filled to the brim with ale.

I stopped and opened my eyes - first looking at Runa and
Zuht. They had their hands on each others shoulders looking at
me, Toree stood beside them looking down at Tripp. I
followed her gaze downward; before me Tripp lay covered in
his blood with his wound healed completely. He was breathing
and no longer pale in color, though he remained unconscious.

"You saved him..." Runa said in disbelief.

"You see, you just need faith!" Zuht said happily.

I had done it, I had healed Tripp... I felt something in me
change... Until this point my powers had only served me
conveniences and allowed me to create destruction... but
now... now they allowed me to save one from death...

"Will he wake up soon?" I asked Toree as I stood up from
Tripp's side.

"His body has been through a lot, and although he is
healed he will need to rest. It is hard to say how long it will
be." Toree answered.

"Then we should get him to the quarry so we can make
camp." I said.

"Yes, but first - kneel..." Toree directed.

"What?" I said in confusion and looking at the others, who
seemed just as confused.

"Kneel down before me." Toree said very matter-of-factly.

I complied with her order and knelt in front of her, despite being thoroughly confused. Toree pulled her sword out and held it over me...

"Jara, Lady and knight of Dragon's Reach, you have now completed the four pillars of a Nystian chivalry. You have risked death for a greater good in the crypts of Enex, you have used your powers to defend those unable to defend themselves when you saved Zuht on the king's road, you showed unrelenting bravery when you put yourself between me, the cythians and the briar at the outpost, and finally you have used your gifts to bring one back from the brink of death here, today.

You have done all of this on your own accord, with no prior knowledge of the pillars. Because of this you have proven yourself worthy of this title...

Here, in front of your peers and friends, I, Lady Toree, royal adviser to Queen Aludia of Nystia and Knight Grand-Commander of the Order of the Moon hereby knight you: Lady Jara, Knight Commander of Nystia and the Order of the Moon." Toree proclaimed, tapping my shoulders with her sword.

Snowed In

Chapter 18

We were nearly at the quarry as the sun began to set. Zuht carried Tripp on his back while the rest of us walked behind, Toree conjured a flame to keep us warm. As we made the last leg of our hike I could not help but feel somehow larger. I had been knighted when I finished my martial studies and came of age in Dragon's Reach, but this felt more special. I did not just learn tactics and how to fight, I made a difference to earn this new knighthood.

Toree had said after that the last person to earn the distinction was Ren. I felt like I had claimed a family honor, made even more special by my companions being there to witness it. Yet all that paled in comparison to Tripp surviving. Alor was an honest and good man, so much so that he sacrificed himself to save surrounding villages that did not know there was even a threat. But Tripp was different... Tripp is still a young lad, not quite twenty years of age, and has yet to fully develop who he is and what he fights for. He was also my friend, and I was honored to heal him.

Ahead the quarry began to show itself, the dusk casting large shadows over the crater that had been carved out. We continued our march to the rim of the quarry and looked out over it. Eroded blocks of stone stood all around, as did an untouched barrack!

"Toree, look! Your theory was spot on, there is a barrack just down the ramp to the first level!" I said joyfully.

"Thank the Gods! The snow around this area is untouched, we will not need to worry about any beasts here." Toree said in relief.

"A whole building?" Runa questioned.

"Toree believes the closer we get to the keep the more complete structures we will come across." I informed her.

"Well that should prove very useful!" said Runa.

"Perhaps we should speak less and move quicker?" Zuht said, adjusting Tripp on his back.

We ran with whatever energy we could muster down a long ramp to the first level of the quarry. There stood a pristine barrack, nearly the size of Gunter's Tower. Toree opened the door and we stepped inside. It was pitch black, except for a few windows purple with the setting sun. Toree and I both created flames and lit the torches and lanterns within the entrance.

The torches and lanterns were different here, they did not use oil or wax and wicks, they held a green stone which held the flame. I was perplexed by them, unsure of how they worked.

"Toree, is there no oil or wick?" I asked.

"No, these stones have been altered to hold a flame until extinguished with water; they will burn indefinitely. Come, all of you follow me, let us light all the torches and find rooms so that we can get out of our wet clothing." Toree directed.

We did as she said and lit the barrack. The building, although built for guards, was just as elaborate and beautiful as every other building from Nystia I had seen, and this structure was completely furnished, as if those men went on patrol and would return any minute. It was both beautiful and unsettling.

We made our way to the second floor where the officer's chambers were. There were three rooms and one privy. We opened each door and lit the fireplaces, which also had the green stones in them. Within a surprisingly short time the building had warmed up. Toree took the captain's room as her own, Zuht took the room next over for himself and Tripp, Runa and I took the last remaining room. They were all beautiful, fitting more for a palace than a guards room.

"All of you, dry your clothes and get some rest, we will meet in the library below in the morning. Zuht, keep an eye on Tripp. In this place he should recover quickly." Toree said, bidding us goodnight.

We were all only too happy to oblige. Runa and I entered our new chamber and immediately stripped off our wet, blood-stained clothes, grabbed a blanket from the bed, and sat on a fur rug by the fire to warm up.

"Knight Commander of an ancient order, that's quite a title..." Runa said in her own flirtatious way.

"Well, I am quite the woman..." I said jokingly.

"You are indeed... in all seriousness, what you did with Tripp...it was incredible. You saved his life, how did you know what to do?" Runa asked me.

"I don't know how I did it, I saw him there and felt like I needed to channel life back into him. I saw light fill his body as it was pulled up from the earth, when I opened my eyes his wounds were healed." I said, trying to explain as simply as I could.

"The Gods know we have had our differences in the past...but being on this quest with you, seeing how you carry yourself on a journey you are personally connected to, and with these powers you've come into... It has made me realize how honest and good a woman you are." Runa said to me.

"The past is the past...unless it's here...in this forest... then I suppose the past is the present...and the past... in unison? I can't quite figure this forest out, but I'm digressing... in truth, I thought you ruthless and a boasting over achiever in our youth." I said, stumbling my words, afraid to say something that might ruin what me and Runa were building, but also wanting to stay honest.

"Ha! I suppose I was all of those things. I thought you brash and impulsive, desperate for more power." Runa replied.

"And what do you think of me now?" I asked her.

"Now...now I see who you really are, not a fascia you present to those not close to your heart. You extended the invitation to solve the riddle at the castle, I know it must have taken a lot for you to do that, and it took a lot for me to agree. Above all else, learning that you have these abilities and have only used them when needed to aid us and not to garner more control, that has shown your true quality." Runa explained.

"I wanted positions of power for so long to prove myself... then suddenly I had the means to achieve it all overnight and it scared me. I did not want to take over or destroy the kingdom, I just wanted to help people. I learned a lot of truths about myself when my abilities activated within me." I admitted to her.

"If I'm honest, being with you has allowed me to let my own walls down. I'm not afraid to show who I am and try to overcompensate for my shortcomings. This is me, this is who I am in this moment...maybe I will change in the future... but right now, here, with you... this is me with no shields up.

I am afraid of these beasts we have been fighting, I worry that we will fail our quest and Nerick will be lost, but I am happy in this forest, with our companions...and I am happy that I am here, with you." Runa admitted to me.

"You are the first person to make me feel truly myself..." I said, putting my hand on her bare thigh beneath the blanket we sat under by the fire.

"And you are the first person to make me feel..." Runa replied, pulling my hand further towards her body.

I nestled into her as we lay down on the fur, I kissed her on the lips as she gave herself to me. My kisses ran down her neck and chest, my hand caressing her body. Now in the light of the fire I could not just feel every muscle of her body, but I could study the shadows of every curve, see every scar inflicted on her. I wanted to show her how she made me feel.

We were lost in time beside the fire as we connected in our passion. I saw Runa in a new light while I kissed and caressed her. I saw her faults, her strengths, her failures. I listened to her breathing go from deep and slow to fast and shallow, her heartbeat rise to a horses gallop until finally settling at a trot.

I lay on top of her, my ear against her chest, as we watched the flames of the fire dance, their flickers now an applauding audience against the walls. At some point we both fell asleep to the flames performance. Runa woke up at some point throughout the night and we slipped into the bed. It was the first real bed we had slept on since the castle and we both melted onto the mattress, soundly asleep.

I woke up to the crackle of the fireplace flames. Runa was already up, standing in a blanket looking out the window. A dim grey light shone through, illuminating the outline of her hair.

"Come back to bed!" I called to her.

Runa turned around with a smile.

"Oh, I think we'll have plenty of time to spend in bed..." she said with a smirk.

"Why is that? I'm sure Toree will want to get a move on." I said.

"She may want to, but the Gods seem to have other things in mind...come, look." Runa said, motioning for me to come over.

I jumped out of the bed and skipped over to the window to look out. The sky was white and grey with snow, so much of it I could not even see the empty stable just outside the barrack.

"A blizzard? I suppose we really will have some time to spend together!" I said slyly as I worked my way under the blanket she was wrapped in.

We shared a short passionate kiss and stood in embrace as we watched the snow come down. I would often sit in the window of my room at Dragon's Reach and watch the winter snows. This was the first time I was able to share the view with someone by my side. As we stood there I imagined being able to watch the snows with Runa by my side after the war; a time in which the only pressing matters would be what to eat to break our fast....

"Should we explore?" Runa asked me mischievously.

"Like this? It might be a bit revealing..." I joked as I squeezed her buttocks.

"You might be right, not to mention we may feel a slight chill... our clothes are covered in blood and dirt though. Let's have a look and see what's in these wardrobes!" Runa said dropping the blanket too the ground and briskly tiptoeing to two wardrobes that stood beside the bed.

We opened the beautifully carved doors and peaked inside. It was filled with tunics and robes. It was the same flowing patterns that we saw in the break at the festival, and in Toree's memories. We each picked a set of robes that we liked and put them on. They were warm and soft to the touch, yet felt dense and strong.

The more time I spent in Nystian memories or places, the more I felt like a primitive brought into the future. It was surreal to see such wonders, knowing that I would be taking two steps back when I return home. I finished dressing and strapped by dagger around my waist.

"What could you possibly need your knife for during a blizzard, stuck inside?" Runa asked me.

"If I had a coin for every time someone has asked me that! When I don't have my knife is when I always find I need it. Watch and you will see!" I said.

"Sure...ready to explore?" Runa asked as she opened the door.

I nodded and we went out our door. The second floor was small, there only sat a table and two chairs at the end of a hallway and the three rooms which we all split amongst us. The two chairs and table that sat at the end of the hall were spectacularly carved with feathers and behind it a painting of mountains.

"I wonder if those are the mountains we're heading towards." Runa said rhetorically.

"Let's see what is on the main floor." I suggested.

We took the stairs at the other end of the hallway down to the first floor. In the light of the day we could see the true grandeur of this place. Three full sets of different styles of armor stood in a study just beside the staircase. In the study were books, a desk, artwork, and a fireplace.

Across from the study was the foyer we had entered through when we found the building; it had shields with a series of coats of arms on the walls. One of them was my own family's. Just off to the right of the entrance was the guards room. Inside there were a dozen narrow beds against both sides of the room. At the foot of each bed was a trunk, and beside the headboards stood a small personal weapon's rack. Against the walls hung tapestries depicting battles.

We made our way through the last of the doorways in the foyer and into the mess hall. There were four large rectangle tables and one medium sized round table at the head of the room. On the walls were intricate patterns made of swords, axes, shields, and spears. They mimicked the sunrise and sunset, others creating patterns of the hills.

Through the mess hall was the kitchen. In it was shelving, on which sat spices, tankards, chalices, and plates. Beneath that was a very simple cooking hearth and a table for preparation.

"We might need this later!" I said, lighting the fire in the hearth.

"I think we might have one more area to explore..." Runa said, pointing to a doorway leading down to a cellar.

"I think you are right..." I said, also lighting a lantern which hung in the doorway.

We walked down the stairs into a cellar. There were bottles of wine lining the walls when we walked in, further ahead were meat hooks and a barrel filled with salt. We looked around the cellar but there were no signs of food reappearing. We checked the wine bottles and those were filled, so we each grabbed two in each hand and made our way up the stairs and to the study.

We put the bottles on the desk and Runa ran back to grab some drinkware. When she returned I handed her a bottle and began to wipe some dust off of the glasses. The tops were stuck on and she was having a hard time getting the bottle open.

"Can I use your knife for a moment?" Runa asked me.

"Aha!" I cried out in joy.

"Oh, damn it! Okay, you were right...please let me use your knife to open this bottle up with." Runa asked, her face turning red.

"I told you! Always carry your knife." I boasted as I handed her my dagger.

She cracked open the top of the bottle and poured some wine for the two of us.

"To the snow." I said in a toast.

"To our bedroom!" Runa said in response with a grin.

Just as we were about to take a sip the front door opened. Runa quickly grabbed an unopened bottle, holding it as club. I made ready my dagger and we stepped slowly into the foyer, ready to defend against whatever intruder had opened the door.

"Ah, ladies. Good timing! I went into the snow earlier to find us some fresh food!" Zuht said, stepping inside with a gutted deer hung over his back.

"Zuht! What were you thinking going out there in this?" Runa questioned, lowering the bottle in her hand.

"I thought master Tripp could use some fresh meat to replenish his energy. I found this bow and quiver in our room last night and thought I would put it to use." he said, holding out a gorgeous gilded bow.

"You are in luck, I just lit the kitchen hearth a few minutes ago!" I said, taking the bow from him so he could more easily hold the deer.

"Great! I will begin preparing this for later." said Zuht as he carried his bounty to the kitchen.

"Now, where were we?" I said to Runa as I picked up my glass of the wine.

"I believe we were about to try a four hundred year old vintage..." Runa smiled and said bringing her lips to her glass.

"Do not even think about drinking that without us!" Toree said as she walked into the room with Tripp.

"Tripp! You are awake!" I cried out in unexpected joy.

"Yes, thanks to you...that's twice you've saved my life...thank you." Tripp humbly said.

"We are companions on this quest, and we are friends. You would do the same for me." I said as I gave him a tight hug.

"Well, I am exceptionally grateful that some of my friends have the ability to heal!" Tripp joked.

Runa poured Toree and Tripp glasses of wine and we all toasted to Tripp's recovery. The wine was unlike any I had tasted before...it was sweet yet complex...full and bold, a mix of flowers, fruit, and summer earth. We each savored the drink in silence. Toree walked to the window in the study and looked out into the quarry.

"I don't believe we will be going any further for a few days..." said Toree, breaking the silence.

"Do you think this will last long?" I asked Toree.

"Nystian winters are beautiful but harsh. This storm will likely continue until tomorrow, it will be at least three days until the snow melts to a level that we can safely journey through the marsh in." Toree answered.

"Well, it's a good thing the cellar is stocked with bottles of wine!" Runa said.

"I think you have the right idea, pour me some more and let's see if anything remains in the armory." Toree said.

"The armory? Jara and I went around the entire building but saw no armory..." Runa said as she poured Toree more wine.

"You would not see it as any other room. Royal guard posts had hidden rooms which housed incredibly advanced armor and weapons. It was kept hidden so that should a post be taken over by an opposing force they could not use it against us." Toree explained.

"Would the guards not just use it themselves?" Tripp asked.

"No, the guards had their own issued armor, this was kept for travelling nobles and knights that may not be moving with their entire kit. Should there be a siege they could quickly and easily arm themselves." Toree elaborated.

"I might have to commission something like that around Dragon's Reach!" I said, intrigued.

"There are already three of them around Dragon's Reach. You have just not known where to look!" Toree said as she walked towards a shield and sword display on the wall.

"How do we find this one then?" I asked.

"Do you remember when we first met at the great hall, and I was looking at the hidden door lock?" Toree questioned.

"Yes..." I replied.

"Look for something in plain sight and pull on it." Toree said very matter-of-factly.

Toree pulled one of the swords out of the wall display, with a click one of the bookcases swung slowly backwards.

"See..." Toree said as she walked in.

We all followed behind her as she lit torches that sat in the room. Around us were pristine full sets of plate armor, sword racks, shields, bows, and chainmail. I was in awe as I walked through, the craftsmen that created these rivaled the best in Nerick.

"You won't need the swords, but this armor is special and will be of use to us. This was created to be stronger than steel and lighter than leather. With it you can move quickly for long periods of time without being weighed down by a traditional harness." Toree began to explain.

Toree grabbed a sword from the rack and swung it at one of the breast plates. The edge of the sword had slightly blunted and there was not even a mark on the armor. I could only imagine the advantages this would give us in any battle, let alone with Wurth.

"I don't know what we will face after the snow settles, but I do know with this we will be protected and our progress will not be impeded by the weight of steel. Before we move on from here we will each suit up in this." Toree said to us.

We did not need convincing, the idea of owning armor such as this was more than enough to win over enemies, let alone friends. We all lit up like small children at a festival and claimed the armor we wished to take as our own.

Eventually we made our way back to the study and poured more wine. Zuht was busy preparing the deer for later in the kitchen, and would likely be spending the majority of the day doing so. Now that we were in a more relaxed environment I could see what Runa had said about Tripp flirting with Toree was correct.

Every chance Tripp had to listen to one of her stories he did, and any opportunity he had to do something for her he took. Unfortunately for him, Toree did not seem to notice the effort Tripp was putting in.

"Tripp, you look exhausted! Why don't you go lay for a while?" Runa said to him.

"You know, I am still a bit knackered from yesterday...perhaps I will shut my eyes for a bit." He said before excusing himself to his quarters.

"He probably just needs a bit more sleep before he recovers completely." Toree said to Runa and I.

"I don't think sleep is what he has on his mind..." Runa joked.

"What do you mean?" Toree asked.

"Tripp has been eyeing you up for some time now...have you not noticed?" I asked Toree.

"Tripp? I'm nearly four hundred, he's just a baby!" Toree shot back.

"Yes, but you don't look a day over thirty two!" I chimed.

"Yes, sometimes much to my detriment." Toree added as she knocked back the contents of her glass.

I poured her another glass of wine and looked around the room. It was exquisite; this guard post felt more like a royal palace. The artwork inside was unlike any I had seen in Nerick, and the colors used all over were bright and vibrant, full of life and energy.

"Toree, what is it like being here, now, with us?" I asked.

She looked at her glass for a minute, then at the room around her. She stood up and walked to the bookcases, running her fingers across the bindings. Making her way to the window to look out, she eventually began to speak.

"It is a strange experience. I know this place intimately...yet not at all. Everything is the same yet different. Burning down Enex woke a sadness in me, camping in the foundations of a town in the forest ignited memories of a distant past. The break nearly broke me...reliving an event of such joy, seeing people that I watched die centuries ago... it made me question my sanity...

And now here I am. The taste of this wine and your company make me feel like I am a young woman in Nystia again, but I know what it is we are fighting for. There is no way I could adequately describe what my life has been like since Nystia fell...other than the memories I have already shown you... but I know that I would not wish any of you to go through it yourselves.

Perhaps at the end of this my curse will be broken and I can live out the rest of my life, perhaps I will walk the world until the end of days, and maybe I will not walk out of this place at all. Whatever happens, I don't want to spend more time grieving than I have already in centuries past. The Winter Marsh will be a sobering experience, so while we are stuck in this place let us be merry and drink, and rest." Toree said to us.

We each raised a glass in toast and drank. We joked and spoke for hours, going through quite a few bottles of the wine. Eventually Tripp returned from his nap feeling more himself and drank with us. It was not long after that Zuht had corralled us into the dining hall for the meal he had prepared.

As we exited the study the scent of cooked venison and spices flowed from the kitchen and into the foyer. Our mouths began to water after filling our bellies with so much wine. We sat at the round table and Zuht brought a platter of venison steaks. It was not on the table for more than a minute before each of us had taken one and carved into it.

Zuht was a capable cook who could easily rival any castle chef. The meat was tender and warm and with each bite a bigger smile grew on my face. By the silence at the table, it appeared everyone else agreed.

"A delicious meal, Zuht." Tripp applauded.

"Thank you, I am still working on a stew for tomorrow. I have also put some in the salt barrel in the cellar so that we can take it with us on our journey." Zuht informed us.

"We were truly blessed to have you join us on this quest." Runa said to Zuht.

We all had finished our meals and sat leaning back in our chairs. The sun had set while we were eating, and now only the lanterns and torches lit the hall. Despite us only being five in this large hall, it felt warm and intimate.

"I think it's time we had some desert!" Toree proclaimed.

"Don't tease us! There's no other food in this place beside what Zuht cooked and what was in our bags." I protested.

"No, no. Not food, a desert wine!" clarified Toree.

"Desert wine? What are you on about?" I questioned.

"Yes, you wouldn't know. It has been centuries since the last reserves that Nerick kept had been depleted... it is a special sweet wine, sweeter than mead. Only Nystia produced it. Other than our steel, our wine was our main trade export! Even a guard post would have at least a dozen bottles in it's cellar!" Toree explained.

Toree jumped up and skipped down to the cellar. A few minutes later she skipped back to our table, three bottles in hand. She put them all down and pulled the cork out of one with her teeth, then poured it's contents into our glasses.

"Go ahead, try!" Toree said, eager to see our reactions.

I took a sip, it was much sweeter than any wine or mead I had ever tasted. Not quite to my liking as I usually preferred strong bitter or full bodied ales and wines. Zuht seemed to have the same thoughts as I, but Runa and Tripp looked as if they drank the nectar of the Gods directly from the teat.

"Not for me..." I said pouring the contents of my glass into Runa's.

"I'm afraid it is the same for me..." Zuht said putting his cup on the table.

"What is wrong with you both? Toree, do not listen to them, this is absolutely divine!" Runa said cradling her glass.

"You know, this is the best thing I have ever put in my mouth?" Tripp said, buttering up to Toree.

"Do you often put things in your mouth?" I asked.

Runa almost spit out her wine and Tripp's face turned as red as the color of the bottles on the table. Zuht silently chuckled from his seat while Toree put her hand on Tripp's shoulder.

"Oh, shut up! Don't listen to Jara, she only asks because she's fond of putting her own foot in her mouth." Toree said in Tripp's defense.

"Toree is right, Tripp. You should feel free to put whatever you want in your mouth! Don't let Jara intimidate you!" Runa joked, cracking herself up to the point she had to gasp for air between her laughter.

It was at this point I knew we had all indulged a bit too much wine for the day. Runa was clearly drunk...and by the looks of it so was everyone else - apart from Zuht. This of course did not stop any of us from finishing the open bottles on the table.

"I think I will get an early night, have a good evening." said Zuht, bidding us goodnight.

"Would the rest of you like to throw daggers?" Toree said standing up.

It wasn't the wisest decision in our drunken state, but then again we were not the wisest in our drunken state...

"Absolutely." said Runa, stonefaced.

"Let's do it." Tripp agreed.

We all got up and staggered to the side of the mess hall where a slice of tree trunk sat against the wall. We grabbed some small eating knives from the kitchen and brought them into the hall. As we took turns throwing the blades at the target it became apparent how inebriated we were. Only a handful of throws actually stuck to the target, the rest hit the wall around it and fell to the ground.

We tossed the knives for a while before Runa was actually able to get one to stick in the target. In celebration she pulled me over and gave me a deep, slightly too aggressive kiss. It was the first time we had kissed in front of anyone else; and by Tripp's expression after, it was the first time he had watched anyone kiss like that.

"Did you enjoy the show?" Runa asked Tripp.

"Oh, uh, well, that uh..." Tripp stuttered.

"Have you never kissed anyone before?" I questioned.

"Oh...yes I've kissed lots of women..." Tripp boasted.

"You have never kissed anyone, have you?" Runa asked.

"Never. Not once." Tripp answered honestly.

"Well, someday I'm sure you will have the opportunity." Runa said as she slapped his shoulder.

"Oh stop making fun of the poor boy! Besides, he's landed more throws on that target in the past five minutes than you have the entire time we've been playing!" Toree rebutted.

"Toree's right, let's leave Tripp be...besides, I think we should be getting up to bed." I said as I put my arm around Runa.

"Go to bed? I'm not even slightly tired yet." Runa protested.

"Yes...which is exactly why we should get to bed..." I suggested as I tried to make my intentions known to her.

"Wha....ooooh! Oh yes, we must be off to bed. Early night, early rise...right?" Runa gaffed.

"Will you two be alright by yourselves down here?" I asked before Runa and I made our way upstairs.

"Oh, I'm sure we'll manage. Go, off to bed with you both!" said Toree as she waved us out the room.

Runa and I stumbled back to our room with every intention of continuing our antics from the night before. We undressed each other and warmed ourselves under the covers...but it seemed we both had over-indulged. Within a minute of getting into the bed to cuddle and kiss we both fell into a drunken slumber.

I woke to a bright sun illuminating the room. It was so bright, that as I stepped out of the bed still naked it warmed me like a blanket wrapped around my body. I walked to the window to look outside; there was snow as far as the eye could see...and it was deep. Toree was right, it would be a couple of days before we could travel again.

I went back to the bed and jumped under the covers again, bringing my body against Runa's. I ran my fingers through her hair and caressed her neck and shoulder. Connecting with Runa like this was still a surreal experience, I sought to take advantage of our time here together as much as I could; what would come after we left the safety of this place I did not know.

I fell back asleep holding Runa in my arms. I don't know how long I slept for, but eventually Runa woke me up as she was stretching out in the bed. She let out a deep breath and rolled to face me.

"Good morning." She said with a smile.

"How are you feeling?" I asked, curious how hungover she was.

"Surprisingly well...but I think I could do with a nice long soak in a tub..." She said.

"I think I can help with that." I said as I rolled out of the bed and to the copper tub that sat in the corner of the room.

I conjured some water to fill it, then flames around the bottom to warm it. In only a few minutes the water was warmed.

"You will have to teach that to the servants at the castle!" said Runa, impressed.

"We'll have to make sure we're at the same castle then!" I hinted.

"And in the same bath; we must stink after the past two days. Come, join me!" Runa said as she got out of the bed and into the tub.

I slipped in across from her and melted away into the water. I could feel the mental weight and physical grime leave my body as my muscles relaxed. We sat there soaking in silence for quite some time before saying a word. Eventually Runa broke the silence and we recapped our evening with the others as we helped to scrub each other clean.

Once we felt clean and proper again we put on fresh clothing and decided to make our way down to the armory and try on the harnesses we chose. It would be important to learn how to put it on and take it off before we were out in the wild again. As we exited the room we thought it best to have Toree come with us. She was familiar with the armor and could help us learn more efficiently.

I knocked on her door and called for her.

"Toree? Are you awake?" I called out.

"What do you need?" I heard her voice call from in the room.

"Runa and I are heading down to the armory, would you join us?" I asked.

"I'm a bit occupied at the moment, I will join you when I'm done." she called back.

"I guess we'll have to make do without her for now..." I said to Runa.

"Maybe we can help her with what she's doing first, help speed it up a bit?" Runa suggested.

I nodded in agreement and knocked on her door again.

"Toree!" I called yet again.

"Yes...." Toree answered from her room, yet again.

Runa and I opened the door and walked through the threshold.

"Runa and I thought we could help you out and.....speed...things...up...." I said; trailing off to a stutter as we saw what Toree was occupied with.

We both blushed and Runa's hand shot up to cover her mouth. Before us was Toree naked sitting on top of Tripp in her bed. Tripp turned his head to look at us, the only thing he wore was a smile that ran from ear to ear. Toree went still and turned to look at us.

"I said 'yes', not 'come in'. And what is that look on your faces?" Toree asked, annoyed by our intrusion.

"We, um...you were...and uhh...with Tripp?" I mumbled incoherently.

"What? Just because I'm a few centuries old doesn't mean I don't have needs...besides he's twenty." Toree spat out.

"Almost twenty, actually..." Tripp mumbled.

"Please stop talking." Toree said to Tripp.

"Yes my lady!" Tripp complied.

"Now, you two... let me give you a more clear response since 'I'm occupied' is too open-ended. I'm sure Tripp would not mind if you helped out, but I'd like to do this on my own, and I would rather not speed things up, I much prefer going at my own pace." Toree rattled off to us.

"I like your pace too..." Tripp added.

"Shh, I said no talking." Toree said putting her finger over Tripp's mouth.

We stood there for a moment more, still shocked by the sight.

"Was there something else? Otherwise you are both big girls, I am sure you can behave nicely in the armory, close the door on the way out!" Toree ordered.

We turned and closed the door as we left the room. As soon as we got into the hall we fell onto each other in laughter.

"I was not expecting to walk in on that!" exclaimed Runa as she began to catch her breath.

We eventually composed ourselves to a giggle and went down to the armory. Zuht was sat on a bench, carving a spear he had chosen to take. I was not surprised, the first time I lay eyes on him, he used a spear to fend off a dozen soldiers from Wurth.

"What are you carving into that?" I asked him.

"Prayers, holy symbols, and a better grip." he said as he maintained focus on his blade cutting across the wooden shaft.

"Why?" Runa asked.

Zuht put his knife down and waved for Runa to come and look.

"These inscriptions are to call Tristi down and connect his power to the spear. These prayers here are to guide us on our mission and protect us." Zuht explained.

"Do you really believe that his power could flow through that?" I asked honestly and without any ill-tone.

"Yes, I have seen it be so." Zuht answered as he went back to carving.

"You've seen it? When?" I inquired.

"When I was a boy there was a group of marauders destroying nearby villages in the mountains. They had pillaged every surrounding village, leaving ours for last. There was only two ways into our village through a narrow path carved into the mountains. When we learned they were coming our priest met them in the path and called on Tristi to give him the power to save the town.

Tristi agreed and filled the priest with his power, the priest hit the stone walls of the path with his bare hands and they began to tumble down. The intruders turned and ran but it was too late; the priest called out with his voice and the mountain filled the pass with stone, crushing the marauders and the priest himself." Zuht recanted for Runa and I.

"He crushed himself too?" Runa asked.

"Yes, we are only given Tristi's power for a short amount of time. The power is too intense for a mortal to survive for long; whether the priest was crushed by the stone or broke apart into light itself, the outcome would be the same." Zuht explained.

"It sounds like becoming a priest of Tristi is quite the undertaking, if that is what an outcome may be." I noted.

"It sounds more than it is because of the priest title. If you take that away it is no different than what you two ladies are expected of every day." Zuht remarked.

I nodded as I watched Zuht continue to carve away, the conversation not slowing him down at all. We all thought of priests as having cushy peaceful roles, but they were far more involved in the traumatic than they let on. For those born into lower class, I suppose they looked up at us as having our own cushy lavish lives. In truth we did have a lot of amenities not given to others, but we also put our lives on the line more than the others in this war.

The spies and soldiers from Wurth specifically targeted nobility and commanders for assassination. It was imperative that our tactics were flawless in battle, and if all failed we retreated faster than they could track. Wurth was already the cause of three ancient houses falling.

This was also part of the reason my family and I all split, if we were not in one place together we could not be wiped out. I was to stay in Dragon's Reach, until Unul arrived that is, my brother was at the pass, and my father at the capital. Many other great houses took the same approach. Runa, being the youngest of four sisters, was groomed to command armies as I was. Our older siblings were taught to run castles and govern the lands in which they stood guard over.

In a sense, the circumstances dictated that Runa and I lived harder and faster paced lives than those of our family. Perhaps that is why we connected so deeply so quickly. There is no time for games, we must be authentic or nothing at all. I suppose in that light we are lucky - whether we live to a ripe old age or die in battle young; we would have lived full and true lives...not unlike the priests do.

Runa and I left Zuht to his carving as we grabbed the armor we selected earlier. I helped Runa put her harness on first; it was exceptionally easy to put on and took only about ten minutes. She stretched about and told me where to tighten her bindings. We switched roles and she then helped me into my armor. We opted to forgo the helmets as we had figured most of our foe would be beast. The strain on hearing and our vision would be far more a detriment against wolfmen and brias.

After I was fitted and in my harness I could not help but notice just how light the armor actually was. It felt lighter than hardened leather and seemed to mold to my body perfectly. I rolled my arms around and jumped up and down, I was truly astonished by the smith's magic. The plate was so comfortable and light that I would choose it over a standard gambeson any day.

"Would you like to have a feel for the armor and spar?" Runa asked me.

"I would love to!" I replied, this would be the first time Runa and I crossed swords outside of tournament.

We exited the secret armory and grabbed two training swords with blunted edges from the soldiers room. The swords were heavier than our Aldonis blades, but that was not a bad thing. The heavier blades would help us be more nimble and precise with our lighter swords.

We made our way to the mess hall and stacked the tables to the side. Once we had adequate space we stood opposite each other. I raised my sword and she raised hers. We circled for a moment before standing at the ready - paused in time.

"I will not go easy on you, and I expect the the same!" Runa called out.

Without replying I lunged at her with my blade. She parried and returned with a downward stroke; which I deflected with the ricasso and guard of my sword. I followed through with an elbow to her shoulder which threw her off-balance. Runa fell to her back and I followed up with a heavy strike down.

Runa blocked the strike with her sword, using one hand on the blade and one on the hilt. She kicked me backward to give herself space to rise up. As she rose she came at me with a flurry of strikes, all of which I defended successfully. On her last strike I caught her blade in a bind with my cross guard and hooked her sword from her hands, tossing it to the ground beside her.

She immediately charged me, burying her shoulder into my gut. I knocked the pommel of my sword against her backplate but she was able to lift me and throw me to the ground. My sword flung across the floor and I rolled before Runa could kick at my chest plate. I swept her legs from beneath her and immediately began to grapple for supremacy.

Runa fought back as we became locked in a hopeless draw. I kicked Runa off of me and stumbled to the side. We locked arms again, each trying to bring the other down first. We pushed and shoved until I was able to get my foot behind her leg and take her down. Her unrelenting grip took me down with her and I fell on top, knocking the wind from her.

"Does that mean I win?" I said, beginning to chuckle after our spar.

"Hmm, Lady Jara on top of me, have you won, or is it I who have won?" Runa said as she regained her breath.

"Perhaps it is a draw then?" I said smiling in her face.

"Perhaps..." she said staring into my eyes.

"Perhaps you two should consider moving the rematch into your bedroom?" Toree said sarcastically from the doorway.

"You are one to talk!" I exclaimed, looking over my shoulder to her.

"You walked into my room! I did not have Tripp bound to a table in the mess hall." Toree rebutted.

"Yes, that is not what we do. I mean, I haven't done that, but if you were open to it I suppose we could try....or no, no we don't do that..." Tripp stuttered, nervously glancing between Toree and I.

Toree raised her hand to her head and took a deep breath, not acknowledging Tripp's input. She shook her head and looked at us.

"In all honesty, that was very impressive. I am glad you are staying on top of your skills. I do not know what we face ahead, but I feel confident with you both by my side." Toree said in praise.

"Thank you Toree, that means a lot!" Runa said as we got up on our feet.

"Zuht said that the stew would be ready soon, so perhaps you should both put this room back together and get changed." Toree suggested, which was more of an order.

Runa and I put the tables back and returned the swords to the rack they came from. We put our armor in our bedroom and changed to eat.

"That was a good bout! It has been years since we've sparred like that." exclaimed Runa.

"Yes, we are every bit equal in the sword! I will have to learn new secret techniques to best you!" I said in agreement.

"I would not count on that...but I must say, you looked ravishing in that armor earlier. Had Toree not come in I may have had my way with you right on one of those tables!" Runa joked.

"That sounds like it could be a lot of fun, perhaps I will take you up on that when we are through this quest! However right now I need something in my belly!" I said as I pinched Runa's buttock and made my way out the room.

Downstairs were bowls of Zuht's stew, in the center of the table was a map of Nystia from before it disappeared. As we ate our food Toree laid out our path to the mountains. She gave extra attention to the marsh, there was a very specific path to take; she warned that we would likely see the apparitions of those from the ancient battle that gave the marsh life. Should we get distracted by them we could steer off-course.

A flower was to be our guide through. There is but one type of flower that grows all year round in the marsh, blue and purple in color. They were planted by monks centuries ago to guide people through safely. Now they would be our guide to the mountains.

After our meals and briefing Toree let us know the day's sun had melted a good portion of the snow. We would be able to resume our journey in the morning. We split up to make the most of our last evening here. Zuht went to the armory to finish his carvings, Runa and I to the bedroom to relax, and Tripp thought he was going to join Zuht in the armory until Toree pulled him by his belt to her side and they retired to her room.

"I don't know who I am happier for, Toree or Tripp." Runa said as we shut our door.

"As long as they are both having fun, everyone is a winner in my book!" I joked.

"Hmm..." Runa sounded as she opened the door to the hallway.

Muffled sounds of Tripp and Toree giggling echoed quietly in the hall and Runa smiled before shutting our door again.

"It sounds like they are having fun...perhaps we should too?" Runa angled.

"I don't know when we will have a chance to speak in private like this again, why not sit by the fire with me?" I suggested.

"Of course, what's on your mind?" she asked softly as we sat in two chairs beside the fire.

"All my life I have itched to play a larger role in the kingdom. When I was ordered back to Dragon's Reach from the front lines and my brother sent to the pass, I felt as if all my aspirations had burned before my eyes. My nights strategizing battlefield tactics became hosting political feasts and bringing strangers to my bed for a thrill.

Then Unul arrives a year and a half later speaking nonsense about magic, fairytales, and orders from the king. I am thrust into a hap-hazard magical ritual the same night and suddenly I was back on the battlefield! I felt validated...but now I am filled with fear and worry.

My machismo attitude has become a mask I put on each day, my sarcasm the strings that keep it tied. I have no aspirations of becoming a conqueror, I have no interest in court titles, but I do want to help the people of the kingdom. I fear now because of my family's involvement and the gravity of what is at stake I will fall short and Nerick will be lost..." I admitted.

It felt like an anvil off my shoulders. Runa looked at me for a moment, then moved her chair directly in front of mine. She sat and looked me in the eyes, grabbing both my hands in hers.

"Your fears are my own; I too have struggled to find my place. With so many older siblings I have not known where I belong aside from the battlefield, there is no future for me in court. I too have felt the pressure of the kingdom's wellbeing.

Each battle has had a tremendous impact, both good and bad - those have all been a result of my decisions. Now I am suddenly on a quest through what should be a bedtime story and the kingdom falls again on my shoulders. I feel the weight you bear...

My solace has been that the weight is shared by you and the others. We have all taken this on together, and it has helped ease the burden...but when this is through I have wondered, 'what then?' Where will I go? If the war is won, what use is there for a commander with no battles? If the war is lost, will I live in exile, unable to save the innocent?" Runa said to me, letting her own fears out.

"It seems like we both have our share fill of fears. I have struggled with where I belong for so long I've lost sight of where I am!" I said.

"And where are you now?" Runa questioned.

"Sitting in a room, looking at my closest friend, confidant and lover, holding her hands and watching the fire flicker on her eyes..." I replied.

"I need to be honest, the first 'place' I've felt I belong is beside you. It started at the capital like a puzzle revealing itself when completed. I could not leave your side when you were feverish at the outpost, and when I thought you were in trouble at the pond I felt that fire stoke itself...that's when I knew I had to kiss you..." Runa admitted.

"I have felt whole when I am with you...it is like I do not care what tomorrow brings, I am happy in this moment...Runa...I would very much like if you would stand beside me as equals and partners - through this quest and whatever comes after..." I said as I gazed into her eyes.

"Jara, there is no place that I would rather be than beside you...or under you...or sometimes even on top of you..." she said with a smile and a giggle.

Runa leaned into me and we kissed passionately beside the fire. We spent our last night in the room making love, unlike the raw lust we shared previously. For the first time I felt truly whole...I nestled my head upon Runa's chest in our bed. She sang the song I remembered from my fevers until we both drifted to sleep.

The Winter Marsh

Chapter 19

I looked out the window as Runa fastened her sword belt around her waist, yesterday's sun had indeed melted much of the snow. I could see spots of grass, rocks, and mud poking through the remnants of the blizzard.

"Are you ready?" I asked Runa, I had already suited up for our journey and was eager to move.

"Yes, but would you mind fixing my braids before we join the others?" asked Runa.

"Of course, come here..." I beckoned.

Runa walked over and looked out the window herself as I undid her old braids, before brushing and braiding her hair again. It was soft and oiled, always smelling like lavender.

"What do you think of the specters Toree has warned us of in the marsh?" Runa asked.

"I think we've already fought three types of beasts from nightmares; if these pose no threat I welcome them!" I answered.

"Yes, but still, it is strange that we should encounter soldiers from an ancient war. Could you imagine if these things happened in Nerick? The whole north of the kingdom would relocate!" said Runa.

"It is a good thing that Nerick is not a kingdom of magic like this place then!" I responded.

I finished Runa's hair and we grabbed our sacks, throwing them over our shoulders to make our way to the mess hall. When we arrived Zuht had already laid out new rations of cured venison for us all to pack. Runa and I took one piece to have now and placed the rest in our sacks.

Zuht was in his armor, he chose a harness gilded with fine gold and etchings of the sun and stars; it was very befitting a priest of Tristi. Runa and I chose simpler armor, which thanks to our prior bout already had been broken in with scrapes and scratches. Then Toree and Tripp walked into the room.

"Good morning, did you both get a good night's rest for today's journey?" I asked.

"I did not sleep a wink! I feel like I can take on the entire world!" Tripp boasted.

"Right...Toree, you have quite the effect on people..." I said.

"What can I say, you learn a thing or two when you have been around as long as I have..." Toree said sarcastically.

"Do you think we will run into anything before we reach the marsh?" Runa asked.

"No, judging by the birds in the sky I believe all will be quiet." Toree replied.

"Right, are we off then?" asked Runa, eager to lay eyes on the marsh herself.

"If all of you have everything you need on you, then yes." Toree answered.

We all nodded and threw our bags onto our backs. Zuht grabbed his spear and we all made our way to the foyer and out the door, into the first level of the quarry. Toree paused as she carried the rear of our column out; feeling the jam of the main door, she then closed it behind her gently.

As we walked up the ramp and out of the quarry, onto the path towards the marsh, I could not help but feel proud of our small group. Leading to this point we travelled in little more than clothing of our choice, some light armor accompanying when needed. Now we marched toward a haunted marsh like the adventurers of stories.

Tripp wore colors of green and yellow, Runa wore white and gold, Zuht his gold, I wore blue, and Toree wore an extravagant red and black floral design made of silks and contrasting bright silver armor. Toree did not tell us directly, but I believe the armor she donned had actually been hers all those centuries ago. It was like the parade before a tournament, and it seemed to invigorate us all.

Toree was correct in her assumption, the only thing we battled for the majority of the morning was the snow and mud that was left. We made our way through a rocky terrain with little vegetation in sight. The sun in a cloudless sky kept our spirits up and our direction steady.

"Would anyone like a song?" Tripp asked.

"I am not great at singing while traversing rocky terrain..." Runa said, assuming Tripp was offering up her services for the group.

"No need to strain your voice, I will sing for us all." Tripp said.

"You will sing? When did you take up singing?" I asked.

"For years! Sir Krinn had a bard travel with us for a time. I asked him to teach me how to sing and he obliged!" Tripp informed us.

"Why keep it a secret all this time?" I questioned.

"Well, it just didn't seem like the right time before...but after nearly dying, being brought back to life, and then being taken to bed by the most beautiful woman I have ever seen...now seems the time." Tripp explained.

"That is very sweet of you." Toree said, rubbing her hand on Tripp's hair while he blushed.

"There are so many things I want to say right now, but out of respect for Toree; I wont. Go on, sing then." I said to Tripp.

Tripp began to sing as we walked through the slushy snow. I am not sure what I expected, but he was actually quite adept at singing. His voice carried beautiful ballads across the bright white landscape on our uphill journey. We all became lost in the song and moved hypnotically towards our destination.

By midday we had reached the top of the hill. In front of our eyes was a massive marsh and a mountain range in the distance. The mountains were clearly visible, but the marsh was covered in a patchy white and grey mist. Tripp's song faded off as we surveyed the sights before us.

"Do you see where the two mountains meet? That is our destination. From there we will follow the canyon between to the center of Nystia." said Toree as she pointed towards the mountains.

"How long is the journey to the keep?" Runa asked Toree.

"With no trouble we can make it in three days." Toree answered.

"Great, three weeks then." I said in a sarcastically bright voice.

"Whatever we find, we will do so together." Toree reassured us.

We began our short descent toward the marsh. On our path were bright purple and blue flowers. These poked through any snow and seemed to be unaffected by the frosts. They trailed into the marsh itself, weaving in and out of the mist.

"Lady Toree, how is it that these flowers bloom even below the snow?" Zuht asked.

"These flowers were 'bred' to survive the coldest winters and the hottest summers. They came to be thanks to the monks that cleared the break that once had a hold over this place. The monks planted them to guide people through the marsh safely. There is only one path that will lead to the other side, without their guidance no one would make it through." Toree explained.

"How magnificent..." marveled Zuht.

"Here that again and take notice; we must follow these flowers! You may be distracted by the specters of the past that reside within the passing mists, do not loose sight of these flowers." directed Toree.

We nodded in understanding. Satisfied with her warning, Toree stepped onto the first section of path through the marsh. We followed her lead for quite some time, winding around and sometimes seemingly heading back towards the direction we had just come in. We had gone on for a few hours before finding ourselves facing one of the passing mists. The colors of the mist glowed with the waning sun lighting the sky a vivid shade of orange.

"What do we do?" Tripp asked.

"Not far from here there is an elevated island above the marsh, it has been a safe haven for me in the past; there is no reason it should not be again." Toree said, ignoring the mist.

"You mean we will make camp in this place?" Runa asked.

"We have no other option, and it sounds much worse than it is. I believe you will find the view quite memorable." Toree responded.

"And the mist?" Tripp asked again.

"Nothing more than a fog, the spirits within a scene from a battlefield, not unlike what we have all lived through already. Jara, come here and put your hand to the ground." Toree said, kneeling on one leg placing her own hand on the ground.

I knelt beside her and did as she asked.

"What are we doing?" I asked her.

"We will need some extra help guiding through this place at dusk. Close your eyes and breathe the lifeforce in from the earth beneath you. As you breathe out see that same energy flow into the flowers we follow, don't stop until you can see the flowers glow in your mind." She directed.

I did as she asked. As my hand was to the ground I could feel the energy flow up into my body. I sent it back down and to the flowers, as I did so I could see the flowers glowing vividly in my mind. After only a few moments I felt like the task was done and opened my eyes; around us the flowers were in fact glowing - just as I had seen in my mind's eye.

"Well done, Jara." congratulated Toree.

"Well this will certainly help us navigate in the low light!" Runa exclaimed.

"Now, let's make our way through the mist, we still have a short way to go before we can rest for the evening. Following the glow of the flowers while we make our way through. The only danger inside is loosing sight of our path!" Toree warned.

One by one each of us made our way into the mist. As I stepped inside I was immediately greeted with apparitions donned in war gear walking around with no clear goal. They did not seem real as those in the break were, they seemed to be made of the mist and nothing more, only the haze allowed them to form their bodies. Some wandered with sword or spear in hand, some holding a wound that no longer bleeds, others just stood - eerily staring at us with blank eyes as we walked past.

None of us gave them any attention aside from our passing gaze. The glow of the flowers shone through the fog and we continued on our path. I had been privy to many sights prior to this quest, and many more since...the sight of these restless souls on this ancient battlefield stood out to me.

They had all marched, fought, and died here for a cause either they believed in or those in control believed in. It was nothing new to me, as a warrior you must be prepared to die in battle; but this was something else entirely. To be killed in battle can be attributed to poor skills or poor luck; but to never find peace after death, even a millennia later, that is a curse I would not wish on any.

We continued through, eventually leaving the mist behind us. Above us was a clear sky in pink and purple. The sun was setting, and as I looked around I could see the face of sorrow upon each one of my companions. The mist, while not physically harmful, was an emotional dagger. For us this sunset marked our first night back on the trail, for the spirits stuck here it was nothing more than a droplet in the ocean of time.

As the sun went down we focused on following the glow of the flowers. Toree and I created flames above us all so that we could walk without loosing our footing in the darkness; the flowers showed us our way but did little to light the path. After a short while longer we could see the island Toree spoke of.

In the darkness the flowers' glow illuminated a raised area of land. It was a hill in the middle of the marsh, it's size was nearly that of the barrack we just left. The moons were full in the sky and their moonlight lit the stone and grass that covered our soon-to-be camp.

"That is it, we make camp there tonight." said Toree.

"There will be no where to pitch our tents on that place...it is just rock and frozen grass." Tripp responded.

"In this armor you will not need a tent. The sky is clear, and the robes and armor you all wear are unlike that in Nerick. They will keep you warm in the cold, and cool in the heat. Use your rucksack under your head and you will sleep well. Go, make yourselves comfortable; we move at first light." rebutted Toree.

Runa and I shrugged at each other and continued onto the island. We walked up to an area of exposed grass on the far side and planted ourselves down. Zuht went off on his own, choosing a small clearing in the midst of dense area of the glowing flowers. Toree and Tripp to a different side of the island, opting to get a view of the moons.

Runa and I did not speak much, instead choosing to enjoy the silence in each others company. We lay down facing the stars, the sight was unlike anything I had seen in Nerick. In the night sky the stars glistened off the marsh beneath us, it was as if there was no horizon, we floated on an island amongst the stars in complete silence. Eventually the stars hypnotized Runa and I as we drifted off to sleep.

I woke early, the sun's light had just begun to paint a pink sky overhead and I felt surprisingly refreshed. I stood and made my way to the tallest part of the island to get a view of our path today. The glow of the flowers had dulled over the night, I was shocked that they still illuminated at all.

I looked across the marsh to the mountains we were heading toward to get a sense of our direction. The haunted mists over this place shifted with the wind; and using the breeze as a gauge I quickly concluded we would be spending some time in the mists today. Given how close we were to the mountains, I saw no reason why we could not reach our destination by nightfall.

I decided we could use some extra guidance in the mists today, so I reached down and performed the motion Toree taught me to illuminate the flowers. It took much less time today than it had yesterday and I felt rather proud of myself, which I wore with a big grin.

"Well done!" Toree applauded as she walked toward me.

"Oh, thank you...I didn't realize you were awake." I said, slightly startled.

"I have not been here in quite some time, and if you ignore the haunted mists passing by- it's quite a beautiful place." Toree continued.

"Since it is just the two of us awake right now I must ask... Tripp?" I questioned.

"I thought you would bring that up at some point..." Toree said.

"Well? Why Tripp?" I asked again.

"His naivety is amusing, his is more noble than most lords and ladies I have met, and his skill and bravery far exceed his position. He is an honest and noble knight in everything but title." Toree answered.

"I would expect that response from someone at court, not my mentor!" I protested.

"Fine, if you want honesty I shall give it...Tripp reminds me of myself at that age, before any events made me cynical and hard. I enjoy spending time with him because I feel like it is pulling that part of me back out. I had put all connection with others aside over a century ago, something about him has opened me up again.

I believe the dagger you carry is not only the key to end to Lucian's nightmare, but also my curse...and in truth I do not expect to return from this journey, nor do I feel like I need to. I have lived many lifetimes over but my appearance betrays who I am inside. I am old and I am tired, but I do not want to see my life end that way.

Tripp is helping me not be that old and tired woman I have felt like for a hundred years. I need not explain to you that feeling, or do you not feel the same sense of home when you have nestled your head between Runa's breasts? Aside from all of that; for someone of low stature, he has rather large assets..." Toree explained.

"You have quite the way with words this morning... 'assets' aside, I do understand. Do you really believe when the curse is broken you will die?" I asked.

"I do, and I am at peace with that." Toree said calmly.

"Have you told Tripp this?" I asked her.

"I will when the time is right." she responded.

"Who will teach me when you are gone?" I asked as I processed my emotions inside myself.

"It is all within you now, generations of your family's knowledge. I am but a crutch now, your mother imprinted all her knowledge in you before we left the spirit realm. Your family is capable of many more things than even I, follow your instincts and when the time is right new abilities will reveal themselves to you." she explained.

"If only there was some more time..." I said to her.

"Jara, after nearly four hundred years there is only one thing I can tell you with absolute certainty: there is never enough time, yet you will always have all the time in the world." she said sweetly.

As cryptic as her response was, I felt like I understood the gist of it. This all was quite a lot to take in, especially now knowing there were more undiscovered abilities within me. I felt the need to lighten the mood before the others woke up, not for Toree (who seemed completely content in herself and the situation), but for myself.

"You know...it has been quite a while since I have heard any worthwhile gossip...just out of curiosity, about how large are those assets you mentioned?" I asked coyly.

Toree cracked a smile and we spent some time talking about things of absolutely zero importance. It seems that was also able to bring her back to days long past as well. I completely understood Toree, and I can not say I would do otherwise in her shoes.

Over the time I had spent with Toree, and the memories she had let me into, I had grown to look at her as an older sister. My relationship to my brother had always been strained; he was far too ruthless and arrogant...not that I couldn't be, but my conscious would not allow me to even think of things he would act on.

I believe that is why I was called back to Dragon's Reach while he went off to guard the pass; he was an ox in a cupboard. What state the court at the castle would be in when I returned I did not know. The best thing I could do is find my father on this journey and return to Dragon's Reach before too much damage could be done.

Toree now filled a void in my life that I did not know was there. I enjoyed our conversations, I looked up to her for guidance, and I respected her greatly. With my mother here only in body, Toree had become my matriarch. I knew that if she was right and did not survive the curse breaking I would take that role.

I could see Runa and the others beginning to rise so I quickly pushed my thoughts and emotions back down. One day I would let them out and deal with it all, but it could not be now.

The others all came to meet us in their own time as they surveyed the sunrise over the marsh. The winds began to pick up and the mists quickly rolled in.

"Right then, if we get moving now we can be at the base of the mountain by nightfall." Toree informed us, corralling us onto the path of glowing flowers like sheep into a penn.

We made our way across the soggy patches of land that scattered across the marsh. We had weaved in and out of the ghostly fog for the better part of the day without incident. The winds had continued to pick up speed as the day went on and the mist seemed to spread across the entire marsh, we only had the glow of the flowers to guide us.

As we made our way through the mist something changed...the spirits stopped paying us attention and instead looked in unison to one side. I was not the only one that noticed, Zuht stopped moving and made his spear ready, Runa drew her sword, Toree made herself ready to use her powers, Tripp and I also drew swords.

"Do you hear that?" Runa asked us.

We all were silent and listened to the silence of the marshland... water was moving...

"Toree, what lives in the waters here?" I asked quietly.

"Nothing...the only thing that inhabits this place are the bones of the dead..." Toree said as she focused intently on where the sound was coming from.

We heard strange animal noises. They sounded familiar but I could not place from where...as the sounds got closer I recognized it...

"Briars..." I said to the others.

"All the way out here?" Tripp questioned.

"It makes sense, they are the only creatures that could traverse the terrain without knowing the path across." Runa mused.

"I wonder how many there are..." Zuht said.

"Two, I can hear the sounds of two sets of legs wading in the water." Toree answered.

"What do we do?" Runa asked.

"We must stand and fight, let us use this terrain to our advantage. The fog, will impede their vision and the mud will slow them down and make their movements sloppy." said Toree.

"They are giants, how will we take them down?" Tripp asked.

"I used nothing more than fire magic the last time, Jara, if you can get a flame in through their mouth you can take them down from the inside out. The rest of you, try to strike the wrists and thighs, their lower legs are too tough even for Aldonis blades. If you can get them on their back strike at the throat and eyes." Toree directed.

We all waited at the ready like statues. There was a loud throat call from the direction we faced. The silent spirits in the mist made it hard to see anything further than a few paces away. I could hear the mud slushing closer to us, then another loud throat call.

We could not see anything but a large shadow in the mist, one was nearly upon us, the other silent... As the the briar in front grew yet closer we could begin to see it's outline more clearly. Before it could react to us Toree let a flame loose toward it's head. Part of the flame landed on the beast and it let out another yell, this time in distress. Zuht charged it with his spear, piercing the briar's thigh, he yanked his spear to the side and cut through the thigh deeply.

The briar fell to it's knees and wildly swung it's arms at us. Tripp managed to cut a tendon in it's right arm, opening it up long enough for Runa to swing at it's throat, which she cut but not deep enough. I ran up and drove my sword through it's eye, twisting it inside the beasts head.

The creature let out it's last breath of life and went motionless. I tried to pull my sword out but it had become stuck on the briar's thick skull. I left it there as I quickly pulled out Alaia, turning to see where the other beast was.

Before we knew what was upon us the other briar charged, knocking Toree, Runa, and Tripp to the ground. It had run out of sight and the others were still trying to get their breath back after having the wind knocked out of them. Zuht and I looked at each other and made ready as we stood back to back, circling and waiting to see where it would come from.

The throat calls of the beast seemed to echo across the marsh and gave us no clear direction. That's when an idea came to me.

"Zuht, get down on your knee." I urged.

Zuht did as I asked without question. I conjured a ring of fire and sent it in all directions around us. Zuht stood back up and we looked at the travelling halo of fire.

"There!" Zuht called.

The flame had made contact with the beast in Zuht's direction. It began to charge us again, this time Zuht planted the base of his spear on the ground and the creature impaled it's own leg on it. The briar fell to the side in a howl of pain.

I felt a cold breeze upon my face and I felt something unlock in me... I conjured a stream of water over the fallen beast and saw it become ice in my mind, as I visualized it became so. Suspended over the briar's head was a massive spear made of ice! I sent it hurling downwards, driving it through the beasts head. The creatures muscles spasmed for a moment before going still.

"Excellent job, lady sorceress!" congratulated Zuht.

"Well done yourself! You had better be careful with these titles, I like that one!" I replied as I patted his back.

The others had managed to pull themselves up and wiped their blades off before sheathing them again.

"You two handled that rather well!" Tripp applauded.

"We all did a good job considering...but I can use someone's help getting my sword out of that ones head!" I said, pointing to my blade sticking out of the briar's eye.

"I think I can help with that..." Toree said as she conjured a wind that pulled my sword from the skull and hurled it across and into the ground before me.

"You will have to teach me that trick..." I said to her.

"In due time! Well done all, now we must not let this deter us from continuing. Onwards!" Toree rallied.

Her energy was encouraging, but not needed. The flowers and mazes of dry land across the marsh, coupled with the soundless specters, had made us all weary. We had grown tired of this place and were ready for a change of scenery.

Everyone shook themselves off and wiped down their weapons before sheathing them. We immediately went back on the move with renewed purpose - for none of us cared to battle beasts in a haunted mist again.

"Toree, forgive me for thinking too far ahead, but is there another way back to Nerick or are we to take this same path back?" Runa asked.

"Worry not, there is another route. None but Jara and I know the way." She answered, much to my confusion.

"You must be mistaken, I have never been until now..." I corrected.

"Yes, you have never been here before - but your ancestors have. When it is time ask and they will show you the way." Toree said.

"Well...why not take that path instead?" Runa asked Toree.

"The other path is much longer and will return us to a different place in Nerick. We needed to handle Enex, this was the only route we could take." Toree explained.

The explanation left them all satisfied and me confused. How would I call on my ancestors to show me a path I've never taken? I suppose I would have to trust that Toree was right and it would come when it was supposed to.

We picked up our pace, only stopping to take a vote whether we would rest before we left the marsh. The vote was unsurprisingly a unanimous no and we immediately pushed forward again.

A few hours later the wind had come to a standstill and our path seemed clear of the mists. It was now late afternoon and we were nearly out. The mountains that had seemed painted against the sky yesterday were now giants overlooking us.

We followed the flower path to the outskirts of the marsh... finally there was solid land within sight! As we made our way across the last of the marsh's maze and onto the hill beyond we all breathed in delight. We had successfully traversed the Winter Marsh. I was unsure of how my father and his men made it across, but then again, it was summer when he left so the conditions would have been more favorable.

"Thank the Gods!" Runa said sprinting up the hill beyond the marsh.

She let herself drop to the ground sprawled out. Tripp walked slowly up until stopping to sit and look at the marsh we had just crossed, Toree soon joined him. I too plopped myself down on my bottom, enjoying a rest from the day's travel and fighting. Zuht knelt beside the marsh waters in prayer. I watched him pray there for a short while until he stood and made his way to us.

"What were you praying for, if you don't mind my intrusion?" I asked him.

"I was praying that when we are through with this quest Tristi would allow the spirits of those trapped there to rest." He said.

"Quite a noble prayer." I said.

"Not noble, just kind." Zuht rebutted.

The priest spoke the truth. Were there a way to bring the spirits eternal rest I would certainly do so. It is a fate undeserved by the pawns of kings' games.

"There is light yet left, are we to camp here or move onward?" Zuht asked Toree.

"You are quite right. We must head for the gorge where the mountains meet. There was once a temple that sat beside a stream that flowed from the peaks, we can refill our canteens and set up camp once there." Toree responded.

"A temple there?" Tripp asked.

"Why would anyone build a temple in the middle of nowhere?" Runa asked.

"These two mountains are powerful places of spiritual power. It was said the stone there holds memories; the peak on the left symbolizes destruction, the peak on the right creation. The temple was a place for monks and pilgrims to learn to harness both. They built a great gate across the gorge called 'The Gateway of the Gods'.

This was also a direct passage to the queen's castle, all the villages and cities to the left of this mountain range could use the path to get to the capital for festivals or a summons' quickly. A great battle for control of the pass took place here, led by Jara's ancestor Ren." Toree explained.

"What was the outcome of the battle there?" I asked.

"Ren and her forces drove through Lucian's army and took control. It was not an easy task and many good men were lost. In the end it mattered not, which is why we all stand here now." Toree lamented.

"And the temple?" Runa asked.

"I do not know what became of the temple, I assume it vanished with everything else here. It is better off, the monks had spent too much time meditating around the energy there and were known to go mad." Toree suggested.

"How fascinating... I would very much like to meditate where the temple stood when we arrive." Zuht said.

"Well, you won't have to wait much longer, it is but an hour's walk from here. We can get to the gate by sunset if we leave now." said Toree.

Finding a spot to camp and get fresh water sounded welcoming. We all got to our feet and followed Toree over the hill and through sparse woods towards the Gate of the Gods.

The Temple of Ilinir

Chapter 20

We had been making our way through the woods when we came upon the stream Toree mentioned. We all quickly stopped to drink and fill our canteens. The water tasted sweet like a mead and we were all eager to get our fill. The setting sun lit the stream in red and pink as it's rays landed around us. The water was made more refreshing by the cool winter weather chilling it as it flowed from the snow covered peaks above.

Toree suggested we continue moving before dark, a suggestion we all agreed with. We continued through, now following the trickling stream. As we exited the woods there was one more hill which the stream cut through. Just over the hill we could all make out a small and steady column of smoke...

"Do you think that's my father's party?" I asked Toree.

"Unfortunately I doubt that very much...nothing living should be here...make ready your weapons!" commanded Toree.

We all drew swords and made ourselves small as we went over the hill...as we reached the top the sight took us all by surprise...

"It can't be..." Toree stuttered.

Before us stood the temple Toree told us about, smoke rising from it's many chimneys. In front were four metal baskets lit with the same flaming rocks from the barracks. The temple sat beside the gorge, which had a large stone wall and locked gate barring us from entry.

"Could this not be another building which has appeared from the spirit realm?" I asked.

"No, the last I saw this place it was pristine... see how the foliage now covers nearly the whole structure? And the guardhouse was not lit when it reemerged..." she responded.

"I do not feel uneasy here, perhaps we should go in and see for ourselves?" Zuht suggested.

"Yes, but do not sheath your weapons unless I say." Toree agreed.

We all walked cautiously to temple doors and pushed them open... as we stepped inside we noticed cobwebs hanging about, the floors were swept and every lantern and fire was lit. On the walls hung tattered tapestries, and in the air was the smell of...chicken?

"Shut the door if you are coming in here! You will let a draft in!" a young man's voice called out from a nearby room.

We looked at each other confused, Toree nodded at the man's request and Tripp slowly closed the doors. We all walked cautiously towards the room the voice came from, swords still in hand...

"Lady Toree, I must say I don't recall you ever having such poor manners! Hurry up now or the food will get cold!" the voice called out again.

"How do you know who I am?" Toree called out.

"Do I not know who you are? Perhaps you're right, perhaps I know who you were, or who you think you are, or who you think I think you are but are not yet? Or maybe who you are no longer but yet yearn to be once again? It is not important, the food will be cold soon and I will have to slaughter another chicken! Come and sit before it gets cold! Tell your apprentice to come too!" the voice called out.

Our faces showed more confusion than words could, yet it seemed Toree recognized the banter of this madman. Her face was perplexed but her eyebrows elevated. She sheathed her sword and walked to the room. We followed quickly behind her with our swords still in hand.

The room we entered had a large hearth with a glowing fire within. The ceilings were arched and covered by wood, in the center a long wooden table sat with a chandelier of the flaming stones above. Food adorned the table and at the end stood a young man in a blue robe.

"Andraas?" She said, staring at a skinny young man in his mid twenties with long blond hair tied back in a sloppy ponytail.

"What is this? By the Gods! He did not tell me there would be other guests! Curse that foul whore's son!" said Andraas, frustrated.

"Who said I would be coming here? And how is it possible that you are here?" Toree questioned.

"Who? That pompous prick of yours! He was shown you would be not far behind him but said nothing of other company!" Andraas exclaimed.

"Who are you talking about?" Toree questioned again, now getting agitated.

"Have these years made you daft?! Lucian! Who else?" Andraas declared.

"Lucian! Where!? Here?" Toree said pulling her sword out again and creating a large ball of fire over her free hand.

"Yes, of course Lucian! He's long gone now, how should I know where to? He came months ago! ...or umm, maybe days ago...perhaps centuries ago? How should I know that either! I stopped counting the days ages ago!" said Andraas, flustered.

"How is that possible?" Toree questioned again.

"Ahh, I see! There is much we must discuss! But first there is much to eat! After we eat I have much to tell!" Andraas said with an eccentric smile.

Toree extinguished the flame and sheathed her sword again.

"The rest of you! Put your swords down and eat! You are safe here from all but your minds! Sit! Eat!" Andraas insisted.

Toree nodded to us and we sheathed our weapons and each took an uncomfortable seat at the long table. Andraas poured us wine and ripped off pieces of the chicken and bread with his bare hands before putting it on plates and handing them to us.

"Where are the rest of the monks?" Toree questioned.

"Shh! Does this look like story time to you? Eat and then we will talk!" Andraas rebutted.

It looked like Toree had dealt with this before. We all did as he asked and ate the meal he had prepared. It felt as if I was in some sort of drunken dream, but the delicious taste of the food proved otherwise.

"It is good isn't it!" Andraas exclaimed.

"Yes, this is deli-"

"Shh! I did not ask you to speak, I simply said the food was good! There will be no speaking until everyone is finished!" Andraas said, cutting off Tripp.

I could not imagine a more surreal and strange situation to be in if I tried. Judging by the look on Runa and Zuht's face, I was not alone. Confusion aside, it appeared we would not be getting any answers until we had cleared our plates.

The meal was quiet, and we all ate our food as we shot off looks of uncertainty to each other. The only two that ate with any normalcy was Toree and this Andraas she seemed to recognize. The food we ate had many of the same flavors that we tasted in the break and the barrack...the thought occurred to me that we may be in a break.

"No, this is no break young sorceress! We are here both now and then, heading towards what has yet to be!" Andraas exclaimed.

Everyone looked at me and Andraas in confusion, we had all remained silent, my thoughts were only just that...thoughts... yet Andraas knew what I was thinking?

"How did you -"

"Shh! I said no speaking. I am the host, so I will speak." Andraas said cutting me off this time.

"But how could you know my thoughts?" I asked anyway.

"Lady Toree, I must say your companions have terrible table manners! I will answer this one voiced question now; because I can hear your thoughts!" Andraas answered.

We all looked at each other concerned... being with someone who could read minds while on a secret quest was not an ideal place to be. We all looked around at each other again.

"Fine! I will answer all your questions! Just please, finish your food after!" Andraas addressed the group as he wiped his grease covered hands on a cloth on the table.

"First, each of you give me your names...quietly..." said Andraas looking around the table.

Toree was the only one that ate her food as usual and seemed to garner no attention from Andraas.

"Ah, so you are the beautiful Runa that is so stuck in your lover's mind!" He said to Runa as he glanced over to me.

"I am a mind reader, not a fortuneteller! I could not possibly know how many of you there would be! What a waste of a question!" continued Andraas as he stared at a now-blushing Runa.

"No, you are not dreaming Tripp. I do appreciate the simple question however!" he said to Tripp.

"Well, it is a pleasure to meet you Zuht, priest of Tristi! I too find this place calm and inviting!" Andraas said to Zuht.

"And you!" Andraas directed towards me.

I did not have any conscious thoughts in my mind aside from how he knew I had Toree's powers with out me thinking or saying anything about it.

"You are full of thoughts, Jara of Dragon's Reach... to answer your first question, all those that possess magic have an air about them. All you need is to listen to your unseen eye and you can pick one out of a crowd! The questions you are not yet aware you have asked will be answered later." Andraas said to me.

I concluded that I was definitely not dreaming, and that this was the strangest dinner I had ever been a part of...

We were all uncertain how the night would play out, but for now it seemed the next step was to simply abide by the madman's directions. We ate the rest of the meal in silence, only the fire cracking on the magical stones and the slurping of food could be heard echoing throughout the surprisingly comfy room.

We had all finished and set ourselves back in the chairs. Andraas was the last eating; still gnawing at a piece of bread and slurping back his wine.

"Very well, I see you all want answers so I will give them, but only to the sorceresses! You two may follow me to my study, the rest of you feel free to wander the halls." said Andraas as he rose from the table.

Runa glanced at me, to which I could only reply with an unsure shrug. I stood up and followed Andraas and Toree out of the room we had eaten in and down a hall. The place was lit with the same stones that lit the other buildings we had seen since entering the borders of Nystia. We turned a corner and continued up a staircase to the second floor. The walls were largely bare and more modest than the dining area.

There was a landing halfway up the staircase, and off of that landing was a doorway, which we walked through. As we walked into the room all thoughts of modesty fell to the ground and shattered. Inside was a warmly lit study, the walls were covered with elaborately carved bookcases and paneling. There sat a desk in the corner and on either side of the room were two large fireplaces, both roaring. Across the floors were animal furs, and there also sat a variety of beautiful chairs across the room.

Andraas motioned for us both to take a seat and closed the door behind. There were no windows in the room, yet it was warmly lit from the fires and chandeliers which hung overhead. Andraas walked to his desk and grabbed a bottle of mead. He handed us both a glass and poured the mead in, we each took a sip of the delicious beverage as he drank straight from the bottle, showing little of the sophistication the room around us implied.

"Let us get straight to the point, what happened to Lucian and how is it you are here now?" Toree said, breaking the silence.

"Each are stories of their own, yet intricately intertwined! Perhaps I should begin with how it is I am here sitting with you, although I could ask the same of you! I have not seen you since before Nystia fell, yet here you sit! There is no need to go over it though, I have seen what has been by using the Pool of Ilinir!" Andraas responded.

"What is the Pool of Ilinir?" I asked.

"Toree, how is it this girl knows so little?" Andraas asked, ignoring me completely.

"Her powers have only just awoken, the world is not what it was. She was not taught our history or our ways. Not that you follow anyone's ways except your own..." Toree rebuffed.

"When I told you the story of how the Winter Marsh came to be, and the opposing energies of the mountains... the armies met here because of the energy the lands hold. Here between the two mountains there is a cave with a pool inside, it was found by the first king of Nystia, King Ilinir. He was shown in the pool how to melt the snow and win the battle, uniting the lands and creating Nystia.

After the battle the break formed. The monks that came to repair it built this temple over the cave; blocking others from accessing the pool and it's prophetic qualities. Only the monks here had access to it, this is how they learned how the break over the marsh would be dispelled...but it does still not explain how it is Andraas is here..." Toree explained.

"Very well, very well! To answer that we need to go back a few hundred years! I'll have to gather all my memories together first! Now where did I leave them..." Andraas said sarcastically.

"Mad and forgetful now?" said Toree, smirking.

"You try hearing everything people think for a lifetime and see how sane you remain! There is far too much to catch you up on. Come, I will just show you!" Andraas said as he stood up and placed his hands on me and Toree's heads.

Without warning Toree and I were transported to the steps outside the temple. The sun was bright overhead and marching forward with an army behind was Lucian. Lucian wore battle armor and carried a sword at his side.

"Where are we?" I asked Toree.

"We are in Andraas' memories...I suppose this is the clearest way to find out what actually happened..." answered Toree.

Lucian walked up the steps to the door where Andraas stood along side two other monks.

"I have no desire to bring trouble to your temple, I just need to see the Pool of Ilinir. Take me to it and I will reward you all handsomely when I am king." Lucian said to the three monks.

"It is forbidden, you can not see the pool." An older monk said to Lucian.

Lucian drew his sword and without hesitation cut the monk's head clean off his shoulders. The monks head rolled down the steps as his body collapsed on itself. Andraas and the other monk stepped back.

"You know we cannot! We are sworn to protect the pool from all those that have not taken the oath!" second monk remarked nervously.

"Your oaths will be useless if you are all dead! A moment with the pool is all I desire...will you reconsider my offer?" Lucian asked again.

"I will not!" the second monk defiantly declared.

"Then you will die too." Lucian said numbly as he used the cross guard of his sword to break the second monk's cheekbone and eye socket.

The monk fell to the ground in agony, grabbing his face and rolling about. Lucian kicked his face with his boot and looked at Andraas.

"You! You are that mad mind reader that has been talked about, are you not?" Lucian asked Andraas.

"I...I am." Andraas stuttered.

"Then look into mine! You will find I speak the truth when I say I will slaughter every last soul inside if I am not taken to the pool. Then who will guard it? The ghosts of the marsh? Take me to it and I will spare everyone else and you can keep your temple." Lucian bargained.

Andraas stood there in silence with his eyes closed for a moment.

"You speak the truth, I will take you to the pool...but only if I look in the waters with you!" Andraas offered.

"I am not hear to cut deals, you will die like the rest." said Lucian as he raised his sword.

"Ah yes, but if you kill me you must know none of my brothers within the walls will take you there! And how would you know if you have found the correct pool?" Andraas rebutted.

"What are you talking about, monk?" Lucian asked, lowering his sword.

"You warrior types are all the same, all you can think with is your sword and your prick! Did you think there was only one pool? Yes! Yes one will show you what will be, the others will kill you when you gaze upon the waters! Perhaps you will reconsider my offer?" Andraas asked slyly.

Lucian became red with anger and paced down the steps to his commanders. He stood there for a moment speaking with them before marching back up the steps, sheathing his sword.

"You will take me to the pool and we will look upon it together. Should you try to trick me, my commanders will leave no survivors and tear this place down... is that understood?" Lucian relented.

"I accept your offer. Follow me, quickly." Andraas said, leading Lucian into the temple.

As they walked in the other monks inside tried to stop Lucian, but Andraas raised his hand and spoke out:

"By the same hand as Ilinir, this too is destined."

And with that all the other monks stood back idly as Andraas guided Lucian to the Pool of Ilinir.

Everything went black and Toree and I were now in a cavern illuminated by torches. Before us Lucian and Andraas stood over a pool.

"This is it, look upon the waters and it will show you what is destined to be." Andraas said to Lucian.

Lucian walked to the water's edge and stared in. Toree and I walked beside him and looked at the waters ourselves. It was black, only reflecting the flames around. Suddenly visions appeared....

In the pool we saw a vision of Lucian making his way to the capital, then Aldonis appeared forging Alaia and the shards of protection. Lucian came back into view with a crown on, only to be followed by Toree stabbing him with the dagger and everything around disappearing. Then...my father came into view with one of the shards hanging from his neck...

He walked through the Gate of the Gods at the entrance of the gorge and set off some sort of reaction.... Lucian appeared back in the castle and Toree appeared before him again....

I looked over at Toree and she was horrified and confused.

"What does this mean?" I asked.

"I do not know, things that have been and have not come to be... it seems there are more questions yet..." Toree said.

Lucian smirked and turned, walking out of the cave. Andraas stayed staring at the water. We were transported again, this time to the chamber we had just eaten in. The room was filled with other monks, Andraas at the table with them.

"Are you sure what you saw was correct?" one monk said to Andraas.

"Of course I am sure! I saw his vision and my own! Nystia will vanish with everyone inside! Someday Lucian will return to conquer again, someone must be here to put a stop to it! One of us must remain!" Andraas said sternly.

"If you speak the truth we must protect this place and the path to the capital..." another monk said.

"I will begin preparations to seal this place from curses!" an older monk called out.

"And what of Lucian's return? Are we to just ignore that?" Andraas asked the group.

An old monk walked over to the table and the room when silent.

"Andraas, it was you that had this vision, and it was you that allowed Lucian to look upon the Pool of Ilinir. So too will it be you that waits for his return and Nystia's salvation!" the old monk declared.

"Have you gone mad!?" Andraas cried out.

The old monk let out a chuckle.

"I can appreciate the irony of that coming from you! I am quite serious. We have all sworn an oath to protect the pool and the mountains. If the only way to uphold that is to channel our life energy into you, so be it!" said the old monk.

There was chattering and whispers between the monks after the old monk spoke, but it was quickly silenced with a clap of the old monk's hands.

"This is the only way. We will prepare the sigils to protect the temple and gate, then we will carry out the ritual. Andraas is the only one of us that can read minds. He will be able to discern the real savior from imposters. Go to your chambers and make peace with yourselves. We begin tonight!" decided the old monk.

The room cleared out and only the old monk and Andraas were left.

"This is your destiny, Andraas. This is how you use your gifts for something good...don't let this place fall into disrepair when we are gone." the old monk said before shuffling out of the room himself.

Toree and I were suddenly outside at dusk. The monks stood before the temple and the gate chanting, and as they chanted sigils drawn on the walls of the temple and gate posts began to shine. The light grew brighter until it just dissipated, the markings now gone completely.

"To the lower chamber." the old monk directed.

"Are you certain this is the right thing to do?" a young monk asked the old monk.

"This is how we upkeep our oath." the old monk said bluntly.

The younger monk nodded and they all funneled into the temple. That is when we found ourselves in a room reminiscent of a cellar. They all sat on chairs that lined the walls of the room, Andraas was laying on an alter in the center. The old monk stood above Andraas and spoke.

"Remember the prophecy you were shown." and with that the old monk shuffled to his seat and sat.

They all began reciting a prayer, as they did the alter began to shake and glow. The deeper into the prayer the brighter the light became. Eventually the light illuminated the entire room and we were blinded, only hearing the monks voices and screams of pain that Andraas began to howl out. The voices reciting the prayer seemed to become less in number until only the old monk's voice and Andraas' screams remained; then silence.

The light returned to the dim cellar lighting, around us in the chairs were mummified bodies of the monks, devoid of all signs of life. It was as if they had been stored here centuries early, yet it had only been a few minutes. In the center of the room Andraas rolled off the alter in pain, crawling out of the room.

We were taken outside the temple again, this time Ren approached with her own army. She looked confused as she approached, looking around for what I guessed were more monks.

"Andraas, where are the others?" Ren asked him as she walked up the steps.

"Lady Ren, it is good to see you again! They are all in the lower chamber!" Andraas answered.

"I must speak to them quickly, Lucian is on his way to the capital." said Ren.

"Well you won't be able to do that!" Andraas laughed.

"What? Why?" she asked.

"Because they are all dead!" he replied bluntly.

"How can this be!?" said a startled Ren.

"Well, I suppose it started a week ago when Lucian arrived and killed two of my brothers, so I took him to the Pool of Ilinir! After that he left and the rest of the brothers channeled their life energy into me! So I suppose you can say the others are in the lower chamber, but they certainly won't be speaking to anyone...or you could say that you are speaking to them right now by speaking with me! Isn't that a curious turn of events?" Andraas rambled.

Ren stepped back and shook her head as she tried to make sense of Andraas' lunacy. She sat on the steps and placed her face in her hands, sitting silently for a while before speaking with her face still covered.

"So you are the only monk left, and you allowed Lucian to look into the pool?" Ren asked.

"Why ask me questions if you don't listen!" a frustrated Andraas answered.

"I listened, I am just in disbelief!" Ren shouted back as she stood.

"You ought to believe a great many things, for there is more yet to come!" Andraas shouted back, waving his finger at Ren.

"What do you mean?" Ren questioned cautiously.

"Come with me, I will tell you all that is and will be once inside, everyone else must wait out here." Andraas said as he motioned his arms toward the entrance.

Ren looked around before nodding and walking inside with Andraas. Once they were through the threshold we found ourselves at the table again. This time Ren and Andraas sat at a corner of the table and spoke.

"Lucian saw the plan you, Toree, and Aldonis created. Lucian is brut prick, but a smart one. He has already come up with a curse to counter and put it in motion. Now you must counter the curse he has used to counter your curse!" Andraas told her.

"How? What have you seen!" said Ren, leaning in.

"Your curse will half work; Lucian will be gone yes, but so will Nystia. Only Toree and Aldonis will breathe the air after. You will perish protecting Toree, and nothing you can do will change that. You will die yes, but worry not, your line will hold the key to Lucian's final fall!" Andraas proclaimed.

"How could that be so?" she asked.

"The pendant you wear holds the key to the world's salvation, and also Lucian's. Some time from now the pendant you wear will cross the Gate of the Gods one final time. When that happens a battle that has not been yet will be again. The wearer of the pendant will be slain, his blood on the pendant the key to restore Lucian, but blood also holds the key to Lucian's destruction.

During the battle you must protect Toree and her apprentice, when they appear you will know you have already fallen." Andraas cryptically answered.

"Curse your riddles, Andraas!" Ren barked.

"Now, now! There is no need to bring more curses into this world!" Andraas protested.

"I will heed the nonsense you spew, the best I can make of it that is. I need you to open the gates to the pass so we may enter." Ren said to him.

"You may pass through...be warned though! Lucian will have the pass heavily guarded. Once you pass the gate it will lock behind until your pendant returns; there will be nowhere to retreat!" Andraas warned.

"Thank you for your warning, there will be no retreating." Ren said standing up.

Toree and I now found ourselves at the gate, we watched as Ren and her army funneled into the pass, as the last soldier crossed through Andraas shut and locked the gates. Then as we looked toward the path we took from the marsh to get to the temple the seasons changed before our eyes, the trees growing older, the ground beneath us corroding away.

Frantically stumbling in tattered and torn clothing, grasping onto a broken sword was...my father...

"Toree, surely that can't be..." I began.

"No, you are correct, that is Mistaan..." Toree replied as she put a hand on my shoulder.

As he grew closer to the temple I could see his hair was a knotted mess, his face overgrown, covered in dirt. He looked behind him as he swung the broken sword around...he had gone paranoid...swinging at opponents not there...

He stumbled up the steps and pounded on the temple doors using the pommel of his sword.

"Open! Open I say! In the name of the king open these doors!" my father shouted.

The doors opened slowly and Andraas stood cautiously, blocking him from entering.

"Show me your jewelry!" Andraas demanded.

"What? This is no time for highway robbery! I will give you all I have once inside, please!" my father pleaded.

"It matters not to me, all will die anyway...eventually." Andraas said with a smirk.

"Are you mad! Very well, here! Take my rings!" my father said, pulling his rings off his fingers and tossing them towards Andraas.

"And what use have I for these?" Andraas shrugged off as he ignored the gold rings on the floor.

"You are mad!" my father proclaimed.

As he said that, my mother's pendant shone through his torn shirt. It caught Andraas' eye and a smile appeared on his face.

"That! What do you wear around your neck?" Andraas questioned.

"This?" my father said as he held the pendant to his chest, "I can not allow you to take this."

"Very well! Come in then and get clean. You are in no state to sit at a table!" Andraas exclaimed.

My father looked confused, as if he imagined the entire dialogue exchange earlier, but went into the temple regardless. We followed them inside where Andraas brought my father to a room with a bath and fresh clothing.

"Bathe! Then come, sit and eat!" Andraas said enthusiastically.

"Thank you, I am Lord Mistaan of Dragon's Reach." my father said, introducing himself.

"Who you are matters not, only what you are. Though I suppose I should give you my name as well. I am brother Andraas, keeper of the Pool of Ilinir." Andraas replied.

"The Pool of Ilinir?" my father questioned.

"Exactly! I will take you too it once you've eaten!" said Andraas.

"What is this pool?" my father asked again.

"It will show you what has yet to be, but only what you need to see. It is a pool of destiny!" Andraas answered.

Suddenly we were transported again, this time to the Pool of Ilinir again, except now instead of Lucian before it stood my father. He was cleaned up and in fresh clothing, next to him stood Andraas.

"These are nothing more than tricks!" my father yelled out at Andraas.

"The only trick here is what you choose to fool yourself with! What you have seen cannot be undone, it is your destiny!" Andraas shouted back.

"I will forge my own destiny, monk. I will take your offer for shelter this night, but come the morning I will continue my journey. The only thing I ask is for a fresh sword if any reside here, and a fresh canteen of water." my father stated.

There was the attitude I remember! Hearing him speak like this again reminded me of where my brother received his vocational skills from. I think in the time he has been gone I genuinely forgot who he was, creating some well rounded and well spoken figure instead. The war had hardened him differently than others like Unul or myself; he had become arrogant and brash, disregarding the opinions and insight of others.

"So be it. I will let you through the gate at sunrise, I shall give you the sword you ask for, and the water. I suggest you savor the taste of the water and the feel of the swords hilt before you enter the pass..." Andraas warned.

Toree and I were not shown the memory of what my father saw, I wondered if this was intentionally done by Andraas or if there was no actual reason to show us. Debating the subject with Andraas would be useless, we instead focused on what was yet to come.

We now found ourselves outside the gate yet again, this time my father was the one to stand before it. It appeared Andraas was true to his word, my father had a 'new' sword and a fresh canteen of water.

"Have you made peace with what lays ahead?" Andraas asked as he opened the gate.

"The only peace to be had is being free of your rants!" my father barked.

Andraas did not respond to the insult, instead he smiled and waved his arm towards my father to enter the pass. As my father walked through the gate a crack of thunder bellowed and the sky shone a bright white. A mist like the one from the break in the valley roared down the hills and filled the pass.

"You should have made your peace, Lord Mistaan of Dragon's Reach!" Andraas said smirking.

"Monk! What have you done!" my father roared.

It was useless, Andraas slammed the gate shut and locked it as the mist made it's way toward him. There was pounding on the gate for a short while before it went quiet.

"Was that a break forming when he walked through?" I asked Toree.

"It appears that way...that would explain the battle riddle he gave Ren." said Toree.

"What do you mean?" I asked.

"Ren and Lucian's armies fought for two days in the pass. More blood was spilt between the mountains than any other battle since Ilinir and the Winter Marsh. When your father crossed that gate the power of the pendent must have triggered a break... one that we must also make our way through..." Toree said.

"Wait! Andraas told Ren about us before she went into that battle..." I began.

"You are right!" Toree exclaimed.

"She will recognize our mission and be able to aid us through!" I remarked.

"My father, do you think he is still in there?" I asked.

All then went dark for a moment until we found ourselves back in the present, sat on the chairs in the study of the temple.

"Oh I wouldn't count on that! He is probably long dead!" Andraas answered in the present moment.

"I don't believe that was a question for you!" scolded Toree.

"Well judging by the pounding he made on that door..." Andraas started.

"Oh shut it, monk!" Toree scolded again.

"It is alright, Toree. He may speak his mind." I said.

"It is possible he yet survives. I do not know the power of this break and how time passes inside it. What I do know is that we will need to get through as quickly as possible." Toree answered.

"And Lucian?" I questioned.

"Why ask her? Why not speak to him yourself?" Andraas questioned back.

"What are you going on about?" inquired Toree.

"Lucian saw that you would return here when he was released back to this world; he bound a mirror in the tower to himself so that you could speak. For what purpose I know not!" Andraas informed us.

"You have had a connection to Lucian this whole time!" Toree blurted out, jumping to her feet.

"No and yes, no more than you have had through the centuries! We are all connected in the web of destiny! Who are you to accuse I of being closer to the spider!" Andraas said in his own defense.

Toree relented and paced to the mantle.

"Take me to the mirror." Toree said bluntly as she stared into the fire.

"No, take us to the mirror." I corrected, standing and putting my hand on Toree's shoulder.

"I shall, but you must make an oath first!" Andraas demanded.

"I have taken enough oaths in my lifetime, what is it you want of me." questioned Toree.

"You and I have lived long past our time... For you, once Lucian is dead your curse is broken. I am not bound to a curse, the lifetimes of all my brothers are bound to me, and I am bound to protect the pool that sits beneath this temple. I may yet live another four hundred years in solitude, and when that time runs out no one will be left to protect the pool." Andraas explained earnestly.

"So what is it you ask of me?" inquired Toree.

"You must end this life of solitude for me! Swear an oath to bring down the temple and bury the pool! In return I will give you the key to the gate, access to the mirror, and I will allow you and all that accompany to look upon the Pool of Ilinir with your own eyes." Andraas answered.

"I will swear it, how does that remedy your lifetime?" Toree asked.

"There are three pools beneath this temple. One sits toward the mountain of creation, the other toward the mountain of destruction, the Pool of Ilinir sits on the line that divides them. The pool of destruction has the power to correct the unnatural life energy I was given. I cannot use it if the temple has been destroyed. You must swear you will bring this place down, when I am gone there will be no more keeper!" Andraas explained.

"Very well, I understand. I swear we will bring the temple down upon the pools before we enter the gate." Toree said with her hand over her heart.

"Very good! Now follow me! I shall take you to the mirror!" Andraas exclaimed as he quickly walked out of the room.

We followed him up the stairs and around a bend, down a hallway and up a circular stairway. Once at the top we entered a barren room. The only object in the room was a huge mirror which took up the greater length of a wall. It was covered with a purple curtain which had a thick layer of dust sat on it.

Toree and I lit the torches which surrounded the room and prepared to remove the curtain.

"I will leave you and make sure your companions have not gotten lost. When you are done, destroy the mirror." Andraas called as he began making his way down the stairs.

Toree walked to one side of the mirror and I to the other.

"Are you ready?" I asked.

Toree nodded and we both pulled the curtain from the mirror. The room immediately grew brighter as the light from the torches reflected off of it. We moved to the center of the room and waited...

"Lucian!" Toree shouted.

There was no response.

"Lucian! Show yourself, snake!" Toree shouted again.

Suddenly a voice from the mirror rang out into the room.

"I can see your temper has not improved over the centuries..." the voice said.

Lucian walked into view within the mirror, with him in the frame it no longer showed a reflection of the room we stood in. Instead it was as if there was a doorway to Queen Aludia's throne room.

"Toree, my love - you have not aged a day since we last saw each other!" Lucian said with a smirk.

"Nearly four hundred years and that is the best you could do?" Toree rebuffed.

"I've been busy ruling my kingdom, something we could have done together had you made better choices... but let's not ignore this beauty next to you! If she made it this far perhaps she would be better suited as my queen? What say you to that?" said Lucian.

"I don't think our courtship would work out, I'm better suited at slaughtering monsters, not marrying them!" I said boldly.

"That attitude! It reminds me so much of someone I once knew... ah yes! Lady Ren! I'm fairly certain my men used her body as a sheath for their swords... Perhaps Toree could confirm that?" Lucian spewed out.

"What do you mean ruling your kingdom? What have you done?" Toree asked.

Lucian laughed and paced around.

"I knew what you had planned all those years ago. The steel you drove into me was the key to your intended curse. I created a counter spell using that steel as my own catalyst. You did not send me to a prison in the spirit realm as I did with Aludia! I bound the kingdom and all those loyal to me to my crown, creating my own kingdom within a separate plane of the spirit realm.

I have spent the centuries ruling, feasting on the endless bounty the spirit realm provides, and bedding whomever I choose. I knew the steel would enter the pass, and the blood upon it would remove us from the spirit realm and bring us back home so that I can finally expand my kingdom.

We arrived back with the mist of the break over the pass. Not all of us have returned yet, but each day more appear. It will not be long before I can expand my borders!" he divulged.

Toree stepped back as if she was about to fall over. I walked to her and grabbed her arm.

"That can't be possible... if that is true how did the beasts appear first!" Toree whispered to me.

"Whispering will not help, I can hear all in this room. I'm sure after the whole kingdom vanished Aldonis went mad trying to figure out 'why'. He no doubt assumed something happened and the curse spreading to the kingdom made it weaker. If he did hypothesize that he would have been partially correct!

The curse could not contain the inanimate objects forever, only those with life in them. Pieces of the kingdom have been finding their way back home for centuries. The soldiers the buffoon that freed me travelled with came across the cursed gold throughout the land. It seemed only the bearer of the pendant was not tempted, the rest turned into the beasts they were inside." Lucian explained.

"Why tell us all of this?" I asked, confused.

"The hour is late, and you have a break not yet crossed. By the time you reach me, my armies will be back at full force. The last time we fought it was Toree and her army against me and my own. Now it is me and my army against the two of you!

Toree, I am prepared to forgive the past should you join me. The invitation would of course extend to your apprentice as well!" Lucian answered.

"An army could not stop me from running you through again!" Toree exclaimed.

"So be it. You know where to find me." Lucian said as he walked out of sight from the mirror.

Toree raged and sent flames toward the mirror! The heat was so intense the mirror melted upon itself, a glowing mess of glass and silver upon the floor, the wall behind charred black.

"All this time I have walked in a world I no longer belong in, yet he lives, eats, and fucks lavishly in what should have been a prison of torment!" Toree shouted as she threw flames at the already melted mirror.

"Toree, you belong in my world... should you have died long ago I would have not known how to control my powers, and have had no higher purpose. This journey with you has given me that purpose and control. You have become the sister I did not have." I said sweetly to her.

Toree stopped her attack on the mirror and fell to her knees, tears streaming down her cheeks. I knelt in front of her and she let her head drop onto my shoulder. We stayed like that for some time before returning to the others.

Downstairs Andraas told us we can use any of the bedrooms in the temple to sleep in, and that should anyone need him he would be in the study. Andraas then excused himself and I stood with the others.

"Come, we have much to discuss..." I said to my companions.

They followed me to the table where we all sat. I told them everything we had seen and learned, including the conversation with Lucian. By the end of it they all seemed worried, except for Zuht.

"My friends, do not look so down. We have made it here, a place so strange and fantastic that even the fairytales do not touch on it! And beside, you have all missed something very important!" Zuht remarked.

"It sounds straight forward to me, we go through this break, which is one big battle, and if we survive Lucian waits for us with an army." Tripp said bluntly in dismay.

"It is not! We will make it through the break! And when we do we will have the upper hand! What is the first thing that happened when we walked in to this place?" Zuht asked.

"The monk asked us all to sit and eat..." Runa answered.

"No! He asked Toree and Jara to sit! He did not know we were here as well!" Zuht said enthusiastically.

"What does this have to do with Lucian?" I asked.

"Everything! Andraas did not know we were here, yet he read Lucian's mind! And Jara, you recalled that Lucian said he had an army against only two! Jara and Toree! Do you see? Lucian does not know there are three others!" Zuht said with a smile.

"You are right!" Runa remarked with a smile herself.

"Zuht, thank the Gods you are with us in this moment! We can use this to our advantage!" Toree exclaimed.

"How?" I asked.

"I will have to put some thought into it, but this does change the tides!" Toree responded.

"I am glad to help, now I will excuse myself to a bedroom. Good night, all." Zuht said as he stood and left the table.

"Yes, he is right. You should all get out of this armor and get some rest." Toree said to us.

"Are you not coming to bed?" Tripp asked.

"I must find a map somewhere in this place, once I have I will join you. Now off with the three of you!" Toree said.

Runa and I made our way to one of the rooms. The quarters were modest, a small fireplace, a simple bed, and a stone wash basin that was built into the walls and had warm water flowing in. There were no ornate extravagancies here as there were in the barracks. We helped each other out of our armor and sat for a moment on two stools beside the fire.

"Do you think your father is still alive? He would have been here over a year ago..." Runa asked.

"I do not think he has died, it does not sit right in my gut." I responded.

"And the prophesy pool below? Will you take the monk's offer and use it?" she questioned.

"It has been a thought in my head, but like my father; does not feel right. I have been led here through destiny, a destiny already written. Even Andraas has said what is seen can not be changed, yet I would strive to change what I see. Beside that, no one has been shown all, only pieces." I answered with careful thought.

Runa looked toward the fire nodding her head.

"And you?" I asked her.

"I do not like to believe in destiny or fate. What I can do or can not do has always been dictated by the higher lords or ladies. This quest is the first time I have been equal to all involved, free to make my own choice. If I look into the pool and do not appreciate what is shown, I would feel that I am fighting a loosing battle against fate my whole life. I do not want my free will challenged, whether it actually exists or not." Runa answered.

"I can understand that." I responded to Runa's explanation.

I smiled at Runa, watching the flames bounce off her hair. Now sat with nothing pressing for the next short while, I had only just noticed how filthy we actually were. There was dirt, mud, and blood from the marshes covering us.

"I think we should use this opportunity to clean and get into bed, I believe it will be quite some time before we have a room like this again." I suggested.

Runa smiled back at me and nodded in agreement. I walked to the basin and rinsed my face with the fresh water that was continually flowing into it. Taking one of the two sponges at the side I cleaned the dirt and blood off my body. As I stood there Runa walked to me, taking the sponge and gently scrubbing my neck and back.

I turned and used the other sponge to wipe off her face, rinsing it and working my way down her body. She smiled and we kissed before making our way to the bed. Knowing what challenges lay ahead, we decided to make the most of the night. We drowned out all the talk of prophesy and destiny as we drank in each others bodies and souls. Was this night destined to happen, or were we intertwined of our own free will? It mattered not; we were content in the moment.

The Gate of the Gods

Chapter 21

"True to my word, any of you that wish to look upon the Pool of Ilinir may. Those of you that do not: share a final drink with me! My story ends here today, yet yours will carry on; for you will be needed again in times not yet here! It has been foreseen, though not seen yet!" Andraas said, raising a glass of wine.

I looked at Runa with a look of uncertainty and concern, she looked back with a face of support.

"Whatever the future brings, may we face it together!" Runa added with a wink towards me.

We all gulped our wine down and placed the glasses on the table. Andraas walked to each one of us.

"Will you look upon the Pool of Ilinir?" he asked Toree.

"I will." Toree responded.

"Will you look upon the Pool of Ilinir?" he asked Tripp.

"I...I will not." Tripp answered.

"Will you look upon the Pool of Ilinir?" he asked Runa.

"I will not." answered Runa.

"Will you look upon the Pool of Ilinir?" he asked me.

"I will not." I said, following the feeling in my gut.

"Will you look upon the Pool of Ilinir?" he asked Zuht.

"I will gaze on the pool, brother Andraas." Zuht replied.

"It has been decided then. Lady Toree, Master Zuht, follow me to the pools below. The rest of you, I bid you well on your adventures and must ask that you leave the temple." Andraas said, showing us to the door.

Runa, Tripp, and I walked through the doors, which Andraas closed behind us. Toree and Zuht remained behind to be taken to the Pool of Ilinir.

"You did not want to look into the pool?" I asked Tripp.

"I thought I would, but when we stood there while Andraas asked us...I don't know... my thoughts went back to the night you and Sir Unul saved me. Had I known something of the future perhaps I would have convinced Sir Krinn to avoid the route all together. Had I done that, well I would still be polishing his armor. Instead I am here with you. I think I prefer going about life by chance." Tripp explained.

"Thank you, Tripp... for coming along on this journey with us. You and Zuht were not summoned to this place, yet here you both are, of your own choice. I do not know many sane others that would do so." I said, grateful he was still with me.

"No, thank you for trusting me on this adventure." Tripp replied.

"There is something I need to tell you both, the dagger the king sent us to find... there is obviously much more to this quest than the King knew. The dagger we seek is my own, Alaia. It has been passed down for centuries in my family and is the key to the curses that plague this place." I divulged.

"Why not use it before and never enter this place?" Runa asked, confused.

"It's power is tied to Lucian, Wurth can not be stopped until Lucian is. Somehow we must connect the two adversaries together, then strike them down with one blow. That is the only way." I went on.

"What is your plan?" asked Tripp.

"I don't have one yet..." I replied.

"We will craft one, I'm sure there are other secrets to be learned in this place." Runa reassured.

I nodded in agreement and we sat waiting for Zuht and Toree to return. Some time had passed before they made their way out the doors.

"Andraas?" I asked.

"At peace." Toree said with a smile.

"Now, how to handle tearing this place down...this place is half the size of Enex!" Tripp remarked.

"Jara, you and I can bring it down if we work together." Toree said to me.

"How?" I asked her.

"This place is connected to the energy around it, we can use that to tune into it. Once you have made the connection to the energy that flows through it see the building as if it is dry clay in your hand, crumbling between your fingers." Toree instructed.

The others moved and I began to do as Toree instructed. We both stood before the massive temple, I focused my attention onto the force that ran through the structure...I could feel it as if it was the pulse of another living creature. The stone temple felt as if it was in the palm of my hand, I looked at Toree and together we squeezed our hands into fists, as we did so dust and pebbles began to trickle from the structure.

"If I was not here to see this with my own eyes I would not believe it." Tripp said.

"I see it with my eyes, yet I still can not believe it." Runa added.

Toree and I continued to work in silence, breathing the walls into our palms. The roof began to fall in on itself, then the walls started to cave. Before long the temple had entirely collapsed in on itself, leaving a cloud of dust over the ruins. The three pools had been successfully sealed by the temple's collapse, and with that our oath to Andraas had been upheld.

"Good work." Toree said to me with a pat on the shoulder.

"We just tore down this place with our magic, and all you can say is 'good work'?" I joked.

"I would give you a medal, but I have none to give out. Come, we have no time to waste!" Toree replied.

"Are you not going to tell me about what you saw down there?" I asked her.

"No, I am not." Toree said with a smirk before continuing to the gate.

I hurried behind her and we all made our way to the gate. The gate itself was a large iron and stone structure that completely sealed off the passage between the mountains. In the center of one of the massive doors was a smaller doorway, big enough only for someone on foot to pass through.

Toree pulled out a key and unlocked the door, then pulled it open with a loud creak. After we passed Toree shut it and used a flame she conjured to melt the frame to the surrounding iron of the gate.

"What if we need to return this way?" Tripp asked.

"Do not worry, we will not." Zuht answered.

"How do you know that?" Tripp asked.

"I have seen it, in the pool." Zuht reassured Tripp.

"What else did you see in the pool...out of curiosity..." Tripp questioned.

"A great many things. Some which you may know, some you may not." Zuht replied with a smile.

"Are you certain the monk did not jump into your body? You are beginning to sound like him!" Tripp remarked.

Zuht chuckled and put his hand on Tripp's shoulder.

"Master Tripp, I will tell you that you shall indeed be a knight, and that your role in this life will hold great importance." Zuht said as he looked Tripp in the eyes.

"Anything about the rest of us?" Runa asked.

"You know, considering the three of you chose not to join us you are all awfully interested..." Toree remarked.

"Well, I don't want to know everything, just some things..." Runa admitted.

"Very well. The three of you are bound together through fate until you each draw your last breath. That is all I can divulge to you. Now we must make ourselves ready for battle, can you see the colored mist beyond the bend ahead?" said Toree.

"I see it, is that the break?" I replied.

"Yes, when we enter, we join the battle that took place here those centuries ago. We must keep an eye out for your father and find Ren. She will be able to help us make our way through." Toree elaborated.

"I suppose we will be fighting this battle in the snow then..." Tripp pointed out, as fresh snowflakes fell from the sky.

"I doubt that, this battle took place in the middle of the summer months. I believe like the other break, when we enter we will end up completely in the past again." Toree theorized.

"Battle or not, if it is warmer in there than it is out here I will welcome it!" said Tripp.

Toree shook her head and began to move towards the mist. As we made our way to the bend Zuht made ready his spear, the rest of us pulled out our swords. We began to progress into the mist, as we did the temperature did indeed rise; and as we moved further into it the sounds of soldiers speaking loudly to each other and cries of wounded filled the pass.

The mist cleared as we walked into a makeshift battle camp. Pikes stood stacked over shields, boxes of food rations sat next to dirty tents, and just ahead were wounded on bedrolls and tables. Some were missing limbs, others with arrows broken off in their bodies, some badly burned and in wraps, others had already expired but were not cleared out yet. It appeared we were not at the front, so sheathed our weapons.

Ahead of us were a group of soldiers standing guard.

"You lot! State your business!" one of the guards shouted as he presented his spear forward.

"I am Lady Toree, these are my private guard. I have an urgent message for Lady Ren, where is she?" Toree stated.

"I am sorry my lady, I did not know to expect you here. Commander Ren is leading from the front. Follow the pass and you will find her. Is there anything else I can help you with?" the guard asked.

"There is one more thing, I sent a messenger ahead of me, older fellow, his name is Lord Mistaan, from Dragon's Reach in Nerick. He may have seemed a bit out of place, did he pass through here?" Toree asked, referring to my father in a manner that would not confuse the guards.

"Aye, earlier today. The fellow just kept going on about some dagger and a king's quest; the lads and I thought he had just gone mad from being in the marshes, or spending too much time with them monks! We let him through ahead, I do not know more than that." the guard informed us.

"Thank you." Toree said as we moved on.

Toree led us through the narrow camp at a quick pace. We weaved in and out of units of soldiers preparing for battle, others fletching arrows, some now limping back with bloodstained armor. We could hear war cries the further forward we moved.

"Volley!" we heard echoing through the gorge as we moved uphill along the path.

Overhead we could make out black dots littering the sky. Toree immediately created a blanket of flames from wall to wall in the pass, covering us all. The arrows rained down, but disintegrated into ash as they hit the flames.

"Me lady, are ye goin' to ta front?" a soldier asked Toree as she kept the flaming shield over our heads, prepared for more arrows to come down.

"We are looking for Lady Ren, we were told she is at the the front. Do you know her whereabouts?" I said to the soldier while Toree focused on the flames.

"Aye, we be headin' tat way erselfs, might we join ya un'er tha co'er o' tha flames?" the soldier asked.

Toree nodded to me.

"Yes, come and join us under." I said to the soldier.

"Ya hear tat boys! Un'erneath! T'ere be alcoves tat li'er tha pass ahead. C'mander Ren havin' a tunnel dug round Lucian's fr'nt line from t'ere." The soldier said as he rallied a dozen of his men under Toree's cover.

We pushed on, the flames scorching the endless amounts of arrows that fell from above. As we moved forward we passed units of soldiers huddling under wooden roofs. The tops of the wall-less huts were covered in a thick layer of arrows, as was much of the dirt beneath our feet. It took some time but we made our way to the area the soldiers mentioned.

We all ducted into the alcove and Toree let the flames dissipate.

There were rocks and dirt thrown in piles all around the rather large alcove. It seemed the soldiers were correct, there was an attempt to mine a tunnel being carried out.

"My tanks m'lady. Ye'll find'er 'n tat tent t'ere!" the soldier said as he rallied his men forward down the pass.

We could hear the sound of steel chipping away at the rock and made our way to the larger of the three tents that stood in the area. Compared to the narrow pass we made our way through, this area was large and spacious, offering protection from the constant barrage of arrows.

Toree parted the entrance to the tent and walked in as we followed behind. Standing at a table was Ren, studying a map, and one of her assistants. Ren looked up surprised, then her face sunk inwards.

"Leave us." She said bluntly to her assistant, who without a word left the tent.

"Ren, it is good to see you again." said Toree softly.

"I thought that mad man coming through was a coincidence, I see now it is not..." Ren replied.

"No, no it's not..." said Toree.

"Then what the monk spoke was true. How is it we speak face to face now?" Ren asked.

"A break formed a year ago over the pass, we entered it today." answered Toree.

"A break a year ago... How long has it been?" asked Ren.

"About three and a half centuries..." Toree responded.

"...how is that possible..." gasped Ren.

"Lucian cursed me to live barren and ageless throughout the years. He knew our plan and countered it. I am here one last time with my companions to end Lucian's nightmare for good." Toree informed her.

"Toree... was I not there to aid you?" Ren asked.

"You and I stormed the keep together, before we could both enter the throne room Lucian's reinforcements arrived. You held them off until the end so that I might live long enough to drive the dagger into Lucian. If not for your help he would have enslaved the world by now." Toree reassured Ren.

"My daughter? What became of her?" Ren asked.

"She took over Dragon's Reach. When she came of age I inducted her into the order and showed her the ways, as I have done for each generation since. You have had a noble and powerful line. This is Jara, Lady of Dragon's Reach, your blood." Toree said as she extended her arm towards me.

"It is good to finally be introduced as myself!" I remarked.

"Jara, it is good to see my line yet continues and follows the ways. Have we met previously?" Ren said with a smile, her hand now grabbing my arm.

"In Toree and Andraas' memories, and then one other time in a previous break... you do not know how much I would like to sit here and speak with you, yet I know we can not... the man all considered mad, he is my father and wears the amulet you and I do. We must find him and make our way out of this pass. There is more at stake than Lucian, without him Nerick will be lost." I said to Ren.

"If the man I saw was your father, he insisted on making his way through the battle to get to the Queen's castle. I sent a unit ahead to scout how far Lucian's troops encampment is, he joined them. Only one of my scouts returned, the rest were either cut down or captured. I do not know your father's fate, I am sorry." she said to me.

"How far is your tunnel?" Toree asked.

"We are nearly through, by nightfall we should be able to sneak around the front line and send them into disarray. You are still a day and half's walk from exiting the pass...Toree, this battle has already ended in your time - how long did it take to push through?" Ren asked.

"Nearly two weeks." answered Toree.

"Two weeks...this is only our third day of battle..." Ren muttered.

"Is there no other way through?" I asked.

"Unfortunately not... come look at the map with me, the others here, they are from your time too?" Ren said.

"Yes, all from my time." I answered.

"Then they may come too." Ren said as she laid some coins out on the map.

"This is where Lucian's front line is in, as I'm sure you could tell by the arrows flying from over the hill. Not far behind is the encampment here." Ren said as she laid the coins on the spots she was referring to.

"Where are you tunneling to?" Runa asked.

"This spot here, between the front and the camp. There should be no more than a handful troops there, and we can take them in both directions by surprise. We should be clear of more resistance until the next bend in the pass. Lucian has had units stationed throughout the pass, it will be stop and go for days." Ren answered.

"And you're certain there is not another way through?" Tripp inquired.

"There is only the pass, we will need to fight our way through." explained Ren.

"What of my father?" I asked.

"If he is alive he will be imprisoned in the camp. Should he have fallen, we will find him amongst the dead." answered Ren.

"Thank you, Ren." Toree said.

"It is nearly sundown and we will be through soon, are you prepared?" Ren asked.

"To go into battle with my ancestor? Absolutely." I exclaimed.

"It is without a doubt that we share the same blood!" Ren replied.

"It would be an honor to join you as well." Tripp said, Runa nodded in agreement.

"I need to brief my captains, you can stay and look at the map while I do so." Ren said, leaving the tent.

Toree looked over the map and studied it carefully.

"I do not think my father has been killed, it doesn't feel right." I said to Toree.

"I feel the same, we should go straight for the camp with a unit, I have a feeling he will be there." Toree said in agreement.

"Toree, we are in a break, like the one that you said used to cover the Winter Marsh?" Runa asked.

"Yes, not quite brought on the same way, but a break none the less." confirmed Toree.

"So even after we pass through it, the fighting will continue indefinitely?" Runa added.

"Unless something so powerful or drastically different happens during a loop to alter the outcome significantly, yes it would continue." Toree admitted.

"Don't you find that sad? The last time we were in a break it was festive and full of joy... now they are all doomed to fight in this place." said Runa.

"Would our presence here not alter the outcome enough to stop it?" Tripp asked.

"No, there needs to be something more extreme. We could speed up the pace of the battle, but it would not be enough to end the loop that it follows." Toree informed him.

"...If we were to do something extreme enough it would lift the break, and we could walk freely through the pass, yes?" Zuht asked.

"Yes, but we could not entertain it until we've found Jara's father, or his remains. Have you an idea?" Toree asked.

"Perhaps, I must pray on it before nightfall." Zuht said, leaving the tent to find a place amongst the stone and dirt to pray.

"Runa, Tripp, go listen in on Ren's orders to her men so that you can convey their plans with us." Toree instructed.

Runa and Tripp both left the tent to go listen to Ren, leaving Toree and I alone in the tent. Toree unrolled a portion of the map that had not been laid out and motioned me over to her side.

"I have come up with a plan, but it puts you and I in great danger...that is why I wanted to discuss it with you before including the others." Toree said to me.

"What are you thinking?" I asked.

"As was said earlier, Lucian only knows two of us are on this quest, and knows nothing of King Ansel's mission. There is an ancient passage and the end of this pass that leads under the mountain and fields straight to the throne room in the capital. It was made by the first king's of Nystia to avoid assassination attempts by those still loyal to the three separate crowns.

I propose sending the others down the subterranean passage with my sword and Alaia. Once on the open roads Lucian's forces that have reappeared will capture us. Make as if I am your prisoner, an offering for Lucian. His ego will not allow him to resist seeing me in chains held by a new young woman. We should get to the keep no faster than the others using the passage.

Once we are there we will lure him close before you break my bindings; the others can then enter and pass me my sword and you the dagger. Even if he has a thought that you and I are acting, he would still not foresee any others." Toree explained.

The plan was perfect...well, as perfect as our circumstances allowed. Ideally I would have spies already in the court, ready to turn; but desperate and unusual times called for desperate and unusual measures. At least we had some element of surprise on our side.

"I think that will be our best chance. Even with the uncertainty of the others being in place when we arrive, it still holds a better chance than the five of us attempting to barge in, swords waving around." I confirmed.

"Then it is decided, that is what we will do." said Toree.

"Shall I gather the others to fill them in?" I asked.

"No, the hour is late and Ren's men are likely ready to begin the attack. We should meet them outside, we will fill them in after we find your father." Toree said.

We left the tent and met the others, Zuht had rejoined Tripp and Runa near Ren's troops.

"You are back, have you thought of a way to end this break?" I asked Zuht.

"I have." Zuht replied.

"Would you care to elaborate?" I responded.

"When the time is right. Now is the time for fighting, not the time for elaborating." said Zuht.

Ren came up to us as her men began to file into the tunnel that was being mined out. The sky had grown blue, and heavy shadows fell unto the pass from the mountains above. It appeared it was time to move forward.

"Are you ready?" she asked us.

"Yes." Toree replied.

"Very well, join me at the front. I have instructed my men to give you any support you need to carry out an important mission." Ren informed us.

"Thank you, we are just behind you." Toree said.

Ren grabbed her commanders and entered the tunnel. The others and I regrouped before entering.

"What is the plan?" I asked Runa.

"We have whoever we need at our disposal, if one of us call six will come running to aid. Ren is sending four units behind the front, she and two other units will join us as we raid the camp." Runa informed us.

"Yes, and also that they are to only engage those wearing Lucian's colors in combat, the rest are to be taken prisoner. She thought it the best way to ensure your father would not be mistaken for an aggressor and killed." Tripp added.

"Are you all prepared?" asked Toree.

Zuht knocked his spear against the dirt and the rest of us drew swords.

"Very well, let us join Ren. Remember, should any of us come across Mistaan we must protect him!" Toree reminded.

We nodded that we understood and joined Ren in the tunnel. We squeezed past the line of soldiers that were waiting for the cue to attack. The tunnel seemed endless, how they mined this out so fast must have been some ancient Nystian technique I was not aware of.

When we reached Ren at the end of the tunnel we could see the light from torches seeping through a crack in the stone fascia. We listened intently but heard no voices, this area must have been unmanned.

Ren silently gave the signal, seconds late a soldier with a large wooden mallet hammered the stone with a few thumps. The stone crumbled in moderate silence and we emerged, looking around.

There were no guards there, supply crates but completely unguarded. We quietly looked around while the soldiers stayed in their queue, hidden safely in the tunnel. We had come out in another alcove like the one Ren had her tent set up in. As we checked the area we heard a couple of voices get closer.

The six of us hid, Runa took a position so she could see the guards coming in, but was concealed by the night's shadow. Toree and Tripp were on the other side of the alcove, Zuht, Ren, and me were against a wagon and in a position to attack the guards if need be.

As the guards grew closer Runa held out her hand close to the ground so only we could see; she held out four fingers. We acknowledged her signal and jumped out from either side of the wagon, attacking in unison. Zuht let loose his spear, impaling one guard through the heart. I mustered a wind which grabbed a guard and sent him hurling towards me, as he reached me I held my sword blade out, skewering him.

As he stood in shock before me, my sword still in his gut; I drew my dagger and slit his throat, then let him fall to the ground to bleed out. Ren did much the same, except with a gust of wind brought the other two guards to her and with one fast flash of her sword took their heads clean off.

Runa gave us a thumbs up and we all joined in the center.

"I will signal my men to join, are you prepared for what we may find?" Ren asked me.

"Finding anything will be a welcomed gift." I replied.

Ren gave me a firm pat on the shoulder and nodded. She then turned and summoned her troops. They emerged from the tunnel like solider ants from the hill, prepared to do their queen's bidding. The first few units moved immediately toward the front, the last units joined us as we grouped and prepared to move on the encampment.

We moved silently along the pass, staying in the shadows where possible. With the sentries taken down and the cover of night, the advantage was on our side. We charged upon the camp, the enemy not knowing what had hit them. Soldiers could not rise from their perch beside the fires before they were cut down.

Ren and I ran through together, looking for any commanding officers and striking them down together, Runa and Zuht paired together and rushed toward the rear of the camp to stop anyone from fleeing towards their next post. Tripp and Toree cut down the tents to ensure no one could hide, all the while keeping an eye out for my father.

The dirt ran red with blood, in just a few minutes Lucian's camp was decimated. There were not even any moans to hear, our attack was quick and ruthless to keep screams and alert bells to a minimum. As soon as we were sure no one survived the soldiers began dragging the bodies to the stock area we had tunneled in from, using the night to hide the smoke that would come from burning the corpses.

"This was not your first time in battle." Ren acknowledged as we scoured the camp for my father.

"No, I have commanded armies myself, as has Runa. In our time we have been in a ruthless war for years, I was forced to learn young and quick." I informed her.

"How is it you have ended up here, in a fight against Lucian?" she asked.

"The war has taken a toll on the north of Nerick, the kingdom we fight is a kingdom of extreme zealots. They do not care whether they live or die, they only wish to spread their lunacy. Where they go they spread their poison and grow in numbers. The king heard of Alaia and what it did to Nystia, he wants to use the same spell to make our adversary vanish. The rest was fate." I explained.

"That is a very extreme measure with an uncertain outcome...is there no other way?" she replied.

"There is not. Without trying the spell Nerick will fall before the summer sun. When we entered the mist of this break it was the middle of winter, what season we exit into I do not know." I answered.

"I wish you and your friends good luck on the rest of your quest then. Do all you can do, for if you fail and you have done all else you will not live with guilt. Sorrow, yes, but sorrow does not poison the soul as guilt does." Ren said.

"Thank you, Ren." I replied.

Runa called out to us and we made our way over. Toree and Tripp were just behind. At the rear of the camp were posts to which prisoners were tied. Some had already been killed and left, others wounded. Zuht was cutting those still living free to join their comrades.

Against one post sat my father; he was covered in sweat and blood, the life fading from his body. I quickly knelt down and cut his bindings, Runa helped me lift him onto our shoulders as we carried him against a crate and sat him down.

"Father, can you hear me?" I said as I rubbed his cheek.

My father reached out and opened his eyes slowly.

"Jara? Is that you? Or am I recalling my life before I shift into death?" rambled my father.

"You are not deceived, I am here!" I exclaimed with tears in my eyes.

"How...how is this so? You should be at home, not on my heels..." he said.

"Father, you have been missing for nearly a year... myself and several others were sent by the king to find you and complete your mission." I explained.

"It is useless, I could not find the dagger." he said to me.

"No, Alaia is the dagger from the stories..." I said.

"Surely that can not be so...the blade has been under our noses this whole time? So much pain and life lost for no reason..." he lamented.

"This has become much more involved than you are aware, but I fear there is too much to tell and you need help!" I said.

"No, I trust you speak the truth. If you say there is more to this than I knew, it was not in vain..." he said, his voice growing weaker.

"I have the dagger, and a task for it. What must I do to connect it to Wurth?" I asked.

"In my jacket there is the king of Wurth's signet ring with a carved gem. Use that to connect Wurth with the dagger, how to do so I do not know. We were to experiment with it when we returned..." he informed me.

"Worry not, Toree is with us, she will know what to do!" I said in reassurance.

"Of that I have no doubts. Your mother and brother?" he asked.

"Mother is...gone... Devin was sent back to Dragon's Reach when I was summoned. I have not seen him since he left for the pass." I informed him.

"Devin will be wed soon, when he is he will be in the south. Here, take my ring. Dragon's Reach is yours, Jara." my father said, shakily pulling off his blood soaked ring and placing it in my hands.

"No, I can heal you!" I exclaimed.

I put my hand to the ground and the other on my father, as I had done with Tripp. I tried to pull the healing energies from below as I had done previously, but I could not channel anything accept frustration. It wasn't working...

"I don't understand!" I said in my confusion.

"It will not work here..." Toree said.

The others must have followed Runa and I, they stood just behind me and looked on in respectful silence.

"Why? Why will it not work here?!" I shouted in despair.

"The mountains are two polar opposites making the energy here balanced. The pass will not allow you to pull from it. I am sorry..." Toree explained.

"Jara, you are ready to take my place; and I am ready to greet your mother in death, but I need your help..." he reassured me.

"What do you need help with?" I asked.

"I can not move my legs and my vision is fading. Give me a noble death..." he said, asking me to end the suffering he was enduring.

I stood up and paced for a moment. There were other healers here, perhaps they could help? No, they would do nothing more than delay the inevitable while we remained in this cursed pass...

"Jara, your father is right. You are not here alone, I am here with you." Runa said as she grasped my arms and looked me in the eyes.

I stood in silence, there was no doubting this was the best way. I nodded in agreement with her and knelt in front of my father. She knelt behind and put his left arm over her neck, holding him him with her other arm.

I fumbled my father's signet ring onto my finger and withdrew my dagger.

"Are you ready?" I asked.

"Are we ever ready? Live a happy and honest life." he said to me, a small smile appearing on his face.

I nodded with eyes full of tears and placed the tip of my dagger under his lifted arm. I embraced him in a hug, while doing so I quickly drove my dagger into his side, piercing his heart. I held him there with Runa as his breath left his body...afraid that when I let him go the weight of it all would bring me to the dirt.

I felt the hands of my companions on my shoulders and found the strength to withdraw the dagger. I stood as Runa took my father and lay him down. Around me all my friends laid their hands upon me, and while I knew the healing energy could not be channeled from the ground, it certainly felt like it was making its way into me.

"We do not have time to waste." I said, returning the focus back on our task.

There would be time to grieve later, until Lucian and Wurth were handled - the world was an open battlefield. We needed to stay our course, however choppy the water may get.

"The ring in his jacket." Toree said, reminding me of what my father had said.

I knelt down and pulled open his jacket. I felt the fabric until I found something solid and heavy inside. I cut open the fabric and pulled out the king of Wurth's signet ring. This seal was as official as the crown itself, those who held it also held the power of Wurth in their hand.

I handed the ring to Toree and looked at my father's body. I could not leave it here like this.

"Stand back." I said to all around.

I conjured a flame and set him alite. The flames engulfed his body, the heat as hot as a forge. I stood there until he became ash, the breeze in the pass taking him with it towards our destination.

"How are you to move forward from here?" Ren asked.

"We must end the break..." Toree said to her.

Ren paused for a moment, thinking about what that meant.

"I do not want to live an eternal life replaying this battle. If I did fall all those ages ago, that is how I should remain. How do you propose it is done?" Ren asked.

Zuht walked over and addressed all of us.

"I saw a great many things in the pool under the temple. I also saw how to aid you best in this quest. When I prayed to Tristi before I was asking him to grant me his power. He agreed." Zuht informed us.

"What do you mean?" I asked him.

"The battle can not continue if the pass is destroyed. You can not pull enough power to bring down the mountains, but Tristi can." Zuht explained.

"You can't mean..." Tripp began.

"Yes, Zuht is right. If the mountains crumble and the pass is destroyed it would alter the events so much the break will...break..." Toree confirmed.

"But you said the priest you saw do that before was destroyed by the power of Tristi within him!" Runa protested.

"It is the only way you will succeed, and it is the reason Tristi spared my life the day my caravan was attacked. It is time to repay Tristi for his generosity." Zuht said to Runa.

Zuht whispered a quick prayer towards his spear and the inscriptions he carved on the shaft began to glow a bright yellow. He knocked it on the ground and the walls around us shook, Zuht's eyes changed and matched the glowing glyphs of the spear.

Suddenly we heard war cries...it seemed someone had gotten through and alerted the next post. Charging in the distance was a battalion of Lucian's soldiers, spears and swords drawn.

"My men and I will hold them off and protect your friend, you stay protected! Jara, it was an honor fighting by your side!" Ren called out.

She rallied her troops and counter-charged the incoming attack.

"Goodbye my friends, may Tristi look over you." Zuht said poetically.

He began reciting a prayer and the walls began to shake again, small stones began to fall into the pass from the towering mountains on either side. We huddled together, Toree and I created a barrier of wind around us; much as I did escaping the crypts. As larger stones and boulders fell we were kept safe.

We looked on helplessly as Zuht then took his spear and thrust it into the side of the pass, the walls cracked and crumbled. He quickly ran to the other side and did the same. The two mountains seemed to howl like an injured wolf from the inside out, then as if in a landslide crumbled.

The stone rushed down in a cloud of dust and began to fill the valley. In the mix of stone and dust Ren and her men disappeared, then Zuht fell out of view, only his glowing spear remained visible. Soon even that was gone. Everything around our shield of wind became black.

The noise and vibration stopped, then suddenly we heard loud bangs, as if a catapult had sent a load into a castle wall. Everything around us became a bright white, forcing us to close our eyes. The world around us shook violently and we were thrown apart.

I blacked out, for how long I do not know. I sat up on the ground from where I was thrown. Around me I could see Runa, Toree, and Tripp, they were all beginning to awaken. There was no sign of anyone else, or the battle that we had just been apart of. The pass was intact, as were the mountains. The sky above was a bright clear blue, and studding the side of the mountains were small trees in bloom...

"Toree, the trees..." I moaned, my head felt like I had been hit with a hammer.

"I see, it's the spring melt...we have no time to loose!" she said, struggling as well.

"Zuht did it! He lifted the break!" Tripp said in astonishment, his face quickly turned as he realized what that meant for his friend.

"Yes, now we must ensure it was for nought." Runa said to him, scooting herself over and putting her arm over his shoulder.

I got to my feet and looked around...all was barren... it was as if we had all been a part of the same dream and woken up in a distant land. I struggled to put a finger on how I felt. My father and Zuht were gone, as was Ren... yet I felt a sense of happiness that the souls trapped here had been set free.

"Runa is right, we should continue on for our friends!" Tripp said, brushing himself off.

We took our time getting ourselves up and stretched. We still had the better part of a day's walk before we reached the exit and got moving. We walked in mostly silence, for none of us really knew what to say after our last experience. The rest of the pass was empty, free of all the fortifications we had dealt with in the break. Eventually the sun began to turn red and was ready to set, the exit of the pass was nearly in view.

"There it is, what is the plan when we leave this corridor?" Tripp asked.

"Near here there is a hidden passage that Lucian does not know about. I only know of it because Andraas told me before he entered the pool of destruction. It was carved during the time of king Ilinir to keep him safe when travelling from his castle to the pass. He would often visit the prophetic pool and feared assassination.

This passage leads directly to the throne room, though I do not know the condition of the tunnels. Runa, Tripp, I would like you both to use this passage and lay in wait for the right time. You will take Alaia and my sword, Jara will bind me and take me to Lucian as her 'prisoner'. Jara will tell Lucian she had a change of heart and wants to join him.

This should get us close enough to strike him down, but we will need you to give us the dagger to finish task." Toree explained.

"How do we link Wurth to Lucian?" I asked.

"When we see Lucian you will give it to him as an offering. Tell him it is a kingdom you defeated in battle, and now you offer the seal to show him your allegiance. When he places it on his finger the kingdom of Wurth will be tied to him, just as Nystia was when it vanished." Toree said.

"What if Lucian has his men strike you both down on sight?" asked Runa, expressing her uncertainty.

"I do not believe he will. You and Tripp are the only advantage we have against Lucian." Toree rebutted.

"It is a very big risk..." Runa replied.

I took Runa by the hand and walked some distance away from the others, then held both her hands and looked her in the eye.

"It is a big risk, but it is a necessary risk. Whether it is Wurth or Lucian, the fate of the kingdom is in our hands. You are a better strategist than even I, you know that this is the best play to make." I said to her.

"And if Toree is wrong and they string you both up before you even get to him?" Runa asked in concern.

"Then I will die happy. You have changed me for the better, you have given me comfort and love, pleasure and happiness... and should I wish for anything before death it would be to end up in a break in the woods, standing at the pond's edge, your lips against mine for eternity." I said to her, speaking directly from my heart.

"If only we could be in that now... I will be there, waiting for the right moment to help you fight Lucian." Runa said, agreeing to go forward with Toree's plan.

"Take this." I said as I handed Alaia to Runa.

"Should I fall, drive this through Lucian's heart." I added.

"We will do it together." Runa replied.

I pulled her forward and kissed her deeply with all of the love my heart had to offer.

"Jara, you have my love." Runa said to me as she broke the kiss.

"And you mine..." I replied before locking her lips again.

Lucian

Chapter 22

Runa and Tripp had entered the subterranean passage sometime ago, now Toree and I stood at the end of the pass. We overlooked a valley dotted with tiny villages, streams, lakes, and in the center the castle I had seen in Toree's memories. The setting sun lit the whole valley in a purple light; it was one of the most beautiful views I had experienced. For a few moments the danger that lay ahead vanished.

We made our way down from the mountain pass and into the fields and woods that stretched between us and the castle. There was no sign that this part of Nystia had only just appeared within the year. To those without knowledge of the kingdom, it would appear it stood here for a thousand years.

"Do you think we are likely to find more beasts on our way to the castle?" I asked Toree.

"No, the spells have fallen apart here and this part of the kingdom has been restored. Lucian would only surround himself by those that were loyal to him, not the cursed." Toree answered.

"So his soldiers and subjects loyal have appeared here too?" I questioned.

"Yes, that seems to be what he eluded to in the mirror room. We will find no friends here. When we get closer you must bind me, there is rope in my rucksack." said Toree.

Darkness crept up fast, we made our way to a ruined tower to use as shelter for the night. Toree told me it was destroyed by Ren's army as they too left the pass, now it would keep us safe from detection. Once inside, we sat ourselves against the walls and pulled out some of our remaining rations to eat.

As I sat beside Toree, I realized how overwhelmed I had been by everything. This journey had turned me from a warrior and lady into a sorceress, a brash and jealous competitor into a gentle lover, a subordinate into the head of a great house, and a girl driven by emotion into a stoic woman. I've made and lost new friends, I've discovered and lost family, and now I sat next to the only person I knew who could relate to the feelings I had been holding inside.

I was an unwelcome guest in enemy territory, carrying out the last mission of my ancestor and Toree...all the while on my own mission to save the only home I have ever known; discovering a part of me I was unaware even existed. It was all intertwined in a complex web of fate, and at times it had been easy to loose track of what it was I was actually meant to be doing.

As I had come under someone's spell, my eyes began to water uncontrollably... My body spasmed and shook, my gut wrenching sideways, my lungs unable to draw air into them, my throat as if a hand was strangling me...

I lost control of my body, overcome with the purging of all I had held inside. All the emotional pain I had pushed down now erupted in physical torment, as if the Gods themselves squeezed and crushed me down. I cried out in every kind of pain one can cry out in.

Toree took hold of my side and cradled me into her lap. She spoke nothing of her experiences, nor gave me any advice. She just let me lay in her lap, with one hand on my shoulder and the other stroking my hair she quietly sang a song. The language she sang it in I did not know, yet the tune and emotion that she carried through her lips mirrored everything I felt inside.

As Toree held and stroked me like a crying babe in the darkness of the night, her song carried my consciousness someplace else. I was both in her lap and looking over a calm sea as the sun rose above the horizon, bringing the start of a new day... then I slept.

The sun rose through the blooming trees, the warm light waking us gently. Toree did not bring up the night before, and neither did I. It was a necessary moment in time, but now it was time we began our trek towards the castle. The towers were tall enough to be our guide even in the wooded areas of this valley. Sticking to the streams and trees was our safest way to avoid being detected too soon.

We stopped to rest often so that Runa and Tripp would have ample time to carry a lead on us. Lucian seemed to expect us, as there were regular patrols of guards over the roads. We stayed quiet as we travelled, knowing there would be plenty of talk yet to come.

By the late morning we had reached the edge of the woods we had traversed since sunrise. Before us was an open field between the woodland and the castle. Near the main gates about a dozen men stood guard.

Toree and I looked at each other, this was it. Our plan would work or we would be tortured and hung from the battlements above. Fate had lead us here, to this moment.

Once we stepped from the cover of the trees there would be no stopping what has been set in motion.

It was time.

"Are you ready?" I asked Toree.

"I have been ready for a very long time." she responded soundly.

I pulled the rope out and bound her hands together so that she would appear my prisoner. As I went to lead her out of the cover she stopped me.

"Wait, this will not work. It looks like there was no struggle, hit me." she ordered.

"You don't think we can do without that?" I asked.

"If you don't it will just arouse the guards suspicion. Do it." Toree ordered again.

She straightened her posture and held her head high. I hit her across the face with the back of my hand, cracking her lip with my knuckle and drawing blood. The simple act made me feel sick to my stomach.

"Again." she ordered.

Again I hit her with the back of my hand, this time from the other side. Another small trickle of blood appeared from her eyebrow. My heart raced as I anticipated her demanding another blow.

"Let us go end this." she said to me.

I nodded and began the act, pulling Toree by the bindings. She gave some resistance, but played the part of a beaten and exhausted woman. As we made our way across the field the guards noticed and immediately went on alert. Two of them came running towards us with spears in their hands.

"And who are you two then?" one of the guards demanded.

"I am Lady Jara, I am here for an audience with Lucian...I bring a gift of goodwill." I replied.

"Oh? And who's that then?" the guard asked.

Toree lowered her head, hiding her face, I pulled her closer and grabbed her hair, pulling her head upwards. She looked at me with contempt and spit a mixture of saliva and blood from her cut lip at me.

"Wait, I know that face! Can it be? Look! It is! It's that treacherous whore! I can't believe she still lives!" the guard said in astonishment.

"Is that sufficient enough for you?" I asked boldly.

"This one killed half my banner herself she did...how'd you get a leash on her?" the guard asked.

I thought for a moment, I could either put a story together for the guard and try and remember it when I see Lucian, or I could risk putting on a display of power... given the circumstances, I thought the display of power more awe-inspiring to the guards.

I held my free hand out and conjured a flaming cyclone which swirled over our heads. I allowed it to grow and block out the sunlight around us...then I snapped my fingers and let the extravagant gesture vanish with a slight breeze.

"Because I am better than her." I said bluntly to the guard.

"Uh....uhh...of course... Lady...Kara you said it was?" the guard said with a tremble.

"Jara." I said emotionless.

"Yes, yes that's it, Lady Jara... well my lady, the king will surely welcome you warmly... please, follow me!" the guard said, turning and leading us toward the gate.

After the two guards turned to lead, Toree looked at me and smirked ever-so slightly. We followed them through the gate, into the courtyard I remember Toree and Ren fighting to take over in her memories. The area was a mix of soldiers and corrupt courtly nobles who's allegiance was with Lucian.

As we walked through there were looks of surprise and disgust in their faces. Some shouted insults, others spoke in a tongue I had only heard Toree speak in memories. Whatever they were saying, it did not seem pleasant, even Toree seemed genuinely upset by it.

The guards did nothing to quiet those around us, instead leading us onwards. I did my best to keep a stoneface as we walked past the unruly crowd. To think these people had been living in some enclave of their own in the spirit realm all this time made me question just how much more corrupt they had grown.

We were led through another gate and into the inner courtyard. This area only had a handful of guards, but again had the corrupt aristocracy of an ancient nation spitting at the feet of Toree.

"Look at her, being led like a rabid bitch on a rope! Fetch dog!" one man shouted, throwing a stick at her foot.

We kept walking, but the man walked in front of us, stopping the guard and blocking Toree and I from continuing on.

"Perhaps you misunderstood me, I told you to fetch..." the man said to Toree.

"My hands are bound..." Toree replied stubbornly.

"Dog's don't use their hands..." the man whispered with a grin in her ear.

Toree stood there, not moving or responding to what the man had said. He turned as if to walk away, but then turned back, grabbed her cuirass and pulled her down to the ground.

I went to protest but she glared up at me, knowing my heart better than even I. My bond with her urged me to step in and end our charade, but her eyes told me to keep the course. I looked around and the guards watched me, seeing if I would help her or not. Against all human nature I stood there, watching; doing nothing to help my friend who just last night consoled me as my own mother would...

"Well get on then! You heard'm!" the guard said.

Toree crawled to the stick on her knees, with tears in her eyes she grabbed it with her teeth and shuffled to the scum that gave her the task. He held his hand out and she dropped it in his palm.

"That's a good dog!" the man said sarcastically, giving her head a rub.

The small crowd that gathered to watch laughed. I thought I would vomit at the sight of it all, but knew I needed to keep it together. The guard yanked her to her feet.

"Let's go, we haven't got all day!" the guard said to Toree.

She stumbled as she was pulled up but caught her balance. I needed to find a way to speed this up and spare Toree the torment of these depraved lunatics.

"Listen, I've come a long way to deliver this gift. As enjoyable these games are, they are testing my patience. Are we nearly there? My throat is dry and I could do with wine." I said to the guard.

"Of course my lady, it's just that a lot of us have been thinking about what we would do if we saw this one again. Some of the fine folks here might have a hard time containing themselves! We'll be on our way then." said the guard.

"It's appreciated." I said bluntly to him.

"Out of the way then, we're to see the king!" the guard called to all in the courtyard.

We picked up the pace, which helped drown the insults to a dull noise. Ahead of us was now the steps to the keep. The two guards which stood there opened the doors as we walked up the stairs and inside. It took a minute to adjust to the light in the keep, and once our eyes did adjust we both noticed some stark differences to the décor since that in Toree's memories.

A statue of Lucian stood in the hall, the colors of the tapestries and carpets changed, and the energy surrounding the halls was dark...gloomy...almost demonic in nature. The hair on my neck stood up as we were led up the stairwell Toree and Ren once fought on.

The guards stopped us before we reached the throne room doors.

"What are we waiting for?" I asked.

"We need to remove the whore's armor, make sure she's not concealing anything, perhaps best to check beneath her boddice too..." the guard said.

"Go on, remove her armor, but should you go further I will take your hand off. I do not want my gift to Lucian spoiled." I warned.

"Of course, your are right my lady." the guard said defensively.

They pulled Toree's cuirass and back plates off, leaving the extremities in place. They looked at me after, likely to see if I would change my mind and allow them to grope my 'prisoner.' One look at my eyes quickly dispelled any ideas they may have had.

"I will need to take your sword my lady." the guard said.

"Very well, if Luc- the king requests it. Here, take it and be gentle. That sword is worth more than you earn in a year." I said as I handed over my blade.

"Of course." the guard said as he took it with more care than it seemed he was planning to.

We were led forward, and now before us was the foyer before the throne room. We were told to wait while they informed Lucian we were outside the doors. Once the guards were out of eyesight and earshot I leaned over towards Toree.

"Are you okay?" I asked.

"I suppose it is a fair punishment... Imagine all your enemies vanquished to a prison for centuries, not alive yet not dead, then they are suddenly freed and you walk through their door. The reception would not be welcoming. It would have been more merciful to have killed them. Had Lucian not thwarted our plan, that would have been their end." Toree said, still a bit shaken after the events in the courtyard.

"I understand..." I said.

"No, you don't... please do not take that the wrong way. I appreciate your gesture, but I hope you never have to understand such things." Toree rebutted.

It was true, I could not possibly understand nearly four hundred years of contempt, hatred, distain, and anger... but she was my friend, and I could not let her think this was all her own weight to bear.

"You may be right, but I am here. I will not leave your side no matter what happens." I vowed.

"You are a good friend, if only we met in better times." she said with gratitude.

"There is no better time than now, despite the circumstances." I rebutted, sneaking a squeeze of her hand.

She let out a smile, and I a smile back. We heard footsteps returning towards us. It seemed the guards were here to fetch us. We resumed our postures and waited.

He opened the doors to the throne room, inside Lucian sat with a crown upon his head and a glass of wine in his hand. Around him a small court of his most loyal nobles and commanders looked on intently. He looked at us with a curious smile.

"Oh my, it has been some time since I saw you last! And you...lady... sorry, what was your name again?" Lucian said with a mischievous grin.

"Lady Jara, your majesty." I said with a bow.

"Ah yes, that's right. Such a different tone from the mirror room! And what is this? An Aldonis blade?" Lucian questioned as the guard handed him my sword.

"Taken, from Toree. My sword was lost in the Winter marsh, after I took her prisoner I didn't think she would have a use for it anymore." I responded.

"Yes, about that...I'm sure you won't mind me questioning what brought on the change of heart." Lucian said.

"I was not long after the mirror room. The mad monk, Andraas; he let me look into Ilinir's Pool." I began.

"And what did you see?" Lucian asked.

"I saw the passage here crumble, I saw the towers of this place through the trees, the world on fire, Nerick overthrown, I saw you on a throne of gold and stone, then I saw myself beside you on that throne...and then under you in our bed..." I said, using whatever knowledge I had gained from Toree and Andraas' memories to play into his fantasies.

"Is that so? And how did that make you feel?" Lucian said as he leaned forward, suddenly listening with more intent.

"It is, at first I thought I was scared...and then I realized it was not me, but Toree that was afraid- afraid of your vision, your power, your ambition. Scared she could not live up to it, that she was too weak.

All I have known is war, and petty squabbles between greedy lords. Nerick has become a joke! If not for me, the kingdom I hail from would have been over run by a nation of religious fanatics. What did I get? A pat on my ass and sent back to my home.

Then Toree approached me with talk of an adventure, little did I know the magnitude of her lies. She painted you as a madman, someone of no vision, just a bloodthirsty beast. But I know bloodthirsty beasts, I have been around them all my life! You do not strike me as that type." I declared.

"What did the monk tell you?" Lucian asked.

"He warned me to go back, he warned of great destruction." I answered.

"Why not heed his advice?" Lucian said, now becoming more curious.

"Go back to what? A kingdom ruled by an old mouse? Wait to be married off for land? Had I heeded every warning I've been given; I would still be in rags suckling from a wetnurse's teat! Besides, I have led armies before the king found me redundant. Without great destruction there can be no creation. Must the forest not be cleared before the stone of a city laid?" I explained.

"You speak as if you are a philosopher. What happened to the monk?" he asked me.

"He tried to stop me, went on rambling something incoherent. I threw him into the pool of destruction and turned the temple to dust. Toree tried to stop me, but she could not best my power." I said.

"You killed the monk?!" Lucian said with an excited laugh.

"Fate is not kind to those that stand stagnant in the path of destiny." I replied.

"You... I have seen you in the flesh for all but a few minutes, yet you and I seem to have the same philosophy. Tell me, how was it you bested my dear Toree?" he said as he stood and walked to us, lifting Toree's chin with his thumb.

Toree spit in his face. He let out a chuckle and then smacked her face, knocking her to the floor. In my heart I knew she had waited centuries to do that, and that the smack was a small price to pay.

"See, this has always been your problem; you act on emotion!" he said, squatting down and speaking over her.

"Exactly. She was so upset that I killed the monk she lashed out in anger; sent objects flying toward me around the room. I easily countered her sloppy attacks and then ended the brawl with a simple and proven technique." I said, using his own verbal momentum against him.

"Yes that does sound like her! What is this technique then?" he asked.

I pointed to her swollen and bleeding eyebrow.

"A fist to the face." I said bluntly.

"Ah, a bit brutish, yet effective. But why? Why turn on her after following for so long? And what of the pass?" he asked, now full of questions.

"The pass was simple, I entered the break with Toree in tow. Coming from behind I was able to turn those around me into ash with my flames. But you are leaving out one important factor..." I said, onto his likely intentional omission of my father in the pass.

"Care to enlighten me?" he said.

"The man that walked through with the same pendant Toree wears. I saw it was he that unknowingly unlocked this place from it's prison. And it was with him that I ended the break and walked through the pass with my gift. The man was Mistaan, and he was my father.

He did not believe in the visions of the pool, but I do. He tried to stop me and rescue Toree. I was forced to kill him with my own blade. I used his fleeting life energy to bring down the walls of the pass, ending the break." I explained.

"That is quite a lot of power you claim to posses..." he said, doubtful it was the truth.

"Excuse me your majesty, me and the boys, we've seen it ourselves - outside the castle walls." a guard unexpectantly chimed in.

The guard's confirmation seemed to smooth over any suspicion Lucian had, for if he had more he did not show it.

"And Toree, why turn on her? For just a vision of destruction?" he asked.

"No, there was more, but I would rather not speak of it before your court." I said, looking around at his inner circle.

Lucian looked around and thought for a moment.

"Very well, all of you, leave." he ordered.

The nobles of the court left, only a handful of guards remained.

"I hope you don't mind my guards, staying. The last time Toree and I were in this room I had a dagger thrust into me." Lucian said sarcastically.

"I would feel better if they were here." I replied.

"Good, before we continue our last topic, you had mentioned you defeated the king of an opposing kingdom...might you have any actual proof of this? Or am I just to believe your word." Lucian asked.

"Of course, where are my manners! Here, a gift for you!" I said, pulling the signet ring of Wurth from my pouch and handing it to him.

"What a beautiful ring...and how was it you came to have this in your possession?" he asked as he studied the ring.

"I led the final charge against him and his army. When I met him on the battlefield we engaged in combat. I cut his sword hand from his arm and ran him through. The king requested only his crown and head, I took the ring as a memento of my own." I explained.

"You know, that story reminds me of myself! Please, where are my manners! Come take a seat, you must be parched! Have some wine." he said as he placed the ring on his finger and led me to his table, handing me a glass of wine and taking a seat across and placing my sword on the table before him.

"Guards!" he called.

I was nervous that he had caught on, but smiled and drank the wine as if all was well. One of the guards came up to him and waited for direction.

"Toree has travelled all the way here, and she's been so polite and quiet. Why not reward her by letting her take a seat on the throne that could have been hers?" he suggested.

The guard nodded and dragged Toree to the throne, tossing her onto the large stone seat. As the scene unfolded I looked for any signs of Runa and Tripp. I could not make out an entrance to the tunnel, nor a hiding place. This room was just two massive stone and gold thrones, a few tables and chairs with wine, and one entrance.

"This place will be your final tomb!" Toree yelled out.

"I knew there was a reason you were so quiet! Have you been thinking of some great escape this whole time? It will not happen. You have been bested." Lucian replied, again playing into our plan.

Lucian turned and looked at me with a smile, as he did I heard the sound of a stone shift, from where I could not see. My heart grew hopeful that Runa and Tripp were ready to spring into the fight, yet I still saw no signs.

"What are you doing over there! Just sit quietly and enjoy it. After this you have a busy schedule in the chambers below this castle. One of the joys of being cursed to live for all time is that all of that time can be spent in the torture chamber!" Lucian called to Toree, referring to the dungeons.

I looked at Toree, she shifted her eyes toward the rear of the throne...that was it! The passage didn't just go to the throne room, it went directly to the thrones! They had made it! Now to bide them some time and try to get the guards out.

"What was it you had asked me before?" I said, reclaiming his attention.

"Ah, yes! Why turn on Toree after travelling all the way to the temple? Just for a vision of destruction?" he asked me again.

"No, it was so much more than that. Toree is too easily swayed by her emotions. I respect those that respect me, and act on logic, not raw impulse. I saw a partnership of respect and power in the pool. I looked in and saw the two thrones of this room.

On one throne you sat with a crown on your head. In one hand a chessboard, in the other a map of the continent. On the other throne I sat. On my head I wore a crown, in one hand a bloodied sword, in the other a child.

Fate sent me to the pool with Toree only to open my eyes! I am to be your sword of destruction against the weak and corrupt so that you may create the kingdom you know you are destined to!

When we are done forging your vision I will give you an heir to entrust our world to!" I explained. It was a gamble to speak of the pool again, but I could think of no better way to explain 'my' actions.

"Fascinating..." Lucian said as he rubbed his chin.

"Have you seen it as well?" I asked, genuinely probing for a direction to go in.

"Yes, but not a soul knew. I too saw the throne room, Toree here, and you... and you did indeed hold a bloody sword...although it appears your vision was more clear than mine. That was the last thing I saw before the monk chased me off." Lucian informed me.

It appeared my gamble had paid off! As Lucian was lost in thought for a moment the stone behind the throne moved again, and again caught his attention.

"Don't mind me, I'm just making myself comfortable for when I sit here myself!" Toree called out.

"Curse this woman... how do I know you speak the truth?" he asked me.

"You know, we have children's stories where I'm from. In all the tales their true loves are found with a kiss..." I suggested.

"Those are stories I believe I would like..." he replied with a grin.

"I wouldn't want our first kiss to be ogled by the hired help..." I said, referring to the guards still in the room.

"Out, all of you." Lucian said.

"And Toree?" I asked.

"No, she stays, I want her to see what could have been hers." Lucian smirked.

"But sire..." one of the guards protested.

"Toree is bound and Lady Jara is unarmed. They are nothing I could not handle." he replied to the guard.

"Your majesty, you underestimate me!" I smiled, knowing well the irony of the situation.

Lucian stood, as did I. He grabbed my face and shoved his lips against mine with aggression. I looked at Toree who nodded silently. I did my best to act enthralled by Lucian's animal-like intimacy while keeping one eye open.

Behind the thrones Runa and Tripp emerged in silence. Tripp snuck around to Toree and cut her bindings, handing over her sword. Toree stretched her back as she made ready, Runa and Tripp at her side.

I pulled my lips away from Lucian's and gave him a large smile.

"So was it like the tales in Nerick?" Lucian proudly boasted after seeing my smile.

"Not quite...to be honest I've had better." I said bluntly.

Lucian's face turned red in rage.

"Better?! Who better than I?!" he raged.

"Me. I'm better." a smirking Runa said nonchalantly from the thrones.

Lucian turned around in surprise and bloodlust to see Runa, Tripp, and a now freed and armed Toree before him.

"Guards!" he called out.

As he did I let out loose a punch to his cheek. The unexpected blow left him stumbling over to the side.

"You played me for a fool!" he yelled to me.

"Yes, and you played your part perfectly my dear." Toree said as she walked toward him and delivered a swift kick to his gut.

It was then the guards rushed into the room with their swords drawn. Tripp and Runa sprang into action while I grabbed my sword from the table. We were outnumbered, at least a dozen to the four of us.

I conjured some wind to disperse them enough to make the fight more even. While Lucian still worked to regain his breath from Toree's kick, the head guard charged his way past and to the both of them.

"I knew it was too easy! We should have cut you both down on site!" the guard yelled to Toree as he swung his blade toward her.

Toree parried and struck back, cutting the guards sword arm in the processes. The guard dropped his sword, grabbing at the wound with his off hand.

"Bitch!" the guard shouted.

"It seems you dropped something, perhaps you should get on your knees and fetch?" Toree said, ready for payback after the incident in the courtyard.

The guard's face changed to worry as Toree made a precise cut behind his knees. The guard dropped involuntarily to the floor and cried in pain.

"I don't think you heard, dog. Fetch." Toree demanded before cleaving the guards head off his shoulders.

Lucian had used the opportunity to regain himself and draw his own sword. I turned from fighting the guards to block a blow from Lucian. Toree came to aid as she struck at him, he blocked it and again tried to take a swing at me. As I dodged his attack my steel pendant was revealed.

"Ah, the symbol of my opposition! You did well to conceal that necklace earlier or my guards would have dragged your lifeless body in here! It matter's not now, none of you will leave this place alive." Lucian said.

"You have not been tested in too long, and that has made you weak!" I said, delivering a kick to his chest.

He stumbled towards Toree, who then drove the pommel of her sword into his side. He turned and elbowed Toree in the ribs, knocking her off balance.

"Jara!" Runa called out.

Additional guards had funneled into the room and they were being overwhelmed. I looked towards Toree.

"Go! This is my fight!" Toree said to me.

I ran to Runa and Tripp, using a blast of fire to scorch their attackers, but the flames proved not enough to turn the tide. We cut down all we could, but it seemed to be a loosing battle. Behind us I could hear the sound of Toree and Lucian clashing swords.

"There must be something else we can do!" Tripp called.

"I have an idea, behind me!" I called.

Runa and Tripp withdrew behind my back. I conjured more wind to push our attackers into a corner, then created a wall of water. I engulfed the guards in the water, their eyes grew wide as they struggled to find air, attempting to work their way out of the liquid deathtrap I had created. While the guards slowly drowned where they stood, Runa and Tripp ran to the doors and barricaded them shut.

The fighting had garnered the attention of the aristocracy within and they would without a doubt attempt to overwhelm us. I released the water and the lifeless bodies of the guards fell to the floor. There was banging at the door, it would not be long before they broke the barricade.

"Toree!" I shouted.

We turned and surrounded Lucian, who now held his sword's point towards us as he turned in place, attempting to keep us at bay.

"You are all fools! You could have joined me! Instead you will all die like animals. Once my subjects break through you will be tortured until you wish you were dead!" Lucian spewed.

"No, we will finish what we started all those years ago!" Toree declared.

"And then what? Your two friends will vanish with me? Only you two wear the pendants you need to survive!" Lucian laughed.

"We will be quite safe." Runa said, pulling a pendant from beneath her cuirass.

"How?" I asked Toree, who stood next to me.

"Your father's pendant and Ren's. Before we left the break I took them. While in the pass I entrusted them to Tripp." Toree said to me.

"You are ever full of surprises..." I said.

"It matter's not, you will all die soon enough!" Lucian called, sending a wind of his own out, knocking Runa and Tripp backwards, I was thrown onto the throne, Toree held her ground somehow.

Toree lunged with her sword toward him but he dodged the blade. He closed the distance between them and they connected blades again. In a flash of steel I heard Toree take a sharp inhale... it was a sound I knew well from the battlefield. It was the sound of one that has been run through...

Toree's sword dropped as Lucian pulled his sword from her torso.

"Toree!" I cried out, just managing to gain my breath after being thrown.

"Now we finish this." Lucian said to Toree, raising his sword for a killing strike.

Toree looked at me as if to say goodbye... but I raised my sword arm, pointing the tip towards Lucan as I struggled to sit up from exhaustion. She nodded, and with a a wave of her hand sent Lucian backwards in a fit of wind.

Lucian was thrown onto me, my sword impaling his abdomen. He looked down in surprise and horror as he saw the tip of my sword sticking out his front. He pulled himself off me, my sword sliding out, now coated in his blood. He looked at me on the throne, sword in hand, covered in blood.

"The vision..." he stammered.

Runa and Tripp had just gotten to their feet again, the banging at the door had become more intense and the wooden barricade was splintering apart. Lucian's reinforcements were nearly through...

"The dagger!" Toree ordered, staggering forward, on hand on her wound, covered in blood.

Runa pulled the dagger out and handed it to her. Toree took it, keeping her eyes on Lucian the entire time. Lucian was now propped up on the steps before the throne, holding his own wound.

"If I die, this all will go with me, and you will no longer be protected from death." he warned Toree.

"I have lived long enough and welcome death, while you have become death incarnate. Now we finish this..." she said as she straddled Lucian.

As she sat atop him she raised the dagger and spoke a spell I could not understand. The dagger glowed with a white light. As she spoke the incantation Lucian tried to grab his sword but I stepped on the blade, he was too weak to fight my foot off.

The barricade on the door splintered apart and Lucian's supporters broke through. The charged swords in-hand! Runa and Tripp turned and readied themselves to fight again. Before they made their way across to the throne Toree drove the dagger into Lucian's heart.

At once Lucian's body began to crack in a bright white light, like a sculpture crumbling apart. Toree rolled off of him as the light running through his body erupted in a flash. His body no longer human, it had taken the form of the ghosts from the marsh. He reached toward Toree with an apathetic look, but as his hand stretched out the transparent white form dissipated like the sun burning off the clouds after a rainstorm. His whole body followed suit until he was no more.

The crowd that charged in also turned white like Lucian. Not realizing what was happening they continued their attack on Runa and Tripp, but passed through them before also vanishing into a mist.

"What now?" asked Tripp.

"We must get out..." Toree muttered.

Around us the thrones and walls began to crack with the white light. I grabbed Toree with Tripp, following Runa out of the keep. The walls around us grew brighter and we picked up our pace. We threw ourselves out the doors and tripped down the steps into the courtyard with no time to spare.

Around us the castle turned into a mist so thick I could not see my hand before my face. We stayed still, unaware of what to expect. I do not know how long it took, but the sun began to show through. The mist began to vanish in the breeze and around us were only trees and grass.

It was done...

It was done!

"Have we..." Tripp began.

"Yes..." said Toree, out of breath.

We looked down at Toree who was laying on the grass, covered in blood. Her hand still holding her wound.

"Your...still bleeding..." Tripp said.

"My curse broke when Lucian died. I am mortal again..." Toree informed Tripp.

"Wait, I will heal you!" I said rushing over to her and placing my hands on her wound.

"No, no I have lived long enough. I am ready." Toree protested.

"But Toree, if your curse is broken, would that not mean you could have children and live a full life, growing old with someone?" Tripp pleaded with her.

"Tripp, is growing old and bearing a child what I want, or what you desire? I have grown old, though my body does not show it...and I have had many children throughout my life, though none have spawned from me...I can see that now. You must find someone in your own time, and you will." Toree said to him with a pat on the face.

"What if I do not want someone else?" Tripp responded.

"You will, I have seen it...when I looked into the Pool of Ilinir. All of you still have important roles to play, and new generations to sculpt." Toree assured him.

"And what of us? Should we care not what happens to you?" Runa asked Toree, who had also become quite close to her.

"Runa, dear...you could wish the moons to stay high in the night sky when in your lovers embrace; yet wish as you might, the sun will still rise. You all have helped me finish a task that should have ended long ago... We have shed our blood, sweat, and tears together on this journey.

I...I have no words to express my gratitude to you all...except, thank you.

Jara, the order is now in your hands... rebuild it, make it strong. That is what lays ahead of you now. All the knowledge you require will be yours. Trust in yourself." she said.

I nodded with tears in my eyes.

"How can we help, if not to heal you?" I asked her.

"I have spent most of my life alone, I would like to see it out in the company of my friends..." she muttered with a smile.

We sat there holding her as she went in and out of consciousness... Runa hummed her song, Tripp rubbed her cheek and hair, and I held her hands...

The sun began to set...and as if her connection with this land could not be broken; her breath faded with the fleeting light of the day. As the last traces of sunlight vanished from the sky in a crimson haze, so too did she.

Home

Chapter 23

Runa, Tripp, and I trotted along on our horses. Coming into view was a bustling Raven's Landing. The banners of all the great houses were draped over the battlements, as was done in tournaments.

The closer we came, the more we could see. Flowers adorned the gates of the lower city, musicians played both in the fields surrounding the city walls and inside. Children were merry and running through the tall late-spring grass. There were travelers from nearby villages making their way to join in the festivities.

It was an odd feeling...there was always some discomfort and adjustment returning from a campaign... but this was the first time I felt like a stranger in my own lands. To the people of Nerick, their enemy simply vanished. They knew nothing of the beasts, the battles, Lucian, our struggles... their homes and families were safe, and they were happy.

I was happy for them too, yet I could not show it. Perhaps I needed more time to breakdown the events that took place, or maybe I just needed sleep and a good meal. For now I was grateful that my horse seemed to know the way on it's own, otherwise I might be temped to gallop into the woods and create a home amongst the treetops.

As we made our way through the city gate and towards the keep my mind wandered to Toree. I tried to imagine what it was like for her when she made her way through the gates of

Dragon's Reach after Nystia vanished... would the Toree of younger years recognize the Toree after Nystia fell?

At the end, yes...and that gave me hope that who I was before is still inside, somewhere.

I was pulled from my inner-thoughts as a young girl pranced down the street with a bucket of flower petals. She tossed them in the air as she sang songs. The petals floated onto my hair and my lap. I picked one up and held it between my fingers, looking at the vibrant color and feeling it's silky texture.

I had not seen anything like this in years...not since the tournaments and festivals of my youth...before the war.

Banners and ribbons hung all over the city, the people laughed and danced, vendors gave their wares freely, and barrels of ale and mead littered the streets. Children played with toy swords made from sticks while their mothers looked on, nursing newborns from the teat. Newborns that would know not of war.

My heart filled with joy... all of these children would be able to be just that - children.

Runa and I were sculpted by the war with Wurth, instead of pursing courtly love we pursued marauders as they raided villages in the north. We did not play with sticks, we played with blunt swords until we were proficient enough to use real blades. A part of me yearned to dismount and join in their games, though they would likely send me to the madhouse!

We had reached the bridge to the keep. It was surrounded by arches of flowers and ribbons, even the halberds the guards held had flowers tied to the shafts. All the gates were open for the first time in years, the guards were not charging at us to stop as they did the first time we made our way through.

A horseman headed towards us, galloping on the bridge.

"Is that?" Tripp began.

"It looks like it." I said, a smile breaking through my lips.

"My friends! Welcome home!" Unul shouted as he came near.

I looked around and could see none of our eyes were dry. Unul was the first friend we had seen since we buried Toree in Nystia. Just his presence here brought us all some joy.

"Unul! How did you know we were here?" I asked him.

"I hear echoes from all over this city. Once I heard you made your way through the field towards the gates I made ready! I wanted to be the first to welcome you all back; the kingdom is indebted to you... but I must ask, where are the others? And your father?" said Unul.

Runa shook her head.

"All of them? Even Mistaan and Toree?" Unul asked again.

"It is Toree whom the kingdom owes their gratitude." I said.

"Jara is right, if not for her more than just Nerick would be lost." Runa added.

"Forgive my confusion, but it seems there was more to your mission than I was aware!" Unul said.

"My dear Unul, there are a great many things we have all been unaware of...but this is not the place." I said.

"Jara, there is something you should know, why you were gone, your mother-" Unul began.

"There is no need, I have known for some time already." I responded before he could finish his sentence.

"I have no doubt that this is yet one more thing I am unaware of...for what it is worth, I am sorry. Your mother and father were close to my heart...but there will be time to reminisce of them later. For now, please follow me. The king has directed that you should be sent before him as soon as you arrive. I will join." Unul informed us before turning his steed and heading to the keep.

We followed in tow to the inner courtyard. Waiting by the water trough was Josan. As we dismounted he greeted us warmly.

"Lady Jara, Lady Runa, master Tripp! It warms my heart to see you all again! I am having your rooms made ready, the king spares no expense, is there anything you would like waiting within?" Josan asked us.

"Wine! Lots of wine, with cheese and bread! The freshest, crispiest bread you can muster!" Runa said.

"I second that." Tripp chimed.

"And if you could have any belongings Runa has in her chambers to mine, I would appreciate it." I said.

"Of course my ladies, master Tripp." Josan said with a cheeky smile and a bow, then turned to make it so.

"Why your chambers?" Runa asked.

"Because my windows have a better view, with a lovely bench below." I answered.

"I see that as an acceptable reason..." Runa said with a sarcastic smile.

Tripp shook his head and walked to Unul. Runa and I followed just behind. It felt like a century had gone by since we last walked through these walls. None of us are the same people we were when we left.

As we walked I noticed we did not head towards the king's secret chamber, or the throne room.

"Unul, where are you taking us?" I asked.

"King Ansel's court has not been in session since Wurth vanished at the battle fields. Since then he has been spending most of his time of late amongst the flowers and trees, so I will take you to his private garden." Unul replied.

The irony was not lost on me. He first gave me King Ansel's message in my own garden at Dragon's Reach, it is fitting that I will give the king my message in his. We walked out the keep and to the king's private area.

The flowers had bloomed all around, the trees full and providing shade. Birds perched on branches, whistling their songs to us as we passed them below. We turned a hedge and there sat the king.

"Your majesty." we all said with a bow.

"You three need not bow down on this day! It was not I that delivered the final victory against our enemy! Come and tell me, where are the others?" said the king.

"Sir Alor, Lady Toree, and Zuht gave their lives in the service of others." Runa said to the king.

"I have here Sir Alor's dagger, he wished it to return home." Tripp said, handing over the linen wrapped dagger from his bag.

King Ansel took the dagger from Tripp and stuck it in his belt.

"And what of the magical dagger?" the king asked.

"Gone, it was destroyed when Toree used it." I quickly responded, Runa glanced over at me.

"That is a shame, had it survived it would have been a powerful tool. What is important is that Nerick no longer endures torment from the north. Tell me, where is Lord Mistaan?" the king asked.

"My father did not survive his wounds...he died for Nerick." I replied, showing him that I wore my father's ring on my finger.

"I see...he was a loyal man, loyal to the end it seems... You wear his ring as your own, did he entrust Dragon's Reach to you?" he asked me.

"He did, your grace." I answered.

"And is this something you desire? Or would you rather have your brother take the oath?" the king asked me.

I looked down at the ring and thought for a moment before responding.

"Your grace...I have learned what we desire is often inconsequential in the eyes of destiny. I accept the responsibilities that have been given to me, I will take the oath." I replied.

I looked at Runa and Tripp. Runa had become more than my lover and friend, she was now my confidant and anchor. Tripp had grown into himself, both as a warrior and as an individual. I now viewed him as a younger brother, and to be honest, I did not care to see him knighted and sent off to another region.

"...There are but three things I ask..." I added.

"You are most entitled after what has been accomplished! What do you ask of me?" said the king.

"Once I take the oath I would like to knight Tripp myself, as a knight of Dragon's Reach." I began.

Tripp looked over to me, in shock and gratitude.

"As is customary with the great houses when forging allegiances through courtship, I would like your permission to bring Runa back to Dragon's Reach...as my partner and wife." I listed second, grabbing Runa's hand as she stood next to me.

"And what is it you desire third?" the king asked.

"Destiny has decreed that I should rebuild The Order of the Moon...in service to your grace and Nerick, of course. I ask for your permission to do so and have a banner drawn up." I added last.

The king was silent for a moment.

"You may dub Tripp a knight of Dragon's Reach. I also accept your request to rebuild your ancient order...however each member must swear fealty to the crown, and I will appoint an adviser to your order. I do not think Sir Unul will object?" the king replied.

"I accept, your grace." Unul said.

"As for a union between Lady Runa and yourself...your houses have both stood as pillars of Nerick's strength for centuries... I can see no reason why this would not strengthen the bonds between your two houses. The strongest of bonds are those forged through the shedding of blood. Lady Runa, is this what you desire?" said the king.

"It is, your grace." Runa replied with a smile.

"Let it be so, you have my permission. Tomorrow Lady Jara and Tripp shall take their oaths, for now we have much to discuss about your quest." the king said to us.

"Your grace, if you would like...I can show you by letting you and Sir Unul into my memories, it is a power I learned from Lady Toree." I said.

"How could you learn such a thing from Lady Toree?" the king asked.

"It would be a very long story to tell, and you might think we are all entirely mad should we attempt to explain it..." I replied.

The king paused and looked to Unul.

"Your grace, I believe we should try this." Unul said in support.

"Very well, show us." the king agreed.

I walked to the king and Unul, and placing my hands on both of their foreheads I let them into the memories I felt were relevant, omitting those too personal for both myself and Toree. It was my first time doing so, and in the process discovered I had the memories Toree shared with me as part of my own...

It was a strange process, sharing memories. When inside someone else's memories time seemed to move as any other day, when sharing the memories it was nothing more than glimpses and flashes of the past...the details being left to my subconscious.

After sharing some of Toree's past I now I understood my mother and Toree when they said I possessed their knowledge. I did not think to look back on anything my mother gave to me when in the spirit realm, and Toree did not elaborate on it. It would likely take years to bring what my mother and Toree imprinted on me to the surface, but I was content with that. This was my path now.

The flashes of the past year ended and my eyes opened. I removed my hands from the king and Unul, who both seemed to look fairly overcome with emotion. Their eyes were swollen, though they would not let out a tear, and they looked at the three of us like a proud mother upon her child's first steps.

"None of you shall want for anything, and your companions shall be honored as heroes. Alor shall have a sculpture at the docks, Toree in the center of the market square, and Zuht shall receive his in the norther temples of Tristi. They will not be forgotten." King Ansel let out as if it was of the utmost importance.

"Your grace, we are grateful." I replied.

"You may all go, I am sure you must need to rest. Should you want anything, but say the word." the king directed, waving us out.

We nodded with a slight bow and made our way back to the keep.

"What did you show him?" Runa asked.

"What he needed to see and nothing more." I replied.

"So, you didn't show you Toree and I...umm..." Tripp asked.

"I don't think anyone needed to see that, let alone the king!" I said with my hand on his shoulder and a chuckle.

"Jara!" Unul called, chasing after us.

"You two go, I will see what Unul needs. Runa dear, don't drink all the wine yourself!" I said.

"Worry not about the wine, it is a warm bath I am after!" she said as her and Tripp continued inside.

I waited for Unul to catch up. We were now in a secluded area and could speak freely without worry of sensitive ears listening.

"Jara, I must take you to the hidden library." Unul said to me.

"What are you talking about?" I asked, confused.

"Before you all left, Toree called for a private audience with me. She told me that should you return and she not, that I should take you there. I did not think it anything more than a scholarly sightseeing tour...but after what you showed us...there is more to it, I can feel it!" Unul said with certainty.

"Very well, if Toree thought it important take me to it." I said, both intrigued and exhausted. In truth I was ready to jump in a warm bath along side Runa; not follow another riddle.

Unul led me to a different area of the castle, it was not the library we discovered Aldonis's blades in. It was in fact below the king's alchemy laboratories. There was no one working there, as everyone was still singing and dancing in the streets. We followed a narrow winding stairwell down to an area that was more reminiscent of a wine cellar than a library.

"There are only tables here..." I said, looking around and seeing no books or scrolls.

"She said you would know the way." Unul suggested.

I suppose I would have to pull her memories sooner than expected. I put my hand to the wall and took a breath, in my mind's eye I could see a false wall moving if I used a rush of wind.

I looked around the area and saw the wall that had come to mind, then walked to it. I conjured a small wind and forced it against the stone; as I did the wall pushed backwards with a creek.

Behind were the flaming stones that we had seen in Nystia...Toree had intentionally left something here...

We looked around together and found shelves filled with scrolls and encyclopedias of magical knowledge, herbal compounds, the explosive compounds Toree used in Enex, and a large book on a table...

I walked to the table and opened the book, inside of it was a list of names. It appeared to be all in Toree's handwriting. The names divided and multiplied, and beside them were locations of birth and death. This continued on throughout, and that is when it hit me!

"Unul! Do you know what this is!?" I said in excitement.

"A list of names?" he replied.

"Yes, but it is so much more! Before Toree died she tasked me with rebuilding the order. And at one point Aldonis mentioned there were others from Nystia that now lived in Nerick...this is a list of all those with Nystian magic in their blood!" I declared.

"We can use this with Nerick's records and see who still has living descendants from these bloodlines...but it will take time." Unul said.

"Yes, time and assistance. Will you help me?" I asked.

"Of course! after all, I am now the advisor to the Order of the Moon...I should make myself useful with something." Unul replied.

"Thank you, Unul." I said.

Unul sent me off to rest while he collected what he needed to do his work. I made my way to my chambers, when I arrived Runa had already bathed and was sleeping on the bed. I couldn't help but giggle at her loud snores. It was the first real bed we had since the temple, and even that one was a few centuries old. The sun was still in the sky but we were all moving on pure adrenaline.

I sat in the warm tub, letting the water sooth my muscles. I stuck my head under the water, as I had done the last time I bathed in this room. The muffled silence of the water around me was welcome. I felt as if I was in the womb, and as my face broke the water's surface it birthed renewed energy into me. I scrubbed the dirt off my skin and from under my nails, I rinsed the dirt and mud from my hair, and I stretched out my toes, now finally free of my worn boots.

I dried off and sat on the bed, too tired to eat and drink myself. I lay under the sheets, it was good to feel the spring and summer silks against my bare skin. As I nestled into my pillow Runa woke up for a moment.

"You asked the king to let me be with you in Dragon's Reach." she stated.

"Yes...you do want that...right?" I asked, unsure of how to respond.

"I love you." she said before rolling over and resuming her snoring.

I smiled and closed my eyes, stretching on the bed. Just as my eyes seemed to close shut they again opened to a new sunrise. Next to me Runa lay away, looking at me.

"Can I help you?" I asked.

"Just admiring your sleeping face. The thought crossed my mind to call in an artist to paint a portrait of you asleep, drooling onto your pillow with your hair covering your face." Runa joked.

"Yes, I know the feeling. I half thought to call a bard in last night and right a ballad to your snoring." I shot back.

We both smiled and kissed. The way Runa looked at me afterwards hinted there was something on her mind.

"Go on, what is it?" I asked.

"You told the king that the dagger was destroyed, yet you still carry Alaia on your waist...why not tell him the truth?" she asked me.

"King Ansel is a good man, but the dagger still holds the power it was created with. Should someone else get ahold of it...well, I do not want Nerick to follow the same fate as Nystia... besides, my family is bound to the dagger, as now are you and Tripp. We must protect it, keep it's powers a secret. If all else think it has been lost forever we can keep it hidden in plain sight." I explained.

"Do you really think someone would try to use it again?" Runa asked.

"We have peace for the first time in over a decade, yet one day there will be those who desire more, like Lucian. That is what my order will stand watch over." I answered.

"Magic and daggers or not, today is a big day, are you ready?" she asked.

"No." I replied honestly.

"Good, let's get ready." she said with a smile.

By mid morning Unul had come to the door to fetch us.

"Are you ready?" he said.

Runa and I looked at each other and nodded. As we walked down the corridor we collected Tripp and made our way to the throne room. Once outside we were asked to wait. Like the city below, the entrance to the throne room was littered with flower petals. From outside the door it sounded like there was quite a commotion within.

"Is it not just the four of us and the king here?" Tripp asked Unul.

"Oh no, all of the court is here. This is a momentous occasion for the kingdom!" Unul informed Tripp.

Tripp looked visibly nervous.

"Calm down, you have fought beasts, men, and helped vanquish an evil sorcerer! You can stand before a group of people." Runa said to Tripp.

"Yes but I was fighting then, now I am just standing...where do I look?" Tripp asked.

"There will be lots of unsatisfied ladies forced to stand next to their politic-crazed husbands. Look at their bosoms." I said.

Unul chuckled for a moment.

"Unul, I did not ask earlier. My ruling over Dragon's Reach will not sow seeds of division between my brother and I, will it? You have likely spoken to him more in these past months than I have in past years." I asked.

"He will see it as a blessing. He would much rather take residence in the warmer southern border. He has never had any love for the snow-filled winters of the northwest." Unul reassured me.

The doors opened and we were led in. Decorations hung everywhere, and around us were standing and cheering nobles and commanders. They all sang our praise as we walked down a red runner toward the king, who stood just in front of his throne. We arrived before the steps to the throne and knelt down.

"Lords, ladies, loyal subjects of Nerick! As you know, after years of war Wurth was defeated. Over two years ago I sent a large expedition led by Lord Mistaan of Dragon's Reach on an expedition to find a way to destroy Wurth. All of those men were lost. Nearly a year ago I sent a group of six to carry on the mission.

Those six were: Lady Jara, Lady Runa, Lady Toree, Sir Alor, Zuht - priest of Tristi, and master Tripp - squire to the late Sir Krinn.

Lady Toree, Sir Alor, and Zuht gave their lives for this kingdom, and everyone in it. They shall be honored from this day forward.

Today we honor the three that returned!

Lady Jara, Dragon's Reach is without a head. Do you swear before me and those here today to rule over Dragon's Reach justly and honestly, to protect those within your lands, and swear fealty to I, King Ansel of Nerick?" the king announced.

"I swear it, your grace." I said with my head bowed low.

"Then to you I bestow Dragon's Reach! Lady Runa, with Sir Unul now undertaking new tasks, I am without a commander for my royal army. Should I ever need to muster a standing army again, do you accept the position as my Knight-Commander, to serve and protect the kingdom of Nerick again?" said the king.

"I do, your grace." swore Runa.

"Then shall the need arise again, you will be called upon to fulfill your oath. Lady Jara, I believe I made a promise myself. Rise, Lady Jara of Dragon's Reach." the king said.

"Thank you your grace." I said, rising up and standing before Tripp.

I pulled my sword and placed the tip at my toes.

"Tripp, you have shown more spirit and chivalry than any other I have known. You have gone from a lone squire to a knight in all but title. You have fought valiantly and stayed true, even after you lay on the brink of death.

It is for all of these reasons that I have the honor and privilege to knight you: Sir Tripp of Dragon's Reach." I said with a smile, dubbing his shoulders with my blade before sheathing it.

"Lady Runa, Knight-Commander of the royal army, Sir Tripp, knight of Dragon's Reach, rise and look upon your witnesses!" the king decreed.

The three of us stood before the court amongst an applause I had only known on tournament grounds. I could not help but feel our companions stood there beside us in spirit.

The celebration lasted for two weeks. Most of which we spent resting from our quest. Unul began his search for those with a connection to Nystia, though most turned up nothing. Before we left for Dragon's Reach Unul swore he would send a messenger as soon as he had a lead.

Rested and fitted with new clothing, Runa, Tripp and I set off for Dragon's Reach. Once there we all began to fit into our new roles. In truth I ran the lands in only name. Runa had a natural ability to run the castle and lands. It did not take long for her to become popular and loved by those within our borders.

Tripp did well travelling our province and carrying out deeds and verdicts where needed. He quickly gained a reputation for being just and honest. Soon the children in the villages pretended to be him as they played games. My favorite was Sir Tripp against the troll. I'm sure should we had ever encountered a troll, he would have done as good of a job dealing with it as the children believe he did.

I spent most of my time studying the scrolls and books Toree left behind; searching through my mother and Toree's memories. I tasked craftsmen to rebuild the ruined sanctum Toree and my ancestors created together. Not long after, I had a monument to Toree built in the gardens of Dragon's Reach. I would often go for walks at night and speak with her there, even if only in spirit. Though he never talked about it, Tripp too would visit the monument each day at sunrise.

A year passed, then two. The kingdom was still at peace and Unul had still not found any living descendants. I continued to hone my skills and learn as much as I could. On the three year anniversary of the victory over Wurth, Runa insisted on throwing a grand feast. We all danced, sang, drank, and ate to those we lost, and then to those we saved. The night ended joyfully and Runa and I went to our bed, passing out in a drunken stupor.

Epilogue

I rolled over with a groan in my bed as heavy knocking began at my door.

"My Ladies" a guard's voice said.

I covered our heads with the blanket, trying to get back to sleep.

"Didn't we tell Welum to make sure we were not interrupted until noon today?" Runa groaned as she raised a hand to her pounding head.

"My ladies, I must speak with you!" the guard said again.

"I did..." I moaned, still groggy from the feast the night before. I stumbled to the quilt hanging over my chair and threw it over my shoulders, making myself somewhat decent while Runa pulled the sheets over herself.

"It seems there will be no rest this morning..." I said to Runa.

I walked to the door and opened it up to see one of the guards stood in the hall.

"What is it that is so important at this time of the morning? Can we have no time to recover from last evenings festivities?" I said.

"I'm sorry my lady, a messenger came, says it's important." the guard explained.

"A messenger from who? Could this not be directed to Sir Tripp?" I asked.

"He said he can only speak to you, says he was sent by Sir Unul. Brought a letter with'm too." the guard said.

He handed me the letter, on it was Unul's seal, and embossed onto the parchment was two interlocking moons...

Made in the USA
Middletown, DE
28 August 2022

71816001R00295